for my father

CONTENTS

A LOOP IN TIME

Book One of the POLIS series

CHAPTER ONE

THE AISLE OF TEARS

Sophia Ludwig loved babies. She loved the sense of infinite possibility. She also loved baby showers, and attended many.

This should have been an extraordinarily happy day for her. She was to attend a baby shower. Since it was spring, there would be daffodils and tulips. All the presents would be wrapped in subtle pastels. Since this was New York, and since the party was being held in fashionable Soho, it was very likely that all the presents would be truly stylish and adorable.

But for one problem — the party was for her. Sophia was to become a mommy.

Most of us know that babies are fragile, and do best in comforting and protective circumstances. Young penguins, for example, hardly stand a chance without devoted parents and the warmth of other penguins. Indeed, in the human world, community and security are just as important.

Sophia's problems centered around just this need for protection and support. For while she resided in a country with secure borders and progressive policies, and in a city with a good selection of flattering maternity clothes and clever diaper bags, she faced a sobering reality. Sophia was to become a single mother, a single mother with very little money. She made her living as a poet and librarian employed by the New York City public library system, which, you should know in Manhattan, can be a hard and meager living indeed.

CHAPTER ONE

Worse, she did not have many friends or family. She was shy. She was most fond of writing stories about people, alone in a small apartment painted with a faded turquoise wash and decorated with tall, skinny pictures of buildings — skinny so as to fit in the very limited width of the walls. The elongated pictures in this cozy space were odd. But more so was Sophia, who stood in the room in a frothy smock, pointy-chinned, with her wide mouth and grave eyes in an expression of intense concentration as she impatiently adjusted her watch.

She was adjusting her watch because she was for once extremely anxious to be on time. This was a party in her honor and she did not want to be rude by arriving late. But it must be said that Sophia was one of those people who are reliably late. So she needed every bit of help she could get; in this case a very special watch would have to do the trick.

At first glance, the watch was just another cheap watch. The band was made of translucent pink plastic with flecks of gold glitter. A pink and gold castle with oddly familiar crenellated turrets gleamed from the watch face. Really, not an extraordinary watch at all; in fact, just an amusement park souvenir, a trinket kids might pester their parents to buy, but sadly destined for neglect and malfunction, as most trinkets are. Except now, as Sophia hunched over her watch, as her long skinny fingers turned the knob and the quaintly shaped hands on the watch face spun about, the room transformed.

The turquoise-colored cabinets in the compact kitchen betrayed nary a hint of strangeness. Tableware and cutlery remained organized in their drawers. The diminutive counter was clear, except for a bowl and a glass representing the remains of breakfast. A writing desk of highly polished, exotic burl wood stood near the window. A miniature statue of a centaur sat on the desk, along with an open book and a pen, two desk accessories with the very same glitter-flecked pattern as on the wrist watch. These items hinted fondly at the souvenir autograph book and pen sets you find when you visit special places.

But now, in this calm and cozy spot, some alarming and most subtle but undeniable things began to happen.

The elongated pictures against the faded blue walls were changing. No longer static and serious visions of famous architectural landmarks, they became infused with light and moving figures, emanating sound. Against its gilt gold frame, the picture of a paneled library room, labeled *The Quintana Castle Query Room*, once stately and empty, was now peopled with children and a librarian who sat reading a book aloud. Within this strangely animated picture, a remarkable event was about to take place. In the far corner of the reading room, a fine old oil painting stood propped against the fireplace mantel; three small figures crept toward the painting and then suddenly disappeared, as if the painting itself were another doorway.

Sophia, still hunched over her watch, trying to get the time just right, uttered a frustrated "Oh, I've done it again." She now reversed the direction of the watch hands, causing those very same three figures to reappear in the picture. But as the watch hands spun in reverse, more odd things happened. In a different picture on the wall, a fine drawing of an old stone building, crowds of people milled about.

Looking up from the watch at the drawing, Sophia sighed heavily and said, "Oh, now I've overcompensated. I've gone too far back." But the spectacle in the picture held her attention, and her gaze fell from the animated picture to the shining placard below, which read *The Aisle of Tears*. She stared at the picture, where crowds stood in lines in a large hall. The picture awoke a train of memories for Sophia. How long ago, and yet we have scarcely changed, she thought. Why, there is Daemon Skye. He had that day lost the glamour of a thunderbolt-wielding god to become a short-order cook for a local diner.

In the picture, a man wearing a tattered cloak argued and gestured strongly at an official. The tattered cloak barely concealed a muscular arm bearing swirling designs and a glimmering gold torque, which drew the curious stares of the crowd, and the suspicious queries of the official.

"Of course, sir. I understand you had a highly prestigious position in your previous society, but here, we want to make sure you can contribute. I am sure you understand. I think your skills, as you said, in spontaneous energy generation will be helpful, but we don't really have a job class for that right now, so I'll just put down *short-order cook* for now. Your talents with fire will really come in handy in frying up sausages and eggs on the skillet, wouldn't you agree?" asked the official politely.

Daemon Skye nodded mutely and suppressed a sarcastic protest as the immigration official completed the paperwork. "So, would you say you are in good health, possessed of normal vision and hearing?" queried the official.

Daemon replied good-naturedly, "I certify that is true. In fact, I am sure I could pinpoint your apartment from where I stand now looking out that window, and assure you that in thirty years, I will have built my skyscraper right over the very spot where you and your Sapling brats now have your morning gruel."

"Excuse me, sir?" asked the official, unabashed, looking up from his paperwork. He was certain he had not heard correctly.

Daemon thought better of his remark. He mumbled sheepishly with a crooked smile, "Yes indeed, sir, of extraordinarily stout heart and constitution."

The official smiled kindly back, handing Daemon his stack of papers, "Here you are, Mr. Skye, welcome to New York. Good luck to you." He then turned to the next people in line, a couple who resembled Mr. Skye in the state of their clothes and their peculiar body accessories.

Sophia watched the proceedings in the picture and thought, oh…there are Sybille and Quint, as in love as ever. The couple stood together like bookends. They barely touched and regarded each other with a cool fondness as if critically contemplating their hidden selves. Other couples in line held hands and clung to each other below their heavy travel coats, exchanging kisses, but not Sybille and Quint. How romantic, thought Sophia, as they faced the official with calm solidarity.

"So, your names are Sybille Nix and Quint A. Senns. And Quint, your previous line of work was levitation, magic carpets, and other inventions for strategic combat. While you, Miss Nix, your specialty was high-spin metals. You are a sort of a jewelry artist, I see. Why don't I put down your line of work as *investment banker*, Mr. Senns. Seems you have knack for spotting winning inventions. And you, Miss Nix, how about *fashion designer* or *jewelry artist*?"

Sybille and Quint regarded the official with friendly if cool detachment, barely nodding their assent. Though they could have easily found reason to protest, they were the sort who abhorred inefficiency and wasted energy under any circumstances. They knew from Daemon's example that it was best to agree with this official, the designated representative for immigration services in their new country of choice.

"Here you go, your official papers. Welcome to New York, and best of luck in all your endeavors," said the official in congratulations. Both Sybille and Quint thanked him.

A large woman stepped up to the registration desk. "Maxine Weaver is your name?" asked the official.

The woman nodded. The official continued, "And you are married to Ray Bender?" The official looked up and searched until his gaze found a short thin man barely visible in the shadow of his wife.

"So your previous occupation, Maxine, was weaving, blankets, carpets, fabrics and nets of all kinds. Well, I am sorry but that is not a major industry here. Weaving by hand is considered a hobby, a craft, rather like knitting," explained the official apologetically.

"But I'll tell you what...we do have a need for people who like to thread things together, so I'll put your occupation down as *tunnel designer*. I'm sure the people at the Metropolitan Tunnel Authority could use your attention to such weighty details."

Maxine smiled graciously in reply and stepped aside just enough for her husband's thin face to peer through. "Oh, yes, Mr.

Bender, you state your previous occupation was manipulation of cosmic bodies, stars, and the like. Well, we don't really have a need for those skills now, but judging from your resume, I think you'd make a fine *optometrist*. They deal with all those tricky things you apparently have a talent for."

With another flourish of his pen and transfer of official documents, he ushered Maxine Weaver and Ray Bender into the local citizenry. But now the official looked toward the next candidate, and a frown crossed his face.

The woman standing before him was uncommonly tall and thin. Her complexion was translucent and her eyes like pools of eternity. Her pointy chin and wide, impish mouth made him think of supernatural creatures. The official was duly trained in what undesirables to watch out for during these interviews for immigration. Here, he knew, was a person who might fall in this category, the undesirables, never to leave this place freely, this place, the *Aisle of Tears*.

He pretended to objectively read her application, then stammered, "Let's see," he said, "Sophia Ludwig, originally of high birth in Bavaria, verifiable lineage dating to the earliest monarchs of the Elledoor world, including membership in a ruling society called the *Ringgolds*. That's all very nice. Hmm, accomplished seer, prophetess, vampire as well…I suppose those could be useful skills."

The official paused. He remembered now from his job training. Among the class of undesirables were those claiming to be involved in supernatural activities — including alps, gnomes, fairies, and vampires. He took a deep breath, and tried to control his anxiety. Here before him was a person who was indisputably in that category. He hesitated to say more lest any remark of his should prompt her to open that wide, beguiling mouth to reveal a set of large, sharp, menacing teeth.

The official now remembered clearly, waking from the tedium of job training when the lecturer explained, "The existence of Elledoor world supernatural beings has never been confirmed."

The lecturer elaborated, "It is said these beings are in hiding after centuries of persecution. These beings have never been demonstrated to be harmful, though stories of their uncanny abilities abound. Though it is hard to identify them, there is a tendency toward uncommonly large teeth, and the presence of highly intelligent animal companions. These characteristics are said to be markers of their very ancient lineage."

But now, the official could not remember whether there was a strictly stated policy prohibiting supernatural beings. I've definitely allowed some major kooks in today, thought the official, what a guy claiming to throw thunderbolts and another claiming to make things fly. What's another weirdo?

He looked down diligently at the application, careful to avoid the eyes of the young woman. Finally, he summoned the courage to look up and say regretfully, "I'm sorry, ma'am, but we have no need for seers or vampires here. We have statisticians, and mathematicians to help us figure out probabilities and thereby predict outcomes. I'm afraid I will have to deny your application."

He looked away, hoping to avoid the wounded expression in those large tranquil eyes, but in vain. The young woman's eyes welled with tears, and the wide mouth parted slightly in a forced smile of acknowledgement and understanding.

Despite her deep disappointment, the woman collected herself and mustered a defensive argument. "But you know, I know much about statistics and mathematics, though we don't call knowledge of that sort by those names," said the woman after a pause. Her sad gaze turned to the window, where she was sure she saw glistening tears of sympathy in the eyes of the statue in the harbor far in the distance.

The official was quiet. He did not want to explain or apologize for the institutional bias against supernatural beings, or point out the objectionable word, *vampire*, on her application. He hesitated.

He had once again summoned the courage to deliver a firm and judicious rejection, when a young man stepped before the desk.

CHAPTER ONE

"Not to intrude," said the man deferentially, "But I couldn't help overhearing. I myself am familiar with the linguistic differences between English and the tongues of the Elledoor world. With all respect, I believe Miss Ludwig made an understandable spelling error on her application. She wrote *vampire* meaning to write *umpire*, you see. She meant to say she is experienced in refereeing, mediation, and research in social conflicts, as opposed to any bloody or predatory pursuits."

The official considered the argument. He stared at the two faces: the one soft but severe, beseeching him with tragic sorrow; the other handsome, irreproachably open and earnest. Finally, he relented. "That's an understandable mistake. And we could definitely use more people skilled in mediation. But the position of umpire may not be particularly appropriate. Why don't I put down *librarian*, since you seem to know something about just about everything?"

Sophia's face brightened. Even then, the idea of spending her days surrounded by beautiful books was all she had ever hoped for. She thanked the official, and in that moment, despite her predilection toward truth above all else, she managed to overlook the half-lie that allowed the official to relent. She happily accepted the pile of official documents and nearly danced to join her friends, Sybille and Quint.

Behind her, the young man who had cleverly intervened on her behalf followed her light and joyous movements. His gaze was distracted, however, as he himself now stood before the quizzical consideration of the immigration official.

"Branch Archer that is a fine name. But unfortunately, archery, like weaving, is not really a calling or job around here, not even archery on horseback. But your other experience as designer of waterworks is very impressive. They may be able to use you at the Metropolitan Tunnel Authority, but why don't I just put down *architect*, and you can see if it suits you," said the official. Then, with hardly a glance at Branch's more esoteric history — Lord of the Underworld, Mischief Maker of the Eons — he stamped the citizenship papers, which he then handed to Branch with a broad smile of approval just as Branch proceeded toward the door where Sophia, Quint, and Sybille now gathered.

Watching this spectacle from the cozy apartment, Sophia smirked and thought, That Branch, somehow everyone liked him. But the thought of Branch saddened her deeply. Even as the picture of the Aisle of Tears resumed its form as a still and static picture of a historic building, and the picture of the warm and comforting library room regained its stately quiet, memories lingered, setting off a train of thought.

She surveyed her apartment, content that her watch was now set to the correct time. The tiny apartment was essentially empty. There was no crib with designer crib linens, or cheerful collection of stuffed animals. There would have been no room, assuming she had the money to buy such things, and assuming she even wanted those things.

Sophia's collection of things already suited her quite well. A miniature statue of a centaur stood on a handsome writing desk, a remarkably exquisite piece for someone such as Sophia, who seemingly lacked the means to collect priceless pieces of art. The muscular torso of a man melded gracefully into the horse's body. The arms were stretched and flexed to shoot a bow and arrow — a bow with a double curve suggesting the outline of a violin. Engraved in the craggy granite base was the inscription:

> To my beloved wife, Sophia,
> The quiver of eternal love
> Through the arrow of time.
> *With love, Branch*

On the bed was a quilt. The quilt was from their close friends Quint A. Senns and Sybille Nix. The quilt featured a border of embroidered herbs: long narrow leaves of sage, the crenellated outline of spearmint, and petite leaves of thyme. In the middle of the quilt was a picture of a garden with a symmetrical arrangement of benches and hedges. There were pools and statues, and a building labeled *The Sagittarium*. The words embroidered on the lower edge read *Sagetooth, Home of the Ringgolds of Eternity*. The initials stitched neatly in the lower corner read *SNL*.

As Sophia headed out the door, she glanced around the living room. Her gaze fell on a large wooden bench made of an exquisite burl wood. Silk pillows in bright, iridescent colors cushioned the bench, and rounded contours in the seat created comfortable spots for slumping. Carved in one such spot, amid the multi-toned rings and swirls of the polished wood grain, was a warning that read:

Property of the Time Terrace.
Criminal penalties apply for defacement of any kind.

The seat had been a house-warming present from her friend Maxine Weaver, quite a nice piece, really.

Among the other things in her apartment was a blue crystal wastepaper basket with five glass petals. The wastepaper basket contained a few crumpled sheets of paper today. Oddly enough, the basket was never emptied, and yet never overflowed, despite the continuous volume of discarded paper. It had been a wedding gift to her from Ray Bender and his wife, Maxine Weaver. Ray was very good with glass.

Now, as she got ready for the party, she took quick stock of what she needed. She had her subway pass. She lived in the West Village and used her subway pass to get everywhere. She had a small present for Sybille's children. She had the pink-and-gold-flecked autograph book that served as her journal and rarely left her possession, and the matching pen. She had her keys and her coin purse. She also brought along a pocket-sized book of baby names.

As she walked out the door, she looked once again at her small, tidy apartment. She had been worried lately, fighting off fears of single motherhood. She knew she would get by; mommies always found a way. Just as she started to feel sorry for herself, she realized that all was not drudgery and despair. For instance, noticing the untidy remains of breakfast left on the counter, she turned to her watch. Turning the knob, she set the time back an hour, and muttered something that sounded like *Counter Unclutter*. The breakfast dishes, now sparkling clean, floated into their designated positions in the cupboards, leaving the counter pristinely clear.

Sophia smiled happily as she once again reset her watch. She felt brave and encouraged by her wondrous, if small feat. She thought there were mommies who were hotel maids, switchboard operators, migrant farm workers, who still took good care of their babies and managed to see their children attend famous colleges and become world leaders.

She had in fact just recently attended a baby shower for the Lujan family, she recalled. They were an immigrant Mexican couple, struggling to get by, working in one of the big restaurants, and yet they were overjoyed. A new baby. A baby boy at that, to be named Miguel. They knew Sophia from the library, and had the generosity to invite her to celebrate their new arrival.

Thinking of this happy event inspired her to hurriedly open her journal to jot down a happy premonition.

> Infinite possibility…infinite, a very hard concept to describe. Symbolically, infinity is the number eight laid on its side. Mathematically, infinity is any number divided by zero.

> But qualitatively, how would one grasp infinity? Infinite possibility would be something like a baby boy born to immigrants in a tiny basement apartment surpassing the achievements of others with every advantage of money, attention, and social position…

Here Sophia stopped to gather her thoughts, which now had a somewhat satirical tone, rather unexpected in such an otherwise enchanting and truly lovely person.

> ...a small boy grows up without the benefit of the most ergonomic baby pram, or bedtime serenades from compact discs designed for developing minds...

This brilliant insight was unfortunately cut short by a strange event. Sophia fidgeted with the pink-and gold-flecked pen, clicking the buttons for changing the pen color. But oddly, when the pen color changed, so also did the decorative glass finial at the top of the pen. Instead of writing in green, Sophia's favorite color, the pen now wrote in red, and the decorative finial transformed into the clearly recognizable profile of none other than Sybille Nix. Sophia's thoughts scrawled rapidly on the page, were interrupted by Sybille's ladylike admonitions.

> My dear Sophia, if you continue to vent your unkind opinions against Saplings, you will miss your baby shower, and all the kind guests will be compelled to return their presents, to universal consternation and displeasure.

Sophia thought to scribble a hasty reply, but thought better of it. Sybille was her longtime friend, doing a well-intentioned favor by throwing this baby shower. Instead Sophia scrawled:

> My dearest Sybille, you are so right. I have synchronized my watch with yours, so as to be neither awkwardly early nor unforgivably late.

Sybille replied promptly with a return dash of the pen.

> It will be unforgivable if you are late. Constance Gordon and Rebecca Poe are both already here...

Sophia read the last bit of information with horror. Constance

Gordon and Rebecca Poe were not only among the more opinionated of Sybille's many friends; they were also known adversaries and reliably caused a scene whenever in the other's presence. Sophia was about to send her sympathy and support, when the writing on the page adopted the distinctive style of yet another writer. Maxine Weaver now wrote in a dramatic black hand:

> Sophia, if you leave right now, without any more silly scribbling, you have just enough time to stop at your favorite newsstand, briefly peruse the latest edition of the *Tunnel Times*, and then be exactly on time for the train to Soho, where in the fourth car, a comfortable seat recently vacated by a Chinese man will be available.

Sophia thought, That Maxine, she does know the MTA trains well. Well, that is her business. But she knows the habits of regular riders and their embarkation and destination points so precisely as to predict when seats will be vacated. What has come of privacy in this society!

Nevertheless, Sophia heeded Maxine's advice, and with one last quick glance about the apartment, she headed out the door feeling hopeful and optimistic. It seemed to Sophia that she really had everything she needed. Though, she thought, a nice blanket and an unlimited subway pass would be nice.

Things would be fine for her child with only one parent. There were wonderful places for children in easy walking distance in Manhattan, noted for wonderful playgrounds, bike paths, and public schools. She made a note to write a letter to the mayor in praise of the city's public spaces and cultural monuments. How else would single mommies get by? No, her child would definitely have the important things.

CHAPTER TWO

A BABY SHOWER

Sophia headed outside, ready at last. Sunshine dappled the trees lining this neighborhood of brownstones. Her neighbor was returning from a grocery trip. He smiled and waved.

What a sweet man, she thought, I feel sad that he suffers from a terrible illness most probably related to his time in service during the Tunnel Wars. She had never really spoken to her neighbor, but she knew a few things about him. She actually knew something about everyone and everything.

She walked down the street and then stopped at a newsstand. Behind the typical glossy magazines with various important world leaders and semi-clothed starlets was a drab, black and white periodical bearing the heading *Tunnel Times*. Sophia peered at the headline, which read:

SKYE TOWER: BRIDGE TO HEAVEN
Manhattan real estate mogul and war hero Daemon Skye announced today the grand opening of Skye Tower, the tallest and most opulent building in New York if not the world. The top floor of this new building is home to the Skye Bridge Spa, which offers services to restore beauty and youth, and the Bull's Eye Restaurant, which serves the best steaks in town.

Below the headline was a picture of a tall, imposing man standing beside a woman with chiseled cheekbones. They posed with elegant detachment before a mural depicting bulls and horses. The caption for the picture read:

> Millionaire Daemon Skye and his wife, the Ukrainian-born model and actress Penelope Heraklova, will host a grand opening party at Skye Tower, to be attended by entertainment celebrities and other New York glitterati. Mr. Skye, one of the most successful *Ringgold* émigrés, is celebrated in New York society for his astonishing rise from short-order cook to high-flying entrepreneur. Mr. Skye returned recently from a tour of duty in the Tunnel Wars, where he garnered many medals for bravery despite tragic setbacks, including the loss of his friend and squadron mate, the noted architect Branch Archer.

The last line drew the faintest glistening in Sophia's eyes, for her husband had never returned to live the rich life Daemon now enjoyed. But her mood, in a mechanism toward equilibrium, returned to the events of the day.

Oh, Daemon, that is impressive, true to your word, thought Sophia, remembering Daemon's determined threat in the Aisle of Tears. However, even Sophia, with her cool, calculating calm shuddered at the thought of Daemon, a ferocious and unpredictable force. Glancing back at the periodical, another headline caught her eye:

ALBERT EINSTEIN, PHYSICIST, AND LEONARDO FIBONACCI, MATHEMATICIAN, SELECTED

CHAPTER TWO

Albert Einstein, famed for his shattering discoveries in physics, and Leonardo Fibonacci, the brilliant 13th-century mathematician, have been selected along with six other noted thinkers to grace this year's *SNL Limited Edition Baby Blanket*.

Einstein's work in general relativity and special relativity changed the common perception of gravity, time, and the universe. Einstein's insights contributed to such modern wonders as the photoelectric effect and the LASER (Light Amplification by Stimulated Emission of Radiation). Fibonacci's discovery of the Fibonacci number series is now associated with everything from flower petal arrangements to rabbit populations, and stock fluctuations.

Below, there was a black and white picture of a man with a bushy mustache and droopy eyelids. Oh, that Albert, such a mischief-maker, thought Sophia. Were it not for him, perhaps the Saplings would still be in blissful ignorance, happy in their rectilinear world of cause and effect, and perhaps we would not have been so worried about Sapling incursions, or been compelled to immigrate and intervene in those dreadful Tunnel Wars, she thought reflectively.

The newsstand sold flowers. Amid her ponderous musings, Sophia spotted a dewy bouquet of sunflowers. "Such a joy, each flower is different and yet the same, optimized design and individuality in one," she exclaimed.

The perfection and organization in a simple flower thrilled her, and she further exclaimed, "I am reminded of Leonardo Fibonacci, such a charming man, rattling on about Hindy-Arabic techniques of calculation, describing his travels in Byzantium. Too bad he had to wait until he was dead to be famous for a magic number series…a magic number series describing many disparate things: rabbit population growth, the spiral patterns of seed heads, and flower petals. Let's see, 0, 1, 1, 2, 3, 5, 8, 13, 21, 34, 55, 89…"

It was true. The small sunflowers had fifty-five petals; the larger ones had one hundred forty-four petals, all Fibonacci numbers. The seed heads in the sunflower were densely packed and scattered in patterns of thirty-four and eighty-nine spirals — all magic numbers.

"Hmm, a brilliant idea…one packing pattern for everything…a pattern allowing each petal the most possible sunlight and rain, and the least shadow; an efficient packing pattern giving strength to each seed head on each stem of each flower," she thought aloud. She took comfort in the idea that the same principle would be true for each child, including her child, single mother or not.

She was so engrossed in admiring the flowers that she was startled, and looked up with a wide-eyed stare of astonishment when the newsstand attendant indicated the price of the flowers.

The price of things these days! I barely make that money in an hour, thought Sophia to herself. She fished in her coin purse for the money. It would have been ungracious to imply that things were unfairly priced, but increasingly she faced the shocking disparity between cost and income.

Sensing that she had a problem, a man behind her asked, "Not meaning to be rude, but may I help?"

Sophia looked up from her frantic search to see a man in a blue suit with a yellow paisley tie and reflective aviator sunglasses that hid his eyes. A typical Wall Street type, she thought to herself, the type to equate cleanliness with godliness, and godliness with faithful digestion of the *Wall Street Journal*.

Then, taking a closer look, she noticed that he was not being at all condescending. He is probably just in a hurry, she thought to herself. But she really knew better, being an astute reader of personalities. She sensed he was simply trying to help. She also noticed the clean line of his jaw, and at once calculated the singular good fortune of this event.

She marveled at the minuscule odds of meeting an attractive

man at a newsstand. She knew this instant, but unspoken connection was a probabilistic impossibility, here in this universe of infinite indifferent interactions.

She wanted to seize the moment, to blurt out something like "You have to be one of the most attractive men in New York!" But instead she said demurely, "Oh, no, I was just counting the petals, never hurts to stop and smell the roses, you know." As soon as those words left her mouth, though, she berated herself. How incredibly trite! How pathetic!

To her relief, he said in reply, "Yes, mathematical marvels in little things. I spend all day trying to predict things that have an irrational rationality." He smiled and removed his sunglasses. He hardly seemed bothered by her rotund shape. In fact, now his eyes followed the line of her neck to the gentle curve of her abdomen. Sophia realized how handsome he was.

She fumbled for a reply, searching for something clever to say. But as so happens with ordinary and even not so ordinary people under stress, she was tongue-tied, and no amount of experience as a vampire and seer would help her now.

Finally she said, "It must drive you nuts to have to do that all day." Immediately, she felt an uncontrollable urge to bite her tongue. What a corny word, *nuts*; he must think I'm about twelve.

He did not smirk, but instead replied reflectively, "Well, it's great when you can predict things perfectly. Maybe you know something about that?"

He looked directly at her.

Sophia looked at him quizzically and replied, "No, not even I predict things perfectly."

In the awkward pause, Sophia's thoughts were scattered; her mind was racing. What could he mean? Who is he? His smile is enough to melt an iceberg. She was just about to ask him his name, when instead she checked her purse again.

Realizing she had correct change, she said, "Hey — thanks, but I think I have it." Flowers in hand, she smiled and waved and continued down the street.

"Later," he said, waving back. When she turned around again, he had disappeared in the crowd.

Sophia was in a daze as she approached the subway station. She felt jubilant. She had almost met someone, someone who wanted to talk to her and seemed to like her, someone who made her heart race and head spin, someone whose odd remark set in motion a string of possibilities and questions — someone who reminded her vaguely of someone else.

But, she thought, it couldn't be. But Sybille and Maxine would know. There must be rules that decide these things. Now she was angry at herself. I didn't even find out his name! I'll never see him again, and all because I am just a gutless little librarian, she thought, berating herself again.

It was true. Sophia definitely had many outstanding qualities: insight into the lives of strangers, a very lively imagination, and friends in all places, here and there, past and present.

But here, as Sophia Ludwig, New York City librarian, she really wished there were things she could change. Maybe she could return to that moment at the newsstand before he disappeared anonymously into the crowd of a huge city, never to randomly meet again. Perhaps if she were a glamorous model like...what was her name...Penelope, from the Ukraine, it would have been different. Perhaps she should turn around now and ask everyone who may have been there — the newsstand attendant, other people in line, anyone who might have a clue as to who he was.

She was so distracted, she barely noticed the faint sounds of Cole Porter from Gnome Records. She barely glanced up when she went by the street saxophonist playing "Windmills of Your Mind." Street performers in metallic blue makeup did a new kind of dance. Pizza makers spun dough in shop windows. The tattoo shop called The Parthian Connection displayed black and white designs featuring exuberant spirals. All over was the waft of stir-fried Thai noodles, and piroshki.

As if in a dream, she entered the subway and boarded the train to Soho. However distracted, she made her way to the fourth car of the train where, as Maxine predicted, she found herself a comfortable seat. Collecting herself under the blank gazes of train passengers, she took a breath. She was headed to a baby shower; she had bought a bouquet of flowers; she had almost met a handsome stranger. She still had in hand her journal, her pen, and all the things she intended to bring, but now she would bring questions.

As Sophia entered through the fire-engine-red doors of the loft on Elizabeth Street, she was greeted by a blur of motion: Elle and Matt, twins who always seemed to be everywhere and nowhere at the same time.

Elle and Matt did not look like most children. For one, despite their short stature and small, round faces, they had a seriousness and intensity that was astonishing. For another, their movements were so quick, you never knew exactly where they were. When they were momentarily still, you couldn't figure out how they got there. It was only from reading signs — a cry or giggle, scattered bubble gum wrappers, trampling feet — that you might guess their presence.

Today, their parents had evidently counseled them about behavior for a baby shower. They arrived at the door and actually both stood still, together, facing Sophia, for several moments. They did not grab her bag in search of a toy or gift; they did not start blurting esoteric scientific know-how mimicking their mother or father. They did not behave like the intellectual bullies they were quite capable of being. Instead, they saw Sophia and raised their arms for the welcome hug that they were accustomed to receiving.

Sybille Nix followed closely behind her children. Sybille wore an elegant, floral dress, high heels, and her signature helical earrings. Her hair was smooth and combed back, and she wore makeup. Sophia barely recognized her.

Sybille's profound knowledge of metals had over the years taken her away from jewelry-making. She was now an assistant professor of physics. Her typical look was best described as high-fashion lab-room grunge: thick glasses, earrings, boots with lug soles, an exquisite quilted jacket in bright red, matching pants with zippered pockets, a pendant for conversations with philosophy-physics double majors. But today, in honor of Sophia and this happy occasion, she looked very much the gracious, society hostess.

Sybille, after all, was married to Quint A. Senns, a Manhattan investment banker whose venture capital projects had helped fuel some of the hottest trends in technology, while making investors very wealthy. Sybille, when she wasn't helping discover the smallest fleck of elemental matter, enjoyed attending fashion shows, hosting parties, and, above all, making quilts.

"Sophia, how wonderful to see you…you look great!" exclaimed Sybille with a welcoming embrace and wide smile.

Behind Sybille was Quint, looking casual and composed in this most stylish and elegant of homes. He greeted Sophia warmly, as old friends. He turned toward the area rug in the pattern of a chess board where opposing chess pieces were already assembled. "Do you still play?" he asked.

Sophia nodded and smiled. But a shadow crossed her face as she noticed the distinctive figures in Quint's chess set. The queen sat on a throne nursing a child. Her expression was stately, and she wore a crown. The king wore a conical crown and a gold pectoral around his neck. He stood in a stiff, unnatural pose as if reposed in a rigid sarcophagus.

Isis, the widowed goddess of magic and prophecy of ancient Egypt, and her slain husband Osiris, god of the underworld, she thought. How fitting. She knew the same thoughts were running through Quint's mind. She felt sure now that the man at the newsstand was no accident; the mythical allusions in this chess collection were no accident. Quint was telling her something. Osiris returned from the dead and was reconstituted in his own body. Branch would be as well, Sophia felt sure of that.

Sophia's gaze now turned to the opposing pieces. She was sure she saw someone familiar in the muscular build and long jaw of the opposing king. As if reading her mind, Quint remarked lightly, "That is the Seth animal, modeled faithfully after replicas that our friend the antiques dealer, Vladimir Poe, dug up for us."

Sophia replied, "Funny, I might have thought you would have modeled the thunder stick and angry temper of..."

"Our friend Daemon Skye?" asked Quint. "Who knows what really goes on in Daemon's heart?"

Just then, as if the name Daemon Skye had been shouted out loud, all the guests turned toward them with looks of intense interest. Sophia continued, "Daemon is opening a spa and restaurant. Last we spoke, he said he wanted most of all to bring the experience of nirvana within grasp of the silly Saplings. He thought they might benefit from the experience."

"You know Daemon Skye?" asked a guest, wide-eyed in disbelief, suddenly looking at Sophia attentively.

"Yes I do, in fact," replied Sophia, "I see him often reading newspapers in the library."

The other guests were at a loss for words. Sophia, with her hesitant manner and frumpy ballerina look, scarcely looked like the type who would be the close friend of a property tycoon. They knew she was certainly being facetious to suggest a property tycoon would read newspapers in the library.

One of the guests, a woman with a serious and proper demeanor named Constance Gordon, smiled politely and then said skeptically, "What would Daemon Skye want to know from the newspapers? He already has the world at his fingertips. He already has what most people consider nirvana."

"Really, indeed...so tell me...what is it that you know about nirvana?" asked a tall, lithe woman emerging from the opposite corner of the room. She wore a fashionable tee-shirt below which could be glimpsed on the slender midriff a distinctive motif suggesting graceful swans locked in embrace.

Unperturbed by the implicit challenge, Constance Gordon arched an eyebrow and returned with a measured and dispassionate response. "Nirvana has nothing to do with frivolous and revealing fashions, that I know," Constance said with an obvious glance at Rebecca's midriff, "especially frivolity and flashiness resulting in a breakdown of the social fabric, in children born of irresponsibility, unwanted children."

With that statement, Constance gulped, but her blank glance toward Sophia carried no hint of apology or sympathy. Sophia self-consciously glanced at her swelling abdomen, so artfully concealed beneath the smock. She blushed in embarrassment. In that moment, she thought to retort, "The miracle of reproduction is a great expression of hope, whatever the circumstances," but instead she shot a silent look back. Constance had turned away.

The other guests smiled weakly at the exchange. One of the guests whispered to her friend, "That's Constance Gordon, you know, a prosecuting attorney, very well-respected, though, a bit assertive. And the woman with the tattoo and long brown hair, she's Rebecca Poe. Her father is a well-known antiques dealer. She's the artsy poet type." They did not mention Ms. Gordon's air of authority, which both impressed and repelled people, or Rebecca's effervescent if eccentric charm. They stammered to change the subject, when Sybille announced cheerfully over the hubbub, "Everyone is here, and the kids are quiet…Let's all sit down. Grab a drink, and we'll do presents!"

Sophia looked around and saw a large, commanding woman in a dark gray suit, seated with perfect posture beside a small, bird-like man. They had a sagacious air, as if they had been the first to arrive and were the only ones who were on time. Sophia was glad to see Maxine and Ray.

Maxine Weaver was the director of the Metropolitan Tunnel Authority. She was there with her husband, Ray Bender, an optometrist. They both looked glad to see Sophia as she took a seat next to them, though they seemed to gauge her flustered state of mind, and were anxious and concerned.

"Sophia, the baby…we are so glad for you. How do you feel?"

CHAPTER TWO

they asked.

"Oh, fine, as always," replied Sophia. She could have gone on and on about the awkwardness of being fifty pounds overweight, the thrill of feeling the baby move inside, the exquisite tickling sensation deep in her groin, or her troubles getting her librarian's salary to cover the cost of supporting herself, let alone a small child. But she did not want to bring up the topic of weight with Maxine nor burden them with her relatively trivial concerns. Plus, she had more pressing questions.

Turning to Maxine, she said emphatically, "Maxine, I think Branch is back. I met someone today at a newsstand. He didn't look exactly like him, but I thought I felt his presence, an aura. Is that possible? Given everything?"

Maxine regarded the younger woman sympathetically, then said with sadness, "What a hopeful idea. But Branch died in an explosion. His body was damaged beyond remedy. Even we, with our advanced healing powers, are not able to reconstruct him under those circumstances."

Sophia protested, "But it was him. I know it!" Her protest was interrupted at that moment by a package that landed in her lap. The package was wrapped with beautiful pink wrapping paper featuring periwinkle cupids. The card read:

> The company you keep
> as you fall asleep
> opens the mind
> to all the heart might find.
> — Best wishes for your new baby,
> *Sybille and Quint*

The gift was a baby quilt, trimmed with white lace, with sixteen alternating squares of white and sage green. In the white squares were portraits in exquisite needlepoint, each with an embroidered label. In the lower corner were the initials *SNL*. Softer than fleece, it felt lighter than a feather.

Sophia was delighted, and being a librarian with a love for books and history, she quickly recognized most of the names and portraits on the blanket. There was a bearded man with a turban, whose label read:

> *Omar Khayyam*
> *Poet and Mathematician*
> *Persia*
> *1123*

Beside him was a woman with upswept hair, in a draped robe; her label read:

> *Hypatia*
> *Discoverer of Specific Gravity*
> *The Serapeum, Alexandria, Egypt*
> *415*

A few squares away was the portrait of a man with droopy eyelids and a bushy mustache, whose label read:

> *Albert Einstein*
> *Physicist*
> *Germany, Austria & Princeton, New Jersey*
> *1955*

"Oh, Albert Einstein," exclaimed Sophia. "Every child should have a chance to speak with him." The guests all nodded and smiled weakly in agreement.

Then she noticed a square with a drawing of a man in a collared tunic, whose label read:

> *Leonardo Fibonacci*
> *Mathematician*
> *Pisa, Italy*
> *1250*

"Oh, Leonardo, I was just thinking about him today, such a fascinating man, such an intuitive and rigorous observer of the ubiquitous patterns of nature," she exclaimed. She was just about to tell everyone about counting the petals on the sunflowers, when she noticed the glazed looks of the other guests. Instead she remarked, "I love custom quilts. Sybille, this is just darling!"

CHAPTER TWO

Finding another package in her lap, she looked down to admire the wrapping paper and read the card. The wrapping paper featured green papyrus flowers and blue water lilies. Opening the card, printed with a large M, she read:

> Best wishes, Sophia, for your new baby,
> that she may
> at each point and date
> travel through space
> with singular grace
> with neither the push of time,
> nor the pull of weight.
> — *Maxine Weaver & Ray Bender*

With anticipation, she opened the small package to discover a round bronze token decorated with a border of cryptic motifs, with a tiny inscription.

Sophia thought to read the very tiny writing but was not sure the other guests would appreciate the humor or charm. Instead, she proceeded to open the other gifts, which were, as promised, of the truly tasteful and adorable sort — things all mommies need: diaper wraps, one-piece underwear, a breast pump, even a tee-shirt printed with the words *Baby Diva*, which the giver assured her was from the latest celebrity fashion line. Sophia thanked everyone profusely.

As everyone gathered to leave, Sophia remembered the gift for Elle and Matt. They had been well-behaved the entire time, and had managed to not collide into each other or any walls once. "Why, thank you. The kids will love it, I'm sure. Though you didn't have to," said Sybille as she opened the gift. She was well aware of Sophia's financial situation.

Sybille read the box: "Marzipan Chess Piece kit. *Model Warriors From All Time.*" Then, looking at Sophia quizzically, she asked, "They do mean the *entire* spectrum of time, don't they?"

Sophia replied, "Naturally."

Sybille exclaimed, "Oh, wonderful…I should tell you that Quint helped with the quilt. You may not need a crib, because the baby will just, shall we say, float off to sleep. You may not need a baby-sitter; there are eyes enough in that quilt. Wouldn't you agree?"

Sophia gave Sybille an understanding look and replied happily, "Sybille and Quint, I never stop being amazed." She gave them each a hug. Then she turned to Maxine and Ray, who asked, "So what are you naming the baby?"

"Well," replied Sophia, "Branch and I had a name picked out, but since things have changed, I thought I'd ask you to help." She opened the book of children's names and read alphabetically:

Amateratsu, Japanese Deity of the Heavens
Atum, Primary Creator God of Ancient Egypt
Ericca, Restorative Plant of the Nile
Horus, Child of Osiris and Isis
Isis, Egyptian Goddess of Wisdom
Osiris, Egyptian God of Water and Regeneration
Seth, Egyptian God of Chaos…

Then, looking up, Sophia said, "Hmm, Ericca Ludwig, I like that," to which Maxine remarked, "Our own little Ericca!"

With the flash of a pen, Maxine amended the inscription on the bronze token in the opened gift box to read:

TIME TOKEN
Valid for Unlimited Trips on the Light Rail
Issued to Ericca Ludwig for the purpose of a
great adventure.
THANK YOU FOR YOUR PATRONAGE
Maxine Weaver
Executive Director of the Time Tunnels

CHAPTER THREE

THε COBRA CAR

Ericca Ludwig was born in a hospital. She was like most newborn babies in every way. She did not debate her wellness assessment or howl too much when set on a scale to be weighed. Neither did she protest when the delivery nurse wrapped her snugly in a hospital issued receiving blanket.

In fact, she was exactly like every normal and healthy newborn baby in the hospital that day. She nursed enthusiastically, burped moderately, and made the sort of baby gestures grown-ups coo over — assuming there are celebratory grown-ups around, which was actually not true in Ericca's case.

There was exactly one adoring grown-up here, and that was her mother, Sophia. For while other babies had grandparents, friends, family, and most important, jubilant fathers, Ericca had her completely devoted mother, which had to be enough.

There was no retinue of well wishers or helium balloons proclaiming congratulations. But there was her mother, who looked at her as if she were the most wondrous miracle ever.

Sybille Nix sent her congratulations but was at that moment receiving a prize for discovering the mysterious entanglement of very small particles. Sybille's husband, Quint was busy convincing investors to build a life-sized simulation of blind chess. As for Maxine Weaver, the level of graffiti in the public subways had escalated, and she was under extreme pressure from the mayor to control the problem.

Sophia was alone in a hospital bed with her new baby. She

could not help being sad. Ericca was so small and vulnerable, with tiny limbs, the softest peach fuzz, and curled, wrinkled feet. Sophia had resisted thoughts of Branch or the handsome stranger at the newsstand, but now she thought, Ericca should know about her father, and finding a page in her journal, she read aloud:

Branch Archer had always been good friends with Daemon Skye. Branch was a well-known architect in New York. Daemon Skye was a successful Manhattan real estate developer and previous short-order cook. They spent a lot of time together in Texas, where they trained to be fighter pilots. They both joined the Air Force during the Tunnel Wars.

Branch was like fresh air. He lived every day the way he wanted to, with confidence and optimism that things happen fairly. He was the person he wanted to be. He was trusting, and always gave people the benefit of the doubt. Because of this, he was almost always happy. He found many things to delight him.

When he moved to New York for the first time, he found that he really liked a huge variety of things, from jazz and Vietnamese food to barbecued ribs. He loved books. Most of all, he loved a woman named Sophia Ludwig.

Branch first met Sophia in New York. They married and were happily expecting their first child...

Here the writing, smeared with tear stains, read, "...when Branch was killed tragically."

Ericca wriggled in her mother's arms. Her mother whispered in her ear, "...though he wishes his daughter the very best for a happy birthday" and kissed her fuzzy forehead.

Sophia felt the flutter of a delicate suckle and gazed in wonder at the small face. She felt a sensation of anticipation as Ericca's tongue pulsed on her nipple. The baby sighed in engorged content as she drifted into sleep.

Sophia put the journal down, opened where she left off, and fell asleep in exhaustion. When the attending nurse came, she closed the pink-and gold-flecked journal, only momentarily glancing at the open page, which was completely blank.

It was only a few days after Ericca's birth and a few weeks since the baby shower that a slender young woman could be seen walking toward the downtown headquarters of the Metropolitan Tunnel Authority.

Sophia Ludwig walked briskly. Along the street were noisy garbage trucks, honking taxis, bicycle couriers dodging cars and busy professionals in suits with coffee cups sealed with plastic lids. People with picket signs and homeless people with shopping carts carrying blankets tried to get her attention. But Sophia was too preoccupied to notice.

Maxine Weaver worked in a tall office building with an elevator lobby veneered in stone. The building had long corridors of doors, and was built above a subway station.

Maxine sat at the center of a large wooden desk. Her mouth was drawn downward in a dour expression as she peered closely at a stack of newspapers and periodicals, the *Tunnel Times* and the *Underground Encyclopedia* among them. She did not look surprised when Sophia knocked at the door.

"Sophia, my dear, how lovely to see you…How can I help you?" she said encouragingly. She reached for the bagel and coffee mug on her desk. She was very fond of bagels and chewed enthusiastically, nodding as Sophia spoke about the stranger at the newsstand and a disturbing uncertainty.

"I've been thinking about our conversation…Branch is a Ringgold. His soul is immortal, though his body is not. He must exist still in some form," argued Sophia emphatically.

"It is entirely possible, in fact highly probable, that he is trying to find a way back to you and has decided he needs to take a physical form," agreed Maxine, as she stood to close the door, bracing herself against the jolt of trains in the tunnels below.

"But," she continued, "he knows that any body he inhabits already has a destiny, a destiny that would be very hard to alter. Generally, possession of Saplings is not encouraged, even in the most desperate situations. Also, we know that he is geographically distant. He was lost in Central Asia. Disembodied spirits, even the spirits of Ringgolds, cannot travel without a vessel. You know that."

Sophia looked away, summoning all the arguments that convinced her that the stranger at the newsstand was indeed Branch. "But I felt a connection, a connection and understanding so perfect as to exist outside the Sapling realm. Also, he made a strange remark. He said I predicted things, as if he knew..." replied Sophia.

Maxine smiled sadly and said, "We Ringgolds living among Saplings feel the same frustrations of love and loneliness. I'm afraid the loneliness and pain of single motherhood are clouding your otherwise infallible judgment."

Maxine continued more sternly, "Branch's plane exploded over Central Asia. No remains of him were found. His soul was lost amid a harsh terrain of mountain and tundra. This is an area he knows well, however. He may find a vessel and a friend to help on his journey back to you. But Branch has to do that himself, and it will not be easy."

"What kind of a vessel can he use?" asked Sophia.

"Well, a buried Ringgold relic will do, perhaps an oil lamp. You have heard of the term *djinn* or *genie*. Those tribes of long ago knew of our kind of technology. These artifacts can still be found. Branch can inhabit an animal. Ringgolds have had a long affinity with animals," explained Maxine.

"Suppose he is able to find a vessel, how will he recover his body? How can he resume his life with me and Ericca?" asked Sophia with a probing look.

CHAPTER THREE

"He needs to find a portal to the time tunnels, loop back in time to return to the moment of his death, and revise history. There are dangers in time travel, and there are low odds of revising the course of events. There are also perils with even the slightest revision, which can have major ramifications. That is why we grant only a few Time Tokens."

"So is there any way I can find him?" Sophia asked quizzically.

"No, I think not. But when Branch is able and ready, he will come looking for you," answered Maxine.

Looking at Sophia's drawn and disappointed face, "I am sorry. I wish I could be more optimistic," Maxine said, sighing regretfully.

As Sophia turned on her way out, Maxine added encouragingly, "You have Ericca. We should all find happiness in her."

"Down," commanded a small girl of about three. She had been floating on a quilt blanket above the floor and spied what she thought was a bug on the floor. "Bad bug," she admonished, as the blanket slowed to a stop. She peered closely at the offending bug. "Good Spike," said she to the obedient blanket.

Spike was the quilt blanket, a baby shower gift from Sybille Nix. As Sybille had promised, Spike had an element of quintessence, and was resistant to gravity when commanded. Sybille, an assistant professor of physics, liked to talk about anti-gravity and a mysterious substance called quintessence that was causing the universe to expand.

There was no obvious explanation for the name *Spike*, though. The blanket was populated by a host of characters, none of them named *Spike*. The only possible explanation was Quint, father of the twins Elle and Matt. Ericca played with the twins at their loft in Soho often and would hear Quint's lively repartee.

Quint liked to say things like, "You should always sell on a *spike*, and buy on a dip," or "The price will climb when there is a spike in demand and dip in supply." He would continue with a remark like "If you predict these spikes and dips, you can out-maneuver the market and come out ahead. You must be able to react and anticipate trends like a well-designed car."

At this point, Quint might launch into a discussion of one of his favorite topics, collector sports cars. Today, in fact, Quint was expected to arrive in one such car to pick up Ericca for a day with the twins.

These financial insights would not have helped her mother, though. Sophia was hunched nearby over a stack of bills, working on a spreadsheet, saying in frustration to herself, "Oh shush, even I know how to balance a budget." In one column, she had written out her expenses. In another column she had added up her income sources, which included revenues from stories and poems sold. This month, as in previous months, the revenue from stories and poems sold once again added up to exactly zero dollars. But all was not bad news.

"Oh, thank goodness," said Sophia with a sigh of relief, "another month of staying out of debt." Her analysis had concluded with the finding that her income once again marginally exceeded her expenses.

"Toy," exclaimed Ericca. She seldom asked for things, since she had learned fairly early not to pester her mother about buying stuff. The object on the floor proved to be not a playful bug, but a subway token. Ericca rode the subway often, though she never needed this particular subway token, a situation her three-year old mind puzzled over.

There was a knock in the tiny apartment. It was Quint with the twins, who made an instant beeline for Ericca and her blanket Spike.

The twins had learned that Spike was not just any ordinary blanket. Like now, when there was a knock in the apartment, there was a low, inflected voice that whispered, "Who's there? Hopefully not those clamorous children, Elle and Matt..." When all grown-up heads were turned away, the head of a man wearing a tunic popped up from the blanket like a bobblehead, making Ericca shriek with delight.

"The name is Leonardo Fibonacci," the bobblehead

announced, "…famed for discovering the Fibonacci series. Do you realize that by doing simple addition you can come up with a glorious pattern…a pattern of numbers that predicts things from the geometry of flower petals to fluctuations in stock prices?"

He elaborated, wagging his finger, "Start with zero, then add one. This equals one. Then take the last number in the equation, the one, and add the one that was the result of the previous equation, and you get two — if you continue the pattern, you might get this —"

Written in the air on an invisible chalkboard was a number series…0, 1, 1, 2, 3, 5, 8, 13, 21, 34, 55, 89, 144, 233, 377, 610, 987…and a poem:

FIBONACCI'S MAGIC NUMBER SERIES
In my very own Book of Computation
Find a series of simple equations,
Successive sums to a ratio convergent
Describing a sublime order emergent.

More than half, less than two-thirds,
A long number too irrational for words,
A repeating proportion in pine cone or seed head,
Spirals and shapes on a loom of magical thread.

"Isn't that amazing? The ratio between successive sums very quickly approaches a single number, the ratio 1.61803…the most magical number of all!"

Seeing that their heads were spinning, he thought to change the subject, "You know, I had a most fabulous adventure once…in Byzantium, a very different place, where there were Hindus and Arabs."

The children were now wide-eyed with curiosity; Hindus and Arabs certainly sounded like fantastic cross-species, like sphinxes or centaurs.

Quint walked in just as Leonardo was launching into a story

about the Hindu god Danu, who was half-man, half-horse. Quint showed no surprise at the talking head on the blanket.

"So glad to see Leonardo is telling you these useful things." He added his own take on centaurs: "The earthbound have always loved speed — the wind in your face, the sensation of graceful and effortless movement. Which is why those ancient Scythians loved horses, and why Ericca loves her Spike and I love my Cobra." With aplomb, he continued, "…bound matter yearns for a lightness of being."

He might have waxed poetic, but happily he was anxious to take the kids for a spin in his favorite Cobra sports car.

Quint collected sports cars, and the bright-red Cobra was his favorite. He knew he would turn heads as he dodged Manhattan traffic in this convertible. He knew the kids loved the feel of the city whirling by. He had no problem with the name, *Cobra*. "You know, you have the imagery all wrong…you should really get up on your Egyptian history," Quint would say.

"Not all reptiles are evil; the cobra is an asp, not a viper like the rattlesnake. The Egyptians venerated the cobra," Matt would chime in knowingly. He was an expert in reptiles and expected everyone to know the difference between an asp and a viper.

His sister, Elle, not to be outdone, would add, "The double cobra appears on the caduceus, the staff of Hermes." Elle was an emerging expert in all things mythological.

Ericca might have found something mean to say to such young smart-alecks. She might have retorted sarcastically, "Yes, but do you know the full Latin name of the cobra species?" (Naja haje for the Egyptian cobra, member of the Elapids.) Or "Was Hermes a Greek or a Roman god?" (Greek; in the Roman pantheon, he was known as Mercury.)

But she knew Elle and Matt were not show-offs. They just knew a lot of things and liked it when people shared their interests. Also, they were fair and kind; this she knew with uncanny perception.

For instance, now they helped her put her blanket in a bag, as their father, Quint, continued his monologue about cars and finance. They did not unearth every possible plaything in the room and leave everything in a scattered mess.

They did not say teasing things about her mother's problems paying for things. In fact, Matt commented on the relative lack of toys: "Some of our friends have rooms that are HIDEOUS, with garbage and toys all over the floor. And they scream at their mommies when told to put things away."

"Especially Tory...she has everything, and she still whines all the time," related Elle.

The twins disliked disorder of any kind. For instance, now Matt's attention was turned to his own toy, a model of a car built with connecting blocks. He was happily snapping the parts together as Sophia and Quint made preparations to leave, when "Argghh!" he screamed.

This was very alarming for everyone, since Matt was not one to scream at little things. But this was not a little thing. The parts were different and not snapping together. A realization that was profoundly horrifying for Matt, and also for Leonardo, who timidly poked his head from the blanket to add his comment: "Would it...if order existed in all things..."

This thought accompanied them as they headed out the door: Matt, vowing there would be no mismatched toys to frustrate small boys; Quint, trying to remember an instance when his prediction for a stock spike failed to materialize; Sophia, in danger of being late for work, wondering how it was that even the best-laid plans seemed to develop problems, a thought that continually haunted and troubled her.

"I'm late. And today is typically Daemon's library day," Sophia mentioned to Quint as she hurriedly headed down the sidewalk. Looking sympathetic, he buoyantly wished her luck, then whizzed away with Elle, Matt, and Ericca smiling and waving in the back of the red Cobra car.

Sophia loved working at the library. But today, she berated herself as she ascended the wide marble steps to the columnar entry and grand entrance lobby.

She was late. She thought of the senior citizens who needed help using the library's catalogues, or library patrons who couldn't locate their library cards. Back behind the checkout counter in the light-filled rotunda, she felt grateful for the anxious faces seeking help, grateful for the distraction which drove from her mind all notions of immortality and changing the past.

What is past is done, she thought. Looping back in time would be difficult, more than impossible.

As if reading her thoughts, a voice asked, "I'd like a recommendation for a good reference on time travel."

Sophia looked up to see the jovial smile of Daemon Skye.

Daemon wore a gray suit that was undoubtedly very expensive and looked as dapper as he appeared in the picture on the newspaper cover three years ago. He looked exceedingly out of place here.

Pretending he was just another library patron, she replied politely, "We have many good books on that subject. You might start in the nonfiction section and search under *physics*."

"Oh, I'm not interested in scientific speculation. I am interested in knowing what can be done to change things, assuming all our destinies are scripted and predetermined."

They locked eyes. She probed his face for the shadow of guilt or mockery. But he did not show anything beyond innocent curiosity

"Then you might be interested in our section on mythology. We have many good books on Eastern mythology, discussing, for example, the *Net of Indra*," she offered with the calm assertiveness of an accomplished librarian.

"Oh, really, that's a possibility. *The Net of Indra*, I can't say I've ever heard of that," he replied with vague interest.

"The Hindus believed that our lives are like individual threads interwoven into a net or coherent whole," she explained before noticing his waning interest.

"That is quite poetic, but I'm really interested in the scientific theory that all matter interacts predictably as if automated by a script or computer code, if you will."

"That is a fascinating idea, but I really am no expert on that topic," Sophia replied, looking away.

With that remark, Daemon looked piercingly at her, and said with the faintest mockery, "That's funny, I thought you would be," then jokingly added, "But…how silly of me."

Sophia turned to help the next customer, a small, frail old woman wearing a very elegant black suit and a black pillbox hat. She was hunched and shrunken. Her hands had purple splotches and were crossed with blue veins that seemed ready to pop.

"Excuse me, dear…but I'm having trouble finding a book on family genealogy," she asked in a faint, coarse voice. She lifted her head slightly, an immense weight on the shriveled, wrinkled neck. She peered at Sophia with lined eyes.

"Of course, we have a good collection of books on genealogy. Or did you need help researching your own genealogy?" asked Sophia kindly.

The old woman's face brightened. She answered, "Bless you, dear. I had a thought today that I'd like to see if I can find someone — someone I haven't seen in years."

"Well, we could start with a name, or a place. Do you know either of those things?"

"I knew him as a baby," the old woman explained. Then, overwhelmed by unhappiness, she sobbed quietly and said, "I…I gave him away. I was a young, single mother…"

This thought tore at Sophia; it was a situation that was too close to her own. In her daily struggles, the possibility of not being able to care for Ericca filled her with anguish. She wanted to help this old woman in any way possible.

"If you know he is alive and how old he would be today, then anything is possible. We have access to large databases and many ways of searching for people," she said encouragingly and offered a set of instructions that read:

Researching Missing or Lost Persons

The task of locating a missing person is difficult, and we can not guarantee satisfactory results. Finding your beloved may be like finding a needle in a haystack.

However, we can offer guidance in this very important quest. In this library, we have the tools to narrow the possibilities and you may query our comprehensive compendium. Look for the compendium in the Q-aisle.

Chief Librarian and Cataloguer of the Q-aisle
Sophia Ludwig

The old woman looked up with a cheerful smile. The line of library patrons had grown. She thanked Sophia and disappeared into the library's maze of books.

Sophia was grateful that the remainder of the day saw nothing unusual.

Schoolchildren from an elite Manhattan private school visited and kept their noise and remarks to a minimum. They looked with indifference at the tables of gray men reading newspapers, and only snickered and pointed at a sleeping old man once. They stifled yawns and kept remarks like "If we can't buy these books… what is the point?" to themselves. They also managed to keep their cellular phones off.

A woman from a book club requested the latest bestseller, titled *From Frumpy to Fabulous at Forty,* and asked Sophia as she offered her library card, "Isn't that Daemon Skye, the property tycoon, over there in that aisle?"

"So it is," answered Sophia nonchalantly, and then added crisply, "We all support the public libraries, you know. Enjoy the book…due back in four weeks."

CHAPTER THREE

Sophia was actually a little alarmed that Daemon was still in the library. It was nearing closing time; the other librarians were getting ready to go home. The library and its aisles of shelves were emptying. The custodial staff would arrive shortly.

She had plenty on her mind herself as she prepared to close the library for the evening: a shopping list and what to make for dinner for Ericca and herself. She barely noticed when Daemon approached the counter and asked to check out a book.

"Oh, glad to see you found something. Hmm…*Blind Chess: Tactics and Ploys*, that sounds interesting," she said as she ran his library card through the scanner.

"Very interesting indeed," he remarked. "Stealth and duplicity are big in the Sapling world. You should know that. You need to be aware of that to cope, and keep the upper hand." He turned and left the library. Sophia watched with relief as his tall gray form exited through the grand doors.

The library was empty now. Sophia searched the aisles for books or sleeping patrons. She had successfully ushered the last patron out the door when she had an inspiration.

At the desk, she retrieved Daemon's library card number, and then typed the command *Show Transaction History*. Immediately the screen was filled with a list of book titles. Then she uttered the command *Matter Mirror*. With that command, the darkened aisles were lit with floor lights that revealed shelves that were hitherto hidden.

She wandered through the maze of shelves, where the book titles read:

> *Seth, Sky God of Ancient Egypt*
> *Pharaohs of the Sun God*
> *Guerilla Warfare of the Overlords*
> *The Scorched Masses*

As she turned down another dimly lit aisle, she found more titles unheard of in most libraries or bestseller lists:

> *Proletarian Armies of the Puppet King*
> *Compassion: the Broken Politics of the Weak*

Electrons and the Power of Negativity
Turning down another aisle, she found the titles:
Assault From the Sky
Divine Intervention

She scanned these titles thoughtfully, until she saw a title that puzzled her:

Castle Ludwig and the Beloved Swan Princess

Looking up startled, she was face to face with Daemon Skye. His gray wool suit was as pressed and impeccable as when she saw him last; his determined jaw was dark with a faint stubble. The hologram spoke:

"Surprised Sophia? Did you expect to find something like *How to Outwit Your Best Friend and Send Him to His Death*? I am disappointed and hurt. Did you expect to find only malice at the core of my heart?"

Sophia was shaken. She had coded the library cards to contain a description of the cardholder and equipped the library scanner to project and enlarge these descriptions as holographic projections. She had never encountered as life-like a projection as this.

Daemon read her mind. "You're wondering if I'm real, standing next to you?" he asked, coming close, lifting his hand toward her.

He continued. "I thought you might want to use your powers to answer your questions, so I thought I'd answer your questions in person. Unfortunately, I can't help you today. It was not I who killed Branch."

"That's not true, Daemon," Sophia retorted angrily. "You grew to oppose Branch and everything he stood for, and you feared his influence in the Council of Ringgolds."

"I agree. I never sympathized with his pathetic attitudes toward the Saplings. I have seen the course of their history, which is destruction and overpopulation. I never shared Branch's hopes for bringing progress to their weak and corrupt kind," he said with thoughtful contempt.

"But I would not murder him. The fate of the Saplings, good or bad, wouldn't be reason enough for me. Really — I couldn't care less," he concluded.

Sophia was beginning to believe him, and was stepping backward in an effort to stop the hologram. But Daemon was stepping toward her. And in the dark, she felt a shiver of fear.

He was now next to her, and brushed a hand through her hair, as he said, "No, for something murderous, I think I'd need a much better reason."

Then he was gone. Sophia stood in the dark aisle of shelves and realized she was trembling. Oh, it's horrible to be a mousy librarian, she thought.

Hurriedly she shut off the library projector, grabbed her coat and bag, and headed for the back exit. The bright sunlight made her eyes squint and she took a grateful breath of fresh air. There was a honk and she turned to see the red Cobra car. There were three small smiling faces, dripping ice cream cones in hand in the back seat. Quint sat in front and shouted, "Hop in!" Sophia slumped gladly into the front seat, as with a loud growl of the Cobra engine, the sunlight and street scene dissolved around her.

CHAPTER FOUR

THE M-GATE

The subway token from Maxine Weaver continually puzzled Ericca during the following years. By now, she was used to taking subways. But she puzzled over a mystery. She found she never needed that token or any other token, for that matter, for the subway trains in New York.

"The trains are free for young children," noted the station attendant one day.

Being then about twelve, she had to ask, "They are free? Meaning the trains go anywhere they want, anytime they want?" She had visions of trains worming around willy-nilly underground.

The station attendant laughed. He was not a typical harried New Yorker, who might have understood this inquisitiveness as sassiness and snapped back in exasperation.

"No, free means that we don't charge small children to ride on the train," he explained nicely.

She beamed in appreciation at the subway attendant's friendly reply, and he beamed back.

That must be it, she thought, New York subway attendants, like most people, are always nice to people who are nice to them. She remembered hearing something like that from her mother Sophia, talking about her father: *He trusted people and found much to delight him.*

But the mystery still weighed on her mind. Not wanting to pester the subway attendant, she wondered silently whether subways were like her blanket Spike, which transported her about the apartment without needing anything more than an occasional word of guidance and appreciation.

For as long as she could remember, she had drifted off to sleep while wrapped in her blanket, lulled into a dreamy weightlessness as the blanket floated freely around the apartment. She had always wondered whether all children had blankets like Spike. She suspected not.

Her friend Elle had explained once, "The quintessence in Spike is a bit of a secret. Most vehicles rely on other energy sources." Elle's twin brother, Matt, followed up by saying, "The New York subways run on electricity, but it's the same amount of electricity whether kids ride or not; kids don't *contribute* much to the load on the system."

Contribute was a word Matt's father used often. He would say, "Rising global need for fossil fuels *contributes* to rising prices here and abroad," or "Diminishing *contributions* from the public will mean a much harder winter for New York's homeless."

That solved part of the mystery. The New York subway was free for children under a certain limit. Free, such a useful word, thought Ericca.

Free...unlimited...infinite...eternal. You could ride the subway for an eternity, just going from one gate to the next, and no one would ever ask you for a token, subject, of course, to the condition that you were under forty-four inches in height and that you were in the company of a paying adult.

Conditions, Ericca found, were all over the place, like gates that allowed certain people to pass but not others. Every once in a while the twins, Elle and Matt, would disappear into the fancy lobby of a Park Avenue building, guests at birthday parties to which Ericca was not invited. There were certain stores that Ericca and her mother never set foot in because there would be nothing there they could afford.

She waited for her mother to come home and felt glum. A long weekend approached, and today at school, the children had all talked about trips to the mountains or beaches with their families.

Elle and Matt had chattered excitedly about going with their mother and father to California to promote Quint's latest project, what he called the Q-Computer.

This was a special weekend for Ericca as well, but not for a fun trip out of town. On Memorial Day weekend, every year since she was a small baby, she would visit a memorial in memory of her father. She looked forward to this, but wished, somehow, that this unhappy memory could be reversed.

She wished that something wonderful would happen for her mother, something to lift the shadow of sorrow from their lives. Sophia, to Ericca's frustration, seemed resigned to things as they were. After all these years, Sophia still visited among her small circle of friends and rarely dated. She still spent most of her free time diligently writing in her journal. The shimmering blue glass wastebasket was filled with a steady stream of crumpled paper, which never overflowed despite the fact that it was never recycled or emptied.

The strangest thing was that her mother never seemed to publish anything or earn any money for her efforts. Every month, the budget chart on the refrigerator indicated zero for the funds earned from published stories and poems. And yet, scribbles continued to fill her pink-and gold-flecked journal, as if a magic muse resided in the pink and gold pen.

Ericca was busy wondering about the unusual things in her apartment when she heard a sob from next door. Leonardo, who often spent these late afternoons with Ericca, bobbed his head out of the blanket and exclaimed, "That is the saddest sob I've ever heard. Could it be…that there really is no solution to Fermat's Equation?"

Ericca shook her head, "No, silly, that must be our neighbor. Mother tells me he just had some bad news." Ericca had heard this sob before. The man in the next apartment lived alone and, according to her mother, suffered from a serious illness.

There was another muffled sob and the rustle of feet and the clank of keys. Her neighbor was leaving, most likely for his daily trip to the park. Ericca was glad for him. The light of dusk and flurry of activity in the park would surely cheer him up.

"You are silly, Leonardo," Ericca remarked. "People don't just care about mathematical problems. Believe it or not, a lot of people just wish they had a friend."

"Well, I can certainly understand that," Leonardo sympathized, "Why, without Albert and my other friends here, where would I be when you're away at school?"

"Albert? Are you really speaking to *him*?" asked Ericca. "Do you two really have much in common? I mean, he really is years, centuries, ahead of you…and a *physicist* at that!"

"Shhh, Ericca," Leonardo admonished. "It's rude, you know, to talk about people in the third person…especially in their presence."

The head of the man with droopy eyelids and a bushy mustache bobbed out of the blanket. He asked crisply, "Maligning physicists, are you? Granted, we physicists owe a debt of gratitude to you mathematicians, but have you ever known a mathematician to have a scant intuition about nature?"

Albert continued, "NO! Those mathematicians are way too happy with their completely abstract world to be ecstatic over the glorious order right before their eyes."

Then, realizing his outburst, he said, looking sheepishly at Ericca, "I didn't mean to interrupt, dear. I completely agree…with what you said about…friendship…"

He trailed off. There was a soft knock from the hallway. Then there was a timid knock at their apartment door. "Sssh," warned Ericca. "I need to answer that." Both Leonardo and Albert silently returned to being flat images in the blanket.

At the door was a young woman in a short skirt holding a gift wrapped with a shiny bow.

"So sorry to disturb you, but I'm Daphne, a friend of your neighbor's. I was just wondering if you knew the man who lives in the apartment next door? His name is Nicholas Bard," she asked tentatively. "If you do see him, could you give him this?" She handed the present to Ericca, who nodded in assent.

"I know it's terrible of me. Today is his birthday, and though we broke up, I still wanted to give him this," she explained with a regretful look.

"Sure, of course," Ericca agreed.

The young woman turned and left as Ericca closed the door. Leonardo and Albert, who had witnessed everything were now bobbing up and down excitedly and chatting on the blanket again. When they saw Ericca, Leonardo asked, "So when are we going?"

"Where?" asked Ericca in confusion.

"To deliver the present, as you promised, of course," replied Leonardo.

"I suppose we could, but I don't really have permission to leave the apartment, you know," said Ericca with hesitation.

"No, she doesn't," agreed Albert in a huff, "You should know better."

"But think of it, how happy he would be…" argued Leonardo. "You know he's on his way to the park. It won't take long."

The idea was tempting for Ericca. She hesitated, then decided. Stuffing the blanket into a backpack along with the gift, she said, "Come now, we'll be back before mother is home."

Ericca knew the way to the park well. She went there often with her mother or with Elle and Matt and Quint. She wandered along happily with a sense of delicious freedom until she reached a busy street, with buses and cars, where the sidewalk widened.

Albert sniffed the air, and said wistfully, "Bratwurst, my favorite." But Leonardo was in a hurry.

"Sorry, not now," Leonardo said, as they passed the hotdog vendor without stopping. There would have been plenty of reason to stop. A woman outside The Parthian Connection tattoo shop encouraged them to step inside, with the special offer of two tattoos for the price of one.

"Just think," joked Ericca, "…you and Leonardo can get matching lemur tails on your backs."

Ericca actually liked lemur tail tattoos. There was just such a tattoo of a spiral striped tail on the back of the centaur statuette in their apartment.

They were heading toward the subway when Ericca realized that she had never before ridden the subway alone. Anxiety was crowded out of her mind, however, when she realized suddenly that she needed to use the restroom.

Leonardo and Albert both complained. But after a frantic search in the busy subway station, she located a women's restroom, one that was not closed for service, with an empty stall.

The metal handle of the stall door was slightly concave, and Ericca was focused on the enlarged reflection of her eyes and nose when she heard an announcement over the intercom: **"Security alert. We urge all subway patrons to exit the station immediately as a security precaution. We repeat, please exit the station immediately."**

Leonardo and Albert chattered in distress. "Hurry, would you please?" exhorted Leonardo. Ericca was ready and flushed the toilet, but the familiar sound of the bowl vortex lingered as a loud hiss.

Ericca was distressed. She knew the toilet had not flushed properly. She knew there were dire consequences for improperly flushed toilets, like, among other things, astronomical water bills. She turned to Albert, who looked away as though he felt ashamed that he had nothing helpful to add.

"Nobel prize winners do not specialize in fixing toilets in New York subway stations," he announced with a miffed air.

"Oh, please, don't be such a snoot," implored Ericca. She jiggled the toilet lever again. To her relief, the hissing noise stopped.

"Of course, the machinery of matter only follows rules of probability. There will always be an anomaly," Albert announced sagaciously.

"Oh, that is enough about this plumbing anomaly. We have a present to deliver," urged Leonardo.

They followed the crowd of people hurrying to the station exit.

Now they realized they would miss Nicholas Bard in the park. Ericca knew her neighbor always visited the Thyme Terrace in the late afternoon, at half-past four sharp.

The Thyme Terrace was a formal garden with clipped hedges and topiaries. The garden was next to the Memorial Monument and the M-Gate of the subway, and quite a long walk from where they were.

As if reading her mind, Albert suggested, "You know, we could always use Spike." Spike was more than Ericca's favorite blanket; it was a magic carpet. But Ericca had never ridden Spike outside her apartment. She knew there were rules against this. Not many New Yorkers were used to seeing a quilted blanket in flight carrying a twelve-year-old girl, in the company of the bobbing heads of long-deceased philosophers.

"Can Spike really help?" she asked.

"Of course...Spike is really not a blanket or a carpet. Spike is more like a drill, tunneling through matter. To think that flight can only be achieved by leveraging an air foil under differential pressure is...well, untimely...pardon the pun. Better to think of movement at light speed as the default, a constant, constrained by the clutter of matter — clutter that can be pushed aside with a sufficiently powerful drill," answered Albert.

Albert tended to be abstruse. But she thought of Nicholas Bard celebrating an unhappy birthday alone for the yet undelivered present. "Let's try it, but don't make a scene," she cautioned.

"Shall we use the trains or the taxi?" asked Albert.

"The trains are closed. You know that," replied Ericca in confusion.

"My dear, the trains we will use are not typical trains. There are trains and taxis and even trams that are part of the *time tunnel network*...for the purpose of saving time, you know," Albert explained.

Ericca thought of the subway warning. She had just experienced a scary security alert in the subway. "We'll use the taxi," she said, before realizing she had no idea what the *Time Taxi* was.

"Then hold on. The only weirdness people will notice is your sudden disappearance," replied Albert.

Immediately, Ericca felt the sidewalk swirling around her, a sensation familiar to her from rides in the Cobra car, only accelerated now. Her body disappeared, until all that remained was her head; even her head shrank to almost nothing, something apparent from a strand of hair on her temple that moved closer and closer. Then suddenly, she was in the back of a yellow taxicab.

Her eyes widened at the sight of Leonardo and Albert bobbing in front of her, each clamoring for the steering wheel. Albert, noticing her alarm, shot a look back and made a sheepish apology: "Sorry, these Tunnel Wars, you know, making it very hard to keep up the metropolitan taxi system."

Ericca grew even more alarmed when she saw out of the corner of one eye, a stylish girl with long curly locks, with a small dog on a leash, staring in astonishment amid the rapidly dissolving street scene. "Oh, no, Tory Skye," Ericca whispered to herself.

Tory Skye went to the same private school as Elle and Matt. Ericca knew Tory from chance meetings in the company of the twins at museums or department stores. Tory showed a cool camaraderie toward Elle and Matt. They were, after all, members of her "crowd." With Ericca, she maintained a haughty distance, and usually looked at her as though she were a small insect, or worse yet, a homeless person, especially when she learned Ericca had no father, and that her mother was, of all pathetic things, a librarian for the New York public libraries.

"Tory will say something to her father about this, and it may get back to Quint, and then my mother," said Ericca worriedly to Albert and Leonardo.

Tory and the busy street had disappeared and now in front of her was the M-Gate subway station set in the pastoral tranquility of Central Park. It had worked. Ericca glanced at her watch. Hardly a second had passed since they stood outside the subway station on Broadway. She was unscathed by the confusing trip.

"Sorry for the bumpy ride," commented Albert cryptically,

"but the Tunnel Wars are degrading service in the time tunnels."

The park buzzed with a medley of activity. Ericca walked along the trails toward the Thyme Terrace. She saw a man painting at an easel. In a clearing around a statue, couples danced the salsa. Skaters and joggers passed by. A man dragged a plastic bag filled with crunched aluminum cans. A woman walked ahead of him with a rolling cart full of pop, which she sold to passersby.

Then she saw him, a man with thinning hair sitting hunched on a park bench near the fountain. It was Nicholas Bard. He was talking to a group of people. Another man in a pressed shirt stood reciting a poem to the group.

Ericca approached timidly, the present in hand.

Nicholas looked up and recognized her. "Ericca, what are you doing here?" he asked before he noticed the present.

"Daphne wanted you to have this and…oh…happy birthday," said Ericca. She sensed that Albert and Leonardo in her backpack wanted to chime in as well, and hissed "sssh…"

Nicholas looked up; his eyes were laughing, his face broke into a smile. He chuckled. "Did she say to open this? I suppose I should," he said. He opened the package. Inside was a small book with a reflecting pool on its cover, bearing the title *Mirrors, Truth, and Tribal Bards*. With a broad smile, he exclaimed, "…that Daphne, she always surprises me." He opened the book and skimmed the pages, reading some excerpts.

> …The ancient Europeans lacked the unifying culture created by modern media. Instead culture grew from the oral tradition of the tribal bard and a medley of venerated nature symbols and icons. Artistically embellished and customized by different tribes, these symbols were used in many places: woolen crafts, mythology, jewelry, and body art. These universal symbols included the pool of wisdom and the world tree of knowledge, and comprised a lexicon of stylized images that is here

today in tattoos and the practice of body painting
with henna called mehendi.

Ericca peered over his shoulder, captivated by the swirling black
and white motifs. Nicholas looked up and said, "Thanks, Ericca.
But now I think you need to head home before it gets too dark."

The park was filled with a dusky gloom as Ericca headed back
to the M-Gate. She passed the Memorial Monument.

She remembered visiting this quiet corner of the park as a
small baby. Set amid the clipped hedges was a glass sculpture in
the form of a ship. Along the sides of the ship were etched in
glass, names in alphabetical order. She touched the etched glass in
a familiar spot and whispered:

> *Tariq Al -Zeer*
> *Ole Anders*
> *Chun Lee Ang*
> *David Angvall*
> *Catriona Anka*
> *…Branch Archer*
> *Reginald Arthur I*
> *Maya Aspares…*

Below the glass ship, the inscription in the stone base read:

> A vessel for the brave,
> A barque in place of a body
> For bodies torn asunder that
> The ka might find the ba,
> The form follow the shadow,
> And the akhu dance
> On the face of the water.

Leonardo and Albert knew to keep quiet here. This was the site
of a war memorial. Ericca was not the only one here. There were

many people, and the base of the ship was strewn with flowers, cards, stuffed animals, even baby blankets, some hand-sewn, all well-worn. On one of these blankets, partially hidden beneath the flowers and stuffed animals, Ericca glimpsed embroidered words in the frayed corner: *may my love always protect you.*

The round pool near the ship reflected the names etched in the glass. Bottles sealed with corks containing notes floated in the pool riding ripples toward the center in the dappled sunlight.

Ericca knelt near the ship, where an elderly woman in orthopedic shoes had left a stuffed bear. The woman asked Ericca politely, "Did you know someone in this memorial?"

Ericca replied, "Yes, my dad. He died before I was even born."

The woman said, "I am so sorry…I lost my son. His name was David Angvall. He was a soldier, one of the ground troops, in the earlier war. He was only twenty years old." She pointed to the name on the ship. "Oh, by the way, my name is Sheila Angvall," she continued, holding out her hand.

Ericca pictured a small boy playing with a stuffed animal. His name was David and he had dark, wavy hair like his mother. Ericca paused, then said, "Glad to meet you, Mrs. Angvall. I'm Ericca. My dad was a pilot. He was killed when his plane exploded. They never recovered his body."

"That is why they provide a vessel here," replied Sheila, nodding toward the monument in the form of a ship, "that the soul might find a way home. That is the meaning of the inscription, you know. The *ba* is the Egyptian term for the soul. They believed in the eternal soul even back then, you know."

Ericca nodded. She knew a little about ancient Egypt from stories her mother told about the deities that populated Egyptian mythology. The Egyptians believed the soul could not enter the afterlife without an intact body, hence the emphasis on mummification and preservation of the intact form. This realization was depressing to Ericca.

"But of course the Egyptians were very sophisticated in their thought. They believed in the upper and lower aspects of self, the lower consisting of the earthbound ego, persona, and corpse; the higher self was the soul and light being capable of traveling to eternity. Of course, not everyone could achieve the transcendent higher self, not even in ancient Egypt." Sheila looked at her sympathetically. "Do you still hope that you might meet your father someday?"

Ericca answered, looking away, "Yes…a part of me does…"

"Me too… I'd like to see my son just one more time."

Sheila now noticed the fading light. She paused. Finally she suggested, "I think the subway is back open…these security scares…Let's take the train together. I am sure your mother is starting to worry."

They strolled together toward the M-Gate. Ericca was glad to listen to Mrs. Angvall's cheery conversation. Sheila identified trees and plants as they walked along. They passed the flowering crabapples in the Conservatory Gardens. The trees radiated gnarled, craggy branches, heavy with profuse rose-colored buds and soft, pinkish-white flowers, scenting the late afternoon with a sweet essence. Ericca looked with interest as Mrs. Angvall pointed to a black walnut tree.

"Look at those green tennis balls," she said. "Those are walnuts, a big favorite with the squirrels, though they work hard for their snack. Under the green shell is yet another even harder shell before the edible part at the core. Talk about a tough nut to crack." Ericca's jaws hurt just thinking about it.

Mrs. Angvall could hardly contain her delight when they passed a rather scraggly shrub with clusters of small, yellow flowers amid scarlet berries and green leaves. "That's a spicebush," she exclaimed. "The berries make a fine seasoning. The leaves and bark are also medicinal. In fact, the Indians used a spiceberry infusion for treating coughs, colds, croup, and measles. The oil from the berries they used in massages for arthritis. They made teas from the leaf and bark, and made compresses for rashes and bruises from the berries. Even the early settlers knew of its restorative properties. They used the bark for medicine to stimulate the immune system."

Ericca knew about croup, having had a recent experience a few years ago during which she awoke in the middle of the night thinking she couldn't breathe.

They arrived at the M-Gate, where a train already awaited them. They both found a seat in the crowded rush-hour train. Sheila Angvall continued her happy chatter about the horticulture of Central Park and her job as a school nurse. Ericca was glad to listen, thinking to herself what an extraordinary afternoon it had been. She had taken a trip through space-time on her blanket, Spike. She was careful, however, not to mention this to Sheila and instead nodded amiably until the train arrived at her stop.

Glancing down at her watch as she exited the subway, she was not at all peeved to notice that the trip took all of sixteen minutes and ten seconds. There were advantages to taking the subway. There was the experience of meeting different people and even learning something, and the added advantage of not having your body compressed to nothing. This thought jogged Ericca's memory of the inscription on the base of the Memorial Monument: the *eternal soul travels through space without the earthly body*. In fact, the lack of an earthly body actually freed the soul in some ways. She thought of Sheila's remarks, *not everyone could achieve the transcendent light body*.

Ericca felt the comforting presence of her own warm jacket and heavy backpack. She went up the stairs and entered the apartment. To her immense relief, her mom was not yet home.

Leonardo and Albert chattered away and offered congratulations. They were jubilant. They had made a trip to Central Park on their own. They rode the subway. They had delivered a gift. They had met a school nurse — a person who knew a lot of things about plants, trees, and the experience of loss.

The Memorial Day holiday was Monday. The schools and

libraries were closed. Ericca had managed to keep the incident with Spike a secret from her mother. She did not see Nicholas Bard that weekend, but happily she heard no more sobs from the apartment next door.

Albert and Leonardo wanted to take another trip out for bratwurst and pretzels, and Ericca agreed after some concerted pleading. Her mother was busy scribbling away in her journal as usual, which was not going well; she continually fired crumpled sheets of paper into the glass wastebasket.

The pretzel man was glad to see Ericca. Business was slow that day, owing to the holiday. He beamed when she requested three pretzels with ketchup and no mustard, though he must have wondered how a girl her size would eat all three.

When the pretzel man was safely out of earshot, Albert couldn't help remarking, "These pretzels, so nice when they're piping hot...They remind me of magnets."

"Geez, enough talk about electromagnets already," complained Leonardo. Apparently, Albert mused about electro-magnetism constantly, and he assumed everyone on the blanket was deeply interested.

"Have you thought about what equation you would use to describe a pretzel?" asked Leonardo.

"Yes, that would be really useful, Leonardo," Albert replied. "The universe might actually be a pretzel knot, which means all those galaxies that are light-years away might actually be much closer if you found a tunnel."

He inserted a toothpick into his pretzel to illustrate. "Kids, please stop playing with your food," Ericca instructed. The two bobbing heads retreated into the blanket in the backpack. There were people around.

Last heard, they were in the backpack, Albert saying, "You know, Leonardo, if you derive that equation, we could write a paper, and who knows, maybe we'll win a prize."

Leonardo said sarcastically, "You mean, I'll write the paper and *you'll* win a prize —" Ericca could not understand this constant bickering; Albert and Leonardo really acted like children sometimes.

Back at the apartment, they found Sophia waiting for them. She wore a green hat and carried a small bouquet of flowers. She was anxious to go. Ericca located a note she had written and stuffed it into a glass bottle, sealed with a cork.

The Memorial Monument was more crowded today than two days earlier. There were more mementos at the base of the ship. There were families with small children, and elderly couples. There were many women there alone, many looking fairly elderly, much like Mrs. Angvall.

Ericca placed the flowers at the base of the ship close to the name of her father. She launched the bottle into the reflecting pool and watched it drift on the dancing ripples. They were about to leave when Ericca turned to see the woman she met days earlier. She was near the ship, wearing a burgundy pantsuit.

Ericca wanted to wave in greeting, except that she saw the gray shadow of a small boy run up to greet the woman. The boy was in her arms holding a stuffed bear; then he scrambled down and ran around the glass ship. Sunlight played on his dark, tightly curled hair and refracted from the glass mast in multicolored rays.

Ericca blinked. She wasn't sure she was seeing clearly. But there was again the shadow of the young David Angvall, a small boy of about seven. But now, with her eyes focused and clear, she noticed there were many small shadows darting around. They leapt around the park glade and wiggled their fingers in the pond, leaving no ripples. They ran around, shrieking with laughter. They jumped up and down, climbed trees, and were picked up and held.

She now noticed graffiti at the base of the ship. Mocking the inscription above it, scratched in a flowing calligraphy, the graffiti read:

Of the Puppet King and the Proletarian Armies

CHAPTER FOUR

Just then, her mother said it was time to leave. Ericca wondered about the strange graffiti even as they headed toward the M-Gate.

The M-Gate was a charming station house set amid the trees. The city subway ran underground, below the station. Next to the station house were the tracks for the Thyme Train, so named for the Thyme Terrace, which was its embarkation and final destination point. The Thyme Train made a circuit around the park, and its open cars were brightly painted. It was a popular tourist attraction. But today among the tourists with cameras, talking in all sorts of languages, Ericca saw more ghostly children. They rode in the company of people whose lined and impassive faces beamed with a new light.

Ericca looked at her mother, who seemed completely unfazed by the spectacle of these ghostly visitors. In fact, Sophia happily chatted about the brilliant spring colors and the pervasive smell of flowers. Sophia looked straight ahead toward the escalator to the underground subway tunnels. But Ericca turned to glimpse something odd in a break in the trees. She saw a red sports car.

The red car followed the tracks of the Thyme Train, and then lurched with a roar onto the street. It was the Cobra car. Quint and Sybille rode in front. Elle and Matt sat behind them, wearing sunglasses and propeller hats, grinning with suntanned faces, as if this were the most ordinary thing in the world.

CHAPTER FIVE

THE Q–COMPUTER

Elle and Matt had indeed ridden the Cobra car all the way to California and back. They were reluctant, though, to admit this even to Ericca when they met again at their Soho loft.

They talked instead about all the different and interesting things they saw in California.

"Oh, you should have seen the Pacific Ocean. The surf was wild!" exclaimed Matt. "When I get older, I want to go back and try surfing."

"We went hiking around Carmel, near Big Sur. You would have loved the redwoods," remarked Elle. She knew Ericca especially loved trees.

They nodded enthusiastically when Ericca told them about her trip to Central Park. They were impressed that Ericca had ridden the subway by herself. "Wow, that sounds fun," they agreed.

Ericca was happy to avoid a discussion of Spike, until Matt accidentally slipped in a reference to their trip in the Cobra car.

He said, "Dad wanted to ride a plane, until I mentioned there would be random security checks on all commercial flights. My dad then did a check using his computer. I must have hit on something, because after that he suggested we go in the Cobra car."

With that remark, he was silent, realizing what he had just implied. Elle looked at him with disapproval and said, "Well, we did take the Cobra car, but we were told to keep it a secret from even our closest friends, but since you have Spike and know about quintessence, it's probably all right that you know."

"Besides — Daddy pointed out that California is very far from New York, about three thousand miles away, in fact. In a plane, the trip is easily several hours long. We wanted to get to California before our joints start to creak," Elle elaborated.

Ericca smiled. The thought of Elle and Matt with arthritic joints was beyond plausibility. They were, after all, paradigms of energy, the Particle Princess and the Wave Rider, as their parents often called them.

"So were you scared?" Ericca asked.

"Oh, yeah," replied Matt. "I knew the Cobra could go really fast, but when we entered the time tunnel it was like flying at the speed of light." He bit his lip again. Evidently the time tunnel was also a thing to be kept secret.

With the mention of the time tunnel, Ericca knew the ghosts she saw over Memorial Day weekend were more than apparitions.

She remembered Albert mentioning the time tunnels before the ride on Spike that brought her across Manhattan in literally no time at all. She pictured the subway token that had been a gift from Maxine Weaver, with the tiny inscription: *Valid for Unlimited Trips on the Light Rail Through the Tunnels of Time.* Now Elle and Matt said they had actually been inside a time tunnel. This was more than coincidence.

"I wouldn't believe that except..." said Ericca. She then told them about her frenzied trip to the Thyme Terrace with the aid of Spike. "Too bad, though, I think Tory Skye saw everything."

"No, not Tory," Elle gasped with widened eyes. They all knew Tory, the daughter of the Manhattan property tycoon Daemon Skye. She could not be trusted to keep a secret and was known for her selective nastiness.

"I'm sure she's told everyone by now," Elle theorized. They looked glumly at each other. The consequences going through their minds were dire.

At best, Ericca's mother would find out from Quint, and Ericca would be punished by being grounded or deprived of Spike.

The worst case was something they could only imagine.

Quintessence produced a state of gravitational repulsion. Gravitational repulsion was very handy for many things besides floating to sleep or beating the subway — things that kids did not meddle in, such as expansion of the universe and travel at light speed. Any publicity identifying quintessence with an innocent baby blanket and a millionaire's collector sports car could be disastrous.

Matt had an inspiration. "Our class is visiting the Metropolitan Museum tomorrow," he said. "I'll try to get Tory to tell me how much she knows and who she's told."

"Yeah, like, right," replied Elle skeptically. "Like, she's really going to tell *you*…"

"Oh, I have my ways," replied Matt.

They were sitting at the kitchen table. The table was strewn with tiny wires and mirrors. Matt was busily snapping parts together. Elle would occasionally interrupt and say, "No, that part doesn't go there — it goes there."

Ericca could not help remarking, "Jeez, you sure are spending a lot of time on that. So far, you've spent two hours, twenty-two minutes, and forty-three seconds."

Ericca was fond of precision, a habit she had acquired by being in the company of Leonardo and Albert. Albert especially was fond of reminding people that it was the smallest fraction of deviation in the position of a star that proved his theory of special relativity.

Albert would say, "Those astronomers and mathematicians definitely helped me by aiming their telescopes at a star during an eclipse and noticing that the star moved from its position before the eclipse. That, of course, was not the true explanation. The star did not pick itself up and walk across the sky. We only see the star shifting because the gravitational field of the sun bends light from the star before the light ray reaches our eyes. It takes a *physicist* to have that intuition."

Ericca, of course, was not concerned with measuring the positions of stars. She did notice things like:

CHAPTER FIVE

The time for a popsicle to melt in your grocery bag on a typical summer day in New York *(5 minutes)*.
The time for fizzy sodas to lose all their fizz *(20 minutes)*.
The time in which hot and delicious macaroni and cheese turned into a cold, unappetizing lump *(15 minutes)*.

Matt was finally done, and smiled as he held up a metal-and-plastic-encased device bearing large letters: *QC*. The device looked like the face of an owl, with probes pointing upward like antennae, and was small enough to be worn as a pendant or stuffed into a back pocket. There was a small Egyptian eye engraved in the metal case, the eye of Horus, outlined in black with a swirling tail attached to the lower border.

"I'll have to show Dad this when he gets back. He had these ideas about a regular, clunky, boring box, but I told him to get a clue. Who is really going to lug around a box just so they can play virtual-reality blind chess in the park?" he said.

"What is that?" asked Ericca.

"A Q-computer," answered Elle. "You can program it to create holographic projections, like your favorite game characters."

Ericca mentioned the ghostly children in the park on Memorial Day. "Do you think those children were holographic projections?" she asked.

"Possibly," answered Matt. "But most computers these days are not powerful enough to create realistic projections, certainly not characters that could pass for real people. This Q-computer will process tons of information, enough for really convincing holograms. But we are the only ones who have such a thing so far. Want to see?"

He pushed a button on the Q-computer and said, "Dad's chess character, Osiris." The antennae of the Q-computer, acting as projection strobes, emitted quivering filaments of light and produced a flickering image of the Egyptian god Osiris. The tiny figure turned and waved at them.

"Oh, do you want to see something really cool?" Elle asked. She pushed a button on the Q-computer and uttered the command, "*Matter Mirror*." The figure of Osiris expanded into the room as the light rays diverged. His presence now filled the room.

"That's spooky," exclaimed Ericca. "Are you sure you guys are supposed to be playing with this?"

"Well, Dad really loves chess, especially blind chess and nothing makes him happier than playing with life-sized chess pieces," Matt explained.

Osiris spoke to them in a low drawl, "Yeah, your father is quite a chess nut, always has been."

They were surprised by his easy Texas drawl. Osiris sensed their disbelief. "Oh, don't worry. I know you borrowed one of the cards from your dad's collection to generate me. You should just know that your dad invented me, as he did all his chess characters; he gave me the personality of one his best friends, Branch Archer."

Ericca thought, He's talking about my dad, Branch Archer.

"But don't you worry, Quint's a great player. He almost always wins, so I won't be suffering the same unfortunate fate as my prototype personalities, Branch Archer and that Egyptian god, Osiris. Poor devils, it's rough being blown to smithereens, and then pieced together with some vital equipment missing."

Ericca and Matt weren't really sure what he was talking about. Elle whispered an explanation, "Osiris was the ancient Egyptian god of regeneration, celebrated for helping the Egyptians develop agriculture and for the regular flooding of the Nile. Osiris was murdered in an act of trickery by his jealous brother, Seth, who scattered the remains of his body. Osiris was reconstructed by his wife, the goddess Isis, who then bore him a child, despite his dismembered form."

Ericca was impressed. "Let's see the Isis character," she said to Matt.

"Sure," he said and pressed another button on the device.

CHAPTER FIVE

The dithering image of a golden goddess with a child at her breast appeared before them, an image that grew larger, more densely pixilated, and substantial as Matt enlarged and adjusted the projection.

The goddess spoke: "You children really should be working on the project Sybille planned for you. Weren't you supposed to be making marzipan chess pieces for your next chess club meeting?"

They all recognized that tone. All mothers seemed to have perfected the art of delivering a nagging reproach as a kind suggestion.

Ericca asked, "Do you miss Osiris?"

"Of course I do," replied Isis. "But I have our child, Horus, who reminds me of him. Osiris is always with me in spirit, as he is with our child."

Isis turned to the lumps of dough on the kitchen table. "Ericca, that knight piece you've made is perfect!" she complimented.

Ericca glowed with pride at the piece, shaped and painted to resemble a knight, decorated with swirls and diamonds; it was not every day you received a compliment from a goddess. Matt and Elle, anxious not to be outdone, turned their attention to their own pieces. At last the squat chess pieces were done, Matt's made of chocolate-swirled dough, Elle's studded with multicolored sprinkles.

"Hey," Matt suggested, "we can make holographic cards of these pieces and use them for virtual-reality chess." Ericca and Elle nodded happily, and another hot spring afternoon passed quickly by.

Spring was quickly turning into summer. Already tour buses crowded outside the Metropolitan Museum of Art. Tourists in shorts and sun hats busily snapped pictures of famous New York landmarks.

This was one of the last field trips of the year. Elle and Matt were not the only ones fidgeting in the air-conditioned halls of the museum; most of their classmates joked among themselves during the docent tour.

Everyone wore their school uniforms, everyone, that is, except Tory Skye, who looked cool and comfortable in a sundress from the Emerging Pop Diva line. As was typical for Tory on school field trips, a chauffeur was stationed outside the museum with Tory's pet Pomeranian, named Pluto. Tory could not be long parted from her favorite pet.

All were in awe of the Egyptian collection. They saw familiar shapes and patterns: the ankh shape seen in jewelry or as the sign of the female, obelisk architecture seen in monuments in New York and all over the world.

The museum docent explained, "The Egyptians built one of the oldest and most enduring civilizations in history. We have here in the museum's permanent collection pieces that date from circa 300,000 B.C. to the 4th century A.D., thanks to the generosity of museum donors who helped establish the Department of Egyptian Art in 1906."

Taking a moment to explain the terms, she said, "Circa means approximately. B.C. means Before Christ, and A.D. means Anno Domine, which is Latin for 'Year of our Lord.' We could also use the terms B.C.E., for Before Current Era, and C.E., for Current Era."

The docent took a breath and continued. "In short, these pieces are very old, some more than three hundred thousand years old."

Tory Skye, still smarting from the docent's reprimand for answering her cellular phone, spoke up now. "So, how did these generous donors come to the conclusion that these pieces are the authentic pieces, and not worthless forgeries?" she asked.

Not at all flustered, the docent answered, "Excellent question! I applaud your investigative mind, dear. Art historians have many ways of dating their finds. One popular method is called radiocarbon dating, which establishes the age based on the amount of carbon-14. Things that are very old have very little carbon-14, because over time, carbon-14 decays to carbon-12."

There were some smirks in the audience, and comments: "Tory

A LOOP IN TIME ❋ 65

really doesn't need any help with dating..."

Tory replied, "Radiocarbon dating does not work for things that are older than fifty thousand years old, though."

The docent was slightly peeved, but she was accustomed to prickly Manhattan art aficionados, many of whom had collections in their own living rooms.

"You are absolutely right my dear. For older objects, radiometric dating is useful. Radiometric dating is based on the same principle as radiocarbon dating, except instead of carbon-14, other radioactive elements are measured: rubidium-strontium, potassium-argon, among others," answered the docent.

Tory was done with her interrogation. She was now admiring a gold necklace with a scarab beetle pendant inside a display case, with a placard that read:

THE HEART SCARAB OF SETI
ca. 1466 B.C.E.; Dynasty 18, reign of Hatshepsut;
New Kingdom Egyptian; Western Thebes
Gold, green stone; 2 5/8 x 2 1/4 in. (6.7 x 5.3 cm)

Tory, peering closely at the glittering pendant on a braid of gold, intently read the placard:

The Heart Scarab was a protective amulet much like the wadjet, or protective eye of Horus. The amulet represented the scarab beetle, the sacred dung beetle that symbolized self-generation and rebirth. The inscription on the back of the amulet persuaded the heart not to invent lies when it was weighed against the feather, the attribute of the goddess of truth, Maat, on the scales during the Weighing of the Heart Ceremony before the tribunal of gods, led by Osiris. This ceremony determined the fate of the soul of the deceased.

"Hmm," Tory whispered to herself. "The famous Heart Scarab of Seti, an enchanted charm to absolve all guilty thoughts and erase all wrongdoing...how useful."

While she read the placard, the docent and her class moved on to other galleries. Looking up, Tory noticed that she was in a gallery that was momentarily empty.

With scarcely a second thought, Tory held her forearm so that the hammered gold armband faced the display. With a flickering flash, the display case lifted and the amulet floated toward Tory's waiting hand. Nonchalantly, she dropped the necklace into her handbag, and would have strolled unnoticed to the adjoining galleries to rejoin her group had she not walked, face to face, into Matt.

"Hey, Matt, how goes it?" she asked casually. She knew Matt as the son of Quint A. Senns and Sybille Nix, Manhattan's premier couple for investment capital and technology ventures.

She also knew Matt because he had helped with some of her jewelry projects, including the Tory Torus, her name for the spiral armband that had so conveniently opened the display case and disarmed the security sensors. She once told Matt she needed a device to manipulate light waves, ostensibly for the purpose of making automated door openers more welcoming to wheelchairs and pets at charity events.

"Hey, Tory," replied Matt. He showed no sign of having witnessed her act of felony grand theft. They walked together to the next gallery of Ancient Near-Eastern Art.

Their class and the docent tour were already ahead. Tory and Matt were among the few people in the gallery. This gallery was a personal favorite of Matt's. The sculpture and jewelry from the ancient Near East reminded him of the centaur sculpture in Ericca and Sophia Ludwig's apartment. All the artwork spoke to him of a deep love and joy in movement and nature: reindeers with antlers that spiraled exuberantly in elaborate headdresses, fanciful winged griffins in hammered gold.

Tory was also fascinated by griffins, especially by a pair of earrings in gold. She read the placard:

> Griffins were popular in the nomadic art of the
> first millennium B.C. in the Black Sea region.
> Griffins were composite animals, made up of
> elements of more than one animal. The griffins
> on these earrings have a feline body with the
> heads and wings of birds. They stand alert with
> their heads high, balanced by the wing tips and
> their tails. The metallic sheen of jewelry reflected
> the light and sparkled in the sun, enhancing the
> wearer's status and power.

Oh, how exquisite, she gasped to herself. Excellent gold crafts
from the smiths of the Caucasus mountains.

Matt would have noticed the greediness in her eyes, but he
himself was preoccupied. The ancient nomadic tribes of the Near
East fascinated him. He read the displays.

Prehistoric Art of the Early Nomads of the Altaic Region

The ancient Indo-Europeans ranged over the
territories of Central Asia, a territory often
referred to in aggregate as Turan. This vast
territory included parts of modern-day Turkey,
Afghanistan, Mongolia, Tibet, Manchuria, Siberia,
Russia, China, Korea, India, Japan, and the western
regions of the former Soviet Union. These early
tribes shared a similarity in language; hence the
term Altaic languages, which today refers to a
family of some sixty languages.

Recent excavations in the Altai Mountains have
unearthed relics from the Scythian-Sakae period

(6th–4th centuries B.C.E.). Most notable are the artifacts found in the mounds of Pazyryk in the Eastern part of the High Altai, at a height of 1,600 meters above sea level. These Altaic burial mounds sequestered a variety of things: clothing, footwear, domestic objects, and harnesses, nearly all with elements of decoration in gold, silver, wood, horn, leather, and fur. The motifs used in decoration are of the famous Scythian-Siberian animal style, with animal heads, horses, elk, and human figures conveying dynamic strength in scenes of engagement. These motifs were repeated in the swirling tattoos found on the bodies of a well-preserved ancient chieftain and priestess found in the vicinity.

He looked up just in time to see Tory Skye drop the pair of gold griffin earrings into her purse. The room was darkened, as if Tory had conjured a cloaking shroud.

The gallery was now deserted except for Tory and Matt. Matt grasped the Q-computer and slid a card into the slot. He pushed a button and whispered *Matter Mirror*. In the darkened gallery, a horse and rider holding a large bow jaunted toward Tory. She looked up with a gasp.

The warrior carried a quiver of arrows on a belt around his waist. The gold pectoral around his neck and the gleaming gold buckle on his belt featured intertwined swirls, a motif echoed in the dark tattoos on his powerful forearms and in the gold embellishments on the bridle. His face, painted blue, was a frightening visage.

"Hello, young lady," said the warrior, addressing Tory with a deferential air. "I don't believe you asked permission. You know, my wife is very fond of those."

Tory gasped and then regained her composure. "I have no idea what you are talking about," she replied innocently.

CHAPTER FIVE

"Just how many Manhattan teenagers, property heiresses or not, have ancient charms and griffin earrings in their purses?" replied the warrior knowingly.

Tory was flustered. She was convinced that her acts of thievery had been undetected. Now, in dread, she looked about the darkened room. Matt was not to be seen. Maintaining innocence, she said, "You're crazy. My father could buy this place. I don't need to purloin this…this…slipshod stuff." She raised her hand to nervously tuck her hair behind her ears. Her exposed forearm gleamed with the light of the Tory Torus.

"I see, the Tory Torus, relic of the Skye clan, masters of thunder and lightning, wizards of automatic doors, museum sensors, and other electron-powered gizmos of the modern age. Well, let's just see," said the warrior. He shot an arrow at Tory's purse and retrieved the purse on the arrow's return trajectory. "Goodness, look what I have found," exclaimed the warrior with mock disbelief. He removed the heart scarab amulet and gold griffin earrings from the purse. "Doesn't look slipshod to me; in fact, this is among the finest craftsmanship of the ancient world."

The warrior continued. "Do you know that a crowd of media and paparazzi are right now crowding around your limousine waiting to photograph Tory Skye as she reunites with her adoring pet? Imagine their surprise when she emerges instead under police arrest for felony grand theft."

Tory was now shivering. She was long a media favorite, a situation that certainly added to the public's fascination with Skye Tower and anything associated with the name *Skye*. The limousine parked in waiting was not there merely to provide proximity to her cherished pet, but was, in fact, helping perpetuate her celebrity aura. The turn of events spelled out by the warrior would be disastrous.

He seemed to read Tory's mind. He made an offer: "Such a sad spectacle, a disgraced celebrity, a sullied family name …The purloined articles will be returned and all will be forgiven in exchange for just a bit of unvarnished truth, and I bid you note, *unvarnished truth* — the heart scarab will not help you now…"

Tory could not imagine what hideous confession he had in mind, but she nodded in agreement.

"You may have witnessed a strange incident, a disappearing incident, involving one Ericca Ludwig, outside the Broadway Metro stop a few days ago. You might have recognized this incident as involving sophisticated manipulation of the fabric of space and time — manipulation not known among mere Saplings. Have you told anyone about this incident, and if so, whom?"

Tory paused, and then sighed silently in relief. For some reason, they were concerned about a completely unremarkable girl who happened to pull a visual trick. "Yes, I saw that. It wasn't a big deal. I told my father, Daemon Skye. He's reminded me a few times to notice things like that, though he did say it would only be alarming under certain circumstances — like among Saplings."

The warrior held a scale in his hand and dropped a feather on the end of the scale that was slightly higher. The scale adjusted; the scale was balanced. "Ahh, truth as light as a feather, which sets the soul free. You tell the truth, my dear. You may go," said he. With that remark, the warrior vanished, leaving the room oddly silent, save for the distant echoes of the continuing tour.

Tory sighed with relief and looked around at a gallery restored to its previous state. The griffin earrings were back in the case as though nothing had happened. When she caught up with her class on their docent tour, she tried to talk to Matt, but he was with a crowd of boys and didn't look in her direction.

Happily for Tory, a crowd of photographers surrounded her when she exited the museum. Reporters interviewed her, anxious for her quips about the museum. But, avoiding this topic, she deftly held Pluto and announced, "The museum was fabulous, but I find magic in today's jewelry. You will be so excited, especially with my line of charms and accessories for pets, called *Enchanted Elements*, locally available in Soho at Tory's Creations, and also online." The reporters scribbled away enthusiastically.

Matt and Elle smiled wryly in the background, as did the rest of

CHAPTER FIVE

their class, as Tory beamed at the fawning reporters.

Later than afternoon, Matt and Elle met Ericca at their loft. Matt had managed to avoid giving any hint of his caper in the museum to anyone, especially Tory, who looked at him suspiciously but stopped short of voicing an accusation.

But now the three of them were assembled about the twins' kitchen table. It had been another hot afternoon. All over the newspapers and television were predictions of a serious drought for the five boroughs of New York City and southeastern New York.

They sat licking Indian ice cream bars from the Spice Market, when Matt announced smugly, looking at Ericca, "Daemon Skye for sure knows that Spike has quintessence, and that you know how to travel in time."

Ericca groaned in despair. She could expect very soon to be reprimanded by her mother. Worse, Spike would be bagged up and locked away, along with her friends, Albert and Leonardo. Spike was right now folded in her backpack, with Albert and Leonardo no doubt waiting for the first sign of misbehavior to pop out and remind them of their mothers' instructions.

The implications could be even more serious. Daemon could confront Quint. Matt knew there was a long-standing disagreement between Daemon and Quint over the uses of quintessence, but he didn't know exactly what was at the heart of the disagreement.

They sat glumly until Elle had an idea. "Well, we can't do that much now about anything. Why don't we show Ericca our vacation videos," she suggested. She gave Matt a small card labeled *The Surf at Big Sur and Spots on the California Coast.*

Matt plugged the card into his Q-computer, and immediately the loft transformed into a beach scene. They felt the cold, pounding surf, and squinted at a brilliant ocean swirling with foam. They ran in and out of the waves and built sandcastles on the beach.

Sitting on a beach with fine, white sand, they laughingly speculated about Tory Skye's magical charms for small pets.

"It would be perfect," joked Elle. "*The Status Equalizing Charm*, for confrontations with larger dogs."

"Yeah, it would have the effect of reducing the frequency of the bark from an obnoxious, high-pitched yap to a thunderous roar," added Matt, who knew a bit about the wave concept of sound.

"The charm could have a tiny Q-computer and make the wearer appear as a big dog, to other dogs that is," added Ericca.

Matt, reminded of his caper in the museum, said, "That would scare Tory out of her designer shorts." He proceeded to tell them about the warrior hologram he conjured in the museum. But, Elle was hardly impressed. She was horrified.

"Do you know what that means, Matt? Tory now knows we can create life-sized holographic projections capable of fooling most people. This is something she will definitely go crying to her dad about, especially since she doesn't have that power yet," explained Elle.

Their joking now ceased. Their mood, despite the tranquil beach and glimmering ocean, became one of foreboding. The power of Daemon Skye, and his alleged role in the death of Branch Archer, lurked vividly in their minds.

"The Heart Scarab of Seti, an amulet that would absolve the heart of guilt, even in murder," continued Elle.

Ericca, reminded of the myth of Osiris and Seth, nodded in agreement and whispered, "His brother, Osiris, out of the way, the Sky God Seth was free to punish the despised mortals at will with drought, famine, and scorching heat, and obliterate all who stood in his way."

They contemplated the glowing red orb sinking below the horizon in a California sunset, each lost in their own dark thoughts.

CHAPTER SIX

BLIND CHESS

The hot, dry spring turned into a hotter and drier summer. Already drought alerts and water conservation measures were in force. The subway bathrooms operated at reduced capacity. The fountains in Central Park were on for only a few hours each day.

The city government offered adapters for toilet bowls to reduce the amount of water used with each flush. Weary commuters debated the merits of humid subway tunnels, rank with the sweat of many bodies, versus clogged freeways gray with smog. Bottled-water purveyors enjoyed brisk business, though many New Yorkers scoffed at the idea of paying more per gallon for water than for gasoline.

The public libraries were busy. Patrons spent many a pleasant afternoon in the air-conditioned stone halls. Sophia Ludwig found herself managing more library users and having even less time to devote to Ericca.

Thankfully, Ericca had Spike and a Metropolitan Tunnel Authority subway pass. Her mother had directed emphatic cautionary words about the use of Spike, but so far, to Ericca's great relief and surprise, did not threaten to confiscate the blanket.

This afternoon, Ericca was to meet the twins at the museum. She carried her backpack, with Spike compactly stored at the bottom, squished by a water bottle and a library book. She passed a playground, where a mirage rippled in the dense, hot air exuding from the cracked asphalt.

She entered the subway and took care to avoid the bathrooms, garbage cans, and drinking fountains. She was indisposed to another plumbing mishap, especially under these circumstances. She turned to descend the escalator to the subway tunnel when she heard a familiar announcement over the intercom: **"Security alert. Please exit the station immediately. Leave no bags unattended. Please alert security staff about suspicious packages."**

Leonardo and Albert heard the announcement as well, and were panicked and strongly urged Ericca to find the nearest exit. "There, I see it, turn here to your right," said Leonardo shrilly, only to be interrupted by Albert, who remarked gruffly, "That exit is already jammed with people. Better to try the exit to your left, though it may be a little farther away."

"Oh, you guys," said Ericca in exasperation. "It is amazing we ever get anywhere with you two constantly arguing."

They were headed to the exit when Ericca saw an elderly woman wearing orthopedic shoes, walking very slowly. The woman was Sheila Angvall. Her walking was so slow and labored, Ericca was sure she was about to collapse.

"Mrs. Angvall, can I help you at all?" asked Ericca.

The woman looked up with a smile and faltered before replying, "How…how lovely to see you…why, you're the little girl from the Memorial Monument…" She grasped for a name.

"Ericca. I am Ericca Ludwig," said Ericca, offering a hand.

"Why, of course, dear, I do remember you," replied the woman hoarsely. She tried to hold herself erect, but instead she hunched over as if with abdominal pain. She was short of breath, and her skin was flushed. Suddenly, she collapsed into Ericca's arms.

Ericca looked frantically around the deserted subway station, staggering a bit to keep Mrs. Angvall from falling to the ground. To her surprise, she saw Tory Skye, with her small dog yapping mercilessly as they hurried out the exit. Ericca breathed in relief as a subway attendant approached.

Moments later, Mrs. Angvall was in an ambulance stretcher with

CHAPTER SIX

Ericca alongside as they rode together to the nearest hospital.

"Mrs. Angvall, can you hear me?" asked Ericca, trying to help the ambulance attendant fill out the forms. But Mrs. Angvall did not reply.

Mrs. Angvall, in fact, did not gain consciousness for several hours, during which Ericca phoned her mother and the museum to notify the twins that she would not be meeting them. The hospital staff was not very worried. "Heat stress, and panic," they commented. They were grateful, though, that Ericca was there to help.

Ericca had this opportunity to make sense of the ghostly children she saw on Memorial Day. "Mrs. Angvall," she asked, when Sheila was fully awake, "When you saw your son, David, that day, were you not surprised?"

"Of course, dear, but there he was that day. He was all there; he even smelled like he did when he was a baby...of course I was surprised."

Sheila looked at Ericca sharply and said, "I know what you're thinking, that I imagined everything. I haven't told anyone because I'm sure most people will think I'm nuts...but since you saw the same thing, I am sure you believe me."

"Did David tell you how he got there or where he came from?" asked Ericca.

"No, he just said he boarded the Thyme Train at the Q-Gate, where there was a pretty pool. The Thyme Train passed fields of checkerboard green, scented with thyme and mint, before arriving in Central Park. He really liked the train, and the other kids on the train were nice to him," answered Sheila.

"Was that the first time you two were able to meet like that?" asked Ericca.

"Yes, unfortunately I've visited the memorial countless times, and never before had the delight of seeing my son," replied Sheila.

"Don't you wonder how he came to be there?" asked Ericca.

Sheila was slightly irritated but answered wearily, "I could worry about a lot of things; I could fret about unjust wars, racial genocide, slave labor, or all the possible contaminants in ballpark food. Thankfully, I have other things to worry and wonder about, such as what I might make for my stitchery club's next get-together."

She continued brightly, "Of course I wonder, and as he boarded the Thyme Train and waved goodbye, I asked him when we would meet again, and he told me sadly, most likely never again."

"Did he say why not?" Ericca asked.

"He said the tunnel was not secure, on account of the protracted Tunnel Wars. The Q-Gate was temporarily open that one time. He had to return while the tunnel was still safe to use or else — " answered Sheila.

"Or what?" asked Ericca persistently.

"He said he had been advised while at the Q-Gate that if he stayed too long, his body would begin to disintegrate and he would be left with his consciousness floating formlessly, trapped here forever. I held him one last time, smelled his hair, and let him go. That is all I know, dear," replied Sheila.

Mrs. Angvall was now settled in a pose of tranquility. She was glad to have shared this with Ericca but did not want to give her empty hope. "Now run along, dear; for all we know, it was all a daydream," said she with her eyes half-closed.

"Thanks, Mrs. Angvall. I'll try to come and visit again," replied Ericca.

Mrs. Angvall smiled a wan smile, waved, and remarked brightly, "I have just the thing for my next stitchery club meeting: strawberries baked with a gratin of lemon-thyme — delicious. I have the recipe if you ever want to try it."

"Sounds yummy…I'll have to try it sometime," Ericca said, turning to wave goodbye. When she looked again, Mrs. Angvall lay with an expression of serene repose, most likely thinking about strawberries with a gratin of lemon-thyme.

Ericca's mind was buzzing. Now she was certain there was a

time tunnel; she had used it to cross Manhattan in the blink of an eye, the twins had used it while riding the Cobra car across the continent, David Angvall had used the tunnel to visit his mother aboard the Thyme Train. It was this last example that puzzled Ericca. David was most certainly like Leonardo and Albert, a traveler in time and space.

This brought another nagging question: Was it possible for her to travel through time to see her father? She fingered the little bronze Time Token that she had since she was a baby. If there were a way to travel to see her father, where would she go? Where would she find him?

She thought to consult Leonardo and Albert about this, but she knew what they would say. First, Leonardo would not get a word in, other than perhaps "Mathematically, time travel is theoretically possible."

Albert might argue in reply, "Mathematicians, with your absurd abstract worlds; as though we lived in an Escher painting of perfect symmetry or a completely rectilinear Euclidean world. Please stop before you totally confuse the poor child." He might launch into a discussion of one of his favorite topics, his general theory of relativity.

He might say, "Gravity creates time and space. Gravity — or more correctly, gravitational potential energy, the attractive force between matter — creates the structure and paths of space, like a chessboard or a grid of streets in a city. Gravity creates causality and a sense of progression, from the gradual droop and wrinkling of flesh to the drip of water in a water clock. Without gravity, if one were to annihilate gravity, like puncturing a very dense bagel, we might find layers of matter in variable configurations, a fluid soup of scenarios of the future, or the past."

It was this last part that fascinated Ericca. If travel to the past were possible, she could "undo" her father's death. It would not be enough for her to see her father alive, as a young man or small boy, in a frozen past. She would want to change the past. She could see no other way. Albert would have said a *fluid soup of scenarios* — not *frozen* scenarios.

She knew her mother was doing her best. Sophia was working many hours at the library simply to support the two of them. But despite all her efforts, she was barely able to maintain the tiny apartment they shared.

They even lacked a television, and the best Ericca could do during those many idle hours at home was adjust the pink-and gold-flecked wristwatch her mother had given her on her seventh birthday. But rather than cartoons, the pictures decorating the apartment showed a series of bizarre dramas.

These intervals in front of the framed pictures on the wall, however, were increasingly more entertaining as Ericca started to recognize the characters. Why, there was her mom, and Sybille and Maxine, looking just the same except for their less-than-stylish outfits. Sometimes she turned the knob on the wristwatch forward and was sure she saw herself and the twins in the animated pictures on the wall.

Aside from this and other odd things about the apartment, which she never tried to describe to anyone except the twins, the summer was shaping up to be another long, hot season. This summer, the twins would be away for weeks in travels to Egypt and in their getaway cabin in the Hamptons.

Not complaining, Ericca knew these were not possibilities for her. She knew her mother was doing her very best as a single parent. She knew there were many families and kids much worse off than she. She saw them retreat into crowded basement apartments along hidden alleyways, rank with garbage.

Now, alone in their apartment, waiting for her mother to return home from work, she was grateful for the cool, curved back of the wooden bench. She fingered the inscription, *criminal penalties apply for defacement*. She was sure that was an inside joke between Sophia and Maxine. She gazed at the picture of the library building framed against the turquoise wash of the walls, a faded print labeled in ornate letters:

CHAPTER SIX

THE SERAPEUM AT ALEXANDRIA
Repository of Ancient Knowledge, Including Egyptian, Ancient European, and Persian Philosophies About the Afterlife and the Eternity of the Soul. Original Home of the Almagest by Ptolemy, and Elements by Euclid. Completely Destroyed in the Fifth Century A.D.

Ericca whispered, "The Serapeum, I've heard of that place. Hypatia told me about it. That would be a fun place to visit." Hypatia was one of the friends who periodically popped out of her blanket, Spike.

She idly fingered her wristwatch. Turning the knob on the watch backward, the empty temple shown in the picture became gradually populated. Ericca grew wide-eyed with horror, however, when the scene transformed to show a mob crowding the stone and marble promenade. A woman screamed as her wounded body was dragged through the streets behind a chariot.

The angry mob closed around her, booing and hissing. Then the stately stone building in the background began to burn. Ericca recognized the ancient library, the Serapeum of Alexandria; the woman dragged through the street was Hypatia. Not a single book remained after fire engulfed the building. Ericca hurriedly set her watch forward, until the picture on the wall was once again a silent architectural rendering and Hypatia another smiling, friendly face on her blanket.

The rest of the afternoon, she dreamed about all the places she would go if she could travel through time, until she heard voices in the hallway. It was her neighbor Nicholas Bard and his friend Daphne heading out for dinner. They apparently were back together. She thought of the birthday gift she had delivered and was happy for them.

Fall returned to New York and with that came relief from the summer's oppressive heat and humidity. The trees in Central Park glowed in hues of burnt umber and saffron. The air was crisp and refreshing. The crowds of tourists had diminished; fashionable New Yorkers donned their fall wardrobes.

The twins Elle and Matt, back from their vacation in Egypt, were bubbly and happy to see Ericca. They listened with interest when she told them about her talk with Sheila Angvall as they munched on hot pretzels while sitting in the park one afternoon. They told Ericca that they had visited Alexandria, but they did not see the ancient Serapeum that once existed there. They did see a lot of ruins, weathered and fragmented structures in stone with chipped and softened edges. They also saw mummies, which were gruesomely ugly.

There was something fascinating about mummies, especially for Ericca. Elle had told her, "Mummification and preservation of the body was important to the ancient Egyptians for entry to the afterlife. It was an extension of the myth of Osiris."

Elle explained, "In that myth, Isis retrieves the dismembered parts of Osiris and reassembles him. Osiris thereafter represented regeneration, and for the Egyptians, he signified the regenerative cycle of the Nile. He also presided over the afterlife and the ceremony of judgment determining passage into the afterlife. Those found worthy, whose hearts were as light as a feather, were admitted to a paradisiacal garden. Those unworthy were eaten. Those in limbo remained on earth and were reassured by the daily appearance of the ship bearing the Sun God."

Ericca was as fond of a good story as most people, but now she thought of her own life. She murmured, "The Egyptians believed the soul could only enter the afterlife with the body intact." She thought of her father, and his death in an explosion that tore his body to unrecognizable pieces. She concluded, "My father was not there to meet at the Memorial Monument on Memorial Day because he has not yet passed into the afterlife. He lacks an intact body, and his immortal soul is in limbo here on earth."

The twins were sympathetic. They could see how Ericca might want to believe her father would be found. They could only imagine how different things would be without their own magnanimous and goofy dad.

But Ericca's speculation about ghosts pushed the envelope of even their imaginations. Ericca persisted, "Don't you get it? The Time Token Maxine gave me is a special token for the Light Rail, not in the subway, but a ride on a light wave that travels through time."

"Well, maybe," said Matt. "There is talk in Mom's circles about a wormhole, which is the intersection of a black hole and a white hole, a tear or anomaly in the fabric of space and time if you will. But these wormholes are never stable. There is such intense gravity at the center of a black hole that all matter, even in the form of a light wave, is crushed."

"We're not talking about current science, the science of mere Saplings," argued Ericca. "We are talking about a kind of super-magical, and secret, technology." She recalled Tory's conversation with the warrior and Tory's allusion to *mere Saplings*. She did not need to remind the twins about the things that happened to them that most kids had no clue about: rides on Spike, jaunts around the world at light speed in the Cobra car, computers capable of generating incredible holograms that would fool most eyes.

Ericca fell silent and looked away. "My father is out there somewhere," declared Ericca. "I intend to find him."

The holiday season was in full swing. The twins anxiously studied for their term exams. "Oh, algebra and French," complained Matt. "Dad took my Q-computer away; no computer games until I get a good grade in French," he whined. Matt labored over textbooks and seemed to have erased the memory of all previous antics.

Tory Skye, in the senior class, once again numbered among their classmates and acted as though the incident in the museum had never happened. She rarely acknowledged Matt, and this holiday season, she was never in class. She was often seen, however, in two dimensions, on the cover of celebrity magazines or on the computer, smiling broadly with Pluto in her arms, promoting her line of jewelry for pets. Elle and Matt scoffed as they read in their father's business magazine:

TORY SKYE, BUSINESS ACUMEN RUNS IN THE FAMILY

Tory Skye, the vivacious daughter of Manhattan property tycoon Daemon Skye, has proved true to her name. Ms. Skye has entered the crowded field of celebrity brand and designer paraphernalia and scored an astounding victory with unprecedented pre-holiday sales of her Enchanted Elements line of accessories. The Enchanted Elements line features charms that evoke mythological themes. The most popular item, the Heart Scarab, sells as a set for pets and owners, and is associated with goodness of the heart. The charm features a beetle pendant plated in 14-karat gold on a gold chain and is reportedly the only accurate reproduction of an ancient amulet available to consumers. The Elements line of pet charms also includes the wadjet, the mythical eye of Horus, said to confer divine protection.

The twins were surprised to see in the picture a necklace that was identical to the Heart Scarab of Seti, the very priceless amulet Tory had attempted to steal from the museum. It was too ironic that Tory Skye, of all people, was selling charms to inspire good-heartedness. They avoided snide reminders of Tory's past behavior: cutting in line in the cafeteria, deriding other kids for their clothes. They were, most important, mystified and curious about how Tory managed to replicate the amulet on a mass scale.

A disturbing possibility lurked in Matt's mind. He was without his Q-computer, but he remembered how he had been a show-off and showed Tory its amazing ability to produce stunningly detailed holograms that mimicked reality.

CHAPTER SIX

Now he recalled his mother enthusiastically explaining the concept of "quantum teleportation." She would expound, adopting the tone of a physicist, "Quantum teleportation could theoretically enable time travel and object replication over expanses of time and space. You would start with an object, or maybe a detailed hologram, and create a matching object where each fragment of matter matches the state of the original. The problem is that in the process of teleportation, the state of the original is destroyed. Quantum replication remains an unsolved puzzle."

Matt mulled over the possibility that Tory had obtained the original amulet or its hologram, and was producing mass replicas with one command on a computer. He wondered whether he had inadvertently helped her. He speculated about the true influence of the enchanted charm. "Probably to get everyone to buy more of that stuff," he later said sarcastically to Elle.

A chance to resolve those questions presented itself when least expected. His mother was invited to a fashion show, and would be attending with her friend, Sophia Ludwig. "You know, Tory Skye will be there. She likes these events, and this year I think her charms will be worn in one of the winter collections. I'm so excited," Sybille said.

Matt had told her everything about the incident in the museum with Tory and his worries about what Tory might be doing. His mother had been surprisingly good-natured, saying merely, "Tory is a clever girl, as you are a clever boy. I'd be curious to see what she's come up with." As she prepared to leave for the fashion show, she said, "Be good to your dad, don't let him get in any trouble, and don't worry, I'll find out what tricks your friend has learned."

The loft in Soho was stocked with all things necessary for staying indoors on wintry days. That day, there were supplies for cookies and for modeling elements of the periodic table in dough, with special instructions for showing the correct number of electrons. There were all sorts of board games, including Ericca's favorite, "Cosmic Trap," where landing on a square identified as *The Trap Hole* caused the board to warp and everything in the apartment to shrink.

Ericca had just landed on a trap square, leaving them all sitting on very small chairs around a tiny table with a microscopic game board with a deep dimple, when Quint came home, dusting fine crystals of snow from his wool jacket.

"Sorry, kids, I'm late, but you know how that goes, pitiful traffic. Everything slows to a crawl with a little bit of snow. You'd think they were in a black hole. Now, let's see, the Trap game, that's good," he said peering at them through his glasses.

As though the word "trap" jogged his memory, he took a quick glance at his watch and exclaimed, "My gosh, look at the time! I was supposed to be at my chess game five minutes ago. Well, I have to go again, kids. Don't make too much of a mess of the place, or your mother will have my head."

With the mention of chess, the twins knew he was off to Central Park. His hurried manner told them that he would rather they did not accompany him. His reluctance to include them told them he was up to something, and they had better come along.

"Hey, chess, can I come along? You know, I aced all my exams. You promised I could have my Q-computer back," pleaded Matt.

"Oh, oh, of course, but come along now," Quint replied.

In minutes, they were all jogging, bundled up in mittens and coats, along the Literary Walk in a corridor of delicately outlined, snow-covered trees. They approached a clearing, the Glade of Games, shrouded in a light, freezing mist, against a backdrop of skeletal sycamore and oak trees. A man in a gray wool suit with a handsome charcoal scarf stood alone there. The man was Daemon Skye.

Quint surveyed the snow-covered ground. Then, as if removing dust from a desk, he made a sweeping motion while uttering the command *Matrix Made Manifest*. The snow cleared to reveal a well-mown lawn with alternating patches of silver thyme and green

Corsican mint in a neat eight-by-eight grid.

The chessboard now ready, Quint strolled to greet Daemon. "Hello, Daemon, good to see you," said Quint as Daemon approached. They shook hands. Daemon looked indifferently as Ericca and the twins trailed silently behind Quint.

"Shall we commence?" suggested Daemon.

"Oh, absolutely," replied Quint. He reached into his coat pocket and brought out two Q-computers, handing one to Daemon. "Of course...the rules of blind chess are the same. We are able to see the location of the opponent's pieces, but we are unable to identify the piece. You can use any set of pieces you wish; simply plug in the appropriate card."

"That's fair and realistic," commented Daemon. "The exact strategy of your opponent is always uncertain."

With that, Daemon commanded the computer, "Generate the Puppet King and his Proletarian Army." An array of gray, rough-hewn characters emerged in the deserted glade.

"Allow me to introduce my favorite chess characters, the Puppet King and his army of slaves, the *proles* of the masses. What can be more formidable than an enemy corrupt beyond a glimmer of personal hope?"

Elle, who liked history and read a lot, explained to Ericca and Matt in a whisper, "The word *proles* means offspring in Latin, a term used during the Roman Empire, when pregnancy and large families were encouraged to increase the ranks of the military. The term *proletariat* is based on the root term, *proles*. In ancient Rome, the *proletariat* were poor, landless freemen. They were artisans and tradesmen working under terms equivalent to slavery. The *proletariat*, or *producers of offspring*, were the lowest rank among Roman citizenry, ranking below the warrior and priest classes, and only slightly higher than slaves, prostitutes, and women. They were the permanent working class critical to expansion of the Roman empire. Marx and Lenin and Mao used the term *proletariat* to unify the peasantry in Communist revolts."

Daemon held his hand toward a small, bent old man with

a craggy nose and a suspicious, leering manner. Daemon said, "My Puppet King, bereft of any moral imperative or concept of absolute good except, of course, his own continued dominion — a weak and aging man, clinging each day more desperately to his empty office, growing each day more capable of vile deception and cruelty to prop up his corrupt regime."

The small, gray man looked up a degree and walked slowly to his place on the board. He smiled feebly, showing a string of broken teeth, and waved as if acknowledging a crowd of well-wishers and supporters. He resumed his pose, supported on a walking stick, head bent, suspicious eyes watching in all directions.

Daemon continued, "Next in the line of power is the king's bishop." A gray, thin man with a long, wiry neck supporting two skull-like heads emerged. The gray robe draped on the skinny frame was held by a ceremonial sash; the man held his hands together in a pose of calm righteousness.

"A lonely, ambitious man convinced of his own moral superiority — the bishop's advice weighs heavily in the king's cunning mind. Though one should be careful with a person capable of uttering two completely different things at the same time." Daemon laughed and said, "Not just deception, but double deception." With that, the bishop moved forward, talking out of both mouths, making a different gesture with each gaunt hand.

"Following close behind the bishop is the king's knight, representing the might of the warrior class," announced Daemon. A rough-hewn, muscular man with the horned head of a bull stepped forward warily.

"Meet my knight, the Minotaur, a man endowed with the strength and virility of a bull. He is stubborn and fearless, but don't be fooled. He has all the agile cunning of mortal men. When equipped with his axe, he hews trees and all that stands in his crooked path."

"Alongside my knight is the rook, a fortress in an enchanted forest, thick with brambles and impenetrable, overgrown vegetation. Opponents of the king suffer slow, tortured death, shrieking in pain in dank, polluted dungeons. Wolves patrol the walls, their ever-watchful eyes gleaming red in the darkness."

The rook moved into position, a stone castle atop a steep rockery. Daemon continued, "I suppose I should introduce the queen before the proletarian army." A tall, slender woman wearing a crown walked forward. She held her head high, her hair fell away from her face onto delicate shoulders, her abdomen swelled forward.

"The king has impregnated her and confined her in chains, so that she may never desert or betray him. She will serve his will and provide proles for his regime until the end of her days. She fills him with self-loathing and a mad twisted desire."

Elle and Ericca, standing together silently in the gray shadow of bare trees, looked on with curiosity. This was not how they had imagined the queen, the most powerful piece of all.

"We should not forget the proletarian army, not until they have served their purpose, anyway," said Daemon, as eight men, bent in poses of attack, moved into place. They held weapons and shields, and wore heavy shackles on their ankles. They bore themselves with demeanors of dutiful aggression.

"Thanks to our queen and her charms, we have a mighty fighting force in ready supply, disposable and replaceable. They place the longevity of the regime before their own meaningless existence. They fight with the fire of the bishop's cloying words, and fear the knight's thunderous axe."

Daemon stood back to admire his assembled pieces. He smirked cynically at Quint and said, "Quite a collector's set, wouldn't you agree? I designed the pieces myself and coded their images onto these holo-cards as I sat watching the evening news. Time well spent, wouldn't you say?"

Quint was not perturbed. He readied his own set and commented, "Daemon, we've had these matches before, and your competitiveness always impresses me." Quint knew Daemon was baiting him for a confrontation, one that would open a long-standing disagreement. Ericca and the twins stood nearby and watched with great interest. They did not yet understand the bitterness of this disagreement. They actually preferred to see this as just another contest of chess expertise.

Quint summoned his pieces. "Meet the Pillars of Light. Appropriately, we should begin with the light of most people's lives, their children. My pawn pieces are children, empowered with imagination, intuition, and science. They are not mere pawns to be sacrificed in a world of conflict. They wear the falcon headdress of Horus and have the divinity of their intrepid souls." Eight small, slender figures, with large eyes and straight hair, moved onto the board, giggling and poking each other.

"Guiding and nurturing them is the queen, Isis," announced Quint as he introduced a woman wearing a headdress containing a bright red disc. A dignified character, she sat upright with a child at her breast. "The queen is determined to ensure the safety and prosperity of her citizenry. She wants all children to find the lives they aspire to. She acts warily, with careful planning and meticulous orderliness to make the most of the strength and resources available to her."

The queen was in place and exuded an air of profound intelligence and compassion. "Next to the queen is the bishop, a wise Sphinx, a composite being with the head of a woman and the body of a lion. She will counsel the queen on strategy. She will serve as a prophet and identify the probabilities of different scenarios." The Sphinx smiled a quizzical grin as she took her place beside the queen.

Quint continued, after glancing at the Sphinx's helical earrings and headdress embellished with a cobra. "My knight is the Egyptian Goddess of the Hunt. She is Neith, and she wields a bow. She is capable of brute force and strategic delicacy. The bow and arrow she wields with consummate skill, and she directs both the arrow of passion and that of punishment."

The slender figure of a woman archer appeared. She had a stern and intimidating demeanor but also seemed to be thinking about her next trip to the ice cream store.

CHAPTER SIX

"My rook is a stone obelisk, a monumental Pillar of Light, a needle piercing the clouds and bringing rain to the desert, a ray of light conveying energy and goodness from the sky. The records and signatures carved on the obelisk commit history to eternity and evoke the might of the word," continued Quint.

The obelisk was indeed inspiring. Ericca turned to Elle and Matt to offer a long, detailed description of all the obelisks in New York and over the world, but Elle and Matt made a "zip it" motion over their mouths.

"Finally, we have the king. The king knows he is a weak piece, flawed by his good nature and trustfulness. My king is Osiris, the deity destroyed and dismembered by his jealous brother. But even for this mishap, he persists, grateful for the queen and her supporters. He fathers a child, Horus, the deity who brings wisdom and foresight to future rulers."

The king appeared, wearing a white conical crown, the plumed atef crown. He carried a scepter and flail. He did not seem the worse for having been hacked to pieces. He looked adoringly at the queen as she nursed their child, while winking at every female on the board.

With Quint's set complete, Daemon commented wryly, "Your dreamy preoccupation with mythology never ceases to amaze me. Naturally, your pawns are so charming. They are the children of plenty, born of the fertile Nile Delta, not the barren, harsh desert. You should know by now that those born of scarcity in the desolate wastelands have a perpetual wariness and paranoia that celebrates force and hierarchy. The world has plenty of these wretches...always has."

"Scarcity and plenty are elusive quantities, Daemon, more achievements than gifts. Plenty diminishes to scarcity quickly under poor leadership and planning. My pawns are so charming because they glow with achievement, not entitlement."

"One would think you were a professor of philosophy, sitting in your university post writing high-minded papers, poring over your esoterica in solitude and obscurity. No one would guess that you've actually experienced purposeful conflict, conflict defining destiny and shaping history. No one would guess you have ever produced anything real, anything successful, or that you enjoy any of the finer things in life," replied Daemon imperiously.

Quint knew Daemon was once again trying to provoke a heated discussion. He coolly suggested, "Let's play — there is nothing more exhilarating than a game of blind chess in the snow."

The game began. Quint granted Daemon the first move. Daemon was a practiced player, and his gambits and sacrifices of pawns and other key pieces in exchange for position put Quint on the defensive for most of the game. Quint was guarded, cautiously advancing pieces, retreating from major piece trades.

In the endgame, only a few pieces remained. This being blind chess, Quint did not know which pieces Daemon had remaining, though he could guess. Daemon still had his queen, but one of Quint's pawns had advanced to the point of converting to a queen.

At the crucial point, Quint wished he could have had two moves in succession. But finally it was over. The Minotaur struck a death blow to Quint's pawn. Quint's pawn had just converted to a queen, a triumph equivalent to the ascension of a member of the proles to the warrior class.

In that window, Quint's remaining pawn took Daemon's queen, who breathed with relief, as though her shackles had finally been loosened. But, even without the queen, Daemon's knight and rook eventually forced Quint to resign the game.

As his chess figures dissolved into the Q-computer, Daemon, pleased with the outcome and behaving pleasantly, accepted Quint's congratulations. "You and Sybille really should come and see the Bull's Eye Restaurant. It's quite a place, and you'll run into a handful of politicians, sports players, and movie stars. Bring in the kids; we're starting up a kids' menu," he said amiably.

Quint, a steak fan, replied, "Great idea. Let me talk to Sybille."

Ericca and the twins, expecting Daemon to mention Tory and

the incident involving Spike, were surprised to see the two men chatting like this. They felt sure something was left unsaid.

Later, Matt asked, "Dad, I thought Daemon was opposed to the things you do, like with the Q-computer, making it available to everyone?"

"Maybe he is. But I've told him and my investor groups that the Q-computer is a powerful computer, capable of great things, solving problems, searching data, even assessing all the moves in chess and coming up with a winning strategy. The Q-computer can also do dangerous things, such as producing deceitful images, or cracking encryption codes. But it is not the fault of the Q-computer, but the user. I just happen to think people will find good ways of using it, like for something really fun, like chess," answered Quint.

Ericca thought, Quint, he's just like my dad, such a good-natured, trusting man. I hope he's never blown to bits. But these dark thoughts were driven out of her mind as the twins pelted each other with snowballs. They all stormed after Quint in a full-fledged chase and snowball fight; though dodging and pelting snowballs in return, Quint handily evaded them.

CHAPTER SEVEN

THE MISTLETOE BARD

For no apparent reason, Ericca had trouble sleeping that night. The day had been filled with happy things. The snowball fight in the fresh snow in Central Park was a riot; seeing her mother dressed up and fashionable was an eye-opener.

Ericca decided long ago that adults dressed and acted in ways that suited their jobs. For instance, her mother was a librarian and usually looked like a librarian, in modest sweaters, skirts, and trousers; she always looked learned and serious. For the fashion show, though, Sophia wore a dress that accentuated her graceful neck and long legs; her curly hair was combed back to frame her cheekbones and chiseled brow. She looked happy and almost as though she was having fun.

Sophia did look forward to the fashion show. Ericca knew this from glimpsing her mother's journal one day when the pink-and-gold-flecked book sat open on the writing desk. She noted the curious dialogue scrawled on the open pages.

Sophia wrote, "Ericca grows stronger and smarter with every day, and I am so glad I have her. But little did I know from that day at the Aisle of Tears what a harsh life it can be in New York, especially as a single mother who works all the time."

Her friend Sybille wrote back sympathetically, "No, New York is not like the Elledoor world, where childcare would not have been an issue with our system for shared nurturing. But New York is one of the better spots to be, really. And there is a lot of fun here. Come with me to the fashion show. Who knows, you might meet someone."

Sophia replied, "I meet people all the time, but it is never quite the same."

Reading this, Ericca knew her mother was talking about Branch. Ericca sometimes felt she knew her father, without having ever met him from everything her mother had said about him. She suppressed a tear.

In reply, Sybille adopted scientific persuasion and wrote back, "In a city of random collisions, the probability of a happy collision rises from nearly nil to encouraging but improbable when the opportunities for collision are multiplied."

Sophia wrote tersely in reply, "Improbable, that I know…" She hesitated but eventually agreed to go.

The holidays neared; Sybille and Sophia arrived home from the fashion show, beautiful shopping bags in hand. The kids buzzed about curiously, certain the contents were for them; they were summarily shooed away.

That night, Ericca should have fallen asleep contentedly, snuggled in her blanket, floating about the apartment, as snow whirled around the trees and brownstones drawn in white. Her mother slept soundly in the next room, wrapped in a quilt decorated with the layout of a garden. But despite the reassuring comforts of home, Ericca was frightened.

Larger-than-life images of holographic chess pieces loomed in her mind. As she drifted off to sleep, thinking about Christmas presents and snowball fights, the gaunt and grotesque figures of Daemon's chess pieces interrupted her pleasant musings. When she did sleep, she dreamt horrible, disconnected dreams from which she woke shrieking in terror.

She dreamt of a dark, impenetrable forest. She was trapped beneath a dense canopy of trees, surrounded by prickly bushes. All around in the darkness, anonymous eyes gleamed, squinted, and threatened. Hoots, shrill calls, and yelps broke the silence without explanation. She was trapped and fearful; a pitiless enemy awaited her in the dark fortress, assuming she escaped the dangers of the forest.

But she would escape. She possessed her own magic, something that the enemy underestimated, she was certain of that. Here Spike and the chattering company of Albert and Leonardo would not help her. But Sheila Angvall, the elderly woman who nearly died of heat stress, this most unlikely guide, she could help. Mrs. Angvall was a plant expert, specializing in wild plants.

"Ericca Ludwig, you poor child, what are you doing in here?" she asked. "You should be with your friends, climbing in trees, and riding your bike. You need a way to clear brambles? Hmm, let's see, my section on invasive and noxious weeds…chemical herbicides would do the trick, also pulling manually, assuming you had an army of gardeners, but those are not options for you, I see…oh, I have it:

> The child of the archer
> Will find the way,
> And send in flight
> The arrows of light,
> And the warmth of day.

Ericca suddenly noticed a leather quiver filled with arrows around her waist and a bow in her hand. And not a minute too soon, because the brambles had come to life; their thorny stems lashed at her like whips. Ericca felt the brambles encircling her legs. She winced in pain at the pinch of their sharp thorns against her skin. She struggled to free herself, but the brambles grew and multiplied relentlessly around her. Just as she felt defeated, strangled under the tightening vise of the vicious vines, she remembered Sheila's words.

She summoned the strength to reach for an arrow, and with her arms taut and flexed, she carefully aimed an orange-tipped arrow at a clump of brambles. The arrow made a furious trajectory to the menacing vines and exploded in an orange cloud. The brambles were subdued, a few stems blackened and withered to the ground.

Relieved and still panting, Ericca gingerly stepped around the withered vines. She spotted a large oak tree in the distance. As happens in dreams, she now saw something very out of place. She saw a heart etched in the tree trunk with the scrawled words:

Nicholas and Daphne Forever

But her relief was momentary, for the brambles attacked again this time more vigorously than before. Ericca shot arrow after arrow, but to no avail. She now noticed that she felt nauseated, and could not longer see clearly; she shot her final arrow. There was no effect. She sighed with resignation, but then, to her surprise, the brambles shrank away to reveal a path and the large oak tree in a light-filled clearing.

This was a dream, and she did not stop to ask why or how. Nicholas Bard and his girlfriend Daphne were seated under the tree at a wrought-iron café table. He was reading a poem to her. Daphne giggled and blushed. They drank from glasses etched with the insignia of bees; they were enjoying an afternoon aperitif.

The happy scene at the oak tree dissolved like a commercial for carbonated water or French linens. Her heart pounded; the rockery loomed ahead, the fortress was shrouded in a dark cloud. Sunshine pounded on the shear cliffs and crevasses. Ericca fired an arrow with an attached rope into a precariously perched tree. She scrambled up the rope and entered the gray and menacing fortress.

The walls at the top of the rockery were patrolled by guards, lone wolves wandering the parapets at will. They were nearly invisible in the dark, except for a silver outline visible to Ericca with superb acuity. Firing rapid arrows, she made her way to the gate and then the great hall.

A fire burned in the fireplace of the great hall. In front of the fireplace sat a man in pajamas with a cat snuggled in his lap, reading a book. From the dark, she could see the silhouette of a once-handsome jaw; the skin in profile sagged from age, the even modulation of the low voice as he read aloud was calm and mechanical. A ghostly woman wandered aimlessly around the room with her abdomen distended and hands behind her back. The clank of chains echoed in the deserted stone hall.

"The invalid king, his vitality eroded by despair, grew to hate all that had once been dear to him. The dreams of his youth became nightmares; his friends, traitors; those he once loved became nothing more than shadows serving a mundane purpose," read the man in the chair.

"But sitting alone in his dark hall, the king brooded, pondered, and planned. The twisted stratagems which emerged from the maze of his deranged mind were cunning beyond the realization of even the keenest opponents. Hardy, strong opponents with high ideals would attempt to overthrow his regime of cruelty and waste to no avail, for with the advantage of his empty soul, he would emerge victorious in the end."

Ericca thought he was reading the plot of a bad cartoon, one of those simple stories with polarized good and evil. She was convinced he was actually the kindly man he seemed, with his warm, fuzzy slippers and purring cat. She crept closer to have a look at his face.

He turned around with a lurch and stared at her. The glow of the dying fire illuminated a horrific face: a craggy nose amid the twisted, leering features of the Puppet King. He attempted to stand, sending the cat off his lap with a yelp, but he collapsed again on his cane.

Ericca ran; the hall echoed with the thunderous laugh of the Puppet King and the sorrowful moans of his queen. She ran faster as she heard the bark of wolves behind her. She dodged into a narrow corridor and sent a round of arrows at the pursuing wolves.

Against a wall in the corridor, she felt the latch of a door and pushed against it, only to find herself tumbling down a narrow, steep staircase. There in the dim, dank dungeon, she discerned the figure of the two-headed bishop, cackling commands at the Minotaur with one head while exhorting a huddled horde of pawns with the other head.

The pawns were bent and silent. Ericca thought she saw children's faces, those of children who lived in rank alleys and fire-trap apartments. The Minotaur guarded the Egyptian king, Osiris, who still stood tall and erect, with his golden mask and plumed atef crown.

"Give the king the axe; let them see what kind of a king he really is," commanded the Bishop. He gestured for one of the pawns to step forward. "You must know the meaning of the term *pawn*...not just a piece in an entertaining board game...though the concept is similar. Think of a pawn shop, of something given up, pledged, something of little value to be sacrificed in hopes of a greater gain. I'm sure it is comforting to know you serve a greater good." The bishop motioned for the king to take the axe.

"Let's illustrate the meaning of sacrifice," said the bishop. The pawns huddled in horror. But, axe in hand, Osiris was motionless. "Sacrifice the pawn, or *you* will be finished," warned the bishop.

Osiris was motionless. The bishop grew impatient and made an offer. "Wield the axe against this single pawn, and the remaining pawns will be saved," he cajoled.

The remaining pawns were now less frightened. Ericca thought the bishop was offering a good deal, except she knew the bishop was very capable of going back on his word, and could not be trusted to uphold his end of the deal.

The moment was tense. The Minotaur raised his own axe. His axe was heavy, shiny, and bright. The Minotaur held the heavy axe in his powerful arms over the pawns ready to smash them with one fell swoop.

In this moment, Ericca saw a trapdoor near Osiris. She sent an arrow on a tether to pierce the door. She pulled the door open, and scrambled through, shepherding the sacrificial pawn and Osiris with her.

Little did she know that the trapdoor opened into the open air; she was now free-falling down the sheer cliff face. She felt a sensation of freedom and resignation; the sky was a deep blue. Such a magnificent blue, she thought.

Osiris and the pawn tumbled with her. Just as she looked in horror at the rapidly approaching ground, a red sports car zoomed through the clouds. The next moment, she was sitting in the leather seat of the Cobra car. Osiris and the pawn were chess pieces again, safe in her hand.

But the sensation of terrifying fall returned; looking, up she saw the hunched figure of the Puppet King, looking into the chasm, yelling, "You fool, to defy me. Let's see how your fine Cobra car does against the Gravity Bar." He pointed the helical end of his cane at the car. The sensation of falling multiplied. As the car spiraled uncontrollably downward, Ericca screamed in horror.

Ericca was awake now. Outside, the snow swirled in gentle patterns around the bare trees. She looked around at the silent and familiar pictures on the comforting walls. Her mother was holding her wrapped in her baby blanket.

Ericca stifled a sob. It had all been so real. Between sobs, she spoke of the menacing characters and forbidding fortress, which now, in the dim light of the warm apartment, captured in words, became nonsense.

"I don't even know why I even think of these things. I don't even know Nicholas and Daphne very well, but I dreamt about them…and the pawns…I saw in the pawns the faces of kids I've never met…except in passing around the city. Why should I care what these people are feeling, so much that I dream about them?" stammered Ericca.

"I'm probably to blame for some of that," replied her mother. "Thinking about what other people might feel and knowing that emotions really do matter is not a universal trait."

Sophia went on, "But it is a worthwhile trait, I think. The hidden order, the subtlety revealed in dreams can be comforting and illuminating."

This did not help much. Still nothing made sense. Not her crazy dream or why she and her mother were alone in the world. She stifled a yawn. Maybe her mother's assurances would have to be enough for now. She lay down and closed her eyes while Leonardo and Albert alternately tickled her feet and bickered over the acceleration rate of free fall.

Albert snapped, "Thirty-two point two feet per second squared. Do you know the energy upon impact of a Cobra car falling at that rate of acceleration?"

Leonardo retorted, "In a simple Euclidean rectilinear world where all that goes up must come down, the impact would be lethal. But in a hyperbolic volume, like a skateboard park, she would have simply ridden back up the side of the cliff."

"Those two, I wish they'd stop fighting," murmured Ericca as she drifted off to sleep.

Across town, the twins went down for the night as they always did, Matt in his Wave Rider pajamas and Elle in her Particle Princess nightgown. They drifted to sleep in the loft and dreamt vivid dreams.

Matt dreamt of Tory Skye, but not Tory Skye the well-bred if snotty Manhattan teenager. In his dream, Tory was an international celebrity whose mega-corporation had created the phenomenon of the small celebrity pet at mass-market prices. Leaping and yapping clones of Tory's pet Pomeranian invaded Manhattan, as ubiquitous and cloying as a coffee-shop chain.

He woke up talking to himself so loudly his mother had to shake him. He woke with a start, wide-eyed, and asked his mother, "Mom, mom, you haven't told me yet what Tory Skye said. Is she making her charms using teleportation or holographic replication?"

"Honey, calm down, please. Your friend has not surpassed you yet. Her charms use a hologram based on the original Heart Scarab, a hologram created in a modeling program on something similar to the Q-computer. She has not achieved quantum teleportation or anything like that. The holograms are translated into plans, which are then shipped abroad for cheap manufacture in an assembly plant abroad, just like any other trinket," answered Sybille.

Matt breathed a sigh of relief. He took care not to tell his mother about his dream. She would've either said he was crazy or worse, obsessed with Tory Skye.

Christmas approached. Lights decorating the department stores transformed the streets of Manhattan into glittering promenades. Ericca admired the scene of holiday bustle and relished the feeling of winter as she strolled along the street. The twins, alongside her, chatted about their busy lives.

"Yes, Dad has all the ducks in place. The Q-computer will be ready for the public in time for summer; all the kids getting out of school can get their Q-computers as a graduation present," remarked Matt enthusiastically.

"Really — everyone?" said Ericca sarcastically. She liked the twins, but sometimes they really had no hold on reality. How many kids could afford a Q-computer, a computer with the singular purpose of generating oversized chess characters? Weren't many kids and families hard pressed just to pay for rent and shoes?

Elle laughed and said, "Don't worry, Ericca, when Matt makes a really cool replicating device, we'll take the money and use it so you can come with us on our next trip. I think we're going to Germany to visit the Neuschwanstein castle."

Ericca replied, "That'd be great. But what would be really cool would be a replicating machine that generates huge ice sculptures at all the street corners during the summer, especially sculptures with a dispenser dispensing really good frosty cones, not the kind with gooey syrup, for free."

Matt looked up and said, "Hey, Ericca, that's a great idea, but I don't think my dad would agree with the idea of giving them away for free." Matt's father, Quint, was very smart about business and would often lecture the twins about careful accounting and how the finest tweaks in efficient production resulted in mammoth profits or losses when amplified to a mass scale.

Quint might say, "If you sold frosty cones for one dollar each, and sold a million of them, you would have a million dollars. But if you spent ninety-eight cents to make each frosty cone, then you would actually only have twenty thousand dollars which is still a lot of money. If, instead of spending ninety-eight cents, you spent a dollar and two cents to make each frosty cone, then you would actually have lost twenty thousand dollars and you would not be happy."

With all this talk of food, they were getting hungry; they motioned to their mothers, who agreed to stop at a coffee shop. Inside the shop, rapt coffee drinkers peered into glowing screens. Ericca noticed one man sitting alone, with thinning hair. It was Nicholas Bard.

She thought of her dream where he sat at the café table with Daphne. But here in this rarefied and stylish coffee shop, he sat alone, brooding over a laptop computer. He looked up when he saw Ericca approaching.

"Oh, hello, Ericca," he said, smiling vaguely.

"Hello, Mr. Bard," she said. He seemed distracted; she had not heard him sobbing next door for a while, so she assumed he was still in a happy relationship with Daphne. She was worried about him nevertheless.

"Getting some coffee?" he asked jokingly. He knew kids their age normally did not drink coffee.

"No, just here with some friends and my mom," replied Ericca, gesturing toward her friends and Sybille and Sophia, who were nearby ordering refreshments. "You are not washing windows today?"

Nicholas Bard had told her his job was washing the windows of tall buildings. This occupation sounded interesting but somewhat hazardous. Ericca thought of her dream and the terrifying sensation of free fall from extreme heights.

"No, I'm working on something more fun. I do freelance

writing for some periodicals," he answered, then added after a pause, "Actually, I'm working on my profile for online dating," sounding a little embarrassed. Ericca peered at the laptop screen; she saw a Web page showing a handsome man with a full head of dark hair sitting in a leather executive chair. The headline read *Handsome Single Lawyer Seeks Beautiful Soulmate.*

Ericca did not know much about internet personals, and she certainly did not want to pry. Nicholas looked up from the laptop and said, "I'm writing a poem, actually, a poem for Daphne. Hey, want to hear something funny? What kind of poet is also a mathematician?"

"Hmm…what?" Ericca replied blankly.

"An upside-down poet, because he writes inverse," answered Nicholas with a mischievous grin. "Get it, get it?"

From her backpack, Ericca could hear Leonardo and Albert choking with belly laughs.

"Oh, yes, ha, ha, that's funny. I get it. Of course," replied Ericca.

She could almost hear Albert saying, "*In verse…inverse…*that's great…like you might say the attractive force of Earth's gravity is inversely related to your distance. The further away you are, the weaker the attraction, and if you get really far away and have enough speed, you can even escape the hold of Earth's gravitational pull. Rather a long explanation of the concept of *inverse*, I know."

Nicholas replied, "Well, I am thinking of funny things to say for my profile. Here's another. What did the yogi say to the dentist?"

Ericca gave him another blank stare.

"I'd like to pass on the Novocaine to transcend dental medication, of course. Ha, ha. Get it? Transcendental meditation — ha, ha."

Ericca managed another nervous giggle. His jokes were really quite clever.

Nicholas now looked back down at his computer, focusing on his typing. "Actually, I'm working on an article for an important periodical. I got stuck and distracted so I figured I'd fill out another Web profile just for the fun of it."

Ericca nodded in understanding, then replied, "I get distracted too sometimes. My mind just starts spinning in every direction." She peered over his shoulder. She could see the neutral colors and clear type of the internet form.

Nicholas sat busily typing, his fingers making clicking sounds on the laptop keyboard. "Let's see, it says here…explain why someone should get to know me. Well, I don't know." He started typing:

> I'm a good friend. I read science fiction. I have an awesome collection of jazz vinyls. I ride a motorcycle. Also, I floss.

> Further, despite my perplexing upbringing by a Communist mother and a distant, apolitical father, I am a fine citizen, and I have managed to serve my country in many capacities, most notably as a fighter pilot on a tour of duty where I garnered some notable medals. I cannot say my civilian life since then has been as illustrious, however. I can say my disabilities give me plenty of time for my favorite pastime, filling out profiles on internet dating sites.

> But in case you were curious, all the information on this profile is true. I'm a great guy. I can make you laugh. I don't advertise to be your partner in crime, or your Prince Charming. I will touch you with the resonance of my poetry. I recognize that personal shortcomings are intrinsic to attraction, and I won't hold you to a bar of celluloid perfection, especially if you don't. So drop me a line, or wink. Life is short.

Nicholas peered closely at the screen as he proofread the profile, but finally, he muttered to himself in frustration, "Some blatant contradictions here. Here in my headline I claim to be a lawyer looking for a hottie, and here in the narrative I admit I'm just another disabled vet with too much time on his hands. I should probably fix that."

Ericca agreed tacitly. The profile was confusing. The headline and picture simply did not match the text. Nicholas deleted the previous paragraphs and started anew. He sat there tapping away. His revised profile read:

> I am as comfortable doing a dress-up night on the town as hanging out on Sunday mornings reading the paper.
> I am known to tip generously and hold doors for people.
> I will be nice to your mother, even if you can't reciprocate.
> I will go shopping with you and hold your bag.
> I like sushi, and am handy with a sushi knife.
> I kayak in Hawaii and ski at Aspen.
> I buy too many ties and books.
> I am very good at my job.

"That last one is a good one," he said to himself. Ericca read the revised profile. She suspected none of it was true. But, not wanting to criticize him for lying to make himself as attractive as possible, she instead asked, "But what about Daphne. Aren't you two still together?"

"Oh, I guess I should tell you…Daphne broke up with me again…when I asked her to marry me," he explained. "She was married before, and she didn't want another serious relationship. I started writing a poem for her but never showed it to her. It starts like this…*Loneliness like the echo of a whisper in space.*"

Nicholas looked down at his computer again. Matt and Elle

had been standing with their mother. They now walked toward them. "Oh, that's a cool computer; surfing the Web, I see," said Matt boisterously.

"Oh, Mr. Bard, sorry, you should meet my friends, Matt and Elle," said Ericca apologetically.

"Hello, Matt, hello, Elle," replied Nicholas, smiling, as though the company of boisterous, nosy kids was a welcome change. "Yes, in fact, I am up on the Web."

"That's cool, man…doing some gaming?" asked Matt.

"No, not gaming, sorry to say," answered Nicholas.

"Nicholas writes poetry, great poetry," said Ericca impatiently. Matt sometimes got on her nerves. She remembered now the day she delivered the birthday present to Nicholas. He was in the park with a group of people who were reading poetry to each other.

Nicholas blushed and said humbly, "I wouldn't say it's great… just honest…and heartfelt."

Turning to Matt, he said, "I'm actually playing a little game with my girlfriend. We haven't called each other for a few weeks. But I was going to post a poem for her on the Web. I know she'll be looking for some message from me, and though it drives her crazy, I just anonymously post a crazy poem or something totally wacky to make her laugh. She'll read it and drive herself crazy wondering if it's me…that's the fun part."

Nicholas grinned at them. Elle said kindly in reply, "You can tell so much from how a person writes. I'm sure your girlfriend will know it's you and be touched."

Ericca looked at Elle as though struck by lightning. It was true, people revealed their personalities in their writing. On the Web, it would be possible to find a world of personalities; souls looking for kindred spirits, souls wanting to make a connection. Perhaps even a trace of her father.

This thought dwelled in her mind. Nicholas thanked Elle and turned back to his computer, clearly signaling the end of their conversation. The kids waved and headed away as their mothers motioned to them.

"That was Nicholas Bard. He and Daphne broke up again," Ericca explained to her mother.

"Yes, I know that. Poor man…but there is more amiss in his heart than simple loneliness, a complexity only poetry can capture. Would it not be wonderful if poetry solved all our problems?" commented Sophia in reply. Her mother always seemed to know about those things.

Maybe poetry did not solve everything. But with the Q-computer, it would be possible to scan the Web's compendium of information: poems, profiles, resumes, news articles. It would be possible to find a soul lacking a persona, a spirit unable to articulate his identity. It would be possible to find her father.

Later, at the twins' loft for some hot chocolate, Ericca brought up the topic again. The twins had heard Ericca discuss the subject of finding her father many times before. They did not want to discourage her; they also did not want to encourage her toward what they saw as very probable disappointment.

"The Q-computer is very powerful. It can process searches, computations, commands faster and more efficiently than any other computer available," remarked Matt.

"But this search ability would not help us unless we know what we are looking for," added Elle. "What do you think your father would say about himself? What do you remember about him?"

Ericca thought, It was true. It would be difficult. She had never met her father. She had never heard his voice or seen his mannerisms. She had only a vague idea of what he looked like, based on a few photographs and the pictures on the wall in her apartment.

She did know her father was interested in things such as architecture, engineering, and water quality. She knew he was a horseback rider and a skilled archer. She knew he was a pilot. She knew he spent time in Texas and adored the gastronomic wonderland of New York.

Elle and Matt nodded sympathetically. "That might be enough

to do a Web search. Let's try a search on keywords like *water*, *engineer*, and *archery*," suggested Elle.

They had the Q-computer in front of them and typed in the key search words. The screen returned an overwhelming number of results. On the projected screen, they read:

Water sports, *archery* bows, fiberglass designed...
Water jet cutter, absorption and adsorption *engineer*...
Archery equipment repairer...

The search results were numerous and mostly unhelpful. "We need to find a keyword that is specialized," said Elle. "What was really different about your dad?"

Ericca thought of the centaur statue and the dedication to her mother. Her mother had never explained the history of the piece to her, but she was sure not many kids had miniature centaurs in their living rooms. Now she remembered her mother's remark: "He was very fond of the parting shot, and was accustomed to riding facing backward on horseback."

"Let's try a search on *parting shot*," suggested Ericca.

Elle, who was fond of mythology and ancient history, perked up and said, "That's interesting, the *parting shot* came from the Parthians, who were nomadic horse people and accomplished archers of ancient history. But what would your father have to do with them?"

Ericca wanted to explain. Her mother had told her once that different creatures had different internal clocks. For instance, mayflies lived an entire life in the time it took an elephant to visit a watering hole. But she was afraid even the twins would laugh at the idea that her dad was a special person, someone who had lived many lives. She merely said, "You never know, maybe he operates a tattoo shop." She peered at the search results.

Poetry and myth...the Parthians were celebrated horse-archers...their mail-clad warriors both male and female surrounded a hostile army and poured in a shower of darts…they evaded any closer conflict by rapid flight, during which they still shot their arrows backward at the enemy…a technique known today as the *parting shot*…

Poetry and myth were fine, but not particularly helpful for finding a missing person. They were stumped and decided to play a board game instead of trying more searches.

Poetry did help some things, though. Shortly before Christmas, Ericca found a small package at her door. The attached card read:

> Dear Sophia and Ericca,
> Best wishes for the holidays and the new year.
> Your neighbor,
> *Nicholas Bard*
>
> P.S. We went to the Green Grotto in Central Park, and I gave her a gift of nested boxes each with a phrase from the poem; the snow fell as we sat there. She loved the poem.
>
> The gift is to scare away nasty dreams, Ericca, part of the lore of folk magic. Don't let those nasty phantoms get to you.

Inside the package was a sprig of mistletoe wrapped in a gold ribbon. This was the first that she had heard the superstition that mistletoe warded off bad dreams. She was surprised Nicholas should mention that. She must have awakened him with her terrified screams in the night. She thought of her nightmare with phantoms from Daemon's favorite chess set — so ridiculous and silly now. That night she slept soundly; the Puppet King did not make a single appearance.

CHAPTER EIGHT

QUINTANA CASTLE

Christmas Day began with a moment of hushed reverie. Rays of early morning light flooded through the window and played on the bare trees and compacted snow. Glass ornaments glistened like teardrops on a small tree.

Ericca was filled with happy anticipation. Her eyes fell on the tree, decorated with spirals of glittering glass. She watched her mother as she slept soundly. She leaned over the edge of Spike, picking up packages and cards as the blanket meandered around the apartment.

The first package had the marks of Matt's special handiwork. For one, the wrapping was not Christmas-themed. There were no cheerful snowmen or rosy, white-bearded characters. Instead, the wrapping had images of reindeer with swirling antlers. The wrapping job was also rather sloppy, as though Matt had scrambled just to find tape and scissors.

The attached note was penned in Matt's hurried scrawl:

> Hey, Ericca,
> Merry Christmas and best wishes for the new year.
> I think you'll like the gift (it's just a start on my new chess set, which will really rock).
> *Your Friend, Matt*

The present was a folded piece of paper with a picture of an archer with blue body paint on horseback. The figure came to life when held to the light from the window. The archer lifted his eyebrows, grimaced, rolled his eyes, and flexed his arms revealing elaborate tattoos. The archer then shot an arrow, sending itself flying into the room, landing as a crumpled piece of paper in her mother's glass wastebasket.

That's cool, thought Ericca as she fished the paper out of the wastebasket. She unfolded the paper and was surprised to see what looked like a grid filled with numbers and symbols. In exasperation, she fished out another. This note unfolded to show a triangle filled with numbers.

Finally, Ericca found the elusive piece of paper, which read, in Matt's distinctive handwriting:

> OK, now for your real gift. News from the Q-computer…Dad inserted his extra memory module, one containing the Q-catalogue. Now our searches will return results from the libraries of all time, literally all time, including even those books destroyed in the past and all books that have yet to be published. Cool, huh? Also, I did another search on *Branch, Osiris, archer, water, engineering* and I came up with this:
>
> *Blue Cup, Green Basket,* by George Sax, is a yet-unpublished novel about leadership in ancient Egypt and the influence of ancient beliefs on modern society. The ancient Egyptians symbolized the divine with elements of nature and considered *water* of utmost importance. The *branches* of the Nile river were associated with deities. Their deities were known as *archers.* The flower of the papyrus plant, *Cyperus papyrus,* symbolized the territories of Lower (Northern) Egypt, where *Osiris* reigned. The blue lotus, *Nymphaea caerulea,* symbolized Upper

CHAPTER EIGHT

(Southern) Egypt, where Seth was popular.

We'll check up on these after Christmas.
Matt and Quint

Ericca was excited. George Sax, a writer about history and politics. She could see her dad occupying that persona. He would definitely have a lot of fun with that personality. She felt giddy with optimism and hardly able to restrain herself from jumping up and down. Her mind was busy conjuring possibilities, even as she unwrapped the next present, which was from Elle.

Elle's present contrasted sharply with that from her twin. The wrapping was neat and sophisticated, as would be expected from Sybille Nix. Conical spirals in gold evoked the shape of Christmas trees against a contrasting background of bright red. Ornaments of different sizes shone on the spiral trees like teardrop-shaped mirrors. A shiny, deep-red satin bow flecked with gold provided a dramatic centerpiece.

Ericca gingerly undid the beautiful wrapping and removed a small box containing a seed. Attached to the box was a note in Elle's careful handwriting which read:

> Ericca,
> I'm so glad we're friends. Here's a little sunshine to help get you through the gray winter. Pssst, you should know we accelerated the growth schedule somewhat to give relief from the frigid cold for poor Albert and Leonardo — remind them to not complain about creaking bones.
> With love,
> *Elle and Sybille*

As light beamed upon the seed, a green sprout appeared. As in an accelerated movie, the green stem shot up and grew into a bright yellow sunflower, radiating full-spectrum warmth into the faded turquoise room.

Ericca basked in the orange glow as she happily read the next card, from Maxine Weaver and Ray Bender. The card featured the M-Gate subway stop in Central Park twinkling with lights and luminous shapes. Inside a message read:

> Dear Ericca,
> Happy holidays. Your mother tells me you are now a regular Metro rider. Please come see me at your earliest convenience, and I'll give you a personal tour.
> Cheers,
> *Maxine and Ray*
>
> P.S. Ray's been experimenting with new coatings and films, which are effective in dim light and for seeing depth in the superficial.

Attached to the card was a box containing a pair of opera glasses. Hmm, I didn't think I needed opera glasses. I don't really even like opera, but you never know, thought Ericca.

Her mother was just waking. She smiled with a loopy grin, eyes unfocused, and sat up with a luxurious stretch when Ericca brought her presents and cards. Sophia remarked happily, "What a nice surprise!" and "I really do need this," as she opened each gaily wrapped package.

Maxine and Sybille, her two closest friends, had sent her things that were not immediately recognizable to Ericca. The gift from Maxine and Ray was a lens labeled *Halo-Projector Replacement Lens*. The gift from Sybille was less mysterious: a floral handbag in green with the motif of bees.

A large metallic envelope embossed with the name *SKYE Enterprises* gave Sophia and Ericca pause. Inside the envelope was a card with a painting Ericca recognized from her museum field trips: Jasper Johns' famous painting *Target*, a composition of concentric circles, updated for the holidays with a tiny red bow against a bright gold background.

The greeting and note on the back read:

**SEASON'S GREETINGS
LIVE THE LIGHT SPECTACULAR
NEW YEAR'S EVE
THE BULL'S EYE & SKYE BRIDGE
SKYE TOWER, SUITE 777**

Hey, Sophia,
No one has ever accused me of having bad taste. Hope you're able to make it. Best wishes.
— *Daemon*

The invitation was amusing and tasteful. Jasper Johns was among Sophia's favorite painters. But Ericca recalled Daemon's chess duel in the park with Quint. Daemon was no fool. He was not one to expend moves without personal gain. Even innocent holiday greetings had a purpose in Daemon's scheme of things.

Ericca puzzled darkly over what Daemon's deeper motivation might be, until Albert and Leonardo started bugging her.

"Lighten up, would you? He's only a guy who wants to date your mom. What's so horrible about that? Get it, get it…lighten up?" said Albert.

"Sometimes your preoccupation with light and gravity is deadening," replied Leonardo with a look of ennui.

Ericca explained about Daemon, about how he was already married, and also about his masterful manipulation of electricity and gravity, or so the twins thought.

"Manipulating electricity and gravity, that would be excellent, but really, thanks to me, we have so many cool inventions, what more could this Daemon fellow do?" asked Albert.

Ericca had no desire to goad Albert into a long conversation about his accomplishments in physics or his contribution to the development of modern-day conveniences. Instead, with her eyes fixed on the glass wastepaper basket twinkling with balls of crumpled paper, she turned again to the note from Matt, turning over and over in her mind George Sax, a writer in the future, *Green Basket, Blue Cup*...a writer about ancient civilizations.

"The subways are open today, as is the public library, but Mom is not working today. She has a librarians' conference uptown," said Ericca. She walked along hurriedly, taking deep breaths, through the crowds of post-holiday shoppers. The twins followed behind, huffing and puffing.

Ericca was excited and grateful. Matt had not only found search results that could lead them to her dad, but he had also borrowed Quint's library card.

"My dad explained that not all users of the library can check out the books catalogued in the Q-catalogue. Only users carrying a special card can use the Q-aisle of the library; my dad said we might find the Q-aisle a little mesmerizing," Matt explained.

They scrambled up the marble steps of the public library, past the Greco-Roman columns, paying no attention to the large white dog tethered to the bike rack or the large black limousine parked in the bus parking zone.

Inside the stone lobby, they slowed to a walk. They shook the snow off their boots on the rubber mats and waited through the security line in Astor Hall. They made their way up the steps, admiring the frescoes in the ceiling of the McGraw Rotunda. After pausing to inspect stone busts in alcoves along the corridor, they reached the Reading Room, a grand, light-filled space. A few readers sat quietly perusing books under green-shaded reading lamps.

Ericca, Matt, and Elle searched about for the Q-aisle. All the aisles looked perfectly ordinary and orderly, grouped by fiction and nonfiction, sorted alphabetically by author name. There were some beloved favorites and also titles that reminded Ericca of the characters that populated her blanket.

But nowhere was there to be found the title they sought. They were doubtful of finding a clue in the library's computer. Most libraries did not officially list books to be published in the future or books destroyed thousands of years ago. They were surprised when the library computer returned a list of articles in response to their search on *George Sax*.

They crowded around the computer and read an article dating from more than forty years past:

THE SAX MIRACLE

Manhattan's celebrated *Sax* family began with a small millinery shop on Seventh Avenue, which grew into the high-end retail chain we know now as *Hats & Sax*, famous for their designer handbags, shoes, and, of course, hats. They hope to expand their retail empire with a strategic partnership with the French retailer, Chapeux Vert, founded by *George* Plantagenet. The *Sax* family plans to add the signature broom flower (*plantagenesta*) of the Plantagenet family to their own store logo to signify the partnership.

They read quickly, anxious to find the names *George* and *Sax* combined in one name. But as so often happens in searches, the exact intent was not reflected in the search results. They were about to examine the other search results when Matt exclaimed, "Of course there is no mention of George Sax or his book; these computers only show results for the present. We don't know very much about the book, but we do know that the book is not even published yet. For that matter, the author has not even been born or is still just a kid."

"Oh, great, Matt," said Ericca in exasperation. Then, remembering Matt's mention of this detail, and feeling bad about blaming Matt when he had already been so helpful, she suggested hopefully, "We can still try to locate the Q-aisle."

At that instant, a squat woman wearing a decidedly unflattering blue pinstriped shirt approached. "Children, if you are here for the children's classics series, you should all hurry along to the Query Room; I would highly recommend it," she said in a stern and condescending tone that would have made any children's story as appealing as cold oatmeal and mushy cereal — classic or not.

Elle poked Ericca and whispered, "That's the same woman I saw once on the street, shaking her head at some street dancers. I mean, wasn't Mozart pretty lowbrow in his day?" Ericca giggled, and nodded in agreement. The twins' mother lectured often about one of her favorite topics, "*Cultural hijacking.*"

The ideas of young philosophy majors had obviously rubbed off on Sybille. She was known to warn the children, "Be careful. Revered icons are often used by people who are at heart cold and intolerant to wrap an agenda based on exclusivity and hate in an attractive cloak." Their mother might then launch into a discussion of the swastika, used by the Nazis in, as Sybille put it, "a horrible distortion of the torque symbol, which was originally a solar emblem of universal reverence dating to the very first civilizations."

What cloaks had to do with icons was not immediately obvious to the twins or any other bright children their age. *Icons* were things museum docents discussed, usually associated with religious painting. "For instance," Elle explained, recalling a docent lecture, "...the term *iconoclast* originated in Byzantine times, where the term *iconoclast*, or image breaker, referred to those who opposed the use of imagery in representing the divine. An icon is a symbolic image with well-understood meaning and association."

The term *cloak* brought to mind figures from movies and books: old men in white beards waving sticks in flowing cloaks, science fiction star-fighters, or adolescent wizards waving wands.

But now, as they went toward the Query Room, they had a glimmer of a clue. "Oh, I understand mother now," whispered Elle, "For example, someone can read *Heidi* and make a story about good cheese, thick bread, and fresh air seem like a story about the superiority of mountain dwellers. Meaning can get twisted or *cloaked* in the strangest ways."

They neared an entrance with a carved, triangular pediment over the doorway and entered a cozy room where a group of children sat attentively in a circle as a story was read.

Matt, who had a streak of impatience, whispered, "We should leave. We're not going to find any clues in here."

But Ericca shook her head in disagreement, and said, "Don't you see, this is the Q-room; Q stands for Query." Matt appeared sheepish, as though that association should have been obvious, and then reminded them, "We need to find the Q-aisle, not the Q-room."

"Yes, but I think the Q-aisle is here in this room," replied Ericca.

She knew this simply because she was a girl with a lot of common sense who did not believe in coincidences. She knew there was a reason for everything; there was a reason they were shepherded to this most unassuming, but charming corner of the vast library. She did not believe that the Q-aisle and the Query Room were completely unrelated; names did not occur in pairs without reason. If there were a Q-aisle, especially one where strange and inexplicable things were to be found, it would certainly be here.

Ericca walked around the room, scanning the titles of books, admiring the high, painted ceilings and the warm, glowing tones of the polished wood shelves. She stepped lightly on the plush carpet, in shades of burgundy and olive, until she came to a painting propped against the carved mantel of the fireplace in the back corner of the room.

The oil on canvas in a heavy gilded gold frame was luminous with color. The painting captured an outdoor scene — a portal of trees that led to an arched stone bridge, over a river with swans. A brightly lit castle glimmered under a twilight sky.

"That is a famous painting in the Hudson River School style of landscape art, a distinctively American style popular in the late

1800s," explained Elle, who, unlike Matt, paid close attention to what art docents had to say. "That castle is unusual for this style of painting; the Hudson River painters were more into lush pastoral tranquility bordering on complacency than whimsy," commented Elle. They read the plaque in bronze below the painting:

**WELCOME TO THE
QUINTANA CASTLE QUERY ROOM.**
Dedicated to the young patrons of the
New York Public Library
that they might explore the shining castles in
their minds.

"Don't you see? This explains everything. This room was named for the benefactor, someone named Quintana, who donated money to have this room built; Q stands for Query and Quintana," explained Ericca.

"Yeah, and this Quintana person was probably someone very rich," noted Matt. This was not a cynical statement but a matter-of-fact observation. "All the rooms and artwork in this library were named for really wealthy people or families. Did you know that John Jacob Astor, the Astor of Astor Hall, was the richest man in the country after making a ton with his trading post in Astoria, Oregon?" asked Matt. He knew a lot about the history of business. Matt was convinced there would someday be the *Quint A. Senns Vestibule*, or even the *Matt and Elle Rumpus Room*.

But Ericca was focused on the painting, watching a faint wisp of smoke emanate from the castle. "Elle, look at the tower of the castle; do you see a little gray cloud, like smoke?" asked Ericca.

Elle squinted and exclaimed, "That is the strangest thing. You're right."

"Let's take a closer look," said Ericca, reaching in her backpack for her new opera glasses, suddenly recalling the cryptic remark on the card: "...to see depth in the superficial." She had brought her opera glasses so Matt could see it; he was interested in gadgets and gizmos of all kinds. She also had an intuition that they would come in handy.

She was astounded as she peered at the painting. Rather than paint strokes, she saw grout lines and cracks in the stone, ripples of water on the river, the fine downy feathers on the swans, the ragged fractal outline of the tree canopy. Ericca scanned the castle for windows and doors until she found the main door, which was open.

Adjusting the focus, she saw through the open door a tall and narrow room, plush and paneled, very much like the room where they now stood, except in the back corner of the room sat a small old woman in a black suit at a desk near the fireplace, periodically tossing crumpled pieces of paper into the fire with an expression of exasperation.

"Quintana Castle," said Ericca under her breath. The small old woman looked up as though she had heard the remark; she smiled and waved in welcome. With that, they felt a breeze, they smelled the scent of a forest and heard the call and rustle of swans.

In a moment of curiosity in which fear and uncertainty took a backseat, Ericca stepped forward over the gilded gold frame of the painting, ahead of Matt. The canvas did not repel her back to the room as well-grounded intuition might predict. Instead, Ericca now found herself looking back at the twins through a wooden frame. She waved to them, and shortly they all stood in disbelief in a shady forest as real as any they had ever imagined.

"Wow, that sure is strange," remarked Matt. They were in a grove of large, old trees, such as might have existed in ages past. They were far from the lofty paneled spaces of the library. The upholstered comfort of the Quintana Castle Query Room was a fabricated fantasy captured in an oil painting suspended before them in midair.

They now found themselves enjoying the warmth of a summer day surrounded by gigantic deciduous trees. A huge black walnut tree, more than four feet in diameter towered over them. "Oh look," exclaimed Ericca, "That is the biggest black walnut tree I've ever seen." Sheila Angvall had taught Ericca how to recognize the deeply furrowed black bark months ago in Central Park.

"Oh, wow," remarked Matt. "My dad said the Cobra dashboard is veneered with a walnut burl wood from a tree like this." He was now very impressed by this magnificent natural specimen. The dashboard of the Cobra car, with its subtle tones and arresting eyes created by dormant buds in the burl wood, was a constant source of pride and admiration.

Elle and Ericca looked at each other with faint exasperation. It was so typical of Matt to think of things like that, without a qualm about the great trees destroyed to veneer fancy cars and libraries. Elle countered, "You're right, Matt, but I think the Cobra has an *artificial* burl wood dash.

"Oh, no, give me a break," retorted Matt. "The Cobra has the real thing. You can tell; the painted plastic dashboards don't have anywhere close to the level of detail of color, and they look fake. The fractals in nature are very hard to replicate, you know. Besides, you should know, Dad wouldn't go for anything fake."

Matt seemed prepared to begin a long monologue exhibiting his knowledge of fractals, but Ericca headed him off by saying, "It's twilight; we should try to find the castle before it gets dark." The twins agreed, and the three headed through the trees toward the sound of the rushing river.

Ericca felt happy in a way she had never before. Here was a primeval forest, pristine and airy, in some ways like Central Park but evolved for survival rather than crafted for human appreciation. These trees were hundreds, possibly even thousands, of years old and destined to live forever, barring an event of violent destruction. She wondered how old these trees were; probably so old as to make counting their rings very difficult.

She enjoyed her reverie as she pushed ahead of the twins until she heard a panicked yelp. She turned around to see Elle looking uncharacteristically spooked, gasping, "It's Matt — they took him."

"Who took him?" asked Ericca. There was nobody else there.

CHAPTER EIGHT

"Vampires, ghostly pale sirens, with billowy curls and white dresses embroidered in red with the letter V. They snagged him with a red ribbon and dragged him into the forest," replied Elle.

Ericca wanted to suggest the total absurdity of this explanation, but instead turned away momentarily to see a team of pinstriped figures running toward them. Ericca and Elle dodged behind trees in the glade to avoid being trampled. Seeing their neat ponytails tucked under baseball hats, Ericca commented, "Of course, it's the umpires versus the vampires."

Elle was not amused. "But what do they want with Matt?" she asked.

The answer to that question was clear as they stepped further into the clearing, where the umpires in blue pinstripes now stood arguing with a band of slender nymphs in candy-striped gowns. Matt stood blindfolded and bound with a red sash, tethered to the tallest of the nymphs. The neatly trimmed lawn, composed of contrasting squares of silver thyme and Corsican mint in an eight-by-eight grid told Ericca the source of the argument.

Giggling, Ericca said to Elle, "They are fighting over Matt. I think they are chess teams, and both teams want Matt to be their king."

That seemed plausible, but Elle had to comment wryly, "Well, studly males are rare, but Matt? You have to be kidding."

They looked back to the scene in the glade. Now it seemed an agreement had been reached to allow Matt to decide. The blindfold was removed and the sash loosened.

The queen of the vampires now replaced her menacing visage with an expression of enchanting sweetness. The throng of lithe and slender nymphs danced around Matt, white gowns swirling, red sashes twirling, a spectacle conducive to hypnotic trance for even someone as well-grounded as Matt. The vampire queen sang to him, approaching him with feline grace until she stood beside him, stroking his chin, her face close to his, while offering him a deep red glass.

To the delight of the umpires, he flung the glass away and

attempted to run, but was then besieged by the horde of stout and sturdy umpires cheerfully offering plates of pie, spaghetti, and roast beef.

Matt ducked this onslaught and dashed away, with Ericca and Elle close behind, followed by the heavy pounding steps of the umpires and the shrill wails of the vampires. The high-pitched siren call of the vampires and the unmistakable thud of the umpires approached. Elle and Ericca caught up to Matt, and motioned to a hidden fork in the trees. As they headed down the narrow diversion, they saw the parade of vampires and umpires head away, their mournful moans and loud exhortations eventually faded in the distance.

They were all panting when they reached the bridge. Elle and Ericca wanted to kid Matt about being nearly kissed by a vampire, but they were out of breath. Plus, they now saw the open, arched door of the castle. They hurriedly crossed the bridge to enter a great hall.

The room they entered was unlike any hall they had ever seen, with an impossibly lofty ceiling. "A fan-vaulted ceiling," Elle informed them. "This style was very popular, and some say it originated with the shape of a corridor of tall trees; the architects wanted to emulate an outdoor cathedral of trees."

Ericca and Matt were more focused on the contents of the room, where infinitely high bookshelves disappeared into the ceiling, a ceiling where the web of support beams resembled a canopy of twisted and braided tree limbs. They approached the desk at the center of the room, where an old woman in a neat black suit sat reading and writing behind stacks of books. She looked up with a kind gaze as they approached timidly and smiled as though she had been expecting them.

"Good evening, my dears," she asked. "How can I help you?"

"We would like to see the book *Green Basket, Blue Cup,* by George Sax," replied Ericca.

"Oh, of course…such a popular book," she mused as she

flipped through a small wooden box filled with cards. "Ah, here it is," she said, looking up and removing a thin, glittering card from the box. "I am so sorry, dears, but that book has been checked out recently, so it will be four weeks before it is due back. But I'm happy to place your name on the waiting list, if you like."

Ericca exchanged long sighs and looks of frustration with the twins. "Sure, please, put us on the waiting list," answered Elle politely and nudged Matt to produce a library card. Matt reached in his pocket and found his father's library card, slightly bent, in his back pocket.

The old woman peered at the card, noted the name, and returned the card to Matt. "I am sorry I couldn't be of more help, but I will notify you when the book is available. Thank you for visiting," she replied.

The three turned to leave when Ericca had an inspiration. "Might we ask who has checked out this book?" she asked with a respectful tone.

The old woman looked at them with a sharp expression, then softened as she replied, "We have a very small group of regular patrons here in the Q-aisle, and many of them value their privacy very highly, so I'm afraid I can't help you with that question."

Ericca nodded in acceptance, but glancing at the shimmering card in the old woman's gaunt hand, she could not help glimpsing the address: 777 *Skye Tower.*

The thought of Daemon Skye was disturbing. They headed out without noticing the beautiful tapestries and paintings squeezed into alcoves between banks of shelves. They did not pause before an exquisite chess set tucked in the corner featuring pieces reminiscent of red candy canes and blue pinstripes. They did not stop to examine the dedication plaque.

They scampered hurriedly back along the trail, not stopping to admire the swans, the arched stone bridge, or the amazing red oak and cherry trees. Thankfully, neither the vampires nor the umpires made a second appearance. Matt, Elle and Ericca were soon back in the Quintana Castle Query Room, which was now empty.

The library was closing as the three exited through the large front doors. They walked down the steps moodily, wondering about the unsettling coincidence and suspicious bad luck that Daemon Skye should obtain the book before them.

A band of people, mostly women and girls, were gathered at the sidewalk at the bottom of the stairs around a black limousine. In the middle of this group stood the unmistakable figure of Tory Skye, wearing a fur-trimmed coat and holding her yapping Pomeranian.

Today, however, Tory and Pluto were not the focus of attention. Instead, all eyes, delighted squeals and chatter were directed toward an old woman in a neat black suit holding a large white dog on a leash.

"His name is Tau. He's a Samoyed. You've heard of the species, how lovely…yes, the species originated as herd dogs in northern climates. They were treated tenderly by the nomadic tribes who bred them, which is why they are so sociable with humans," the frail old woman could be heard saying. "Yes, of course, you can pet him. He is very gentle, but just one at a time." The crowd packed around the old woman for a closer glimpse of the dog, Tory among them.

Suddenly, there was a shrill, angry shriek. All eyes fastened on Tory, who now had a pronounced red scratch across her delicate face. Her little Pomeranian, so accustomed to sitting still on her arm, was now yapping and squirming in uncontrolled agitation. Tory's chauffeur immediately shooed the crowd away, ushered Tory, irritated pet and all, into the limousine, and drove off.

When Ericca and the twins arrived in hopes of finding the old woman they recognized from the Q-aisle, the crowd had dispersed and they were left in the dim light of a cold Manhattan evening.

They wanted to know who the old woman was in the black suit. She was someone like themselves who lived in the hubbub of New York. Yet she was also in a painting containing a forest of primeval trees, a stupendous castle, and voracious vampires. As the three made their way to the transit station, they explored all the possibilities.

"Of course she's Quintana Castle," remarked Ericca.

"That's crazy," refuted Elle. "Quintana Castle was probably one of the long-dead philanthropists from the turn of the century in New York, much like John Jacob Astor."

"No, maybe she lived long ago but she has an extraordinary life span, rather like those great old trees we saw," explained Ericca. "I just have an intuition about that."

Then, getting another idea, she asked, "And isn't it strange, the similarity of the names Quintana and Quint?"

"Don't you believe in coincidence? There are millions of people in New York from all over the world. Of course there will be similar-sounding names," argued Matt, finding it hard to fathom a connection between his father, a brilliantly successful venture capitalist, and an old woman whose main role was that of librarian to ghostly, obscure books that for most people did not even exist.

Ericca silenced them with a significant look and reasoned, "Think: just how often do two people with similar names have access to a hidden library aisle containing books yet to be published?"

With that remark, they boarded the train and sat glumly for the rest of the ride home without uttering a word.

CHAPTER NINE

THE BULL'S EYE

They could not believe their incredible bad luck. Somehow Daemon Skye had found the Q-aisle and checked out the book minutes before them. The decisive advantage of even a small increment of time disturbed each of them deeply.

Matt went to bed that night with the firm intent of devising an invention that would produce royalties and patents to put his name alongside that of John Jacob Astor. But instead, his thoughts drifted to female faces amid coronas of shiny, curly hair, soft lips parted slightly in a whisper of threat and invitation. Ugh, he thought, I don't even like girls.

In his dreams, he held a hand-drawn sketch of a device and stood in a cramped and dusty government patent office. A bespectacled clerk unhappily informed him that a patent for such a device had been issued just minutes ago. A delicate face appeared inexplicably, as so often happens in dreams. But here, the fair face was mocking and leering, towering over him while holding a small, yapping dog.

But the scene from the dusty patent office dissolved to reveal the scene of a fashionable Upper East Side apartment. In a room with fancy moulding and vanilla walls, Tory Skye contemplated a gold statuette. "Darling, look what I found today. It's an original figure of Isis. Isn't it remarkable?"

Matt winced in his sleep as he pictured himself replying, "Sweetie, what a wonderful piece. Did you win it in an auction?"

Tory looked up with an angelic expression. "No, dear, Daddy

said I could keep it. There weren't very many Persian pieces, but his Egyptian collection is quite good."

"Of course there wouldn't be, my love. Alexander the Great managed to burn all those civilizations to the ground and wiped out every vestige of those cultures. The Egyptians were smart. They just proclaimed him pharaoh and he let them be." Matt pictured himself answering Tory with an air of calm reassurance.

"Well, it's a good thing Daddy saved what he could," Tory replied sweetly. She held a glass of wine to him. Matt turned to embrace her, but as he did, her lithe form turned into the shape of a squat matron and her countenance turned into that of a stubborn bulldog. Matt was petrified with horror and woke with an agonized shout, "No, not the dog. No, I thought of that first."

Then, shaking his head in the cheerful and familiar surroundings of his bedroom, he thought, That is so absurd. Nahh…Tory has nothing over me. He rolled back to sleep.

His twin slept soundly in the room next door. Elle's mind wandered the corridors of the Q-aisle, stopping to admire fabulous paintings she had only glimpsed fleetingly during the day. There was an exhibit featuring a sled and harness next to a doorway framed with a pediment carved with the Greek letter *Tau*. She peered at the plaque next to the exhibit, which read:

WELCOME TO THE T-GATE
Dedicated to the magic of words and the courage
of the Samoyed sled dog Etah, who accompanied
the adventurer Roald Amundsen
in his successful quest for the South Pole.

She glanced into the adjoining, light-filled room. The parquet wood floor glistened. Grand paintings hung on the walls. Two rows of columns defined a center corridor. Gold capitals adorned the tops of each of the round columns, marked with symbols even Elle could not recognize. Metallic sconces perforated with stars illuminated each column. In the back, a large display showed a diagram resembling a subway map. Elle wanted to step farther into the room but stopped when she heard Ericca and Matt call, "Elle, where are you? Are you OK?"

Matt's shout in the night roused Elle from her dreams. With no clue why Matt was so alarmed, Elle muttered to herself, "Matt …the dashboard is really plastic," and fell back asleep.

Ericca wondered endlessly that evening about Daemon Skye. There were, she reasoned, thousands, millions of books, past and present, about ancient Egypt. It was no mere coincidence that Daemon should happen to choose the exact same book at the exact same time.

No, she thought, Daemon must have had a clue. It was now apparent that Daemon, like Quint, had access to the Q-catalogue, and the Q-aisle. That fact did not alarm her. What was puzzling was how Daemon might have picked out this book, a special book by one *George Sax*, without following the same path she followed with the twins.

Then an idea struck her. Perhaps she was not alone in wanting to find Branch Archer. She knew Daemon and her father, Branch, had been good friends and buddies in the same close-knit Air Force squadron. Perhaps Daemon had a reason for finding Branch.

Even so, Daemon would have had to do the same searches, read and filtered the same results, exactly as she did with the twins. That was unlikely, because Daemon did not have the same kind of collective intuition. He might have eavesdropped on them, but again, that was impossible, because her conversations with the twins were always in the private surroundings of the twins' loft.

Except, she thought, when they were huddled over the computer in the Reading Room, whispering within earshot of several library patrons. Then she recalled that Tory Skye was nearby that day, possibly in the library where they were, listening at a distance as they searched on the name *George Sax*.

Ericca thought of Tory's iconic face disfigured with an unsightly gash and felt a pang of sympathy. Hey, Tory was never really that bad, she thought. In fact, she almost felt sorry for her. But Tory was the type of person who thought nothing of stealing rare artifacts. She was the type of person who thought nothing of using a small dog as a fashion accessory.

Yes, Tory was a clever person, completely capable of deception and cruelty. Tory would be the two-headed bishop from Daemon's chess collection, a vile and scheming cheat beneath the guise of a sweet debutante. Now the image of Tory's scarred face gave Ericca a vindictive satisfaction.

She berated herself for what she knew was a very unkind thought. She recalled the scene on the checkerboard lawn with girls in pinstripes and candy ribbons clawing at each other. All over Matt, she thought. What a joke. The tension and aggression was real. She knew this feeling and whispered to herself, "No, this time, Daemon, I will get there first."

Ericca looked forward to a busy day. She was to meet Maxine Weaver at her office today for the promised personal tour of the MTA offices. MTA was short for Metropolitan Tunnel Authority. Maxine undoubtedly knew a lot about Manhattan's personal mobility systems. Ericca suspected Maxine could also comment on a transportation system only a few New Yorkers knew of.

There had been no mention of the time tunnels for some time. The twins avoided further discussion of their cross-country trip in the Cobra car, and Ericca had no inclination to repeat her adventure with Spike. But now, as she stuffed her blanket and opera glasses into her backpack, Albert and Leonardo popped their faces out of the blanket and immediately launched their familiar repartee.

"Good morning, Albert, I trust you are well," said Leonardo, as the Albert peered back at him through droopy eyes.

"I have been better, I must say," replied Albert. "My poor bones, they tend to creak and complain with this unconscionable weather."

"Oh, arthritis, the agony of old age," answered Leonardo with lugubrious sadness. "If we were all young and spry like Ericca…"

"There must be a remedy in this enlightened age, perhaps deep soaks in warm jets, or…I have it…a levitation room," said Albert. "…a respite from toil and time, an antigravity chamber for laughing your heartaches away," continued Albert excitedly.

"What are you two yammering about?" asked Ericca. "Aren't you excited? We are going on an outing today."

Albert and Leonardo were happy. All too often, as residents of a baby blanket, they found they were increasingly excluded, as Ericca found more things to do outside the apartment. "Yes, it is just too bad, rather like being a pet, or even…a really old person," ventured Albert. Albert and Leonardo disliked being characterized as "old," so this remark caused a welcome silence.

As Ericca headed out of the apartment, Albert and Leonardo giggled quietly in her backpack, filled with delight and anticipation. They examined the contents of the backpack. "Oh, a *Spectocular*," remarked Albert, seeing Ericca's new opera glasses. "…a Ray Bender original…Ray periodically comes by and asks me about the speed and behavior of light," continued Albert as he studied the initials *RB* engraved in the case.

"A *Spectocular*…really?" asked Leonardo. "I've never heard of such a thing."

"Oh, of course not…Ray is a very private person. You would be too, if you were a genius…not to imply you're not a genius…because we all know that you are," fumbled Albert. "Yes, a Spectocular, for witnessing spectacular things…that should be fairly obvious."

Albert now shut up. He had put his foot in his mouth already. Also, he recognized the voice of Ericca exchanging greetings with her neighbor Nicholas Bard.

"Hello, Mr. Bard…happy holidays," said Ericca. "Thank you so much for the gift." She hesitated. Nicholas had overheard her shrieks in the night from her nightmare about the Puppet King. She did not want to bring up that subject, but she did not want to seem ungracious for the gift.

Happily, Nicholas was with someone. She wore a dark, stylish jacket and matching boots. Her shiny hair fell lightly on her shoulders. Ericca recognized her as Daphne, from their first meeting that spring.

He smiled. "You're quite welcome…oh…and I don't think you've met my friend, Daphne. She's visiting from Seattle," he said, introducing the young woman beside him. Daphne smiled and said, "You must be Ericca. We've met before."

Daphne smiled a sweet smile of recognition. Ericca could see why Nicholas was so infatuated with her. Ericca turned down the hallway to exit the building, feeling strangely happy at the thought of them together.

In the muted sunshine of the winter day, Ericca headed toward the subway stop. The pretzel vendor looked her way. The newsstand attendant waved. She stopped to glance at the headlines, ignoring distressing news about wars in foreign countries and investment scams. Instead, she picked up the periodical her mother frequently read, the *Tunnel Times*. On the front page was a picture of a young woman with a black pillbox hat over her elegant bouffant hairdo. The headline read:

NEW YORK HEIRESS MISSING

Quintana Castle, the reclusive heiress to the Sax family fortune, has been reported missing. The widow of the Sax heir and political activist Taliesin Sax, disassociated herself from her husband's family following his assassination thirty years ago, and has lived privately in Manhattan since. She is known by her maiden name, Quintana Castle, in her low-key bequests to the Midtown Public Library. Quintana Castle was last seen with her dog, Tau, a white Samoyed, outside the Midtown Public Library. In this picture, she is shown some thirty years ago before she retired from public life.

Ericca read the article again. She could not believe the stunning coincidence of names. "Quintana Castle, Taliesin Sax, George Sax," she recited to herself. There had to be a connection between the heiress Quintana Castle and the author George Sax. She was sure of it. And there was yet another connection, one between George Sax, the writer of a yet-unpublished book about civilization and leadership and Taliesin Sax, a department-store heir assassinated for political reasons.

Ericca was now in a tearing hurry to talk to someone, perhaps the twins or maybe Maxine Weaver. Surely the twins had seen the latest headlines and would see the connection between Quintana Castle and George Sax. Quintana Castle would lead them to him.

Then a frightening thought came to mind. What if Quintana Castle was kidnapped? What if the fate which befell her late husband threatened to claim her? Ericca ran to the subway station frantically. She needed the advantage of time. She needed to find Quintana Castle.

Ericca was grateful for the staunch columns and calm of the Metropolitan Tunnel Authority lobby. The elevator arrived promptly when summoned by a push of the up button and only lurched slightly while climbing to the ninety-eighth floor offices of Maxine Weaver, director of the MTA.

Ericca checked her watch. She was right on time for her lunch appointment with Maxine. Everything was as it should be. Except, as she exited the elevator to the corridor of offices, she couldn't help noticing that all the offices were empty. There was not a soul to be found amid the paper-strewn desks, banks of metal file cabinets, and humming computers.

Maxine Weaver's office was deserted. Ericca looked at the wide wooden desk and stupendous view, anxious to find a note of explanation. Then, in the piles of paper on the desk, Ericca spied not a note, but the corner of a photo of a teenage girl holding a small dog. Ericca recognized the face instantly as Tory Skye's.

The note attached to the photo alarmed Ericca even more, and set in motion a train of theories.

TUNNEL STABILITY AND
SECURITY THREAT SUSPECT:
TORY SKYE

Tory Skye, juvenile female residing in Manhattan often seen in the company of a Pomeranian by the name of Pluto, noted for nipping and possessive behavior. Tory is suspected of setting off security and stability sensors with an unknown substance in the suspect's possession. Continued surveillance advised.

It was no coincidence. Tory had caused the security evacuations Ericca experienced that past spring. Ericca pondered what this could mean. She knew Tory wore the Tory Torus almost all the time. Tory could be setting off a security sensor innocently, or there could be a more sinister explanation. She looked at the dossier; her suspicions of Tory mounted.

Ericca was turning to leave when another folder caught her eye; the note sticking out of the folder read:

PROPERTY DEFACEMENT SUSPECT:
EMPIRE POETS SOCIETY

Various instances of graffiti in Central Park, at the Metropolitan Museum of Art, and at MTA facilities have been linked to the Empire Poets Society. Quotations of political import scrawled on various structural and artistic pieces have been traced to the literary efforts of this group. This group has no previous criminal history but is under surveillance at this time. Two members of the group are under suspicion.

The picture sticking out from the folder was familiar; it was a photo of the glade in Central Park where she had found Nicholas Bard with his poetry group. Another picture in the file showed a statue of a ghoulish woman with a headdress of serpents. The words *Of the Hollow Patriarch and the Stuffed Mandarin* were scrawled at the base. Oh, my gosh, Ericca thought, Nicholas is linked to a crime too.

Ericca leafed through the folder with a sense of tense secrecy, listening warily for approaching footsteps. She heard the click of heels growing louder. She froze in panic.

She closed the folder and hastily collected herself as she left the office. Uniformed policemen were headed toward Maxine's office as Ericca walked toward the elevator. "Excuse me young lady, but were you given permission to be here?" asked one policeman gruffly.

"I had an appointment with Maxine Weaver today, but she never showed up," replied Ericca innocently.

"Maxine Weaver has been missing for several days, and her staff has been temporarily dismissed by order of the mayor. We would advise you to leave now," replied the policeman curtly.

Ericca nodded in dutiful agreement. The elevator was empty, eerily so, which did not help the odd sensation in her stomach and ears as the elevator dropped to the lobby level. Outside in the sunshine, she found her way through throngs of protesters and pedestrians. Ericca now felt a sense of serious urgency and waved the slogans and signs away. She needed to find the twins right away. She needed to get help.

The twins hovered over the kitchen table, littered with the pudgy and colorful shapes of marzipan chess pieces. The twins, concentrating on their pastry projects, looked up with alarm as Ericca rushed toward them shouting, "Tory did it. Tory wants to punish that old woman and her dog. She wants to sabotage the time tunnels and she has captured Maxine Weaver."

"What old woman, what dog?" asked Elle with surprise, trying to fully grasp what Ericca was talking about.

"Quintana Castle, of course…Haven't you read the papers?" explained Ericca with impatience, before hurriedly searching the loft for a copy of the *Tunnel Times*. Pointing excitedly at the headline article, she said, "Look, she's the same woman from the library, from the Q-aisle, only much younger. She's missing and I'm sure Tory has something to do with it."

Matt and Elle looked closely at the photo. "You're right. Geez, Ericca, you were right from the beginning…how did you know?" asked Matt.

Ericca hid her smugness and replied, "I just know women who wear black hats have unusual names like Quintana. It's actually been proved…scientifically."

Elle chimed in, "We women have an intuition about these things, Matt." She then turned to Ericca and asked, "But what makes you think Tory has anything to do with this?"

Ericca fumbled for an explanation. "Tory was there at the library. Tory had her face scratched when Quintana's dog caused a scene. Tory has good reason for disliking Quintana Castle, mostly for her dog, who caused the trouble…and worse, stole all the attention from her adorable Pluto."

"Hmm, Tory is a spoiled brat and a petty thief, not a vindictive lunatic," Matt interjected.

Ericca and Elle exchanged knowing looks. "Oh, Matt, never under-estimate the seriousness of damage to a woman's vanity. We are talking about payback with a capital P," remarked Elle.

"Plus, look at the circumstances, it is beyond coincidence. Some person residing at Skye Towers is very interested in George Sax. This person is also interested in Quintana Castle, and has reason for detaining her or …" Ericca paused. She did not want to spell out her worst fears.

"Let's see, you're saying that there is a connection between George Sax and Quintana Castle because Quintana was once married to someone named Sax, and that there is a *conspiracy* against the Sax family?" queried Matt skeptically, trying not to scoff. "A bit far-fetched. Don't you see the quantum leap you've made?"

"Yes…of course…I just know it," stammered Ericca, knowing now there was no way to prove her theory. "We have to find Quintana, fast…I just know it."

Then Ericca remembered the invitation sent to her mother. "I know. There is a party at Skye Towers on New Year's Eve, the Light Spectacular. We'll sneak in and look around disguised as…" Ericca fumbled for an idea.

"I know," she said with her face alight, as her gaze fell on the marzipan chess pieces, "We will be pastry chefs delivering candy-cane chess pieces, a festive centerpiece in a gala party, a holiday gift from Quint A. Senns."

The twins groaned but nodded in agreement. Ericca's enthusiasm was infectious; plus, they couldn't think of anything more fun to do on New Year's Eve.

Ericca watched, blanket in hand, as her mother dressed to attend the New Year's Eve party at Skye Towers.

"Remember, Ericca, brush your teeth and try to do some reading, and don't stay up too late watching movies. I may be late coming home," instructed Sophia.

Albert and Leonardo popped out of the blanket and chimed in together, "Don't you worry about a thing, Mrs. Ludwig. We'll make sure she stays out of trouble."

Sophia smiled wryly and replied, "Of course you will," as she gathered her purse and cloak and headed out the door. With the click of the door closing and the fading tap of Sophia's high-heeled shoes in the hallway, Albert and Leonardo turned to Ericca and said, "OK, now we need to go."

Ericca crept about the small apartment as she prepared to leave. She had her blanket, Spike, her Spectoculars, and a warm coat against the frigid evening. "Shh," she said to the blanket in her backpack as she warily slid along the hallway walls, careful to avoid being seen.

Thinking she had made a clean getaway, she breathed a sigh of relief, happy to be out in the chill evening air. But looking up in the dim light, she discerned a familiar shape. It was Nicholas Bard, returning home in the company of his friend, Daphne.

He was in good spirits as they stopped to exchange greetings. "What a pleasant surprise, Ericca. Out for an evening stroll?" he asked.

"Yes, yes, that's exactly what I'm doing, Mr. Bard," answered Ericca nervously. "I am actually meeting some people, my friends, Matt and Elle. We are going to see a movie tonight."

Nicholas scrutinized Ericca. He seemed concerned. He was not sure Ericca had permission to be out alone at night. He replied, "That sounds fun...hey, you know, Daphne and I were thinking of seeing a movie too. Mind if we tag along?"

Ericca replied, "Sure...I suppose." A few minutes later, the three of them were at the base of Skye Tower.

"Sorry, I think I need to go find my friends now," said Ericca hastily as she headed into the gilded lobby.

"Sure I can't help you find your friends? You know I cleaned the windows of this building today. I know it pretty well," replied Nicholas.

Ericca shook her head and turned to go when, with a fleeting inspiration, she turned around, and asked, "When you cleaned the windows today, did you happen to see anything unusual on the seventy-seventh floor?"

"Unusual...what do you mean? Let's see, I suppose you've never seen the Skye Bridge Spa. It's sort of unusual, seeing a bunch of women bouncing around in laughing fits."

Albert perked up and said audibly, "Oh, wonderful, a levitation room, let's go there now."

Hearing this, Nicholas looked sharply at Ericca and said, "Excuse me. Did you say that?"

"Say what? Oh...yes...that was me. Of course...did you happen to see a woman in a black pillbox hat in this spa?" answered Ericca.

"Hmm, come to think of it...there was...I think," answered Nicholas, quizzically furrowing his brow. Ericca silently cheered and turned again toward the elevator, waving goodbye to Nicholas and Daphne.

The twins were already at the appointed meeting place, the women's restroom outside the service entrance of the Bull's Eye Restaurant. "Ericca, we're in this stall," whispered Elle.

They were huddled in the handicap stall, with cake boxes, and already wearing chef's uniforms. Ericca donned a chef's uniform, stuffing her jacket into the backpack, which she tucked under the front of her chef's coat.

"Hmm, Ericca," said Elle, giggling, "You're going to have to stop eating all those bagels," as she poked her inflated mid-section.

"C'mon, let's go," urged Matt. "The head chef is expecting us in a few minutes. Oh, wait, I nearly forgot these —" He dug out three sticky-back tags from his pocket embroidered with the logo *Polis Pastries*.

"Polis Pastries?" asked Ericca.

"Oh, yes. Matt and I decided we needed to look professional, so we came up with a logo. What do you think?" asked Elle.

"That's great, but — " answered Ericca.

"You're wondering about the name. Well...we thought of something like *Metropolitan* or *Megalopolis Pastries*, or *Uncanny Cakes*, but we liked the sound of *Polis Pastries*. It has a nice alliteration to it...and in case you were wondering, a *polis* in ancient Greece was a city-state...hence words today like policy, police, politics, and metropolis."

Elle was fond of reciting the etymology of words, and Ericca had to admit it was helpful to see words grouped by related meaning. But right now, Matt was waving for them to hurry up.

"How do I look?" asked Elle as they put on the final part of their costumes, white chef's hats with attached wigs.

"Just stunning," said Ericca with a giggle after a quick glance in the mirror.

The portly chef of the Bull's Eye Restaurant was supervising the kitchen staff when they entered through the service door, cake boxes in hand. Elle announced, "Delivery from Polis Pastries."

The head chef stopped amid his frenetic activity and remarked, "Oh, thank you. My gosh, pastry chefs get smaller every day…well I suppose it helps to have small, dexterous hands…please set them aside there."

As his back was turned, Elle and Ericca set the cake boxes down, and then silently dove under the table skirt of a large display case. They were there just in time to hear Daemon Skye, his patent-leather shoes in slate blue visible as he strolled by, followed by a parade of guests.

"We are so delighted you could join us this evening. You will find that the Bull's Eye Restaurant really has the best of everything. For instance, the steak here is superb. Our chief chef will tell you more."

"Oh, yes, our steaks come from truly select cows, from certified organic ranchers. Our Tajima beef, or Kobe beef, as you may know it, comes from an ancient stock of black-haired Japanese cattle. These cows are pampered with sake mash and make wonderfully marbled steaks. You can even request our very popular steak tartare."

Elle whispered, "Raw, thinly sliced…" to Ericca's questioning look. The head chef continued.

"Another popular entrée here is boneless eye of round, and also the rib eye steak, which we marinate in Marsala wine. The eye of round, from the round section of the hind-quarter, is one of the best and most tender, along with the rib eye, from the backbone. But really all our steaks are delicious, and we have a great selection, including porterhouse and filet mignon."

Ericca made a face and whispered, "You mean they section up the parts of the cow's butt?" Elle nodded in confirmation.

"But don't forget our other specialties, including Canine Biscotti, created especially for Pluto."

Amid the appreciative remarks, Ericca heard her mother's voice, "Truly a remarkable place, Daemon." Sophia and Daemon strolled together out of the restaurant. Ericca motioned for the twins to follow as they dodged out from under the table to a hiding place behind a large planter. They were there just in time to see Daemon and Sophia disappear down a hallway painted in terra cotta, with horses and bulls suggestive of cave paintings.

The three followed Daemon and Sophia. They slithered along the walls until they reached a doorway where they heard voices. Daemon and Sophia were inside a paneled office with a stunning view of the lights of Manhattan. Jasper Johns' *Target* painting hung above the desk.

"You've never seen this photograph? Well, Branch and I were friends before everything. We flew two hundred and thirty-three combat missions together. Branch was a great guy; even in the darkest moments, he always had a joke. Teamwork and friendship were everything to him," remarked Daemon.

Sophia was silent as she looked at the framed picture of two young men in fighter-pilot gear.

"Let me show you the sculpture garden and the Skye Bridge," offered Daemon. They strolled out of the office into the adjoining room, an airy atrium with big potted plants and works of art that looked like museum pieces. Ericca and the twins stayed hidden in the office but were within earshot.

"What a wonderful collection, Daemon…I recognize all these pieces from throughout history and from all over the world. This is magnificent." Ericca could her mother's voice from the next room.

"Well, I try. Works of art, like great books or lost love affairs, are powerful, like jewels turned over and over in private moments, to expose new facets of delight each time," replied Daemon reflectively.

Ericca seethed with anger. Daemon Skye, who was most likely instrumental in her father's death, was now conveniently befriending his best friend's widow. She scampered past the twins to look at the photo on the desk.

She recognized the cool half-smile of Daemon Skye; next to him stood a smaller man with a long slender jaw, smiling broadly.

CHAPTER NINE

As she turned to find the twins, she saw a book on a chair. The title on the spine read *Green Basket, Blue Cup*. She quickly opened the jacket, just long enough to note the publication date. My gosh, she thought, this book will be published in just eight years.

There was a thud of footsteps. Ericca closed the book abruptly and dashed into the adjoining room, a room paneled in marble with a high glass ceiling. All around were pieces of sculpture, many of which she recognized as monuments from around the city. These must be replicas, she thought. She gasped at the sight of the Memorial Monument, its smooth hull inscribed with names. There was no sign of graffiti, but a familiar whisper from the next room kept Ericca from looking closely.

Matt and Elle were already in the next room, hunched behind the planters that stood next to the round door. Ericca dashed to join them. "That is the entrance to the levitation room...Daemon and your mom have already gone ahead," whispered Elle, pointing through the round door.

In the dim light through the circular door, they saw an atrium where stars and constellations twinkled brightly in the glass ceiling. A large round window framed a view of the glimmering city skyline. Bouquets of flowers, bunches of grapes, books, and bottles of perfume floated in midair. Strangest of all was the sight of two women: a frail, old woman in a black suit and pillbox hat, and a rotund woman in pumps and a tweed suit. They floated in midair, taking nibbles from grapes at whim, laughing in fits. Ericca immediately recognized them as Quintana Castle and Maxine Weaver.

"And what is wrong with this?" asked Albert in a muffled voice from underneath her coat. "That looks like wondrous fun... especially for those of advanced...status..."

"What's wrong is that they are being held against their will," asserted Ericca. But she could not help admitting to herself that it did look fun, especially when she spied Tory Skye, in a lavender leotard and black skirt, her shiny locks tied in a ponytail. Tory swung from a diaphanous tether, executing graceful somersaults in midair. They heard faint notes of classical music. "Hmm, sounds like Albinoni," remarked Elle.

Suddenly, they froze, when they heard Daemon Skye say, "What a pleasant surprise, our little pastry chefs are actually none other than Tory's inquisitive pals." He stood there eyeing them with suspicion. Ericca and the twins froze; they felt a chill of fright run down their spines when they realized that Sophia was not there, that they were here by themselves in the lair of Daemon and Tory Skye.

"You're wondering what happened to your mother. Well, she said she had to go, to tuck you goodnight. Which reminds me, isn't it a bit late for the likes of you three to still be up?" asked Daemon dryly.

Ericca had had enough. "Let them go, Daemon," she demanded.

"Ericca Ludwig. I don't believe we've ever been formally introduced. You do have your father's fire, but truly, simmer down. Things are rarely what they seem," replied Daemon coldly.

"It will never work, Daemon. George Sax's books will be published no matter what you do. Maxine Weaver will fix the time tunnels no matter how long you hold her in this trap," accused Ericca.

"Temper, temper, and jumping to conclusions." Then, with a heavy sigh and in a resounding voice, Daemon replied, "Very well, to make light of the matter... *Vacuum Evacuate!*"

The round window shattered with an ear-piercing din. Quintana Castle and Maxine Weaver plunged downwards; they screamed in alarm as they were sucked uncontrollably toward the gaping hole left by the shattered window. Ericca sprang into the room, frantically trying to grasp the two women before the black vacuum and terrifying height spelled their end. Tory Skye watched impassively, held aloft by the tether.

But to no avail. With a loud whoosh, the unsecured contents of the rooms went flying out, Ericca, Quintana, and Maxine among them. Ericca flew abruptly into the frigid night sky and glimpsed in horror the lights of buildings and cars far below. The cold air sent blood coursing away from her hands and face. She felt numb, then panicked as she noticed the gushing red gashes on her hands. The shattered shards of the exploding window had ripped her skin, and now she tasted the saltiness of warm blood in her mouth.

She was falling quickly. Below she glimpsed the hard pavement and throng of headlights. She saw Maxine and Quintana above her still clutching plates of grapes as they twisted in midair. They were screaming. In that moment, Ericca forgot her horror as she agonized over her rash remark, a remark that thrust these two dear old ladies out of a heated heaven into the blistering cold vortex of night.

The pavement was now closer. The successive levels of Skye Tower flew by in a blur. Ericca searched her mind, but neither the counsel of Sheila Angvall nor Leonardo nor Albert came to her aid. Now her suspicions of Daemon Skye, her loud accusations in the levitation room, all the events that led up to this moment seemed hasty and mistaken. The tears that welled in her eyes tasted of the bitterness of personal defeat. Then suddenly, looking forward, she saw headlights, weaving through the sky towers. It was the Cobra car.

Maxine fell with a loud thud into the backseat, with Quintana landing in her lap. Ericca was not far behind. "Well, right on time as Daemon said, but where are the twins?" asked Quint, not looking at all disconcerted.

"The twins are back at the party," explained Ericca, pointing upward to the shattered window, where Daemon now stood, watching at a distance.

"Oh, of course, I should have warned them, the Bull's Eye can be quite a trip; Daemon hates for his guests to be bored," explained Quint as he looked up and waved.

Daemon waved back and yelled, in a wry tone, "Don't forget to tour the Gravity Bar, on the thirty-second floor, to rap with Doctor Gravity."

The Cobra car was slowly descending. Ericca saw inside the

boxy rooms of the skyscraper, and then heard the funky beat of rap music. Then, to everyone's surprise, the Cobra car started to rattle and drop rapidly. Quint manipulated the controls on the dashboard, but nothing worked. He grimaced with frustration and grumbled something about the fortuitous appearance of a *Time Tram*, but nothing slowed their dizzying descent. They were certain to crash violently into the sidewalk, were it not for a sudden inspiration.

"Albert, do you have any experience with aborting free-fall catastrophes involving a quintessence-equipped car with three adults and one juvenile passenger?" asked Ericca.

Albert popped out of the blanket and peered at the rapidly approaching sidewalk. "You know, Spike has been known to work with massive objects, though this situation may strain the limit. But we should try, and now." Thankfully, he did not make any pointed remarks about Maxine.

Ericca unfurled the patchwork blanket like a parachute, while grasping Maxine's hand. The Cobra car's fall slowed dramatically. "Quickly, to the T-Gate," Quintana instructed Quint.

Quint apparently knew what she was talking about and steered the car down Park Avenue, past the crowds around the Big Apple in Times Square, toward Midtown. Ericca looked down and saw they were approaching Bryant Park and heading directly toward a large window in the library.

She ducked, expecting a violent din and another rain of glass shards. Instead, the window opened, allowing the Cobra car to land gracefully between two large columns. When Ericca looked up, she found she was in a subway station.

Quintana breathed a sigh of relief, smoothed her hair, and said cheerily, "Ericca, welcome to the T-Gate." Not thinking to ask about this remark, Ericca stepped out of the Cobra car, and sighed with relief at the feel of solid ground.

CHAPTER TEN

ΣMPIRΣ POΣTS SOCIΣTY

Ericca's jubilation was short-lived. Maxine and Quintana collected themselves after their hair-raising escape from the Skye Bridge. Maxine straightened her jacket and smoothed her wrinkled shirt. Quintana adjusted her pillbox hat.

Ericca felt smug and pleased for her daring rescue, and was completely surprised and caught off-guard when Maxine and Quintana turned to her with ruffled expressions.

"Young lady, can you please explain what that was all about?" asked Maxine.

"Well...of course...Daemon Skye held you captive, and I rescued you," replied Ericca. This seemed obvious.

"We were being held captive?" asked Quintana.

"Well, yes," answered Ericca. "Daemon wanted to punish you for that accident with Tory." Turning to Maxine, she explained, "Daemon and Tory are trying to sabotage the time tunnels."

Maxine and Quintana looked vexed, but then their irritation turned to bemusement. "Ericca, where have you been getting these fantastic ideas? Daemon did not harm or kidnap us; he actually invited us very graciously for a complimentary visit to the Sky Bridge Spa, a respite we both really needed...very invigorating and rejuvenating," replied Maxine.

Albert poked his head out and said, "Totally agreed...when flesh and bone disintegrate under the pull of weight, a little levity can reverse a grave fate...hmm...quite poetic, if I say so myself."

Maxine and Quintana were not at all surprised at the talking head. In fact, they found Albert charming and funny.

"Such fluency, and from a physicist," said Maxine in approval.

"Albert, I'm sure you would have enjoyed yourself," added Quintana. "Laughing with Maxine in the levitation room certainly took years away…and that is not all…Maxine and I were treated to massages, sea scrubs, fresh and healthy food. We even had our nails done as part of the Isis Signature Pedicure." She displayed her hand. Her cuticles were trimmed, and her nails polished and shaped.

Maxine admired Quintana's nails, and then flexed her neck with an expression of relief. "Oh that massage was simply wonderful. All that cervical strain from making left turns and parallel parking has just been killing me," remarked Maxine, stretching herself.

Quintana nodded in agreement. "You poor dear…the weight of our busy brains does take a toll, I agree."

Quintana and Maxine continued to gush over their spa experience. They also discussed their plans for a follow-up visit. "Did you try the Cleopatra Milk and Lavender Soak? It was simply divine," asked Maxine. Ericca wondered what ancient Egyptian queens had to do with therapy for modern day Manhattanites. She slunk sheepishly into the shadows.

She was sure she would make the situation much worse by trying to justify her actions. She still believed the accusations she had blurted out. She knew in her heart that there was a connection between her father, George Sax, and the rash of security alerts in the subways. She knew that Daemon had a role in all this.

She also knew there were psychiatric labels for people who acted on their every fear. Quintana, with her level of learning from many hours in the library, might be one to advise professional counseling for paranoia. Ericca would not welcome such a label, so she refrained from further argument.

The Cobra car had landed in an obscure wing of the Midtown Public Library. Since they had been cloaked by the trees of Bryant Park, Quint was sure there were no witnesses to the spectacle of a gliding car. Quint was now backing the Cobra car through the double glass doors. "I need to pick up Elle and Matt at the Skye Tower," he explained. "Ericca, do you need a ride?"

Ericca felt dispirited at the embarrassing turn of events. She declined the ride. She thought of her angry words and began to wonder whether she had played into Daemon's hands. Maybe Daemon knew all along that she would be there to rescue her friends and contrived the situation to mock her.

As the Cobra car roared away, Ericca followed dejectedly behind Maxine and Quintana as they headed out the T-Gate. She remembered getting a glimpse of this wing of the library when they exited the Q-aisle. What planning, she thought, to locate a subway station right next to a popular civic attraction. Except, she mused, there were not many users of either the T-Gate or the Q-aisle today.

The T-Gate was certainly built for high traffic. Ericca was reminded of the departing and arriving platforms of subway stations. Two rows of columns defined a wide central corridor. Between the columns was a large sign with some sort of map. The columns were decorated with metal sconces that illuminated the corridor. Looking more closely, she noticed that the stars perforating the metal sconces were different on each column. She passed one sconce with the pattern of Orion, and then another with the constellation Taurus. The column capitals were simple round rings, plated in gold.

Ericca was tired and wanted to sink into one of the carved wooden benches along the corridor or even stop to admire the paintings on the walls. As they went through the Q-aisle, she stopped to look at a chess set with blue pinstriped pieces. Below the display was a plaque, which she fleetingly read:

UMPIRE CHESS
Dedicated to the Principle of Fair Play
A Bequest from the
LOGOS Corporation on Behalf
Of the Late Hammond Spiro

Ericca scrambled to catch up with Quintana and Maxine. The spa experience had really lifted their spirits; they chattered excitedly and strolled briskly together. They only stopped momentarily at a fountain near the end of the corridor. "As charming as I remember it," remarked Quintana.

"We do try to keep it in good shape, but these public waterworks are a hefty maintenance issue," replied Maxine.

They were looking at a round reflecting pool; the water was still except for a spiral of ripples which rotated almost imperceptibly around a shiny ball in the middle. In the capstone bordering the pool, Ericca spotted the chiseled outline of symbols, symbols she recognized immediately as Egyptian: the ankh key composed of a circle joined with a plus sign, and the wadjet eye of Horus, an outlined eye with a flourishing lower swirl, which also appeared on the Q-computer.

"Come along, Ericca," called Maxine. "Quintana needs to close the Q-aisle." Ericca scrambled away from the pool. She had already been chastised once this evening. She knew better than to act out.

For the next few months, Ericca diligently devoted herself to schoolwork. She avoided the twins. She did not want to admit that her conspiracy theory had been disproved, conclusively.

It would be a perfect spring day before she saw the twins again. The mail that day contained the usual array of bills and advertisements. But today she found a letter addressed to Nicholas Bard, mistakenly delivered to their mailbox. The letter was from the Veterans Administration Hospital and was stamped *Urgent*.

Albert saw the letter and exhorted her to deliver it immediately. "Do you know what *urgent* means?" asked Albert. "It means right now; time is of the essence."

Leonardo, remembering their escapade at the Skye Tower, warned, "Albert, are you goading Ericca on to another crazy wild-goose chase? What if Nicholas isn't where she thinks he is? What if Ericca gets in trouble for leaving the apartment?"

CHAPTER TEN

This constant bickering was beginning to wear on Ericca's nerves. "Shush, enough of the fighting, both of you," she admonished in irritation. She had to admit her surly mood was not entirely their fault.

Nicholas Bard, she thought, what an unfortunate man. He seemed destined to perpetual unhappiness. Ericca knew this from the muffled sobs from next door.

Nicholas' unhappy turn of events echoed Ericca's own frustrations. There was no such thing as happy karma or obvious inevitability after all. There was no plan or happy coincidence leading to wondrous discovery.

But she contemplated the word *Urgent* again. Maybe she could make a difference, a difference for the good. She grabbed her jacket, Spike, and her backpack and, against Leonardo's protests, was soon out the door in the warm sunshine of a spring day.

On the subway, she sat next to a woman with a dark mole on the side of her face. There was a hair in the middle of the mole, and she clutched a plastic shopping bag. Tattooed and pierced passengers with earphones vibrating with a heavy bass beat sat nearby, oblivious to the press of humanity around them. The man across the aisle wore a dark blue suit and read a paperback. Ericca wondered what everyone might be thinking.

Ericca suspected that the woman with the mole was silently appalled at her fellow riders' tattooed midriffs and pierced belly buttons. These passengers were in turn contemplating other ways of tagging their bodies. The man in the suit found escape from this predictable scene in the adventures and intrigue of a fictional action hero. The idea of this motley group brushing shoulders and breathing the same air was quite a happy thought, actually.

The park approached, and Ericca breathed with a sigh of relief. There were no security alerts today. She exited the subway at the M-Gate and strode outside, past the Thyme Terrace, the Metropolitan Museum of Art, and Belvedere Castle. Her foul mood began to seem silly.

Couples sitting hand in hand on park benches, or waltzing in a glade, were charming to the point of innocence. A man stood painting at an easel in happy solitude. She spied the same man she had noticed last spring, in baggy pants and a tee-shirt, walking around with a plastic bag, picking up empty aluminum cans. A woman in a suit and high heels walked ahead with a rolling bag filled with canned drinks, which she sold to passersby. A line of skaters in colorful, close-fitting lycra uniforms zipped by. The play of light on the fountains filled Ericca with delight.

In front of her was a group of tourists, or so it seemed from their cameras and casual garb. They chatted cheerfully. "The Central Park Conservation society has done a beautiful job!" remarked an elderly man. "Oh, did you just see that, that is a rare blue water lily, I believe," exclaimed a woman in a cardigan sweater. The elderly woman at the head of the group turned around. Ericca recognized her right away as Sheila Angvall.

"That is indeed a rare blue water lily," agreed Sheila. "If you are interested in rare lilies, though, I would recommend visiting the Botanical Garden in the Bronx, where they have the rare corpse flower, now in bloom, for one day. Residents of the Bronx are especially proud of this plant. The corpse flower, along with many species of lotus and water lily, is believed to have existed millions of years ago, dating back to the time of the dinosaurs and the ancient Egyptians. You really should see it. The tuber in full bloom is…quite impressive."

"That is absolutely fascinating," replied one of the members of the tour group. "I have heard of the corpse flower, known for its horrible smell of rotten eggs when in bloom…hence the name. The smell is evocative of dead bodies and is repugnant and sickening to all sentient beings except for flies. Thankfully, the flower only blooms once every few years."

"Oh, my goodness, what could possibly be so fascinating about such a plant, and what is their connection to water lilies? Water lilies are the epitome of loveliness…and the rare blue water lily was celebrated as the logo of Upper Egypt and in many famous paintings," remarked the woman in the cardigan sweater as she strolled away from the group toward the lily pond.

"Water lilies are indeed lovely and I count Claude Monet as one of my favorite painters. And though we do not have the Gardens of Giverny here in New York, we do have ponds, several lakes, and of course, you are certain to find Impressionist souvenirs in the Metropolitan Museum," offered Sheila. "In fact, if you would like, we can take a small detour and visit the lily pond. We'll visit the Alice in Wonderland sculpture and the Conservatory Water along the way."

The group nodded enthusiastically. Ericca would have liked to follow them on this detour. She wanted to say hello to Sheila, but glancing at her watch, she realized she needed to hurry to catch Nicholas Bard at his usual spot at half-past four at the south end of the Literary Walk.

She scampered through the Glade and past Bethesda Terrace. But as she approached the street crossing at Terrace Drive, she saw two kids skating at the end of a pack of speed skaters. Their long, skinny limbs were bent and graceful as they pushed in synchronicity with the pack. They passed in a blur. Ericca recognized them as Elle and Matt.

Ericca was about to continue on her way when she saw Matt trip on his skate and crash to the ground. The pack of skaters stopped and turned around in concern. Elle helped her twin up and led him toward the glade where Ericca now stood. Ericca waved. Elle, seeing her for the first time, smiled and waved.

"Hi, stranger," called Elle.

Matt was now on his feet, looking somber and rubbing his elbow. "Hi, Elle," replied Ericca. "Matt, are you OK?"

"Yeah, I'm all right. I hate it when I trip on twigs," said Matt, grimacing as he inspected his scraped knee. "What are you doing here?"

"I'm trying to deliver a letter to my neighbor Nicholas Bard," replied Ericca.

"Yes, and against my better counsel," chimed in Leonardo,

suddenly poking his head out of the backpack.

"Calm down. Calm down," interrupted Albert, "It's just a walk in the park. We are not bombarding particles today, unfortunately."

Ericca ignored this background commentary and showed the twins the letter. "Wow," said Elle, "That could be really bad news. You'd better hurry and deliver that." Ericca agreed and headed toward the Literary Walk.

"Hey, Ericca, wait up," called Elle and Matt a few moments later. They were no longer in their skates and were running to catch up with her. Huffing and puffing, they said, "We've been meaning to tell you something."

They walked hurriedly under the canopy of elm trees along the Mall toward the Literary Walk. Had they had more time, they would have stopped to admire the various distinguished busts and statues along the tree-lined promenade. Ludwig Van Beethoven stared at them from his stone pedestal. Sir Walter Scott sat reflectively beneath graceful drapes in bronze.

At the sight of Sir Walter Scott's bust, Elle broke her train of thought and commented, "Oh, yes, there's Walter, the writer of *Ivanhoe*. What a great story, with love, chivalry, a fair maiden named Rowena, an evil king named John, the usurper taking over the government from the rightful king, Richard the Lionheart."

Returning to her train of thought, Elle said, "Ericca, we've wanted to tell you something."

Ericca waited silently, expecting Elle to say something like, "We were such fools. Quintana and Maxine were there entirely of their own accord."

Instead, Elle had some startling news. "Our dad said engine failure in the Cobra car that night was caused by a strange pull from something on the thirty-second floor. He says Daemon snidely hinted at this when he said to visit the Gravity Bar."

"Well, of course, the Gravity Bar is on the thirty-second floor," replied Ericca, recalling the evening as clearly as if it had been just yesterday. "But I thought the Gravity Bar was, well, just a bar."

CHAPTER TEN

Ericca conjured the image of a stylish Manhattan nightspot.

Matt nodded in acknowledgement. "No, the Gravity Bar is more than a nightclub. Dad suspects Daemon is working on a project, maybe a super-magnet, being stored at the Gravity Bar. Maybe Daemon needed some test subjects; the Cobra car conveniently made an unsuspecting subject."

"What could he be testing?" asked Ericca.

Albert, who had restrained himself for too long, now popped out of the blanket to explain: "That should be obvious. Suppose Leonardo and I were getting tired of being carried around like helpless papooses, and wanted to go back to being dead in some philosopher's heaven, or even to rest in peace among the familiar faces and places of our own time. We would now need a time tunnel of sorts. Maybe we could exploit an anomaly, a wrinkle, or a tear in the fabric of space and time. We could create this time tunnel, and then...whoopee...we would be out of here."

Ericca understood Albert's train of reasoning and fully comprehended its import. She felt hurt. "You're not happy here? You want to leave me?" asked Ericca, dumbfounded.

Leonardo, clearly touched, said in admonishment, "Albert, would you please not startle the poor child like that. No, Ericca, we are not leaving. Albert is merely trying to explain things by analogy."

Matt had been listening as well, and he now asked, "But Albert, how does this explain what Daemon is up to?

"Heh, heh, my dear boy, I would expect that a budding inventor like yourself would catch on right away. It's obvious. Either Daemon wants to build a time tunnel, one which he controls, or he wants to sabotage an existing time tunnel that competes with or threatens him. But then again, he may just be developing a force field for fun, maybe to protect that marvelous apartment and laughing room he has. Maybe he fears the Tunnel Wars will cause some serious destruction and he is preparing a defense."

"This makes no sense," protested Ericca. She was tired of talking about Daemon and the time tunnels. She had learned her lesson and was not interested in repeating the experience.

Elle, however, was curious and asked, "What reason would Daemon have for operating a time tunnel?" Albert opened his mouth for a rousing explanation, but shut it immediately and tucked himself back into the backpack. They were now at the Literary Walk; several people sat attentively on benches, among them Nicholas Bard, listening as a man in floppy pants and a muscle tee spoke.

"Mr. Bard, I have a letter for you," said Ericca, approaching the bench. Nicholas looked up, and took the letter. Looking at the envelope, he grimaced. He anxiously tore open the envelope and hurriedly read the letter. He did not comment as he stuffed the letter into his back pocket. He smiled at Ericca cordially in thanks, but turned away again as though relieved to divert his attention.

Then, realizing his rudeness, he looked at Ericca and said, "Ericca, you really should stay. I don't think you've ever met my friends. We are the Empire Poets Society, and we meet here every week to share our poetry...our thoughts...even our rap. That guy talking now, he's pretty good."

Ericca was not a huge fan of rap, but looking to Elle and Matt, she saw they had found places to sit and were listening in fascinated attention. "His name is Regi. His dad is actually a famous rap artist and music producer who started out in Brooklyn. His stuff is not preachy, but not the typical rap either. He kind of reminds me of the Black Eyed Peas or even Nas," continued Nicholas.

"Way to go, Regi," exhorted a tall, slender woman wearing dangling, filigreed earrings and a pendant featuring an Egyptian eye. "Her name is Rebecca; she can be the typical overbearing, outspoken feminist, but she's pretty nice usually," commented Nicholas, noticing Ericca's gaze.

Oh, no, thought Ericca, even feminist-philosopher types are fans of Tory Skye. She recalled ads for Tory's Creations and her Eye of Horus pendant and pet charm. How sad.

"Thanks, thanks. Well, today, I have just one more piece, one I've been working on for a while," said Regi in a serious but casual tone. He then adopted the defiant stance of a hip-hop performer and began rapping.

No one sleeps.
We, kings of the heap,
Doctors of the street,
Succor of the weak,
Suckers of the week,
Fillers in the fleet.

Everyone clapped and Regi took a seat. "The next piece is from George, a guy I've known awhile. He's one of those shirt-and-tie financial guys, but it's rumored he comes from a really rich family in Europe, though you'd never guess it from his stuff," explained Nicholas.

Ericca's heart skipped a beat at the name *George* and at the sight of a man in a button-front shirt and pressed trousers. Ericca guessed he had come here directly from any one of the air-conditioned office towers around the park.

"I have the dubious pleasure of coming after Regi," said George. The audience chuckled. "His is a hard act to follow, but hopefully I can enliven my subject matter a bit for you this evening. What follows is what lurks in the back of my mind while I decide where to park other people's money. If you've ever had the job of parking other people's money, you'll understand why some distraction is helpful..."

He continued, "This may become a book or a collection of essays, but don't expect to see it in the Hip-Hop Top 40, though hopefully the ideas will strike a chord or two..."

> *All the King's Horses*...we all know this familiar line from Lewis Carroll's *Through the Looking Glass*. Of course, Lewis Carroll was not his real name; there are serious consequences to writing acerbic commentary even when cloaked as nursery

stories...but I digress.

This line reverberates with us today as a whimsical but pointed reference to the fragility of government. Humpty Dumpty chatters to Alice about his *cravat*, or sash, given to him as a *Happy Un-Birthday* present by the King and Queen.

There have been many gifts bestowed, sashes, titles, and tithes awarded in militaristic hierarchies, past and present. In ancient Rome, members of the proletariat advanced through cunning warfare, or perhaps plain cunning. It was possible to be the Bridge to Heaven incarnate by back-scratching and bureaucratic skill. With the array of not-so-inconsequential trinkets at stake, it is no wonder that so many Humpty Dumpties have ascended to power, past and present.

Unfortunately, hundreds of years of inspiration by acquisition has ingrained a monolith of trite and empty ideas: right of might and mass appeasement. Starting with the Hyksos takeover of Lower Egypt and their militarizing influence on the easy-going Egyptians, the trend continued with the slaughter of the tribes and their ruling elites in the New World, so effectively eliminating indigenous cultures that in this day and age, we cannot imagine anything different from what we know. Dissent has been long silenced, and a culture of suffocating sameness spreads like a weed.

CHAPTER TEN

George looked up and remarked, "Hopefully I haven't ruined a perfectly good nursery rhyme for you…"

The group applauded in approval. George smiled faintly in acknowledgement; the fading spring sunshine cast a warm glow on his pronounced cheekbones and illuminated the corners of his eyes.

Ericca looked significantly at Elle. Ericca could not precisely read her expression, but she was sure she was thinking, This must be George Sax, the writer of the future book *Green Basket, Blue Cup*. She turned to Nicholas and asked, 'What was his name again?"

Nicholas turned to her and answered, "Uh…his name is George Plant. Do you want to meet him?"

Ericca hid her disappointment. It was difficult to admit that yet another theory was disproved. Albert sensed her disappointment, and whispered, "Ahh…take heart…it is the most outlandishly profound ideas that are the most difficult to prove."

Nicholas looked up. "Excuse me?" he asked.

"Oh…nothing," she said squeamishly.

She was saved from further inquiry by the sudden appearance of policemen, who proceeded to cordon off the area. "We request that everyone here remain still. You are wanted for questioning."

"Questioning? And what is the justification?" asked George Plant.

The policeman produced a piece of paper and answered, "Suspicion of defacement of public property, especially an incident in the past few hours."

"And what incident is this? All of us were either at work or on our way from work," asserted George.

"Some wise guy thought to scratch an offensive phrase, *All the King's Horses,* on the Alice in Wonderland statue. Would you have any information about this crime?" replied the officer.

"No, I've been here this past half-hour, and everyone here can attest to that. Before that, I was in my office at Fibonacci Capital. I have many witnesses who will corroborate that," George answered. Ericca could sense Leonardo tingling with delight at the mention of his name. She hoped he knew better than to blurt out an explanation of his mathematical findings and their use in financial analysis.

The officer looked at George significantly and said, "All right, young man, I believe you. You may go…this time, but I must ask that the others stay for further questioning."

He proceeded to question Regi, who was packing a bag just as George left the glade. "Young man, do you have any knowledge of this incident?"

"Hey, man…I wish I could help you, but I've been at the recording studio all day. But if you need to talk to me some more, here's my card. Call me anytime," answered Regi. Then looking away and waving his hand, he said, "Sorry to be in such a rush, but my girlfriend is waiting for me."

The officer looked at the card and said, "Hey, I thought I recognized you. You're Doctor Gravity from Doctor Gravity and the Pharaohs. Hey…I've downloaded all your songs. Could I get you to sign a picture for me, for my kids?"

Regi pulled a pen from his bag and said jokingly, "I'm not signing my life away, am I?"

Just then, a slender girl with curly hair came up to him. She held a yapping dog; both pet and owner wore sun hats, matching shirts, and matching pendants. She asked Regi affectionately, "What's going on?"

The officer immediately recognized her as Tory Skye. He could not believe his luck, two celebrity sightings in the space of minutes. He fumbled in his pocket and produced another wallet-sized photo. "You know, Ms. Skye, my daughter just adores everything you do. Would you mind signing this for her? Thanks."

"Oh, of course," replied Tory. She put her dog down while she searched for a pen. The small dog, without a leash today, scurried around, sniffing the ground, stopping for several minutes near Elle and Matt. The officer had now resumed his questioning, focusing on Nicholas and Rebecca.

Ericca, waiting her turn, watched curiously as Tory and Regi embraced and chatted happily. She was distracted from her thoughts by a familiar voice. "Ericca, is Nick in trouble?" Ericca turned to see Daphne looking concerned and alarmed.

"Hi, Daphne, what brings you here? Oh, oh, Nick, I don't think he's in trouble. The police are just trying to find information about a graffiti incident," answered Ericca.

"Oh, thank goodness, I was afraid it was something related to Nick's — " said Daphne, who then paused without completing her thought. "Oh, oh, me...well, I had a conference in town and thought I'd steal a few minutes to see Nick."

"Oh, neat...a painting conference?" asked Ericca.

"Painting? No, no, it's a software conference related to my job, which is to write software," replied Daphne.

"Software?" replied Ericca, with surprise.

"Oh, didn't Nick tell you? I write software, you know computer code, that automates processes, actually the process of stripping the parts of chickens...you know, the nice, neat, perfectly sectioned chickens shrink-wrapped in grocery stores. Well, you need really smart algorithms to assess the individual weak points and joints of each chicken precisely."

Ericca suppressed a laugh of ridicule and disgust. Daphne actually seemed to take some pride in this. "Oh, that's really interesting...but for some reason I thought you were a painter?" replied Ericca.

"Oh, how funny...but come to think of it, that's what I put down in my Web profile. I wasn't about to put down *Designer of Poultry Dissection Processes*. I doubt I would have gotten any responses with that," said Daphne knowingly. She laughed and looked more relaxed.

Ericca smiled weakly in apparent understanding. The world of online personals got weirder the more she learned about it. The oddest thing was that people managed to find worthwhile things in each other despite all the deceptions and illusions. "Well, I thought you two broke up because you didn't want to marry him or something?" asked Ericca cautiously.

"Nick told you that?" answered Daphne with a big laugh. "That never happened. We just have trouble having a relationship because, well, we live three thousand miles apart." As Nick came toward them, Daphne added "That Nick…you have to be careful…he can be a real joker."

All this was too much for Ericca. She fought the conclusion that all her impressions of people were completely wrong. She thrashed about the contradictory personas of Tory Skye: snotty celebrity teenager and political radical.

Ericca was trying to figure this out, when she looked down to see a small dog with a curious pendant leaping at her. "Oh, Pluto, I don't think Tory would like it if I played with you," said Ericca.

She was right. At that moment, Tory scooped up the yapping dog with scarcely a glance at Ericca and strolled away with Regi.

Ericca looked up to see that the officer had left. Elle and Matt rushed toward her. "Ericca, we're in trouble. Matt can't find his Q-computer," said Elle worriedly.

"Oh, no, Matt…where did you last see it?" asked Ericca trying to use the tactic her mother used in these situations.

"I took it out of my back pocket when I sat down, and I was fiddling with it because I thought I might have broken it when I had that crash on my skates. Then the officer came and we spoke to him, and when I turned around, it was gone," explained Matt.

The three looked around and focused on the rapidly diminishing shapes of Tory, Regi, and Pluto. Ericca obeying her first instinct, said, "Tory."

Elle and Matt looked at each other for a moment, and then said, "Let's find out."

They sprinted after Tory, anxious to keep up with the stylish teenager, her dog, and her rapper companion. They did not notice the soft pad of footsteps behind them or the clink of metal bangles and beads on slender arms swinging in agitated hurry.

Rebecca, among the last of the Empire Poets Society to leave, now followed closely behind. But her intense gaze was directed not at the three kids in front of her, nor the celebrity teenager in the company of the rap-world scion. Instead, she murmured the name *Padma* as she trailed behind them, not removing her eyes from the small dog held securely in Tory's arms.

As the crowds in the park moved in front of her, she held her gaze unwaveringly on the increasingly more distant dog. She accelerated her stride and maneuvered her way through the opposing traffic without effort. Her breath continued its relaxed and even pace even as her stride quickened to an athletic and graceful sprint. And when Tory Skye and her companions turned a corner, Rebecca Poe knew where they were.

CHAPTER ELEVEN

THE GRAVITY BAR

Matt was on the verge of tears as they tore through the park. The Q-computer was where he kept the things he considered most important. He fought back the lump in his throat and an overwhelming sense of sadness and anger. The last thing he wanted was for Elle and Ericca to see him crying.

But he was upset. He thought of the things he stored in his Q-computer, including the characters he had just created, based on Scythian warriors. He had spent many hours imagining these characters and then creating their every expression on the computer. The Q-computer even had the beginnings of something so secret he had not told anyone.

What worried him most was the possibility that the Q-computer's authentication mechanism, which checked the iris of the user's eye, had been disabled. He knew the computer was damaged during his high-speed crash. He had heard a cracking sound in the fleeting moments after he lost his balance. Darn, he thought, the brittle fragility of today's materials.

Elle said reassuringly, "Don't worry, Matt, Dad designed these things to take a beating. Even if the thief tries to use it, they won't get past the authentication routine."

But Matt was deaf to reason. He wanted his Q-computer back right away. This sense of urgency made him stop suddenly and look angrily at Ericca, asking in frustration, "What are we doing? Why are we chasing after Tory?"

Ericca scrambled to find a good reason. "Well, as you said,

there is something suspicious going on at the Gravity Bar, and, you know, that guy she's with, that's Doctor Gravity. They are up to something, and I'm sure finding your Q-computer would just be something more for them to crow about."

Ericca panted after the twins, who were older and extremely athletic. She thought, All that skating does come in handy. "That makes sense, Ericca," replied Elle between short breaths.

"Look, they've crossed the street, and are heading toward Skye Tower," remarked Matt.

They stood at the entrance to the park, near the museum by the M-Gate, waiting for the light to turn. Ericca kept a steady eye on Tory's long, curly hair. They had stopped to browse in a shop window. To her irritation, she heard someone call her name, "Ericca, Ericca…"

Ericca turned to see Sheila Angvall's round, beaming face. "Why, hello, Mrs. Angvall…what a pleasant surprise," said Ericca with a polite smile.

"Yes, yes, I'm pleased to see you too. I'm leading a tour today. These people have come from all over the world and they are a truly fascinating bunch," replied Sheila enthusiastically.

"Oh, yes, and Sheila has been just wonderful. We came all the way from Louisiana and have traveled all over the world, but Sheila is definitely the most amusing and knowledgeable guide ever," chimed in a man wearing a plaid rain jacket. The plump woman wearing many shades of pink standing alongside him agreed heartily, saying, "We are members of the Dahlia Club and the Friends of the Arboretum Society in Baton Rouge, but we just love New York and Central Park."

This was too much for Ericca and the twins, who wanted to scowl in the face of such unequivocal warmth and good cheer. Inwardly, they were each guilty of nasty thoughts, which they successfully suppressed. Matt was still mad but managed a vague cheerful up-curling of his lip.

Elle, usually prodigiously diplomatic, smiled fleetingly with a quick "Welcome to New York…we hope you enjoy your stay."

Ericca waved happily to Mrs. Angvall, calling, "Great to see you, Mrs. Angvall," as they rushed across the street.

Tory and Regi disappeared into the lobby of Skye Tower. Elle looked around frantically and in frustration asked, "Well, what do we do now?"

Ericca thought for a moment and then suggested, "Well, I'm sure they are headed to the Gravity Bar. I think Regi has a nightclub act there. Let's go see."

Matt, still in a foul mood, said darkly, "Yeah...right...the bouncers are just going to let us in."

They looked at each other and agreed; they were a bit short, and they weren't dressed right at all. They were about to turn around and head home, when the loud brakes and heavy fumes of a large truck caught their attention. The truck had the name *Tepes Antiques* on the outside and was now pulling into the loading dock.

"Wait, I have an idea," said Ericca, scarcely waiting for Elle and Matt to follow as she dashed back into the lobby and opened the door in the back corner labeled *Loading Dock*.

The large truck had stopped at a loading bay adjacent to the freight elevator. Ericca whispered and gestured. In the dim light of the garage, they snuck into the freight elevator and cloaked themselves in the blankets protecting the sides of the elevator. "A piano for Eric MacPhail on level twenty-five," shouted one of the loading-dock attendants.

"Eric MacPhail, didn't he play for the Knicks at one point?" asked a burly voice.

"Yeah...I think that's him. He also played for the Celtics in Boston...or that is where he came from at least."

"Oh, these professional athletes...is it really so important to be able to drop a ball into a basket?" asked Albert from the backpack. Matt had told him the Knicks were a professional basketball team.

"I completely agree with you, Albert," replied Leonardo in an unusual display of camaraderie. "We may not be jocks, but we have something just as important to offer."

"This next one's for D. H. Rider on the forty-eighth floor. I can't tell what it is. Maybe a huge exercise bike," shouted the mover. "Oh, him...didn't he play for the Celtics too?" asked the loading-dock attendant as he helped move another heavy item.

"Nahh...I think Rider is one of those physicist eggheads who helped develop the bike they used for the Tour De France. He's an expert in something called *boron carbide*," came the reply.

Elle whispered, "How exciting. That must be the same D. H. Rider who developed the latest frictionless bearings for our speed skates."

Albert and Leonardo groaned. "Doesn't anyone care about anything other than sports around here?" asked Albert with exasperation.

"What was that term *egghead*? I'm sure it only applies to physicists, not mathematicians," remarked Leonardo with a huff. *Egghead* they knew instinctively was not a term of flattery.

"This small one's for the Petersons on the thirty-seventh floor and this one's for the Skye dock at the Gravity Bar on the thirty-second floor," yelled the loading-dock attendant. The freight elevator lurched under the weight of a massive object. Ericca, squished in the back with the twins, felt her stomach drop. They heard another yell: "OK, I think that's all that will fit in this trip." The elevator doors closed leaving them in tense darkness.

They all breathed a sigh of relief that quickly turned to tense silence. They could not imagine an elevator capable of hoisting such an enormous weight, and each silently listened for the first sign of a failed cable. The elevator lurched and began a wobbly ascent. The elevator opened at level twenty-five; they heard shuffles and grunts as the movers unloaded the piano. The elevator door closed again, and Ericca's mood was buoyed momentarily.

Panic overwhelmed her again, however, when Elle whispered, "We have to figure out a way of hiding ourselves." Matt nodded, and pointed at the object draped with a heavy moving blanket. They stepped onto the pallet supporting the object, tucking the blanket around them.

In the dark, they felt their way under a cold, metallic object. As their eyes adjusted, they could see that they were hiding under a sculpture. "This is a bronze sculpture," whispered Elle. "You can tell by the rich patina. Also," she continued, knocking softly, "...it's hollow, as most large bronze sculptures are."

Ericca looked around under the blanket and ran her hand along the smooth, cold surface. "I know what this is...This is the Alice in Wonderland sculpture from Central Park."

The twins gasped. Crawling out from their hiding place, they discovered that they had been stooped beneath a mushroom, cast in bronze. On top of the mushroom perched the figure of Alice herself. Ericca straightened out from her position curled at the Mad Hatter's boot. Now she ran her hand along the top of the mushroom, polished to a slippery smoothness by countless hands and bottoms, expecting to find telltale signs of defacement. To her surprise, there was no graffiti anywhere.

The next stop was the thirty-second floor. The elevator lurched to a stop; they silently huddled around the base of the sculpture as the pallet was lifted onto a forklift. Peeking from under the moving blanket, they could see they were in a storage room littered with paraphernalia of all kinds.

"Over there, near that loading elevator; we'll move it up to the sculpture garden on the seventy-seventh floor once Mr. Skye has had a chance to inspect it."

Ericca gasped. They would need to find another hiding place, and soon. Mr. Skye would not take too kindly to the sight of three meddlesome intruders in his private warehouse.

The sound of voices and steps diminished. They peeked into the room; the lights were out and there was nobody in sight. "Sssh...let's climb out and see if we can sneak into the Gravity Bar," said Ericca as she tiptoed out from underneath the mushroom.

They slunk around the dimly lit room. In one corner was stored a wide array of sound equipment and lights. "Wow, look, those are some awesome amplifiers and speakers. And look, there's the turntable I've been bugging Mom about," exclaimed Matt. Matt counted music among his hobbies and liked to experiment with hip-hop hooks using a specialized scratching turntable.

"That's all for Regi's show tonight," said Ericca. Next to the sound equipment stood some racks of clothing. Looking more closely, they realized the racks held costumes, pharaoh costumes with gold headdresses, blue and gold flails and crooks, wide gold collars, and long gold cloaks.

Alongside the rack of pharaoh costumes stood another rack of costumes. These consisted of white-and red-striped halter tops attached to sheer bodysuits and long white-and red-striped skirts.

The next rack held costumes with blue-and gold-striped halter tops, also attached to sheer bodysuits. Translucent blue and gold veils made up the flowing skirt.

"Oh, no, you'd better not be thinking what I think you're thinking," said Matt, looking at the pharaoh costume.

"Oh, don't worry. You'll have something to cover you up," said Elle as she removed a plastic bag from the hanger. She read the attached note:

> Pharaohs,
> It's important you be ready at least thirty minutes before showtime. Please have all your makeup on. The blue paint should be applied to all parts of the body that show. And don't forget the eyeliner. You guys are awesome.
> *Regi*

Matt groaned and asked in dismay, "You mean I'm going to be wearing makeup?"

Ericca nodded and replied, "Well, it's not so bad. Look at what we have to wear." Elle removed the plastic bag from the costume with red and white stripes. The note read:

> Calling all Vamps and Umpires,
> Spooking hour is at hand. Be sure you've
> used your antiperspirant today; these
> bodysuits show everything. And don't
> forget the silk slippers; makes twirling a
> lot easier. I love you. You're beautiful!
> *Skye Diva*

"Skye Diva? You have to be kidding...Tory now has a singing career?" scoffed Elle.

"And we're supposed to be her backup dancers? Well, I suppose we don't have a choice if we want half a chance of getting into the Gravity Bar," said Ericca.

A few moments later, they were dressed and made up in complete costume. "My gosh, you are the spit and image of King Tut!" exclaimed Elle to Matt.

"Yeah...like my emblems of power?" said Matt wryly as he wielded the crook and flail.

"Careful with that," said Ericca, stepping toward them in a white and red halter top that fit loosely about her chest.

"Hmm, we need to make some adjustments," said Elle. They noticed that all their costumes were a little long, and the tops noticeably baggy.

"Well, we can do something about the tops," said Elle, stuffing a nylon stocking under her bodysuit to round out the bosom.

"Well, that doesn't help the height issue," replied Matt.

Ericca agreed. They would not pass as members of Regi and Tory's dance group without a lift of sorts. "I know, let's use Spike," she said.

"Oh, no, no...we shouldn't do that," protested Albert. "With the three of you standing on Spike, someone is bound to stick a foot in my mouth."

Ericca thought snidely to herself, Albert, you always have a foot in your mouth but instead said, "Oh, don't worry, we'll turn Spike over...though you do bring up a good point about shoes...they need to be visible under Spike."

"Trust me...neither Albert nor I have any experience holding the shoes of juveniles using a levitating blanket to sneak into a bar," said Leonardo with a huff.

"Oh, fine, we'll just use tape," replied Ericca, determined for this to work. She found a roll of packing tape nearby, removed Spike from her backpack, laid Spike on the ground on top of the shoes that came with the costumes, and taped the shoes to the blanket.

"*Levitate Along*," she whispered. Adhesive tape, a wondrous thing, Ericca marveled. The blanket lifted itself several inches from the floor. Ericca and the twins stepped onto the blanket, adjusting their robes and skirts to fall to the floor, covering everything except the toes of their shoes.

The bouncer at the entrance to the Gravity Bar hardly blinked and said simply, "You're early, but you're welcome to hang out. There's a dressing room backstage where everyone meets about half an hour before the show. Mr. Skye likes it if you socialize with customers. Helps the atmosphere, you know." They nodded, not wanting to betray their adolescent voices, and glided through the doors.

Inside a few people were seated in cozy lounge areas, talking and sipping from cocktails. They spotted Tory standing at the bar, dog in hand, smiling up at Regi, who stood near her, holding a drink. Ericca spotted the handbag Tory had been carrying in the park and whispered to Matt, "We need to check inside her bag."

"Oh, like that is so simple...I'll just go up to her and say, 'Can I see if you dropped my Q-computer into your bag, by accident?'" replied Matt sarcastically.

"Well, maybe we'll have a chance later," suggested Ericca hopefully.

"Let's go sit down over there...so we don't look like sticks in the mud," said Elle. She glanced toward a dark, empty corner.

They glided toward the empty corner, behind the backs of two people seated and in conversation. A large statue of a Buddha blocked them from most of the room, and now seated, they had a chance to relax.

"This is kind of fun, to be in a bar," said Elle brightly. She was yet fifteen, soon to be sixteen, but many of her friends already knew of dance clubs.

"I suppose…" replied Ericca with hesitation. She really could not see why people considered nightclubs enjoyable.

They were quiet for a moment and feeling happy with themselves. The two people nearest them talked quietly, though Ericca found she could hear their conversation distinctly over the din and background music.

A man in a slate blue wool suit held up a glass and said, "Welcome, Vivian…and happy birthday."

"And to you, Daemon, and a very happy un-birthday to you!" said the woman seated across from him.

Daemon chuckled, "Funny you should say that…on this day of all days…but tell me, how are you, Vivian? How is the LOGOS Corporation doing?"

"Well, we've had our share of troubles. But we've had some success. I am really excited about a few new products coming down the pipeline."

"Really…tell me more," replied Daemon.

"Well, many of our labels are in the last stages of approval, but here and abroad we've had the usual round of pesky activists."

"But you've had some experience with dealing with those, haven't you?"

She smiled and said with hesitation, "Yes…or rather, my father did."

"Your father, Hammond, was a brilliant strategist. I've heard much about him," replied Daemon.

Vivian acknowledged the tribute with a cool smile and commented, "Without him, LOGOS Corporation would still be run by a bunch of West Coast hippies, good for creating their *ever-blooming sunflowers* and not much else."

"Yes, amazing the naiveté of a sheltered upbringing," remarked

Daemon reflectively.

"Well, Taliesin was brilliant, but you know brilliance and idealism can be dangerous, especially when combined with influential family connections."

She paused, looked away and continued. "Well…that is in the past."

"We would hope. Are you finding your own ways of dealing with this pesky activism?" asked Daemon.

"I am, and I'm also finding the right people to help." Vivian paused again, then changed the subject abruptly. "Daemon, everything here is just fabulous…the artwork, the restaurant, the bar, the spa — "

"Well, I've always believed in the civilizing influence of stately surroundings."

"Especially in this day and age, where we have no idea what unruliness the next day will bring. What you provide here, this wonderful, protective environment, is just wonderful."

"Thank you…I propose a toast to stability and perpetuity." Daemon smiled and raised a glass. They sipped their drinks, vaguely looking at each other, as though signaling a silent agreement.

They now turned toward the stage, where bright lights flickered and the speakers shuddered with a low bass riff. "That's little Tory?" asked Vivian.

Tory was on stage in a red candy-striped costume; her white halter top shrouded in sheer veils of red and white.

"That's Tory. She's making quite a name for herself," affirmed Daemon with pride.

"She's grown to be a beautiful young woman."

"She has…and an exceptionally talented and ambitious one as well," replied Daemon.

"Without the usual teen acting-out issues then?"

"Well, of course, there's always that…I hope you're not talking about Regi? No, I like Regi. I like better that Tory has a mind of her own," answered Daemon.

The mention of Tory and the preparations onstage signaled

Ericca to whisper to the twins, "We should get onstage…before we are noticed here."

The twins nodded in agreement. They wanted to hear more of Daemon's conversation, but sensing the situation, they summoned Spike to usher them toward the backstage area. Already the bar was filled with people, women in clingy dresses, men vaguely scented with cologne, all drinking at the dimly lit bar.

"Hey…if we go backstage, we might end up onstage…I'll look like a dork up there," whispered Matt nervously.

Elle and Ericca exchanged looks. Matt was right; he would be conspicuous onstage. He was not famous for his improvisational skills and definitely had no experience in hip-hop dancing. They imagined themselves onstage with the group of Tory's handpicked backup dancers with a sense of dread.

"Well, we really just want to check Tory's purse. Maybe we should try the coat-check area, or the dressing area backstage," suggested Elle.

Ericca and Matt considered this and nodded in agreement. "Let's wait until the show has started and the backstage area is pretty much deserted," suggested Ericca. They did not have long to wait; already Tory was onstage welcoming the audience. The hum of conversation lowered as all eyes turned toward the figure onstage, whose energy and youth created a magnetism that was irresistible.

"Ladies and gentlemen, in this, the fabulous creation of my father, Daemon Skye, please welcome this evening Doctor Gravity and the Pharaohs!"

A line of Pharaohs danced onstage with severely stylized and synchronized motion. Their sinewy muscles and lean frames tinted metallic blue exuded a raw energy. Their impassive faces projected an intense assimilation to the beat that mesmerized the audience.

All eyes were now diverted to the whirl of frenetic motion onstage. Ericca and the twins saw their chance and dodged into the backstage dressing area, which was now dimly lit and empty.

Ericca scanned the rows of hooks and cubicles filled with

purses, coats, and shoes. Everywhere were strewn stray socks, underwear, and makeup bags. At last Ericca spied a large green floral bag with a gold clasp and leather strap. A matching shirt hung alongside the bag in a neatly arranged cubicle. Quietly pointing, Ericca signaled to the twins. Somehow she was not at all surprised by the orderly state of Tory Skye's cubicle.

Elle quickly undid the clasp of the bag while Matt peered over her shoulder, certain he would spy his Q-computer among the contents of the bag. Elle warily fumbled in the purse, discovering surprisingly mundane and not-so-mundane things — breath lozenges, lip gloss, cellular phone accessories, a Tiffany jewelry box containing a strand of teardrop-shaped pearls.

Finally, failing to detect the cool, thin shape of the Q-computer, she looked up with a sigh and gestured her disappointment. Then, holding up a book, she looked excitedly at Ericca, who now guarded the door.

Ericca recognized the book right away; a papyrus flower and a blue lotus were featured on the cover, which read *Green Basket, Blue Cup*. A train of possibilities now raced through her mind. Perhaps Tory was a subscriber to the secret Q-aisle, perhaps Tory had reasons for discovering the identity of one *George Sax*, perhaps Daemon truly had nothing to do with any conspiracy to harm Quintana Castle.

They clustered over the book while Elle flipped the pages, scanning for notable excerpts. "Oh, look here, this is interesting," said Elle softly, pointing to the foreword.

> As we wrestle with issues of the day, we might look into the past for insight into our conflicts.

> The papyrus plant in ancient Egypt signified the Nile Delta, also known as Lower Egypt. The blue lotus signified the Nile Valley, or Upper Egypt. The ancient Egyptians celebrated the union of the two areas with the red and white crown of Horus.

However, the need for this symbolic union underscored deep political and philosophical divisions, divisiveness that is with us today as we grasp for the decisive power of technological superiority, all the while yearning for the subtle magic of diversity and understanding...

...Throughout history, conquest required not just annihilation of armies and individuals, but also the destruction of whole cities, of all vestiges of cultural differentiation, all claim to property, intellectual merit, and national identity — libraries burned, voices silenced, history erased. This is the direction in which we head with our focus on technological warfare.

Ericca did not pretend to be an expert in either ancient Egypt or political philosophy; neither did the twins. But since they were older than Ericca, they were in a position to comment. Elle noted wisely, "Mom is really into that Egyptian symbology stuff. It's true, though, the areas of Lower and Upper Egypt had distinct identities."

Not to be outdone, Matt chimed in, "Oh, yeah, there was constant political backstabbing even back then. It got pretty gory. I read somewhere Osiris was actually a pharaoh who was assassinated; the fourteen pieces of his dismembered body were sent as gifts to each of his priests. Afterward he became a martyr and was more influential in death than in life, though his son Horus was evidently hounded by Osiris' enemy, Seth. Seth, by the way, was very popular, a cult figure in Upper Egypt."

Oh, great, thought Ericca, here we are rummaging in Tory Skye's purse, practically under Tory's very nose, and all Matt can do is tell stories about bloody assassinations that may or may not have happened thousands of years ago. She peered more closely at the book and whispered to Elle, "Let's see what it says in back, about the author…"

There was no picture. Disappointed, they read further.

> George Sax draws inspiration from the events
> around him, both large and small. He extends
> his thanks to Maxine Weaver of the Metropolitan
> Tunnel Authority, and the Swan Maiden of
> Schwangau. *Green Basket, Blue Cup* is published
> posthumously.

Their eyes widened at the mention of Maxine Weaver. "We need to talk to Maxine now," said Ericca emphatically.

"Hold on; remember, this book has not even been published yet. She may not know anything about this book or any George Sax, not yet anyway," said Elle in reminder.

Matt, who stood on guard, motioned to them. The dancers were returning to the dressing room before the show finale. The lights came on. Ericca and the twins turned to face the mirrors, pretending to adjust their wigs. Looking at herself and the twins in the mirror, Ericca could not help noting how grown-up they looked. Hey, good job, she thought smugly. But the sight of her rounded bosom beneath the sheer skin-suit, dark-outlined eyes, and painted lips disturbed her. She looked away.

There was a noisy medley of voices and shoes as the dancers returned, sweaty and excited from their performance.

"Hah, I missed that last part, where we shake…hope Tory didn't notice…"

"Whatsa matter with you, girl? You can't be doing stuff like that. Remember, you have to dance with attitude."

"Hey, can I borrow your hairbrush?"

"Hey, whatcha doing with my hairbrush?"

There was the sound of a tussle and a sudden hush in the room, as all turned to see Tory Skye pop her face into the room. "OK, divas, let's go…show them what you got!"

Ericca and the twins were swept along as the group headed

onstage. "Oh, no, what do we do now?" whispered Matt.

"Improvise, make something up. Remember, it's all about attitude," replied Ericca, a trying her best not to crack under the pressure.

Thankfully, their time in the spotlight was short, as the dance troupe moved to the back to showcase Regi, who now stood front and center in a shimmering gold cape and gold pectoral, rapping to the hypnotic hip-hop beat.

Yeah, it's great to be
Kings of the heap,
Doctors of the street,
Suckers of the week,
Posse for a treat,
Fillers of the fleet.

As a finale, Tory Skye, in her white halter and shimmering veils raised her forearm to reveal her gold arm torque, the Tory Torus. With that motion, the gold scimitar in the Buddha statue in the far corner of the bar floated in midair into Regi's waiting grasp.

Regi twirled the scimitar like a flail, finally spinning himself while flinging the shimmering scimitar into the air and catching the curved blade with a dramatic sweep. The crowd was roused to thunderous applause.

"Oh, of course," smirked Matt, making exaggerated motions to mock the jerky movements of the hip-hop artist. "Doctor Gravity, wielder of the scythe...the Grim Reaper."

"...and harvester of souls..." added Ericca in a hush.

The applause diminished, and they moved with the crowd, now rapidly dispersing into the bar. Ericca, huddled with the twins pretending to be in a private conversation, was startled to hear a voice behind her.

"Miss, you were marvelous onstage. If we could talk a moment, I might have some modeling or other opportunities you'd be interested in."

CHAPTER ELEVEN

Ericca turned sharply around in surprise to see an amiable middle-aged man behind her looking at Elle. She whirled back around and turned away without a word as the crowd packed around them.

They were headed for the elevator lobby when out of the elevator emerged a woman marching angrily, flailing wildly, breaking away into the bar, despite the bouncers' efforts to obstruct her.

"Tory Skye stole my dog. Padmasambava sees all, past, present and future. You cannot hide him from me any longer," screamed the woman, dodging past security guards toward the booth near the stage where Tory now stood with Regi. Her lithe form, shiny long hair, and array of bangles and beads were familiar. The woman was Rebecca from the Empire Poets Society.

All eyes were now fixed on this spectacle. Security personnel scurried into the bar. Glad for the distraction, Ericca and the twins boarded the down elevator and were soon rid of their costumes, mingling anonymously with the street life of a pleasant Manhattan evening in springtime.

They boarded the subway just as Rebecca was escorted out of the Gravity Bar by Skye Tower security guards. They sat silently on the hard plastic seats, Matt scrubbing the blue metallic paint off his face, glad for the blank impassiveness of late-night subway riders who hardly noticed the odd trio.

As the subway snaked underground below the towering city, Ericca, too distraught for words, mulled over the thought *George Sax...published posthumously*. She knew the meaning of this. George Sax died before his book was published.

Now, as the events of the evening unfolded in her imagination, Daemon's private conversation reverberated in her mind: *pesky activism...brilliance and idealism...a sheltered upbringing...influential family connections*; and with that, the passage written by a man who would die before his voice was heard by the world: *throughout history, conquest required not just annihilation of armies and individuals, but also the destruction of whole cities, of all vestiges of cultural differentiation, all claim to property, intellectual merit, and national identity — libraries burned, voices silenced, history erased.* Suddenly the steel and plastic confines of the subway train no longer seemed safe. She clutched her blanket.

Ericca turned to Matt, who was lost in thoughts of his own. Matt had been as certain as Ericca that Tory had his Q-computer, pilfered as a practical joke, a malicious attempt to steal his inventions, and payback for his little trick in the museum a year ago. He even hoped it had fallen into her hands; the idea of a clumsy stranger prying apart, and eventually discarding the device filled him with agony. He was sorely disappointed they hadn't recovered it and dreaded the thought of explaining the loss to his dad.

Elle was the more upbeat of the two. Cautiously relieved, she repressed nervous giggles at the thought of Matt in his pharaoh costume trying to dance to hip hop. Darn, should have had a camera, she thought.

But a nagging question distracted her from her musings; she recognized the woman responsible for the scene as they were leaving. She knew the face, the voice, the beaded bracelet. Then she remembered. The turquoise and red amber copal beads were unmistakable; her mother, in fact, wore the same beaded bracelet once. The bracelet came from an antiques dealer, a man who traveled in Afghanistan, Kazakhstan, Tibet, and the Far East. She had a sudden flash of memory: The woman at the Gravity Bar was the antique dealer's daughter, a devotee of Eastern philosophy, a woman named Rebecca.

That night, the events of the day crept into their dreams amid fragments of fear and speculation.

In Matt's dreams, he was once again in the tall old growth forests of the Q-aisle, but this time he was dressed as a pharaoh with the throng of red candy-striped and blue pinstriped dancers twirling about for his pleasure. The sensation of sweating bodies so close to his, gyrating to the hypnotic beat under hot stage lights made him squirm in his sleep.

Elle's dreams were bewildering; Tory Skye browsed around a department-store jewelry case, nonchalantly dropping beaded bracelets and jewels into her large green bag. Elle yelled in vain, only to be taken away kicking and screaming.

Ericca's dream was perhaps the strangest of all. As she slept, a line of chickens, yellow and straggly, stripped of all their feathers, were skewered in an assembly line while being systematically dissected by an array of knives. In the middle of all this, she stood silently as though in a trance, wielding the remote control.

CHAPTER TWELVE

SYBILLE NIX LABEL

Ericca awoke refreshed the next morning to the sight of spring sunshine streaming through the trees. Floating on Spike, she crossed the room to the curved wooden seat strewn with cushions where her mother now sat, lounging in a silk kimono, cup of coffee in hand, reading the paper.

Sophia looked up in alarm as three heads, Albert, Leonardo, and Ericca loomed large in front of her. They exchanged glances in silent empathy, as four pairs of eyes now focused on the news of the day as reported in the *Tunnel Times*. The headline read:

Metropolitan Museum's Egypt Collection:
Victim of Bold Defacement

"Who would scratch such obscenities on such beautiful, irreplaceable artifacts?" asked Sophia between sips of coffee. She read further.

> Members of the Empire Poets Society are suspects in the Central Park defacement of the Alice in Wonderland sculpture, and also the incidents at the Met, reported Maxine Weaver of the MTA Committee on Defacement.

Sophia commented, "That couldn't be. Maxine is wrong. No one in the Empire Poets Society would do such a thing."

CHAPTER TWELVE

Albert and Leonardo chimed in, "Yes, philosophers love ideas and believe in the power of ideas to influence not in brutish methods like despoiling public works."

Sophia read further. Her eyes widened when she read:

> George Plant, Manhattan financial analyst and member of the Empire Poets Society asserts the complete innocence of himself and his fellow word-spinners in the society. "We are strong believers in the civilizing influence of public art and its power to inspire contemplation and community. We abhor these attacks, and we are fully cooperating with authorities to find the true culprit."

Ericca glanced briefly at the man in the small black and white photo, whom she recognized as George from the park. Albert and Leonardo wondered at the fashion of the day, which required that respectable men wear trimmed coifs. But Sophia lingered on the photo and the face she first saw more than ten years ago.

Their fleeting meeting at the newsstand, lodged in her memory, now awoke with the image of his striking features, blurred in the newsprint photo yet more vivid than ever. It had been a brief meeting, a moment of serendipity and silliness with the colors and fragrances of spring, compared to which everything else was gray and surreal. A snatch of a conversation months ago in a deserted sculpture court came to mind... *works of art like great books or lost love affairs...are like jewels turned over and over in private moments to expose new facets of delight each time.*

What a revelation, the picture, the quote, like an endless nest of boxes or a fractal pattern under repeated magnification, never ceasing to reveal a surprising intricacy of design, yet identifiable at first glance.

Sophia's thoughts were interrupted by a knock at the door. Of course, today was a big day. Quint was here with the twins. They were to attend a gala fashion show showcasing Sybille's latest pet project, her new line of fashion and accessories, under the name *Sybille Nix Label.*

Ericca scrambled to open the door. Matt and Elle, no worse for their late-night escapades, tumbled into the apartment much as they had since toddler days when every friend's apartment held the promise of new and fascinating toys.

"We'll need to head out now. You never know about freeway traffic. Also, it'll be nice to get a good parking spot, though the Cobra car will definitely have an advantage in squeezing into those compact parking spaces over those wide trucks they tend to favor in the suburbs," remarked Quint.

Soon they were outside on the street under the shade of trees. They passed a newsstand, where Quint stopped. "Well, today's a big day for Sybille, I think I'll get her some flowers," he said.

Looking at Quint buying sunflowers, Sophia thought of herself, of the meeting at this very newsstand over ten years ago, and the stranger she had never seen again. She thought of the picture in the newspaper. George Plant, she thought. Could it be?

Albert and Leonardo were chattering away as they strode to the parked Cobra car. "It really is amazing that for all the years since the invention of the combustion engine, we are still relying on this clunky contraption of spark plugs and pistons."

Matt said in defense, "This clunky contraption is actually a British muscle car with six cylinders. This car has raced in the Le Mans."

Albert knew better than to criticize the Cobra car too much, but he did want to make a point. "What I meant was there is so much strain today on limited natural resources, it behooves us to continually innovate and find a sustainable paradigm for transportation."

Ericca was familiar with Albert's ideas and actually found them tedious, but Matt found the topic fascinating and egged Albert on in his soliloquy. "Well, you know I demonstrated that mass and energy are interchangeable; an apple holds enough energy to power any one of today's vehicles." Sophia barely looked up at this remark. She was lost in her own thoughts.

With the familiar roar of the Cobra engine, they merged into street traffic, zipping through the tree-lined brownstone corridors toward the freeway. Soon they entered a large paved parking lot. Still wrapped in her private thoughts, Sophia looked up as Quint expertly wedged the Cobra car between the wide bumpers of two large vehicles.

Ericca and the twins scrambled out. Quint dropped his key chain into his trousers, dapper khakis today, and held the door for Sophia, bouquet in hand. Sophia felt herself pulled from her brooding thoughts. Regret and speculation gave way to a happy sense of anticipation.

Her happy mood was disrupted once more, however, by a very unpleasant sight. A large vehicle idled near a parked car slowly inching out of its very small parking spot, when suddenly out of nowhere, another vehicle pulled in from the other direction, filling the coveted parking spot just as it was vacated.

A woman with red curly hair, severely angry, stormed out of her large car just as the driver of the now parked vehicle walked away, black pumps clicking sharply against the hot asphalt, blue pinstriped shirt smoothed over with a nonchalant gesture. There was the shrill whine of raised voices, angry agitation vaguely veiled with politeness. Finally, the driver with the red hair returned to her idling vehicle in apparent defeat.

Ericca and the twins strode away, hoping the scene was over. Seeing adults behaving badly was not to their liking. They felt only kids had this prerogative.

They turned back, though, in time to see the driver of the idling vehicle, raised baseball bat in hand, threatening to smash the back window of the offending car. The woman in the blue pinstriped shirt returned to defend her car. There were angry voices, and then the sound of bodies thumping and seams ripping as Sophia and Quint rushed to restrain the two women.

Ericca and the twins looked in alarm at the spectacle of flailing limbs, discarded baseball bat, and disheveled hair, not knowing what to do but reluctant to interfere. "Well, those nails, they're really long," remarked Matt. Elle agreed, and Ericca tried to restrain a delicious mirth. Finally, Quint and Sophia stood up, smoothing their clothes, as department-store security guards arrived to escort the two women away.

"Well, let's hope fashion show audiences aren't all like that," remarked Quint as he straightened his tie and recovered the bouquet.

"You know, a pilfered parking spot is no trivial matter," replied Sophia.

"That's true," remarked Leonardo, "but if they hadn't been blinded by emotion, these ladies would have known that everyone's purposes are better served with behavior that is not directly competitive."

"How insightful," said Sophia. "But wasn't John Nash a little after your time?"

"Oh, we mathematicians always intuit orderly and optimal resolution; if there were proof of this intuition, so much unpleasantness could be avoided."

"Yes, that is very nice, guys, but you see there was only one parking space, a physical reality, so enough talk about optimization theorems. Besides, don't we all know from Kurt Godel, that nothing mathematical can be proved?" interrupted Albert.

Sophia nodded in pleasant agreement. They were near the entrance and were soon in the hallowed, air-conditioned halls of the store, surrounded by the mirror and glass counters of the cosmetics section. Perhaps tempers would be cooler here, she hoped, thinking with dismay of the ruffled hair and lined faces of the parking-spot combatants. Perhaps it was good that she had never had the big house in the suburbs with the flat lawn and large car.

The elevator opened to the top floor atrium café. Quint and Sophia stepped into the marble lobby to the smiling acknowledgement of the hostess, who was followed by Sybille, smiling broadly and waving raffle tickets.

"So delighted to see you," said Sybille, giving Quint a quick peck on the cheek, as he gave her the bouquet. "My goodness, what happened?" she asked noticing the faint red scratches on his face.

"You wouldn't believe it. Parking-lot altercation of the worst kind," replied Quint.

"Oh, sweetie, how awful," said Sybille as she kissed him consolingly. Ericca and the twins giggled nervously; public displays of affection still embarrassed them.

The hostess offered them glasses of champagne. Sophia gladly held the glistening cold glass to her lips and scanned the room. She recognized some faces from the baby shower of so many years past. More surprising was the flurry of faces that smiled back in recognition.

Hello, Sophia, how's the baby girl?
Not a baby any longer? Of course, she must be about twelve now?
Sophia, you look wonderful. Are you still working at the library?
Sophia, I love those earrings.
Fabulous dress...

Sophia smiled back. Despite the upsetting incident in the parking lot, she still believed in the affinity between women. She loved these events, events celebrating the pleasure of pretty things, conversation, clothes, shoes, hats, scents, bags, jewelry — a concept lost on the male gender which tended to comprehend gatherings for the purpose of sport and appetite, and not much else.

What a great bag, she thought, as she noticed a woman with a green bag with a gold clasp. What fabulous shoes, though they require pretty fastidious pedicures and perfect nails. That dress is the perfect shade of saffron, though on her it looks like a big unflattering tent. She immediately retracted that thought as she realized the woman was none other than Maxine Weaver.

Maxine was taking an unheard-of day off from her duties as the director of the Metropolitan Tunnel Authority. Beside her was her husband, Ray Bender, a small bird-like man who today had forsaken the typical low-key uniform of a respected Manhattan optometrist for a silk tunic in bright blue.

Sophia thought to take a seat next to her old friends, when she found herself accosted by Sybille, who, taking her arm, murmured, "Sophia, don't look that way. That's Constance Gordon, she'll recognize you." Sophia managed a quick glance and saw out of a corner of her eye the woman in the pinstriped suit. She was standing near Maxine now, chatting and smiling courteously as though the altercation had not happened at all; on the other side of the room stood the red-haired woman who had wielded the baseball bat.

"We need to keep those two separated," whispered Sybille, without hinting favoritism toward either.

Indeed, it would have been a shame to spoil the event with a disruptive catfight. Preparations for the show were in full swing, with designers, models, and celebrities mingling with the other guests. Hors d'oeuvre trays circulated, piled high with cheese, crackers, salmon spreads, and prosciutto speared with olives; not very inviting fare for Ericca and the twins at all.

Their eyes widened, however, at the sight of trays with chocolate-covered strawberries, and marzipan chess pieces fashioned in the shape of mounted archers. Matt's jaw nearly dropped; he was certain these interpretations of ancient nomadic warriors came from the secret collection on his Q-computer. His glance fell on Tory Skye chatting with a group of teenage girls in the latest spring fashions. Regi stood near her, and near them stood Daemon Skye, who was talking with a woman with severely painted arched eyebrows. He recognized her as Vivian from the Gravity Bar the night before.

He signaled to Ericca and Elle, who did not understand his

look of fury. But now they all perked up their ears, overhearing Sybille remark, "Oh, there's Daemon. How sweet of him to come, and he's brought Vivian Spiro with him. Have you met Vivian?"

Sophia shook her head.

"Well, Vivian is the heiress of the LOGOS Corporation, which was originally called the Spiro Company and was founded by her father Hammond Spiro. The Spiro Company was originally a pharmaceutical company, but now they're very much into the latest genetic technology. They helped develop the transgenic watermelon; you know, the seedless kind that is smaller and less sweet than the seeded variety. Sterile watermelons. Quint knows her pretty well," explained Sybille.

"Hammond Spiro…I've heard of that name," replied Sophia.

"Oh, most people have. His foundation has made contributions to a lot of public institutions, including the New York Public Library, but he was also very active in politics during his time, though rumor was his tactics were pretty heavy-handed."

Sybille looked away momentarily as the runway lights flickered and the room darkened. Evocative strains of chanting and drums silenced the hum of voices. Tree branches that joined to form the shape of a gothic arch were the backdrop for a parade of models in flowing floral dresses.

Over the hushed applause, a low voice announced, "Ladies and gentlemen, welcome to Empires of the Ages, the spring collection of Sybille Nix Label."

Matt groaned. Fashion shows were never his favorite, but now Elle mentioned, "You know that green bag that Tory seems to like so well? Look, it's in the show along with the matching green shirt."

Matt looked and wanted to laugh. Sure enough, the model slinking down the runway had slung over her shoulder a sage-green bag with a yellow bee motif, the very same bag they had rummaged through just the night before. The model wore a matching green shirt trimmed in satin, which was made more comical than alluring by the matching shirt on the small dog perched on her arm.

Matt wanted to scream. Not only was his mother following the laughable trend toward accessorizing pets, but she was apparently on good terms with Tory Skye. He wanted to shake some sense into her. He was sure there were more important things in the world than making look-alike costumes for pet and owner.

The announcer continued. "Sybille Nix, recognized as an emerging talent in the design world, is pleased to bring you the symbols of the ages updated for every day." Elle and Ericca sat in fascination. Here was a glimpse of a world beyond plastic dolls and fantasy princesses. Parading before them were icons of feminine power re-created in sophisticated and alluring ways.

"Sybille Nix Label is pleased to present age-old motifs — swirling vortexes, bees, lilies, cosmic orbs, the elegant geometries of nature — in exuberant frocks, sensible handbags, and flattering shoes, celebrating our rich pastoral history," exclaimed the announcer.

Matt sighed and made a face, while Elle whispered excitedly, "I love those colors and motifs. Mother was explaining how ubiquitous these motifs are, like corporate logos or religious icons."

Matt made another face, as if to say, Really, like dogs need to be decorated with motifs. He was increasingly peeved that no one seemed to understand what a sellout his mother was, hocking the folklore of nature symbols to entertain the obscenely rich and worse in apparent cahoots with his rival Tory Skye.

Elle and Ericca now admired an ensemble in dark-blue satin, with a flouncy tiered skirt and matching shirt, paired with blue satin sandals with criss-cross lacing, resembling ballet slippers, whimsically framing the delicate bare ankle.

Matt saw that the situation was hopeless. He was drowning in a sea of female fluff without a life preserver. He looked around the room hoping to find an item of interest, perhaps a weapon, computer, or vehicle of some sort, and turned again to see something curious, a parade of models in red and white candy-striped gowns, with the letter V embroidered on the bodices.

CHAPTER TWELVE

Elle pointed excitedly. They were the very nymphs from the Q-aisle, except now they carried themselves with calm and dignity, spreading their arms in graceful half-pirouettes that displayed their transparent veils in artful billows, fairy-tale ghosts floating down the runway. "My gosh...the vampires again," whispered Elle in astonishment.

"No I think it's the vegetarians and the victims," commented Matt wryly, alluding to their skinny forms and expressions of bland melancholy.

Elle and Ericca rolled their eyes as if to say, Matt you're hopeless. They knew better than to expect a boy to have any appreciation of the efforts here. They turned their attention to the runway just as the announcer commented, "...and to appreciate just how old these symbols really are, we bring you back to the ancient civilizations of Egypt, where five thousand years ago the bee was the logo for the Nile Delta, the fertile region of Lower Egypt, where Osiris, Horus, and the archer goddess Neith reigned."

Matt turned in amazement to see male models in pharaoh costumes: gold pectorals, gold cloaks over blue trousers and blue and saffron-striped shirts, cone-shaped hats in blue and white. They were followed by a retinue of women in dark wigs and pleated white linen dresses with gold sashes, holding blue lotus flowers, carrying green raffia bags. "...ancient Egypt, where the pleasures of life and the plenty of the earth were celebrated, the fragrant and intoxicating perfume of the lotus and the versatility of the papyrus used for food, paper, and medicine."

"In the mystical world of the Indo-Europeans, the lotus signified birth, rebirth, and transcendence — the padma incarnate." Chanting mantras to the twang of a sitar, a procession of models in bright silk robes, twirling multicolored ribbons and saffron-colored umbrellas, danced down the runway.

Following them two rows of men bore a palanquin. Their shin length trousers were hemmed with a repeating pattern of swastikas. On the palanquin, under a saffron silk turban in a red and gold robe, a model sat in a pile of silk lotus petals, gesturing with four arms. On the soles of her bare feet were painted the crossed lines of a swastika.

"Well, we all know you can never have enough hands," joked the announcer to chuckles from the audience. "The famous third eye of intuition also comes in handy, as well as the swastika symbol, a sun symbol among the Hindus."

Elle explained, "The third eye is the bindi, that red dot on the middle of her forehead." Noting the beads around the model, Elle pointed excitedly, whispering to Ericca, "Those beads, those are Rebecca's beads."

Ericca gave her a perplexed look. She was not one to notice details like this, though she was better than Matt. Elle then pointed to the short, balding man standing near Sybille and Sophia. "Vladimir Poe, the bead dealer," noted Elle. Ericca shrugged.

The announcer paused as the colorful procession exited and another astounding sight mesmerized the audience. "The fabulous golden sun, Ra among the Egyptians, Surya for the Hindus, Siddharta, Ahura Mazda, Mithradates, Zoroaster in the Near East, as important today as in ages past."

The next train of models strode in a double row, each holding golden propellers, wearing pointed caps covering their ears that reminded Ericca of ski hats. Their outfits, in alternating colors of red and orange, were decorated with tone-on-tone motifs of round vortices, rectangular swastikas, reindeer antlers, and paisley teardrops.

The models chanted and whirled while sprinkling the runway with flower petals. "...the dynamism and secret magic of nature evoked as fantasy in art, and now, in the everyday," commented the announcer.

This was almost too much for Matt, especially the sight of men wearing paisley. But his attention was captured, as down the runway came horses, flanked by models arrayed in black carrying spears. The models manipulated talking puppet heads like ventriloquists.

Matt did not know whether he wanted to laugh or scream in horror at the odd spectacle of pierced skulls capping bronze spears. The maidens with their unfortunate victims had pallid white faces; wide, bright-red lips; and silver chokers that looked like chains of teeth.

The armored horses wore cataphracts decorated with checkerboard, fleur-de-lys, and serpent motifs. The tunics on the mounted models were yellow and blue, with the bee motif in a diamond pattern, which reminded him of Tory's purse.

Following this martial procession was a train of winsome dancers, long light hair trailing as their heads turned slowly. They wore fluffy white wings reminiscent of swans, and their long white dresses were trimmed with fur.

Finally, the announcer exclaimed, "Sybille Nix Label is proud to present a timeless and elegant evening wear collection, inspired by the dynamism of red and the mystery of black, evoking the eternal complements: life and death, birth and reincarnation, time and space, ego and transcendence."

A checkerboard rug in black and red unrolled on the runway, followed by models, their chiseled cheekbones and defined jaws in expressions of solemn impassivity. Their gowns, some short and some long, were in variations of black and red, with contrasting sashes of red, black, and gold.

Finally, the last model proceeded down the runway. She wore a simple floor-length dress of black chiffon which flared in translucent clouds about a red sash. She lowered her eyes under a green straw hat as she walked on the arm of a man in a dark gray suit. Ericca was so absorbed she did not notice her mother's soft gasp. The man was George Plant from the Empire Poets Society.

There was loud applause, followed by another wave of claps and cheers as Sybille came down the aisle, grinning and looking relieved. "George Plantagenet, chairman of the board of *Hats & Sax*, is pleased to announce that Sybille Nix Label will now be available in all their New York stores."

Ericca looked at Elle in amazement as if to say, What? George *Plant*, from the Empire Poets Society, is actually George *Plantagenet*, the head of a department-store chain? She was about to blurt out this question when she saw a familiar figure in the crowd clustered around Sybille and Sophia. The small, fragile old woman wore a neatly pressed black suit and black pillbox hat. The woman was Quintana Castle.

Ericca and Elle meandered their way through the crowd of grown-ups. Ericca hoped George Plant would recognize her from the Empire Poets Society meetings in the park, but she now felt too shy to approach him.

In the crowd, they looked up from the blue slate shoes below them to see the cleanly coiffed head of none other than Daemon Skye. He stood with Vivian with their backs to them. He leaned into Vivian's ear and whispered, "I am frankly as surprised as you. We were very curious about this one George Plant. He may have developed quite a following, but this is a very surprising development."

Vivian replied in a whisper, "Well, maybe this is a fortuitous moment — an outspoken poet and influential heir in one."

Ericca looked in alarm at Elle and Matt, who had also overheard the conversation. Apparently everyone who had read the *Tunnel Times* today now knew that George Plant and George Plantagenet were the same person.

Daemon continued in a low voice, "Well, I can see how he might want to masquerade as George Plant; notoriety can be a bothersome...and dangerous thing." Vivian looked at him, noting the word *dangerous*, but said nothing.

Ericca and the twins wanted to hide in a corner far away from these insinuations. But all around was a press of bodies, some anxious to find an exit, others trying to congratulate Sybille, who still stood next to Sophia in the thick crowd. Stepping away from Daemon and Vivian, they found an opening from which they could see Sophia, who now stood close to George. Sophia looked into George's face, and they stood talking quietly.

The years since their meeting at the newsstand had been full of the typical things in the life of a busy Manhattan financial analyst.

CHAPTER TWELVE

He had his bachelor apartment, sparely decorated, a television, some favorite pieces of art, and an extensive collection of books. He generally avoided the glitzy events that involved his family and the family business, opting instead to mingle anonymously as George Plant with people he happened to find interesting.

Today's event, following so closely on the heels of his appearance in the papers, was a last-minute arrangement. The marketing directors of *Hats & Sax* coaxed him into representing the store, promising a more creative display than usual.

He was impressed, and found the subtle blending of earth themes with the business of fashion tasteful and clever. But more than that, the occasion proved to be a reunion in many ways. He recognized, of course, the faces of Manhattan celebrities and cognoscenti, Daemon Skye and Vivian Spiro among them. He recognized Tory Skye and Regi, mostly from tabloid covers and entertainment television.

But now, looking into the clear eyes and delicately parted lips of the woman before him, he was transported to another moment. He had thought often of that moment, knowing random meetings happen in big cities all the time, people who disappear as soon as they appear, moments never to be revisited.

But the reserved woman fumbling for correct change at a newsstand had made an impression on him. He often wondered whether there might be a way to contact her, an option he dismissed as he turned to the multiple distractions demanding his attention.

But now, of all unlikely things, she stood before him, her thin frame lacking the fecund quality he recalled, a frame that held a tantalizing combination of rounded and angular geometries, a face with the effervescence of youth and the pensiveness of age, a persona at once stately and silly. He marveled at the balance of shapes with an airy lack of redundancy, creating an exquisite line ending in the delicate ankle. She spoke to him.

We've met before Mr. Plantagenet.

Oh yes, I remember, at the newsstand, ten years ago.
Still fascinated by Fibonacci?
Yes, that, and street poetry as well.
Funny you should mention that...

They were in a sphere of their own now, the hum and clatter of voices and stage assistants in a separate realm. They barely looked up when the room became quiet as all eyes turned to stare at an unseemly spectacle: a fluffy Pomeranian wearing a green shirt and neck charm, struggling in the arms of Tory Skye, barking shrilly at the couple in the corner. Pluto was prone to fits of possessiveness.

Matt stared and commented, "Oh, it's that darn dog again. Doesn't Tory know that this is an adult event?" He then smiled snidely. So far the afternoon had been one long exercise in boredom and agony, except maybe during the display of ancient warriors.

Elle and Ericca chattered about the show, and everywhere were shrill voices of delight, praising the fashions and accessories. Matt wondered whether there was a baseball game on.

Finally, Elle turned to him and said, "Lighten up, Matt. Life isn't just about competition and conflict. Believe it or not, some of us are capable of cooperation and bonding."

"Yeah, right, unity under the universal cosmic roof of eternity," Matt replied mockingly. Elle made a face. He teased her, "You know, Elle, what they say...girls always grow up to be their mothers." He ducked as Elle turned to deliver a well-aimed blow.

Elle managed a searing retort despite the failed blow. She commented smartly, "You know, Matt, boys don't become men until they stop thinking of only baseball and warriors."

Matt would later receive another reprimand. Back at home, packing busily for a family vacation, he confronted his mother. "Mom," he said, "Tory was carrying one of your purses, and I think some of her phony charms were in your fashion show."

Sybille raised an eyebrow at the accusing tone but was inwardly impressed by her son's attention to detail. "Tory is a big fan of my bags. They are great bags, lightweight and casual, but stylish. And yes, we used some of her jewelry in our show."

Matt was not to be appeased. "Tory is an enemy; we shouldn't be friends with her." He stopped, knowing he would sound paranoid if he tried to explain his suspicions of Tory.

Sybille rolled her eyes; she had seen this kind of obstinacy many times before. "Well, it's like this: Your dad may have differences with Daemon Skye, but they still enjoy a good game of chess. Fashion, like chess, is something fun where we forget our differences…"

But Matt was on a mission. "Oh, yeah, and all that stuff about symbols, that is all just for fun…kind of a high-culture fun for rich people?"

Sybille turned again in surprise; her son's fearless criticism impressed her. "I think of it as a way of filling the void left by empty or corrupted symbols; think of arches. Now, when we think of *golden arches*, we think of fast-food and convenience, rather than older and more profound associations. But you are wrong. It will be for everyone. I've managed to get quantum replication to work."

With this remark Matt's eyes widened. Maybe his mother had found a crucial piece for his secret plan. But his mother had already turned to organize her packing. Soon she would be reminding him to brush his teeth and pack some reading material. The question of the whereabouts of the Q-computer would possibly come up, a question he was anxious to avoid. He went back to his room to fume in private.

CHAPTER THIRTEEN

THE PROLETARIAN PRINCE

The next day, Sophia Ludwig found herself singing to herself as she went through her day. She could find no definite reason for her good spirits; the news of the day was filled with the usual unhappy stories. Occasionally an encouraging story or provocative headline caught her eye: *Stave Off Aging With Rejuvenation of Mitochrondrial DNA*, *The Cradle of Civilization Unearthed in the Chaos of the Tunnel Wars*, *Rainforest Plants Offer Hope for Modern Disease*.

But all the news of the day was inconsequential as her mind returned constantly to the day before, a discreet gaze, a shy smile. He had asked for her name. He wanted to know where she worked. They said how pleasant it was to meet again and then turned away much as they had twelve years before. She had no idea whether she would ever see him again.

Sybille was encouraging, of course, having spent many years trying to find her a date. "He is very attractive, you know, considered one of the more eligible bachelors in Manhattan. Being a department-store heir definitely doesn't hurt. Constance Gordon, remember her from the parking lot…well, she has been pursuing him for years. Though her duplicity and pettiness would be enough to wither a titan or pave a jungle." Constance Gordon, a prosecuting attorney, with evident predatory instincts in parking lots and elsewhere. Sophia thought of her matter-of-fact demeanor and plain suits. Constance Gordon would be a sensible choice for any man.

But George Plantagenet was not just any man. "He has a grace and maturity that belies his years, yet he has a spark and authenticity that is refreshing," commented Sybille in encouragement. In her own state of wedded bliss, Sybille was always happy to offer her insights into modern love, weighing in on such eternal questions as:

Is he interested only in fun or is there any potential for commitment?
Do people always find the people they deserve?
Are all men freaks from Mars?

Sybille found the hidden dynamics of love as curious as the entanglement of invisible particles. In fact, she liked to draw parallels between random collisions on the quantum level and the world of haphazard liaisons. "I am certain overall there is a plan, rather like Einstein's quantitative description of relativity. There is an overall elegance and order, despite the seeming randomness." This she would say consolingly to female philosophy majors after a series of bad breakups.

Sophia chuckled to herself; any analyses of the vagaries of love or quantum physics were inconsequential in her new mood. Especially as, later that day, she recalled with a strange tingle his visit to the library. "Just wanted to get a book," he said innocently, approaching her as she stood at the counter. "Do you have anything about Robert Oppenheimer, the physicist who spearheaded the Manhattan Project?"

There were many books on that topic: Robert Oppenheimer mastermind of the atomic bomb project, later to be humiliated for his opposition to escalation of the arms race, dishonored by the very country he had given the decisive advantage of weapons superiority. Prometheus and Pandora.

"Not a surprising turn of events, actually. Civilization has always followed this pattern, like a wave advancing and retreating," commented George.

"But now we are amid an unstoppable wave…begun with Mr. Oppenheimer's determination and presumption," remarked

Sophia dryly.

"A wave, yes, but unstoppable…it's not really helpful to be so pessimistic," he replied.

She smiled wryly, logging the book into his transaction history. Hmm, such a long list of books, she thought, glancing at the list of previously checked-out books. He took the book and thanked her courteously. She watched him leave without further word. As he walked away, her stomach sank. Now she was certain he was not Branch; he was something more, something secret and elusive. She would have been surprised to know she would be seeing him again that very evening.

Ericca, Albert, and Leonardo would have been happy to witness the meeting of Sophia and George in the library. They might have smirked and giggled nervously at the tentative signs of attraction, but Albert would most certainly have ruined the atmosphere. He would have blurted out, at the first mention of Robert Oppenheimer, something like "Oh, of course, the famous Los Alamos physicist Mr. Oppenheimer, a driven, ambitious man who of course owes a small debt of gratitude to *moi* for his historic achievements."

Leonardo, a lover of peace and order, would be compelled to launch his own diatribe. "Humph, some achievement! To reduce warfare to its current state, the bloodless interaction of machines and a blind race for more efficient destruction."

Ericca, still in a state of awe from the fashion show, lounged around the apartment, thinking of swastika tattoos and saffron umbrellas. Feeling an urge for something sweet, she went to explore the pantry and refrigerator, and then suddenly noted the time.

This afternoon she was determined to speak with George Plant, to warn him about the insinuations she had overheard. She also mulled over another more extensive theory, but with recent history in mind, she was in no mood to share her conspiracy theories with anyone other than Matt and Elle.

But most important, though, she had to see George again because a small voice in her heart still held out the hope that George Plantagenet was actually Branch Archer.

It was nearly half-past four, the time the Empire Poets Society met in Central Park. She gathered some books, her subway token, and reluctantly stuffed Spike into the bottom of her backpack. Albert and Leonardo were now in a passionate argument that would have degenerated into a fistfight if they had been more than bodiless heads in a blanket.

"Of course, a remarkable benchmark achievement, if I do say so myself," said Albert, clearly miffed. "My insight into the explosive potential of matter saved countless lives on both sides; think of the unending carnage, regression in technological progress, and quality of life that might have ensued if the war had not been decisively ended."

"Even today our colleagues debate whether Oppenheimer's achievement was a boon or a curse...you know that, Albert. Mr. Oppenheimer himself opposed further development of the fusion bomb as being a genocidal weapon," argued Leonardo.

Ericca had only a vague idea what Leonardo and Albert were arguing about. She did know their strident voices were getting on her nerves. Also, this adversarial tone of voice was something she herself had been chastised for many times.

She recalled times fairly recently when she had one complaint or another for her mother: Why couldn't they live like other kids, with family vacations, roomy homes, household help, and video games? In these outbursts her mother seemed sad, as though silently granting the validity of the complaint. But even so, she would firmly request a rewording of the complaint. "You'll find, Ericca, that you're much more likely to get a positive response when you use a nonadversarial tone of voice."

As they headed toward the park, Ericca wanted to coax Albert and Leonardo from their harsh and embittered stances but was reluctant to be seen talking to herself or her backpack here among many strange eyes. Approaching the Literary Walk, she did notice one familiar person. Sitting on a park bench near the customary gathering place of the Empire Poets Society was Nicholas Bard's friend, Daphne.

Daphne sat there reading a book, her dark hair nearly hiding her round tortoiseshell glasses. She wore a boxy blue raincoat with numerous velcro and zipper closures that reminded Ericca of a ski parka. Oh course, thought Ericca, she's not a New Yorker; she's from a place called Seattle. Daphne was not the type of girl you'd expect to be wearing hip-huggers, midriff-length tee-shirts, personalized body art, or tailored raincoats.

Daphne looked up and waved hello. Though it was half-past four already, there were no other people there from the Empire Poets Society.

"Why, hello, Ericca…how pleasant to see you," said Daphne in greeting.

"Hi, Daphne, have you seen the others?"

"No, I was just wondering about that myself. Nicholas said he would meet me here. I wanted to see him, as today is my last day in New York."

"Really…why?" replied Ericca.

"I'm going back to Seattle. My conference is over."

That sounded like "Nicholas and I are over." But Ericca merely commented, "You're done learning about dissecting chickens?"

"Oh, that and more…there was some fascinating discussion about computer security and such," replied Daphne.

Ericca tried to look interested. She occasionally heard talk about the vulnerability of the Web, usually from the twins. "Well, you know, there are people called hackers who specialize in mimicking valid users and can do things like guessing passwords to break into secure computer systems," Matt would say.

Elle might add, "Potentially someone could hack into the central military systems and start a war or destroy an entire city just for fun."

"That does sound fascinating," replied Ericca flatly as Daphne pushed up her thick round glasses, which were slowly sliding down her nose.

"Oh, where is that Nick?" asked Daphne, anxiously glancing at her watch. "Well, that would be so characteristic of him."

"What do you mean?" asked Ericca.

"Well, I told you Nick is a real joker, and…he also has some health issues," replied Daphne with a sigh.

"And you like him anyway?" asked Ericca.

"Yes, I do, of all amazing things," said Daphne. "Even though he lied to me from the beginning, portraying himself as a Manhattan lawyer on the Web, and ever since has been kind of a flake."

"He lied on the Web?"

"Oh, yeah, a lot of people do. I have to admit I wasn't entirely forthright myself," answered Daphne, glancing down at her generous midsection and padded thighs. "But, you know, he's really sweet, a fine thinker, a great guy, a real original…"

Daphne and Ericca sat on the park bench for another hour before deciding it was hopeless. Nicholas Bard neither called nor showed up. George Plantagenet did not make an appearance either. Ericca got up to make the trip back to the apartment. Trying to hide her disappointment, she hugged Daphne and wished her a safe trip to Seattle.

Little did she know she would be seeing Daphne again the very next day.

Nicholas Bard surveyed his empty apartment, befuddled by the dusty, cluttered corners. He had stuffed in one pocket the poem he had just written and was headed out the door when the telephone rang. He was surprised because, as a single man living alone, with fairly solitary habits, he was not accustomed to phone calls in the middle of the day.

Over the phone he heard the crisp voice of George Plant.

"Nick, it's George Plant. I've been arrested on suspicion of defacement of public property, and also some more serious charges related to national security."

Nicholas gasped. "That sounds serious, George," he said.

"Well, I am a little worried. I'm in jail, something I've never before had the pleasure of experiencing. I actually have access to some pretty competent legal representation, but I suspect the people behind this have some good hired guns also," replied George over the phone.

"Anyway," he continued, "it'd help if you warned the others. I don't know what this is about, whether it's a crackdown on the Empire Poets Society, or free speech, an attempt to frame me, or all of the above. But it might make sense to start finding people to corroborate your whereabouts, pretty much to say you weren't anywhere near the Metropolitan Museum of Art."

"The Met? You mean you're suspected of carving offensive phrases on that famous Egyptian sarcophagus? What was it... *the blue lotus will rise above the muddied wasteland* or something like that?"

"Well, that's the main crime. I swear I didn't do it. But for some reason, the district attorney's office thinks it was me, that some of the things I've written indicate I oppose the government and sympathize with our enemies."

"That's pretty gruesome, man," sympathized Nicholas. "Hey... get yourself a good lawyer. I'll call the others."

Nicholas spent the remainder of the day contacting members of the Empire Poets Society. Only at the end of a long series of telephone conversations did he remember his date with Daphne, at which point she was already aboard a plane thousands of miles away.

Sophia Ludwig was anxious to close the library. She knew Ericca was waiting at home; with the twins on another faraway holiday, Ericca was bereft of real companions and spent the day alone in the apartment. Sophia was therefore unpleasantly surprised to see a group of poker-faced people in suits enter the library and approach her.

"Are you the head librarian?" they asked.

"Yes I am. Can I help you?" replied Sophia

CHAPTER THIRTEEN

"As a matter of fact, you can. We would like a printout showing the library usage of one George Plantagenet, books checked out, Web sites visited..."

"I'd like to help you, but you know the New York City library system has strict confidentiality policies," replied Sophia.

"We understand that, but we have a special subpoena for this case."

"And what is this case?" asked Sophia.

"Mr. Plantagenet is a suspected threat to national security. He has been arrested."

Sophia felt her stomach drop. All day she had thought of the serendipitous events of the past few days. They had met again. They were attracted to each other, or so she intuited. In all her happy thoughts, she was completely unprepared for this news. George Plant, actually George Plantagenet, was now sitting in a grim jail cell accused of horrible acts signifying betrayal of the worst kind. She tested herself by allowing herself to believe for a moment that all the accusations were true, that her long fascination with this strange man was delusional. She fought back a sense of heartbreak.

Sophia stared impassively at the subpoena before looking up and stating firmly, "The Midtown branch has a long tradition of honoring the privacy of library patrons. I have no wish to break this tradition under these circumstances."

"That is your choice, ma'am. But you'll find yourself in some unfavorable legal straits if you do not comply."

Sophia faced this threat with calm resolution. They would return shortly with a piece of paper and lead her away in a police car.

It was at that moment that Ericca returned to the apartment. She was now hungrier than ever and actually was hoping her mother was already home with dinner ready. But this evening was unusual. The apartment was exactly as she had left it, with pillows and books and toys exactly as they were more than an hour ago.

She explored the refrigerator; she drank the half-empty glass of milk and ate the remaining peaches. As the hours dragged on that evening, Ericca began to get anxious. The phone was silent, and there was no note of explanation. Ericca sat in the empty apartment getting more worried by the minute. The minutes turned to hours, and the orange light of late afternoon succumbed to the hazy darkness of evening. She was hungry again. Checking in the refrigerator, she scrounged and made a satisfactory meal from the leftovers she found in plastic containers.

"Lonely as the echo of a whisper in space..." said Albert wistfully.

Ericca looked at the melancholy face and asked, "What's the matter, Albert? You don't usually miss people, do you?"

"Of course I do. But I wasn't thinking about that. I was thinking about the cosmos, this vast dark milieu where our own monumental woes and worries have no consequence."

Ericca thought, I might have known. He has no clue what I'm feeling. He thinks it helps to know that we are just inconsequential specks in a vast universe. He has no idea I feel like crying.

But rather than cry, Ericca thought, I should go out to the library and see if Mom's still at work. Battling a paralyzing uneasiness, she once again packed her backpack, and was soon facing bright headlights and street signs. She navigated unwaveringly among the evening pedestrians, anxious to discourage interlopers and glad for the reassuring presence of Spike. As she rounded the corner onto Broadway, she ran right into a familiar face.

Miguel Lujan, another twelve-year-old and one of the best students at her school, was walking briskly along, bag of groceries in hand, when he collided with Ericca. In the unfortunate crunch, groceries were tossed on the sidewalk as the bag tore. "Oh, sorry, I didn't see you coming. Hey, aren't you Ericca?" he asked.

"Oh, yeah...Miguel, is it? I'm so sorry," said Ericca between breaths, scrambling to pick up scattered tomatoes and tortillas.

He calmly dismissed the apology. "Don't worry about it. I should've seen you," he said. They picked up the remaining grocery items, which Ericca volunteered to carry in her backpack.

"Sure, that would be great. I don't live very far," said Miguel.

Soon they were climbing down an alleyway stair to the entrance of a small basement apartment. Miguel opened the door to reveal in the dim light two people snoring on the couch in the cramped living room.

"They're my aunt and uncle from Mexico. They get up really early to turn on the sprinklers and tidy the washrooms in Central Park," explained Miguel. That didn't sound like very interesting work to Ericca. She was accustomed to people who helped launch companies or directed transportation systems or investigated particle physics.

"Hey, it's great, they might finally have health benefits and union representation," remarked Miguel, as though reading her mind. He moved to the refrigerator, which was already stuffed, and began reorganizing the contents to make room for the new things in Ericca's backpack.

"Well, my parents aren't home yet; they both work in some of the big restaurants, which open late," explained Miguel. Being on his own every night, going to bed without a comforting kiss and hug, or even the philosophical ramblings of talking heads, was routine for him.

"Well, my mom didn't come home tonight. I have no idea where she is. I was on my way to the library to find her when I ran into you," explained Ericca.

"Well, if you want, I can go with you to the library to check, if you like, or we might try looking up the missing persons files on the Web," suggested Miguel.

"Sure, let's try that," agreed Ericca. Soon they were milling about on Broadway, which was still busy. "There's an internet café and coffee store I like to go to down half a block. If you wait for someone who's already paid for time, you can usually talk them into letting you surf for free," commented Miguel.

Sure enough, as they entered the burgundy café, a group of teenage girls sat giggling, hunched over a computer screen. They giggled and joked among themselves as they browsed a Web site for online personals:

> ...lonely as the echo of a whisper in space...
> Sounds like a real winner...
> Giggle...you have got to be kiddin'...that's a pickup line?
> Oh, look at this one, Mirror Maid, Intrinsic Dialogue...
> That is so lame.
> Well, is this better?...Hot and Heavy in Brooklyn Heights?
> How about this?...Ceci n'est pas une pipe?
> Is that French?
> Yeah...I think it means would you like to smoke my pipe?

The teenagers cracked up. They were about to leave when they saw Miguel and Ericca. They giggled, remarking to each other, "Gosh, they're so cute...sure you can surf using our login."

To Ericca's surprise, the headline on a Web site dedicated to local news read:

SAX HEIR ARRESTED

This afternoon, George Plantagenet, chairman of the board of *Hats & Sax*, was arrested on charges of defacement of public property relating to the graffiti on important ancient Egyptian pieces in the Metropolitan Museum of Art, and notable public art in Central Park, including the Alice in Wonderland sculpture and the Memorial Monument. Mr. Plantagenet denies all charges and is in police custody. Morgana Sharp, the attorney representing Mr. Plantagenet, asserts her client's innocence. "Without naming names, we believe there are forces at work anxious to implicate Mr. Plantagenet," said Ms. Sharp. When asked for comment, Constance Gordon, the prosecuting attorney, reported, "Mr. Plantagenet's fall from grace is as surprising as it is tragic, but we have mounting evidence of his hostility toward the public and our governmental institutions."

In a related incident, Sophia Ludwig, head librarian of the Midtown branch of the New York City Public Library, was arrested late this afternoon for her refusal to reveal records material to the case.

Ericca read the article over and over in disbelief and dismay. Her mother was arrested. Ericca had never known anyone who was arrested before. The article didn't say how long they were keeping her. The article didn't even explain why they arrested her. Her mother had not hurt anyone. Then she thought of George Plantagenet, a man she was convinced would lead her to her father. He now sat in jail, accused of hostility toward the public, of being a danger to society.

Miguel looked at her sympathetically. It was bad having parents who had to work all the time and left you alone at night, but this, an arrest and imprisonment for an indefinite length of time was much worse.

Finally, Ericca turned away from the screen with a brave smile to Miguel. The article might not have helped her situation, but it did explain things. Her mother was alive and safe, but she would not be coming home for a while. Ericca now felt completely alone in the world. This realization would have brought her to despair, had it not been for the presence of Miguel. She did not want to seem self-pitying in front of someone who faced problems with such resourcefulness.

Ericca and Miguel headed back home. Ericca thanked him for showing her the internet café and apologized again for spilling his groceries. That night, Ericca contemplated the shadows in her room. Had it not been for the lulling motion of Spike, she would probably have sobbed quietly to herself all night.

The next morning, Ericca awoke to the sound of a knock on

the door. Still wearing her clothes from yesterday and bleary-eyed, she opened the door to see Nicholas Bard. He was unshaven and seemed preoccupied.

"Sorry to bother you, Ericca. Glad to see you're home," said Nicholas. "Your mother called me and asked me to check to see if you're all right, and also to tell you that…she's been arrested."

Ericca's spirits lifted as she looked into his familiar face. She felt less alone, despite Nicholas' less-than-polished presentation. "I know," replied Ericca.

"She asked me to look after you, but I said I couldn't…too many of my own problems at this time. But I did mention I might be able to get Daphne to help. I know Daphne left for Seattle, but your mom said that might work out. She said you have ways of traveling on your own. I called Daphne and she's expecting you," said Nicholas.

Ericca's eyes widened. She was to stay with Daphne in Seattle? "How long can I stay with her?" asked Ericca timidly.

"Daphne said you can stay with her as long as you like," answered Nicholas. "So, I take it you'll be all right?" Ericca nodded, and Nicholas gave her a reassuring pat on the head: "Give Daphne my regards."

Ericca closed the door behind her. Immediately, Albert and Leonardo began jabbering with anticipation.

"When do we go? It will be so exciting to have a change of pace. Seattle, isn't that the West Coast, where they have fish ladders and ferry boats?"

"Oh, and don't forget the outstanding coffee, worthy of an Italian!" crowed Leonardo, who was from Pisa.

"Well, you know the command," said Albert to Ericca. "We're ready whenever you are." Ericca uttered the command, "*Anomaly Amplify.*" She felt a familiar shrinking sensation, followed by the sensation of a swirling vortex, from which she emerged with Spike and backpack in hand in a hallway in front of a bright orange door. Ericca knocked.

"Ericca, what a pleasant surprise…Nick said you might be

coming," said Daphne as she opened the door.

Ericca looked around in amazement at the periwinkle-colored room, and the large window, which opened to a view of impossibly blue water glinting in the sunshine on this clear spring day.

"That's Puget Sound, and those white-capped mountains in the distance are the Olympics. Come take a seat. I'm working on a security issue for my clients now, but make yourself comfortable and help yourself to anything from the fridge," said Daphne amiably.

Daphne sat happily tapping at the keyboard looking intently at the glowing screen. Her apartment was clean and spare. Very cool, thought Ericca, noting the posters on the wall and mementos displayed artfully on the desk.

"What are you doing?" asked Ericca.

"Oh, just some computer stuff…"

"How'd you start doing that?" asked Ericca. It didn't seem so laughable after all. Daphne had a really cool apartment. Apparently Daphne did some pretty neat things.

"Well, while I was growing up, my mother worked at a start-up computer company in California called the LOGOS Company. LOGOS was an acronym for *Language of Gentle and Orderly Sensation.* Supposedly the company was developed by a hippie working from his garage in Menlo Park who wanted to create an ever-blooming sunflower for his wife," explained Daphne. "Well, the company was really successful, at least, until it was bought out. I grew up around some really cool technology-geek types. That's the long story, anyway."

Ericca thought of the fragment of conversation from the Gravity Bar…*left to his own devices, Taliesin Sax would just have used his inventions to create his ever-blooming sunflower.* "So, was the founder of the LOGOS Company someone named Taliesin?" asked Ericca out of the blue.

"Hmm, it's been a while. Yes, I think you're right, Taliesin Sax. How did you know that?" replied Daphne, looking up from the screen.

"Well, I heard from someone, actually the head of the LOGOS Corporation, I think her name is Vivian…anyway, I heard her talking about Taliesin."

"Well, the LOGOS Corporation was taken over in a rather hostile way, I am told. So this Vivian person probably represents the new company, which I think is into genetic research. Anyway, enough shop talk. Let's try to go somewhere fun for lunch, shall we? The Pike Place Market is just a few blocks away," suggested Daphne brightly.

They did have a fun lunch. They visited the Belltown P-Patch, where Ericca admired the tile mosaics. Radishes had already put out their green tops. Tulips and daffodils were in bloom. They walked to the Pike Place Market.

The crisp clear air, buzz of activity, and medley of sights and sounds were cheering. She surveyed the donor tiles on the floor of the fish market, but the engraved names brought too many unhappy thoughts of the Memorial Monument back home. She managed a smile anyway, because Daphne was fun and obviously trying to brighten her gloomy mood.

Looking back on those days in Seattle with Daphne, Ericca would feel a warm and wondrous glow.

The days passed. Finally, one rainy afternoon, two people were seen walking together along Park Avenue, careful of not touching the other, yet with an air of familiarity. They entered through the heavy double doors of the historic apartment building and disappeared into the elevator.

"Would you like to come in, maybe for some coffee or beer?" he asked, noting her weary, distracted expression.

"Sure that would be great," she replied.

The elevator stopped with a thud, and they walked down the hall. Inside his apartment, he took her coat at the entryway. They strolled around the sparely furnished apartment as he pointed out things of interest.

"Oh, this painting here is one of my favorites. It's called

The Sun by Yue Minjun, a living artist in China. Look at those expressions…what a crack-up."

Bright pink faces with exaggerated smiles squinted in profile in three rows of continuous clones, set against simple shapes suggesting a red sun and yellow sky. "Kind of a self-mockery and mockery of the Chinese state…It's amazing artists can get away with that over there."

Sophia recalled his reading list, the list she refused to publicize. *Dragon Ladies and Gorgons, Eastern Empire to Westernized Wasteland.*

"Well, this must be boring, all this talk about art…how about a beer?" asked George as he bent over to peer inside the refrigerator, which was nearly empty: a few bottles of beer, pop, a styrofoam container of leftovers, an orange. The sink had the dull sheen and vague smell of sinks that have not been used for days. Papers littered a desk where a computer monitor sat in a nest of wires and computer peripherals.

Sophia walked casually around the room. Standing by the desk, she caught a glimpse of a letter written in flowing calligraphy.

> No one sleeps
> Not the hollow patriarch in his sleepless night
> Nor the stuffed mandarin in dreamless sleep
> Nor the brittle sultan in his scorching nightmare
> Not the bishop in the maze of black
> Nor the sphinx in the matrix red
> Nor the fallen prophet in his net of twisted lies
> No one sleeps.
> — *Rebecca Poe*

Sophia found herself wondering about the poem and the poet, a woman named Rebecca. She moved to the counter in the kitchen and graciously accepted the glass of beer George offered. "Did you do it, then?" she asked as she took a sip.

George looked at her quizzically. There were many reasons to believe he was guilty. He had been in the Met just last month as part of a private charity event. The graffiti echoed his very words.

But he was innocent and he knew there were forces that worked in secret to drive policy in certain directions.

"No, I did not."

"I knew that."

"Hey, would you like some pretzels? Sorry for the state of the kitchen. I don't really cook much, though I do make crepes, having grown up in France..."

"No, I'm fine, I really should be going."

"No, no stay. You said you're fond of books; tell me who are your favorite authors?"

"Well, I'm very fond of self-help books, you know the ones with pink or violet covers like *How to Marry a Manhattan Millionaire*."

He laughed. Then remembering his family's history as artisans of fine hats for high society, he asked "Hey, how about a proletarian prince? I happen to know one intimately."

And thus Sophia Ludwig and George Plantagenet passed the afternoon following their release from prison.

Nicholas Bard still very much liked flirting online, and he checked his e-mail often. So he read the late-afternoon e-mail from George Plantagenet only minutes after it had been sent:

Nick,

I'm glad to report that I've been released. You'll probably hear about this on the evening news. In the middle of my lawyer's efforts to establish my innocence, a woman by the name of Sheila Angvall confessed to all the incidents of defacement. She is now under police custody. I don't know this woman yet, but I intend to.

Long and short of it, I'm back at my apartment.

CHAPTER THIRTEEN

Drop me a note.

Later — *George*

That evening, Nicholas telephoned Daphne, who was in the middle of a game of chess with Ericca. Ericca returned to her apartment that night to find her mother home with her favorite dinner on the table. Granted, her mother did not cook that much. Dinner was Chinese takeout, steamed buns stuffed with duck, arugula, and plum sauce from Chinatown. Munching on her bun, her mother said half-jokingly, "Next time I'm not home, you can assume I am either dead or in jail." Ericca managed a wan smile and said nothing; the mere thought of a next time made her very quiet.

CHAPTER FOURTEEN

PLUTO

The next days were clouded by disappointment. Ericca was jubilant to have her mother back. The short separation made her appreciate her mother in a way she hadn't before. But an oppressive sadness engulfed her as she tried to accept an unsatisfactory answer that now stubbornly asserted itself.

At dinner after her mother's return, she finally found the courage to ask about George Plantagenet. Was there a link between George and her father? Was George an *avatar*?

Her mother was impressed that Ericca knew the word *avatar*. She was also impressed that Ericca had pursued the question of her father's existence to an astute if incorrect conclusion. "No, George is just what he seems, a charming and intelligent man, but not the host for your father's soul. George is completely his own person."

But now, her mother insisted on knowing how she came up with the question. Soon, Ericca found herself explaining how a keyword search came up with the book *Green Basket, Blue Cup*. Sophia laughed when she heard how they disguised themselves as pastry chefs to sneak into the Bull's Eye restaurant. She was, however, somewhat annoyed that Ericca and the twins had overheard her entire conversation with Daemon.

Sophia issued some very motherly admonitions: "I do not want you to stay out late again, especially not at the Gravity Bar or any other adult nightspot." Then, having a second thought and silently reproaching herself for her parenting shortcomings, she added,

CHAPTER FOURTEEN

"I'm so glad you find the library interesting. The Q-room is a wonderful place for children, and yes, the Q-aisle is restricted, but I'm sure you and the twins will find much to enlighten you there. As a matter of fact, I'll let you use my library card to access the Q-aisle, just so you don't have to keep asking Matt. That book you find so interesting may be back in circulation by now."

Ericca brightened momentarily at the thin card placed in her hand. "What is the Q-aisle anyway?" she asked.

"Well, you should know that by now," answered her mother. "It is the quiet corner of the Quintana Castle Query Room. You met Quintana at the fashion show, didn't you?" answered her mother. Ericca shook her head.

"Quintana Castle is the benefactor who donated money to the New York City Public Library to build a dedicated reading room for children. You said she was the librarian in the Q-aisle? Yes, well, she's a retired old woman with time on her hands, and she likes to volunteer there," explained Sophia.

This was information Ericca had already gleaned. "But wasn't she also at one time married to Taliesin Sax, the guy who founded the LOGOS computer company?"

"Hmm…I think you're right. That was a long time ago. Taliesin Sax died tragically, reportedly by his own hand."

"Did Quintana and Taliesin ever have children?" asked Ericca.

"That I certainly don't know. Those are things people usually don't share with their friendly neighborhood librarian. I would guess not, however. He died more than thirty years ago," replied Sophia.

"Isn't it strange that only some people have access to the Q-aisle and others don't?" asked Ericca, not wanting to recount her visit to the grand T-Gate or the forests outside the Q-aisle, but curious beyond the depth of the question.

"Not at all…Many libraries are exclusive: law libraries, medical and research libraries, for example. The Q-aisle happens to have a comprehensive compendium of published work of the past and the future, archive and prophecy in one. As you can imagine, it would not do to allow everyone access to such a collection."

"But why not? Who gets access and who does not?" probed Ericca, clutching the proffered library card tightly under the table.

"That is a question that I can't explain now, but I'm sure you will find a good reference there, maybe after doing a search on the term *Ringgold*," answered her mother with a significant look as she stood to clear the table.

Ericca muttered the term to herself, and later at school she visited the school library and searched on the term. She had been in a listless mood since the end of spring break. Though she completed her homework with ease as always, she felt her mind wandering and the days in class dragging like eternity. Today, her feelings of disappointment sharpened. The search yielded no results.

Miguel was in the library that day. He turned to sit at a different desk at the sight of her pointy-chinned pout. He himself was not very happy, and as Ericca looked his way, he glanced back with an expression of weariness.

Ericca thought about the tiny apartment he shared with his parents and aunt and uncle. She could not imagine how anyone got any sleep there with people coming and going at all hours of the evening. It was a remarkable feat that so many people fit into that cramped space without everyone tripping over each other constantly and tempers flaring. She could see why Miguel seemed to know all the spots around town to stay warm and entertained at all hours, day or night. She gathered her things and walked to where he sat.

"Hi, Miguel, what are you doing?" she asked.

"Oh, just looking up some stuff for science...how about you?"

Ericca hesitated. Then, to her surprise, she found herself spilling the entire story of her search and its disappointing conclusion. Her thoughts, so long the province of her own solitary, fantastic mind, burst out with a fluency that surprised her.

CHAPTER FOURTEEN

Miguel listened sympathetically, without ridicule, even as she explained her theory. The Egyptians believed in the eternity of the soul and the importance of an intact body. There was something to that beyond mythology she was sure. She paused briefly to catch her breath.

"You know, I've heard of that, must have been something I learned on a field trip to the Met or something. Yeah, the Egyptians believed in nine aspects of self preserved in eternity: the ba, or soul, which resides in the ka, or persona; the ankhu, the transfigured self, spirit or intellect; the shadow; and the secret name," commented Miguel sagely. He was not one of those types of boys to fidget in boredom during docent tours.

"Wait, that's only five," replied Ericca with a grin.

"Yeah, I know. I forgot the other four," Miguel answered sheepishly. He listened to rest of her theory with a straight face, as though he believed every word.

Finally, Ericca remarked, "Now I'm supposed to find out what *Ringgold* means, and I'm coming up with blanks."

"Well, think about it. It's a composite word, made up of *ring* and *old*, or *ring* and *gold*," suggested Miguel. "Now think: where are these words associated?"

Ericca racked her mind. "Of course, trees, where rings signify the age of the tree. The more rings, the older the tree. Or gold rings, like wedding rings, signifying a promise." She felt herself turning pink.

"Well, that should be the answer. Maybe *Ringgolds* are associated with old trees, promises…or wishes. Maybe only *Ringgolds* have access to the Q-aisle, or whatever that hidden corner of the library is," answered Miguel matter-of-factly.

"Does that mean I'm a *Ringgold*?" asked Ericca incredulously. She did not think of herself as being old. She did not think of herself as a tree.

"Well, maybe you're descended from *Ringgolds*. Who you're born to decides a lot of things, you know," replied Miguel with a worldly air.

Ericca swallowed a hasty reply and looked away uneasily. She did not like to think of herself as an elitist. She thought of Miguel's situation; his parents were immigrants. He certainly had no claim to a tradition of high birth, as did the many other kids in Manhattan who claimed membership in the dynasties of political families and department-store chains from the moment of conception. She changed the subject. "So, how's your family doing?" she asked.

"Well, my aunt and uncle are probably going to be deported. Their work visas have expired and they can't get them renewed," he explained.

"Well, don't you have people who can help, maybe your parents?"

"Well, my parents can stay here mostly because their employers have sponsored them," replied Miguel.

"Oh…what do your parents do?" asked Ericca.

"Well, my dad works as a pastry chef at the Bull's Eye restaurant. He specializes in spun-sugar decorations."

Ericca wanted to laugh. For some reason, she was constantly amazed at what people did for a living. She pictured amber threads of sugar hardened into the shapes of swans, turtledoves, or puppy dogs under the careful direction of a conscientious chef. At this comic thought, she felt her mood lifting. She spent the rest of the afternoon wondering what fantastic things could be created with spun sugar.

Later, she would have reason to not only laugh, but smile as well. Her thirteenth birthday was celebrated at school, with kind remarks from her teacher and handmade cards from her classmates. But later, as Ericca walked up the stairs to her apartment with the twins, Miguel came bounding down the street, pastry box in hand. "Ericca, Ericca, wait up," he called.

Miguel offered her the pastry box with a small smile, "I wanted you to see this. My dad made it for you." Ericca opened the silver box to find inside a small cake decorated with the delicate figurine of a girl drawing a bow. The amber threads of spun sugar were translucent like glass. "Well, you said your father's name was Branch Archer. So I thought this would help when you think of him," replied Miguel.

Elle and Matt looked on admiringly. The figurine was exquisite. They also knew Miguel. He was in the papers as one of the winners in the Young Scientist contest sponsored by the LOGOS Corporation, a contest Matt had entered as well. Ericca looked up with a broad smile, an expression she hadn't worn in weeks. She wanted to say something, but as she searched for words, a barking sound came from Miguel's backpack.

Ericca was accustomed to noisy backpacks. She was afraid the voices inside her own backpack would sound an alarm. But before that happened, Miguel turned to remove a small, yappy dog from the bag, saying apologetically, "Sorry, but I've been told to take care of this dog until we find the owner." Ericca and the twins stared incredulously at the fluffy dog, a Pomeranian they recognized at once as Pluto.

"My dad found him in his bag after coming home this morning. I think the dog actually belongs to Tory Skye, and for some reason, he wanted to hitch a ride home with my dad the other night," explained Miguel. He evidently did not keep up very well with celebrity news. He could not even give the dog's name or breed. Ericca wondered what reason Pluto would have for running away.

It was only when they were all gathered in Ericca's apartment that the reasons for Pluto's running away became clear. Ericca invited Miguel and the twins to share the birthday cake. This would be the closest thing to a birthday party she would get, though she did not mind this fact.

Her friends sat around the small round kitchen table as Ericca rummaged through turquoise cabinets for plates and silverware. In the clatter of dishes and silverware, they heard a faint thump on the floor. Turning, they saw a small metallic object near the floor where Pluto now stood quietly. It was Matt's Q-computer.

Matt was overjoyed. He had managed to avoid the subject of

the Q-computer with his parents and had been on extremely good behavior since that day in Central Park when it disappeared. Now he jumped from his chair and picked up the device, just as Pluto started leaping and barking at him.

"Pluto, where did you find this?" he asked. The dog merely whimpered and looked blankly back. "Hmm...still works," said Matt as he pushed the button to activate the iris scan and then began testing the functions of the device. He was not prepared at all when at the command *"Matter Mirror,"* a figure immediately projected onto the turquoise walls.

Ericca, Elle, and Miguel watched in amazement as the form of a man with brown hair and tanned skin materialized before them. Ericca recognized the outline of the angular jaw and square shoulders immediately. He was her dad, Branch Archer.

Countless times before, Ericca had rehearsed in her mind what she might say if she ever met her dad in person. She would be sure to show him her favorite books and latest school projects. She even had a note she had written to him, detailing all the things they might consider doing — camping in the Redwoods of California or kayaking in Puget Sound near Seattle, where Daphne lived. But at this moment, all Ericca could do was stare.

Branch laughed, showing the wide, toothy smile she remembered from photos, his head tilted back angling a shock of hair from his face, eyes crinkled. "You didn't expect me to miss your birthday again, did you?" he asked. "Or miss the culinary delight of Mr. Lujan? I think not."

Not saying a word, Ericca leapt from her seat to be lifted up for the first time, in her father's arms.

"Well, I didn't plan on being an accessory to Tory Skye forever," explained Branch as they later crowded around the table. "But I had to wait for Matt to drop his Q-computer so I could appear as myself. You know how that goes, when your body is ripped apart and baked beyond recognition."

Ericca had heard this scenario before. Her mother had explained years ago that her father was killed in the explosion that destroyed his plane in midair. But now her speculations were confirmed. It had been true all along. Her father was alive all this time; his spirit survived the explosion and had been searching for a way to take physical form. Now he was back, not as himself, but as a hologram, a programmed representation so accurate only he himself could create it. If the Q-computer were destroyed or turned off, her father would again disappear.

"Amazing, wireless data transfer taken to new heights, telepathic synchronization. Send my kudos to your dad, Matt, or, better yet, let's go there later and I'll congratulate him myself. Worked like a charm, though I have to admit it took a singular strength of mind to keep the connection going. I just was sitting there in Tory's lap recreating myself, and lo and behold, here I am, back in my own body, or pretty close anyway," said Branch jubilantly.

He looked in admiration at his transfigured self. He certainly was all there: his carefree personality, acute intelligence, and laughing eyes. Ericca could not contain her jubilation.

There was a nagging thought, however. He was not real. He was the creation of a computer gadget, an illusion as beguiling as a dream and as ephemeral as a cloud. But as he sat there talking, it did not matter. Ericca fought back tears as she watched his every move, savoring every inflection of his voice, every mood that crossed his face.

Matt, who had been quiet, finally summoned the courage to voice a question that perplexed him. "Well, my dad will be thrilled to hear it worked so well. But, umm, how did you get around the authentication schemes?" he asked. Branch had been inhabiting the body of a dog until he was able to generate his human persona, a dog whose small brown eyes definitely did not match Matt's.

Branch hesitated, then laughed. "I see your parents haven't told you everything. Well, it so happens that part of the benefit of having an eternal soul and having lived a long time is that you pick up little relics along the way. Like this useful trinket, something you may recognize," he said.

He opened his hand with his fingers splayed like a starfish

to show a gold ring, embossed with a jeweled eye, an eye they all recognized as the *wadjet,* the Egyptian eye of Horus. "You know this as the protective eye of Horus, shown also on the Q-computer to represent its security feature. Well, I happen to know that protection works in many ways. I like to call this my *Every Eye,* a very handy thing if you have the mind for it."

They looked spellbound at the glittering green gem, so beautifully carved and deeply colored that it gave the entire room a surreal glow. "Yes, but what does it do? For the Egyptians, the eye was something from mythology, not part of their technology," asked Miguel after a long, awestruck silence.

Branch spoke as though he knew everything about Miguel. "Thought you might ask that, and that's good, distinguishing myth and magic from technology. I'd like to explain things in a way you can relate to, like quantum mechanics or string theory on the super-sub-microscopic level, but let's just say for now this unlikely trinket is a key, much like the ankh. Only instead of unlocking time, it unlocks intuition, passwords, and secrets, hidden or destroyed. Like for instance, we all have heard a lot about those unfortunate incidents of vandalism and graffiti around the city. It would be nice to know who, of the millions of people in New York, would do such a thing. The police recently arrested someone based on completely circumstantial evidence, with no witnesses at all to corroborate their accusation."

The mention of this event jogged a fragment of conversation from Miguel's mind. "Oh, but *there were witnesses,*" he said. "My aunt and uncle, who are in the parks every morning before dawn turning on the sprinklers and cleaning the fountains, said they saw a man with an unusual walking stick around the Alice in Wonderland sculpture just before the graffiti was discovered. He was the only one there in the park at that hour."

Ericca whirled around to look right at Miguel. She had recently heard the startling news: her friend Sheila Angvall had confessed to all the crimes and was now under house arrest. She had not believed the story at all. Sheila loved the parks and was incapable of violating the law.

Miguel continued, suddenly finding credulity in the story he had earlier dismissed. "Yeah, they said they thought they saw the man point his walking stick at the sculpture, and then with a bright flash of light, the sculpture was gone. Seconds later, with another bright flash of light, the sculpture reappeared. I told them they were nuts; maybe just the streetlights playing tricks on their eyes."

Matt interjected, "No, I have reason to believe they saw what they saw." He did not want to explain the details to Miguel, who hitherto knew nothing about levitating blankets, flying cars, life-like holograms, or matter-transforming arm torques.

Ericca did not want to explain details either. She was distraught with a horrible realization. "Sheila Angvall will be convicted and imprisoned for something she did not do. We have to do something about that," she declared.

They all looked at her blankly. "We have to go see her. Let's go now. I know where she lives," she exhorted, standing up from the table and grabbing her jacket and backpack. "Dad, are you coming?" she asked, turning to Branch. It felt strange and wonderful to utter that word, *Dad*.

"Absolutely, I'd love to meet the famous Sheila Angvall," he said. "But someone else should hold Pluto's leash. I think my presence is confusing that poor dog." Elle volunteered for that task, and soon they were out walking toward the subway station, with Albert muttering quietly in the backpack, "Quantum mechanics and string theory…they should have asked me."

George Plantagenet sat in his apartment, glad to be home, glad to be sending e-mails notifying everyone of his release from jail. He was not happy with the apparent conclusion to this ugly episode, however. He had never met Sheila Angvall, but sources depicted her as an upstanding citizen, a nurse, a plant enthusiast, and a leading expert on the horticulture of Central Park. The charge against her was based on the thinnest of grounds: She was often seen watching the Empire Poets Society's meetings in the park, and she was the mother of a slain soldier.

Constance Gordon, the prosecuting attorney on the case depicted the alleged perpetrator as a woman embittered by the death of her twenty-year old son some thirty years ago. "She has a deep cynicism and resentment, and scrawled the words of George Plantagenet, *of the Puppet King and his Proletarian Armies*, on the Memorial Monument. This was her way of expressing anger against the government for the loss of her son," asserted Constance on television to explain the resolution of the case.

George winced at the use of his own words taken radically out of context. There were many puppet kings in history, emperors and figurehead statesmen pushed to horrible acts of warfare and civilian repression by cabinets, ministers, priests, and generals. There were many proletarian armies, generations of young men with pent-up energy dedicated to murderous agendas taught from infancy: the Japanese regime before the second World War, today's terrorists. What cruel use of his own eloquence, he thought, to frame an innocent woman and impugn his own allegiances.

There was a silver lining to Sheila Angvall's complete confession, however. The case was considered resolved. This quick resolution had allowed him and Sophia to go free, a turn of events that was a surprise and a tremendous relief to him. They had been treated like any other suspected hoodlum or thief pulled off the streets as a menace to society. They were handcuffed and assigned prison garb and cots. They would have been subjected to a battery of medical tests and interrogation if he had not objected strongly. He was glad they had not forced the issue.

Looking back, he thought of his childhood with an adoptive family in southern France. He was told early on that he was an orphan, adopted from the United States to live with a branch of the Plantagenet family. He knew his biological parents were from the United States, New York, he was told, to be specific. That was all he was told.

He would later learn that his adoptive family was none other than the Plantagenets of the highly successful international retail chain *Chapeau Vert*, later to become part of the even larger conglomerate *Hats & Sax*.

But growing up, he whiled away his early childhood amid the languid and relaxed family life of his adoptive French family. He was just another French country boy. He developed an abiding love for sunflowers, pétanque, clear skies, allées of trees, narrow stone streets, old stone houses with thick walls as buffers against searing heat, thundering wind, and bone-chilling winters.

It was only later, when management of the family business fell on his shoulders, that he moved to New York, to a world of sleepless, frenetic energy that at once thrilled and wearied him. The array of cultures and lifestyles and the endless inventiveness in matters of personal enjoyment were astonishing. The universal fixation on success and material acquisition, however, soon seemed shallow and tedious. He found that things tended to go better when he hid his position in the Plantagenet family, hence the alias George Plant, ordinary Manhattan financial analyst. He did without the usual trappings one would expect of a department-store scion. No designer-decorated apartment, private plane, or getaway cabin.

His gaze lingered on the rug below the mantel, something his last girlfriend had picked out about a year ago. He missed her now. They were still good friends. The rug had come from the Altai Mountains, the region at the conflux of Russia, Mongolia and China, an antique two thousand to three thousand years old. Her father had found it. What a strange combination, he thought, the Mao culture caricature above the mantel next to this relic from the time of Scythian nomads. He was sure most interior designers would never approve.

His eye dwelled on the intricate motifs of winged griffins, horse riders, and elk in faded vermilion, delighting in the child-like exuberance and simplicity. The *Pazyryk* carpet, the oldest known hand-knotted carpet, he thought. The ancient nomads of the Indo-European steppes existed at the same time as the Egyptians. They covered the ground in their tents with beautiful wool carpets.

They rode expertly with the wind on strong horses. They moved their dwellings with the seasons. They tended their herds and delighted in warfare. Women were accorded status comparable to men and were honored in death as they were revered in life. They made astonishing artifacts of solid gold: combs, buckles, torques, and jewelry of all kinds.

So long ago, yet the influence of these ancient people was still seen everywhere: a deep reverence for nature, tribal leadership through inheritance, ritualized death and rebirth. They were the first guerrilla fighters, before Genghis Khan, Mao, the Viet Cong, or today's terrorists — highly adapted to their environments, specialists in grassroots activism and small-scale warfare.

He thought of the essays he wrote, the ones that seemed to attract the wrong kind of attention, the kind of attention that landed him in the papers and in jail just days ago. He thought of his very own words, recited half in fun and half in earnest for what he thought was a nonjudgmental audience: *a culture of suffocating sameness...spreading like a weed.*

He understood how those words might be interpreted as sympathy for foreign adversaries and their indigenous cultures. There was an ounce of truth in that. There was a part of him that stood in abject revolt to the world that had given him everything on a silver platter. This was partly revolt, a need to define himself, but mostly he steadfastly believed in cultural preservation; he would be a good guerrilla fighter, one well-adapted to harsh environments and adept at intellectual improvisation.

He recalled a snowboard trip once, several years ago. He was in the Colorado Rockies on a frigid day where even temperatures during the day were well below freezing. There was a blizzard at the top of the mountain, and the lifts were practically closed. He was among the few people still on the mountain that day. He rode his snowboard deftly over the light snow, careful of minimizing sudden shifts in weight that would have landed him knee-deep in the accumulating drifts.

The trail was deserted and signs indicating the way down were covered in blinding snow. He panicked. Somehow he had gone off the trail and was now in a steep and rocky area that was impossible to navigate. The ski day ended and the gloomy clouds turned to night, a frigid night. He found shelter from the howling winds and accumulating snow in a tree branch. He did not know how he survived that night.

When they found him the next morning, he was nearly dead, barely breathing. His hands and feet were so severely frostbitten, the paramedics thought they would need to amputate. But that did not happen. To everyone's amazement, including his own, his feet and hands regenerated. The cells in his extremities, robbed of circulation, came back to life spontaneously. Thereafter, George knew he was far from ordinary, a finding he shared only with his tight-lipped physicians.

He always suspected he had some extraordinary physical strength, but never knew exactly why. Little things happened while he was growing up that perplexed him: a cut that healed almost instantly, an ability to see faraway things with stunning acuity, a tolerance for temperature extremes. Now he thought of the ancient Scythians and how they were adapted to their harsh environment. Perhaps part of the answer lay there.

This thought brought to mind a happier thought. This afternoon, in fact, just moments ago, a beautiful woman had sat across from him on this sofa. They contemplated the painting on the mantel. He told her how he loved going to art auctions, not necessarily to buy anything, mostly to contemplate things of originality.

He told her that he also liked opera, and put on some opera music as they talked, *Nessun Dorma* from Puccini's last and unfinished opera, *Turandot*.

George explained the story: "The Prince of Tartary, in the Eurasian steppes, anticipates his victory over the Ice Princess. He sings..."

Sophia knew the story. It was among her favorites. She completed his thought, "...this evening, icy princess...in your cold chambers, watch all the bright stars that tremble with love and with hope..."

"The Princess Turandot of Turan...called the Ice Princess for a heart that is cold...or a heart that has died?" he asked.

"For a heart that is unconquerable. She is, after all, a princess, the monarch of a vast territory stretching from the Caspian Sea to Asia. She cannot give her heart to just any prince who comes along. She also possesses magic, which she is loath to share with any man," replied Sophia solemnly.

"But she will relent in the end?" he asked, with a flirtatious look.

"Or she might discover his secret name and slay him at sunrise...Puccini never finished the opera," replied Sophia, looking right at him.

"But until then, the royal court bemoans their fate. *Nessun dorma*, no one sleeps until his secret name is discovered."

He at that moment touched the back of her neck with his fingertips; soft tendrils swept his hand as he gazed on her clear brow. Death, love, conquest hinged on knowledge: disclosure of the riddle of the Sphinx, betrayal of a secret name. He played with this thought as his fingertips grazed her neck. He mused, she would be the first and last to know him, his secret name, his elusive self.

Sophia spoke, disrupting the moment of amorphous silence. "But then at sunrise, the princess has a change of heart; the court is spared and she surrenders to her prince." She smiled whimsically as she got up and took her glass to the kitchen.

Sitting in his living room hours later thinking about her, George felt lonely. He wanted to see her again. But it was too late to call. Her young daughter was sure to be asleep already. He took the empty beer bottle to the kitchen, walked to his bedroom, and was soon sound asleep, a deep, pleasant sleep interrupted only by vague visions of grinning clones under a scorching sun.

Matt talked excitedly as they made their way to the subway.

Branch had seen the warrior characters stored on the Q-computer and complimented him on his work. "That's really awesome, Matt," said Branch, "I can't wait to play that game with you. When are you going to be ready?"

Matt looked around. Elle and Ericca were a few steps behind talking with Miguel. He wasn't sure he wanted to share his inventions yet, but he was glad Branch was so encouraging. "Well, my game is going to be called *Ultimate Warrior*. It'll be about building the best warrior possible using a bunch of weapons, strategies, and strengths — stuff from mythology, archaeology, and modern technology. Currently, my favorite character is called *Ultimate Axeman* who wields a collection of battleaxes that range from the Japanese *naginata* to the Swedish *halberd*. Pretty cool, huh?" replied Matt with a beaming grin.

"That's fantastic," replied Branch. "I could tell you some stories about incredible battles I've known, but it looks like your research work on your own is pretty intense."

"Well, I've had a little help," confided Matt. Sure, the Web was useful, but the amazing imagery and realism of detail was from a source not easily available to most. He had been to the Q-aisle a few more times with his dad's library card, and had found incredibly vivid and entrancing descriptions of ancient warfare.

"And most important, I think I've captured the spirit of different battle scenarios," said Matt, spurred by Branch's infectious enthusiasm, "...from the early hand-to-hand conflicts between nomadic horsemen before the advent of guns to modern-day tests of rival technologies, to the warfare of tomorrow, an apocalyptic fight fest using warrior clones, guerrilla terrorism, unmanned smart bombers, and biological weapons." Matt looked up at Branch with a wide grin.

Branch hesitated before replying flatly, "Sounds like a fun game. Good work."

They were almost at the address Ericca had for Sheila Angvall. They made a strange parade, a rather diminutive man in a checked cowboy shirt and cowboy boots, four children, and a small dog.

They rang the doorbell. They heard a man's voice over the intercom. He asked the reason for their visit. He was the security guard on watch. Sheila Angvall was under house arrest and was only allowed select visitors.

They looked at each other, trying to think of a good reason for their visit. Finally, Branch spoke into the intercom, "We are here from *Polis Games*. We have a contract with Mrs. Angvall for consulting services on our latest game involving horticultural monsters."

There was silence before the man's voice returned, "OK, come on up."

They were soon past the security guard posted outside the apartment door and in Sheila's living room, a small but charming room with dried mushrooms hanging from the ceiling and a wall mural depicting Central Park. Sheila smiled from her wheelchair. She took Ericca's hand. "Ericca, how lovely to see you. I'm sure I can be a valuable consultant on your game project," said she with a knowing look.

"Mrs. Angvall, what happened?" asked Ericca, noting her frail condition. It was just weeks ago that she had seen Mrs. Angvall on her walking tour.

"Oh, my dear, I have been better," she replied. "A broken hip. I fell a week or so ago, and now I have trouble supporting myself, old tired bones, you know," answered Sheila with a sigh.

They looked at her sympathetically. "But now, dears, tell me how I can help you?" she asked.

"We're here to help you. We happen to know that you're not guilty," said Ericca emphatically.

Sheila merely smiled and looked down at the array of dried flowers and half-filled papers in front of her. "Of course not, my dear, but neither was that young man from the Empire Poets Society, and certainly your poor mother, Ericca, did not deserve to be put in prison."

Ericca did not understand. Sheila Angvall was a willing scapegoat, sacrificing herself for two relative strangers.

"But you see, Mrs. Angvall, you don't have to do this to save George and Sophia. We know who really did it; we even have witnesses," argued Ericca.

"Witnesses who will shortly be deported, sent out of the country before the truth can be disclosed," answered Sheila, looking right at Miguel. "No, what I'm doing is for everyone's good. I know that for a fact." She turned back to her papers.

Ericca persisted. "And how would you know that?" she asked.

"I had a visit shortly after my accident. Someone prominent... and well-connected explained to me what was at stake here and how I could help," answered Sheila.

She trailed off; she looked tired. Ericca noticed under the pile of papers and dried plants that cluttered Mrs. Angvall's desk the familiar pattern of flowers in green and blue, the cover of the book *Green Basket, Blue Cup*.

Ericca's eyes widened. She now recalled Mrs. Angvall's words, *someone prominent and well-connected*. She knew immediately that this person was Daemon Skye. But as her gaze turned to everyone around the room, she grasped for a reason. Why would Daemon turn to Sheila Angvall to save George Plantagenet? She turned a quizzical gaze again to Mrs. Angvall, who sat placidly refusing to provide further details.

CHAPTER FIFTEEN

RAINBOW SPRINKLES

Mrs. Angvall avoided Ericca's look and moved her elbow so the pile of papers once again hid the book from view. She turned to Matt and Elle and smiled warmly. "I've entirely forgotten my manners. We haven't been introduced. You must be Elle and Matt. I've heard so much about you." She pressed their hands to hers when they came closer to her wheelchair.

Then she turned to Branch and said, "I don't think we've ever met, but I think I know you best. Ericca has talked about you constantly."

Branch was not at all fazed. He took her hand and said, "Likewise, Mrs. Angvall. The pleasure is all mine." She beamed back at him.

Then, turning to Miguel, she said, "We haven't met, but I think I recognize you from the newspaper."

Miguel shyly extended his slender hand. "Pleased to meet you, Mrs. Angvall. What you saw was probably something about the Young Scientist award. I won an award for a theory I had about travel at speeds exceeding light speed, riding manufactured waves of space-time."

"Goodness, that sounds very advanced," she replied, "But I happen to find that just fascinating. The unseen is the most astonishing and difficult to prove. I, in my long years of studying plants, have always sensed a subtle intelligence among them that is dismissed by science today. Sometimes I think I can even talk to plants." She gave him a mischievous smile.

CHAPTER FIFTEEN

Then, noticing the guard's presence, she looked up and said, "Absolutely, monster plants, that is a terrific idea for a computer game. Let's see, so you are looking for ideas for your game, creatures, I imagine. Well, you can create a creature, but you should also create an antidote, a reversing agent."

Matt who had been looking a little bored, suddenly took a keen interest in the conversation. He perked up and said, "Yes, so far I've only thought of conventional weapons, you know, stuff people recognize, but I thought it would be cool to have something totally off-the-wall."

"You are a clever boy. No, no one wants to play the same war game over and over. How about Morphing Monsters, and the antidotes will be called Rainbow Sprinkles," suggested Sheila enthusiastically. That name had immediate appeal for all the kids; they thought of multicolored toppings for cupcakes and ice cream cones.

Sheila raised her eyes to glance at the guard, who walked discreetly around the room. She adopted an exaggerated, playful tone, widened her eyes for emphasis and gestured with her hands.

"Let's start with a blue monster that we'll call Viridian Venom, a water snake that lurks in rice paddies and morphs into a variety of forms — a killer horde of mosquitoes, a grim reaper with a sharpened scythe. The antidote for this monster will, of course, be Blue Sprinkles, a powerful agent poisoning the water in which the snake dwells, causing it to wither and burn in a gray cloud."

Matt nodded enthusiastically. He could almost hear the terror of computer gamers when Viridian Venom was invoked. Sheila Angvall continued, "The next monster is called Orchid Osmosis, a tropical flower that releases toxic vapors from its pistils, vapor that penetrates the skin membrane, causing horrible, disfiguring and painful acne…"

Elle and Matt were teenagers. They knew what acne was and how horrendous and gruesome an affliction it could be.

Sheila continued, after a pause, "The antidote for Orchid Osmosis is something called White Sprinkles, which renders the bloom sterile and unattractive by blackening the colorful petals."

"The next monster is called Coriander Corrosion for the plant that grows in hot, humid jungles. While coriander seeds are used to wonderful effect in Indian cooking, Coriander Corrosion is a cruel distortion of its namesake, emitting a pungent smell that spreads for miles, accelerating the oxidation process in everything from living cells to metals. Bodies wither under the attack of free radicals; vegetation and all organic substances grow mold and fungi; pipes, artillery, and aircraft rust and deteriorate," continued Sheila.

"Thankfully, we have Green Sprinkles, the most potent plant-killing agent in hundred-fold the concentration available at your local hardware store. Strong stuff for tough situations," explained Sheila.

"Now, we can't forget about Ivy Pinks, a transgenic crossbreed between the invasive vine known as English ivy and the popular flowering perennial dianthus also known as pinks. This unassuming ground cover adopts a personality of its own when near any vertical structure, whether it be another plant, a tree trunk, a wall, a human leg, or an animal. Its climbing personality enables it to smother and choke its host in a matter of minutes. For this menace, we have Pink Sprinkles."

Sheila was evidently having as much fun as any game developer might in envisioning these wicked plants. "The final monster is called Saffron Suffocation. Like Coriander Corrosion, it is named for a valued herb, saffron, the priceless threads of seasoning derived from the stigma of the *crocus sativa* flower. When agitated, this monster gives off a cloud of fine orange dust, bypassing all known physiological or mechanical filters, disabling machinery, and fans, and suffocating all living things. The antidote for this monster is called Orange Sprinkles, as the color of saffron is a very seductive yellowish-orange."

Sheila smiled and asked, "What do you think?" The kids were awestruck; Pluto was pulling on his leash. Matt clapped enthusiastically. Branch, however, was silent and looked away into the distance.

"That's wonderful," said Matt, "Where do you get such great ideas? Far out!"

"Well, let's just say my research has a way of inspiring all sorts of ideas," said Sheila, trying to be modest and acting subdued suddenly. The discussion had evidently tired her. She coughed and rested her head on her hand. Then looking back up, she said, "I'm in the process of recording my memoirs, so these ideas are constantly occurring to me."

Ericca looked down at the stack of papers. She was glad Mrs. Angvall was taking the time to record all her expertise. She had a sobering intuition that time was one thing Mrs. Angvall did not have much of.

The security guard entered the room and looked distractedly at them. Soon he would motion for them to leave. "Don't worry, I'm a big girl. I know what I'm doing. Thanks for visiting. See you soon," said Sheila with a note of finality as the guard ushered them out.

They were once again on the sidewalk outside Mrs. Angvall's apartment. "Well, that wasn't very productive," remarked Ericca gloomily.

"I think it was," replied Matt. "Who would have guessed she would have so many awesome ideas. I wonder whether she's a gamer?"

Elle protested, "Is that all you can think about, gross things with no real purpose except suffering and destruction?"

Matt was annoyed at his twin, but that did not dampen his enthusiasm for this, his invention, which he knew would be the most popular computer game of all time. "Get a life, Elle. Remember, I put up with all that nonsense at the Gravity Bar. I even sat through one of Mom's fashion shows. I deserve some fun too, you know," he said.

Branch interjected, "Matt, I think you'll find that Sheila's monsters and antidotes don't live purely in the realm of illusion;

they are more real than we'd like." They were quiet, especially Miguel, who had not said one word since introducing himself.

As they started on their separate ways toward home, Ericca asked, "Dad, do you want to come home with me? Mom's not going to be home, but I'm sure I can fix you something." She felt this was a tad ridiculous, inviting a hologram for dinner, but then she thought, Well it really is him, his soul and personality anyway.

Branch looked at her a moment, then replied, "Sophia won't be home?" His face clouded over.

Ericca hesitated. She was not sure this was the moment to say it. But after a deep breath, she found the courage and said, "Mom is actually going out on a date tonight to the opera with George Plantagenet."

Branch had anticipated this; he had seen Sophia chatting with George at the fashion show. "Thanks for the offer, but I think I'll stay with Matt and Elle and visit Quint. I can't ask Matt to part with his Q-computer again," he replied cheerfully, careful to conceal his sadness.

As her friends left at their respective subway stops, Ericca reflected on the events of the day. She was happy. There was nothing but serendipity today, serendipity that brought her father back to her in the image that she loved.

But she still could not fathom why Daemon Skye would ask Sheila Angvall to shoulder the guilt for crimes she did not commit. Then she thought about the book she glimpsed on Sheila's desk. She felt the library card her mother lent her, still safe in her pocket.

There were still a few hours left in the day when Ericca entered the halls of the Midtown Public Library. Her mother was not working late today. She was getting ready for her date with George. Sybille had talked her into visiting a hairdresser and makeup artist for the occasion and had a recommendation for a wonderful manicurist.

Ericca made her way past the remaining library patrons in the

Reading Room, basking in an orange glow from the sunset sky. She entered the Quintana Castle Query Room and nonchalantly stepped into the painting that marked the entrance to the Q-aisle. After scampering hurriedly over the bridge, she was alone in the hushed quiet of the Q-aisle. There was no librarian today sitting at the desk in front of the fireplace.

She surveyed the neat collection of items on the desk: a few wooden boxes labeled with library codes, a statuette of the falcon-headed Egyptian god Horus. The miniature statue wore a headdress consisting of a red disk between two gold prongs. She tried to open the wooden boxes, but they were stubbornly closed.

Frustrated, she looked for a tool to pry the boxes open, but to no avail. Then a phrase entered her mind, *the eye on the Q-computer represents its security feature.* She looked closely at her mother's library card.

Next to the logo for the New York City Public Library system she noticed another logo, a logo absent from her own library card. The logo showed the outline of the eye of Horus, an eye that shimmered like water dancing in sunlight. She raised the card to study how light bounced and reflected off the mesmerizing eye. When the eye on the card aligned with the round red disk on the Horus statue, a light flashed in the empty hall and the jeweled eyes of the falcon statuette moved and glistened.

Ericca was startled. She didn't understand what happened until she moved the card down a fraction; the statuette of Horus was once again motionless. She now dropped the library card between the two gold prongs so the red disk aligned with the eye on the library card. Once again, the statuette's eyes came alive. The wooden boxes on the desk opened to reveal a card catalog of impossibly thin sheets of film, organized by library call numbers.

She remembered the call number from when they visited last. She summoned the film so it aligned with the red disk; the transaction history was now projected as swimming text before her eyes. Ericca's eyes widened as she read the card. *Green Basket, Blue Cup* was checked out to Daemon Skye, residing at 777 Skye

Tower. At last, her suspicions were confirmed. It was Daemon who had visited Sheila Angvall; Sheila got the book from him.

Ericca pondered all the possible reasons Daemon Skye could have for choosing Mrs. Angvall. She could not guess how Daemon would even know someone like Sheila Angvall. Then she remembered Sheila's words: *I'm in the process of recording my memoirs.* She had a flash of intuition. Sheila wrote a book that came to Daemon's attention in a visit to the Q-aisle. Ericca now tried to summon the book, trying out any conceivable title: *Edible Foliage in Central Park, Urban Horticulture for Fun and Food.* There were no relevant search results.

Frustrated, she decided to buckle down to the original purpose of her visit. She summoned all documents concerning *Ringgolds* and to her surprise, a multitude of documents appeared. The longest and most clearly written article was one from the *Underground Encyclopedia*; it read:

> Not much is known about Ringgolds. They existed in prehistory and scant trace of them remains; the lore surrounding Ringgolds is often considered mythology.
>
> Ringgolds are reputed to have lived tens of thousands of years ago, possibly before the last Ice Age. They were a humanoid species adapted to Ice Age climates. They understood the cycles of nature on many levels and the parallels between reproduction in plants, animals, and humans. This esoteric understanding resided in the earliest tribal rulers, usually three women who collectively oversaw reproduction, child rearing, and resource management.
>
> The Ringgold tribes developed and acquired further knowledge of the natural world aided by finely tuned intuition and patient observation of nature. They

became expert horseback riders and archers, fine metallurgists, and weavers. Like other nomadic tribes, they developed agriculture and transitioned from a nomadic to a settled existence. Settlements grew, and with that a need to defend territory; militarism evolved, and with that a shift from matriarchal cooperation to patriarchal rule of force.

This dramatic change affected all early nomadic tribes. But among the Ringgold tribes, the seat of power and knowledge remained as it always had. It was long understood that those who had a deep emotional stake in the perpetuation of the tribe would be the most far-sighted rulers. The deep attachment between mother and child represented an innate inclination toward rational and humanitarian leadership.

These early rulers understood the profound order of the natural world, the hidden dimensions of space and time, and promotion of strength and longevity. Because of their esoteric knowledge, Ringgolds took advisory roles in the governments of early civilizations.

Occasionally they donated their own Ringgold mitochondrial DNA in the form of a royal consort to a deserving Emperor to help ensure the longevity and prescience of the ruler's descendents and the stability of future governments. However, they never disclosed their most valuable secrets, time travel and eternal life, to the younger human species. This species the Ringgolds referred to among themselves as *Saplings*, a term related to the current scientific nomenclature *Homo sapien sapien*.

Saplings differed from Ringgolds in being relatively

short-lived and prone to sickness. Mortality and inherent weakness created emotional impairment of all kinds, and unfortunate propensities like lying, cheating, stealing, murder, and greed. These propensities led to constant conflict over resources and an endless stream of material waste and pollution. While condemning the constant violence and want among Saplings, the Ringgolds sympathized and sent two Ringgold emissaries to help alleviate suffering: Isis and Osiris, who then lived among the ancient Egyptians and helped optimize their systems of agriculture and belief.

Isis and Osiris promoted belief in the afterlife, the pleasures of community, and the mathematics of building, trade, and resource conservation. Isis and Osiris developed cult followings in Egypt, influencing other belief systems, including the cult of the Holy Sophia or Holy Wisdom among Eastern Europeans. The mythology of Sophia continued in this century, with some believing in the transcendent wisdom of an unassuming librarian.

As the Sapling population multiplied, the Ringgolds diminished because, despite their long life spans and stouter constitutions, they bred very infrequently. Also, there was a major migration of Ringgolds. Following the discovery of a black hole in the middle of the Milky Way Galaxy, ruling members of Ringgold society developed ways of stabilizing this cosmic feature to create a refuge of beauty and calm free from the ravages of gravity and time. A refuge equipped for disassembling and reassembling all life and matter. This refuge they called *Sagetooth*, and the system they devised to travel there was known as the *time tunnels*.

CHAPTER FIFTEEN

A few Ringgolds are known to still exist as of the writing of this article, among them D. H. Rider, Sybille Nix, Quint A. Senns, and Daemon Skye. Only a few Saplings are now known to exist, hidden in the few corners of the Earth left untouched at the conclusion of the protracted Tunnel Wars. The Tunnel Wars, known by various names in the Sapling world, incited the participation of many Ringgolds, who feared that Sapling skirmishes would result in the discovery and destruction of the time tunnels.

The Ringgolds that remain may well be on their way to Sagetooth, provided they are able to rebuild the time tunnels. It is reported that Daemon Skye continues, much as he always has, in a specially developed force field-shielded cocoon that houses his restaurant, spa, bar, and extensive art collection, an art collection he hopes to transport to the gardens of Sagetooth. Among the few other vestiges of civilization is a small wing of the Midtown Public Library in New York City, a room once called the Query Room, a children's reading room that houses a collection of archive and prophecy and a gateway to the time tunnels.

Ericca read the article multiple times before its meaning really sank in. Then she read the date on the article. The article was from twelve years in the future. Then she read the article again. Somehow this all made sense, as though she had known all this from the very beginning. There was only one part that shocked and surprised her...*only a few Saplings are now known to exist*. She read again the list of Ringgolds known to exist and then sighed with relief. *Among them*...she thought, that means the list is not necessarily complete.

Ericca read the final paragraphs over, trying to comprehend the horrible portent. The light from the falcon's eyes shifted, startling her. The figure of a woman approached her as she sat at the desk. She recognized the face and voice at once as belonging to her mother. The woman spoke:

> Ericca, by now you will have read an article explaining the differences between Ringgolds and Saplings. By now, you know that most of your speculations have been more right than wrong. You are probably wondering why I hadn't explained anything until now.
>
> I'd like to say the daily reality of working in a library meant I had insufficient time to educate you about what it means to be a Ringgold. The real reason, though, is that I wanted you to have your childhood as long as possible.
>
> Now, you may think a talking blanket is no substitute for a real family. That living with a working single mother is no childhood at all. But hopefully you'll agree that your adventures with Elle, Matt, Leonardo, and Albert have been everything childhood should be: challenging, surprising, and, not incidentally, preparation for what lies ahead.
>
> What lies ahead for a Ringgold child, I'll admit, involves a more serious responsibility than you might have imagined or wanted. The mixed blessing of being a Ringgold should now be painfully obvious. You have seen the return of your dead father's soul, a possibility not available to Saplings. Now, if I'm not mistaken, you wonder whether you might change history and return him

to our lives whole and complete.

I have to admit I do not have all the answers. The Ringgolds here on Earth are self-determined with powers unheard-of in Saplings, both a boon and a curse. They have other mixed blessings, as you may have noticed: magical relics not available to Saplings.

But my purpose was not to counsel you on the use of magical relics or the perils of tinkering with time. I have pondered how I might console you for years of loneliness. I do understand that you, having lived so long among Saplings, have a concept of love that requires demonstration and expression.

The image of her mother dithered away. The falcon's eyes shifted, sending its beams of light to the frescoed ceiling. She heard her mother's voice fading.

I want you to know that Ringgolds as we are, you were conceived in love by your father and myself. We meant for you always to have the kind of family life you now envy among your friends. Know this, no matter what happens.

She saw on the ceiling the ghostly images of her mother and father playing on the beach. Branch rode a bicycle over the sand while Sophia sat on the handlebars. They were giggling. His shirt blew around his lean, muscular form. Her bare toes were curled as she tried to keep her balance.

Then the ghostly projections faded to make way for a series of flashbacks Ericca did not completely understand. There was the image of an astounding castle set among dramatic mountains and lakes populated by swans. Then she saw the image of a woman talking to a man at a newsstand: Sophia and George.

Ericca turned away from that. Her mother had said it herself: She was a Ringgold, blessed with magic relics, self-determined. She picked up her bag, removed the library card from the gold prongs. She remembered the article…*Sagetooth, a place of refuge for reassembling all life.* She knew that was where she needed to go.

Three children, one small dog, and one cowboy entered the loft in Soho. Miguel had been invited along, and he was happy to come. He was excited. He had heard of Quint A. Senns and his wife, the famous physicist Sybille Nix, but had never had the opportunity to meet them.

He was still a little distracted by the conversation with Sheila Angvall. Branch had remarked…Sheila's *monsters and antidotes don't live purely in the realm of illusion.* He recalled the special ceremony to honor winners of the Young Scientist award held at the glass and steel headquarters of the LOGOS Corporation. He remembered being shown the colorful displays highlighting the long, illustrious history of the company.

The LOGOS Corporation was once a small pharmaceutical and pesticide business called the Spiro Company. After acquiring LOGOS Computers, the company was able to make strides against its competitors with their newly acquired computerized analysis methods. The merged company earned large government contracts during the war.

The merger with LOGOS Computers expanded their brand to the West Coast. They made *LOGOS Corporation* their new name, and continued to grow as a multinational conglomerate holding patents in things from transgenic seeds to lethal herbicides and the latest DNA-splicing techniques.

Miguel remembered his moment at the podium along with only a handful of other young scientists from all over the country. Vivian Spiro, the granddaughter of Harold Spiro, shook his hand and made a short speech praising his insightful findings. He remembered his barely contained sense of pride and exuberance. He was among the youngest of the kids honored that day. His parents and his aunt and uncle were there, among the few brown faces in the crowd. He had beamed and waved at them.

But now he recalled the displays in the atmospheric lobby. What once awed and inspired him now troubled him deeply. The display read LOGOS…*living organism genotype ownership and simulation*. Below were pictures of gleaming, spotless lab rooms located all over the world, specializing in gene manufacture and cloning. Cloning and the combining of body parts for therapeutic and other purposes will achieve mankind's dream of immortality, the displays boasted. Looking over the posters showing the company's history, he had noticed the heading *Rainbow Herbicides: A Decisive Weapon*.

"Miguel, Miguel, I am so honored to meet you," said a smiling, winsome face. He recognized the woman as Sybille Nix. He knew her from the many research papers he had mulled over before writing his award-winning theory on space travel.

"Hi, Professor Nix. I'm Miguel Lujan," he said in reply as he extended his hand, trying to appear as tall and grown-up as possible as she towered over him in three-inch-high designer sandals.

"Mr. Poe, I have someone you really must meet. Miguel, meet my friend Mr. Poe. Miguel is one of the most promising young minds I know." Miguel held out his hand and turned to look at a man whose walking stick fit exactly the description he heard from his aunt and uncle…*a man with a wooden walking stick with a carved coiled serpent.*

"Mr. Poe has been bringing the most spectacular beads from his travels for use in my collections," said Sybille warmly. The man peered at Miguel from behind round wire glasses. His thick gray brows lowered and his eyes wrinkled as he shook his hands.

"Pleased to meet you, Mr. Lujan…wonderful, wonderful work," said the man enthusiastically. "Vivian mentioned you to me."

Miguel was perplexed for a moment. Then, thinking of the only Vivian he knew, he replied, "You mean Vivian Spiro? You know her?" he asked.

"Oh, oh, yes. I know her," replied the balding man. "I help find relics that are very hard to find. I myself am an explorer. I have a small, specialized antiques business that takes me all over the world, but most recently to Central Asia and China." He presented Miguel with a business card that read:

Tepes Antiques
Vladimir Poe

Miguel tried to recall where he had seen that name, *Tepes*. He knew the historical association with Vlad Tepes, the Impaler. But he had also seen the name recently, but he could not name where. He silently pondered. Then he remembered. There was a large moving truck outside the LOGOS Corporation the day he was there; the name on the truck was *Tepes Antiques*.

Elle peered over his shoulder. She saw the business card and looked sharply at Mr. Poe. She wanted to leave immediately to find Ericca, because at that moment everything made sense. But before she could do anything, a slender young woman with long dark hair and an array of beaded bracelets approached her as she stood next to Miguel, with Pluto on a leash.

The young woman casually shook her hair to reveal dancing, filigreed earrings. She said pleasantly, "Hi, you must be Elle. I don't think we were ever introduced at the Empire Poets Society meeting, but I am Rebecca Poe."

Elle looked up at the striking, angular face with beautiful eyes. She smiled in acknowledgement. She now recognized her as the woman who was taken away by security guards, screaming and flailing, as they escaped from the Gravity Bar.

"Excuse me, but could I hold your dog?" she asked. Pluto was now leaping and barking relentlessly at the slender young woman.

"Why, of course. He's not really my dog. My friend Miguel actually found him, and we're now trying to return him to his owner," replied Elle.

"Oh, really?" replied Rebecca, "You mean to Tory Skye?" She evidently kept up with celebrity pets, a good sign.

The fluffy dog with the green shirt now snuggled in Rebecca's welcoming arms. She scratched the fur under his chin and spoke soothing words as she stroked him. Elle could not make out her exact words, but they sounded like *Padmasam…so wonderful to have you back.*

Suddenly, Rebecca said with a serious look, "This dog is actually my lost dog, Padmasam, who has been missing for about a year, right about the time Tory Skye started coming to Empire Poets Society meetings with Regi Arthur. I'm so glad you brought him back to me."

Then, turning to Mr. Poe, she said happily, "Look, Papa, Padmasam has returned to me." Turning once again to Miguel and Elle, she said, "I suppose I should show you proof that he's really my dog and not Tory's. Well, look…" There was a small amulet of the eye of Horus on a chain around Pluto's neck. On the back of the amulet was engraved *Padmasambhava sees all.*

Elle and Miguel could only imagine Tory's anger at the loss of her pet, Pluto. But they were convinced Rebecca was telling the truth. The amulet might have been the reason Tory was so interested in the dog to begin with.

"Just a trinket," said Rebecca, noting their interest. They both smiled at Rebecca as she thanked them, and turned to the corner of the loft, where Matt, Branch, and Quint stood chatting.

Matt glowed with pride. The idea of *Polis Games* now completely occupied his imagination. He felt encouraged, convinced his dad was going to help him with it this summer. He would not stop thinking about it until the next day.

The next day, Ericca awoke to find her mother in a remarkably happy mood. She found herself being unusually respectful and helpful as they finished breakfast. At school that day, she tried to pay attention, but inwardly she wondered whether the T-Gate was still working …*as a gateway to the time tunnels.* She knew the M-Gate worked at least once, on that day a year ago when she first met Sheila Angvall at the Memorial Monument. The thought of Sheila made her sad, and she was glad when she was called on during math to explain the concept of parallelism.

After school, she hurried back to the Midtown Library; her mother was busy with a library patron so she didn't stop to say hi. She was back in the Q-aisle again, only today sitting at the desk was none other than Quintana Castle. Ericca sighed. She had wanted to explore the contents of those wooden boxes in private. The withered old woman looked up with kindly eyes.

"Why, hello, Ericca...what a pleasant surprise," said Quintana. Ericca suspected she was not at all surprised. The comings and goings in vaults of secrets like the Q-aisle were probably very closely monitored by the Ringgolds.

"Likewise, Quintana. What a pleasure to see you," replied Ericca in the tone she reserved for elderly women who are actually members of an ancient magical lineage.

"It has been a happy day, remarkably so," replied Quintana as she glanced down at a series of scribbled notes on the desk. Ericca glanced at the tremulous scrawl; Quintana's gaunt and shriveled hands hardly looked strong enough to hold a pencil. This thought made Ericca wonder: Quintana was a Ringgold, yet she was aging like any ordinary Sapling.

Looking more closely at the spidery scrawl, she could make out the words...*George Plantagent...Horus...Caesarion...Ptolemy XIV...Taliesin Sax...dynasty under attack.*

She looked up querulously at Quintana, who explained matter-of-factly, "Sometimes, the heart seeks closure in the form of evidence, evidence that is indisputable and conclusive. Ringgolds who live among Saplings for long periods of time acquire this tendency toward stubborn attachments." She looked up into Ericca's perplexed face.

"I was young and strong once like your mother is. I had a child by myself, just as she did. But instead of choosing to bear the hardship of being a single mother like your mother, I chose to give my child away to be raised by another family. I did not want to know his name or where he lived. I did not want him to know me...or our shared history."

Ericca saw Quintana's agony and asked, "But why, why not?" She knew Quintana was the widow of the slain Taliesin Sax, a wealthy New Yorker, and founder of the very successful LOGOS Computer company. She would not have been the typical destitute young mother.

"I have wrestled with this question for years, between wanting to find my son, and wanting to leave him be for his own sake. This is where being a Ringgold helped. Ringgolds have the strength and presence of mind to wield magical relics that exert changes on the atomic level, at the deepest levels of nature. Ringgolds can also focus their minds and block out distractions and unhelpful emotions. That was what I did when my son was born. I knew the killers who stole Taliesin's company and left him for dead in his study in the mountains of Santa Cruz would track down his son to the farthest corner of the globe. It's historic. Usurpers never allow the sovereign's heir to survive and inherit his rightful legacy," said Quintana sadly.

She brightened. "But today," said she as her spotted hand brought the book back into view, "I know who my son is and what he grew up to be with certainty." She opened the cover of the green and blue book to the dedication which read:

For my mother, Quintana Castle

"And I am so proud of him, of the man he is and will become," she said slowly flipping the pages of the book with delight. "I have even visited all the moments in his childhood, growing up in an old French country farmhouse blissfully and securely removed from the perils of his lineage. I gave my newborn baby son to my closest friends, you see. The Plantagenet family was happy to help, and I hid all record of the adoption, even from myself. You know, Sapling secrets are easily compromised."

"But now look at how he's grown. Did you meet him at the fashion show? A gorgeous, charming man and a wonderful poet rather like his father," gushed Quintana as she stopped to pet the large white dog placidly curled under the desk. "And now it's as thought we are all one happy family; well until that unfortunate Sapling eventuality. Well, we can't help that, can we Tau?" she said amiably, feeding a biscuit to the dog.

Quintana stood up with a smile, and bid Ericca goodbye. "I have some errands now on this most remarkable day." She strolled out, handbag and dog in hand, just as Miguel, Elle, and Matt ran toward them.

"Ericca, Ericca, we've figured everything out," exclaimed Elle breathlessly. "Miguel said you would be here. It was Mr. Poe, and Tepes Antiques. Remember that truck from the loading dock in Skye Towers? Vladimir Poe, he did it. He stole the original pieces of art from the park and the Met, and delivered them to Daemon Skye. Then it was he who replaced the originals with replicas and etched the graffiti, making it look like Mr. Plantagenet did it."

"But why would Mr. Poe do such a thing?" asked Ericca.

"He works for Daemon. That's his job. He obtains relics and buys and sells them," answered Elle.

"But why would Daemon want to frame Mr. Plantagenet?" queried Ericca. She knew Daemon was a Ringgold with no strong favorites in Sapling rivalries and conflicts.

Matt hovered about the desk, holding the green and blue book *Green Basket, Blue Cup* that Quintana had left on the desk. He had an air of solemnity today, making the gleeful boy of yesterday seem like a different person. In his hand he held a large envelope. He flipped through the pages, and now looked up and said quietly, "Daemon did not want to frame Mr. Plantagenet. That was someone else's doing."

Then noticing their blank looks, Matt asked, "And how do I know that?" He took a deep breath and explained, "Mrs. Angvall died alone in her apartment last night, an apparent heart attack. She left me all her papers. I read through them. I suppose Daemon must have arranged for the return of the library book shortly after she died."

Ericca stifled a tear. Matt continued, "But I think you'll find an answer to your question here." He pulled an envelope out of the book, embossed in sparkling letters with the name *Skye Tower*. The notes on the envelope were in Daemon's distinctive hand:

The white bishop serves two masters. He may not yet know the true motives of those who seek his services. He may not care…George Plantagenet must be freed.

Ericca thought of the bishop with two heads. She racked her brain. Who was the other master? As if reading her thoughts, Miguel looked at her and said, "Vivian Spiro, of the LOGOS Corporation."

The combination of the two names rang with cruel irony. Vivian Spiro was the director and heiress of a predatory corporation that would stop at nothing for market dominance, not even murder. She had no right to LOGOS Computers, the creation of a dreamer and poet. She remembered Quintana's words… *usurpers never allow the sovereign's heir to survive and inherit his rightful legacy.*

Ericca approached Matt to peer over his shoulder. He handed the book to her with a sad expression. Finally, the book she had been so curious about was in her hands. She was sure she would have a fun read that evening.

That evening Matt was quiet for most of dinner and went to bed without teasing his sister. He remembered being summoned to Sheila's apartment earlier in the day. He and Branch had stood looking around as the attorney gathered the papers she had willed to him. He stood in the room, noticing for the first time the simple black charcoal drawings of hollowed faces in numb despair. Käthe Kollwitz, this he knew from his museum visits.

Later he read her memoirs, stapled together with a cover sheet which read *Rainbow Sprinkles*. Sheila Angvall had spent the year since the previous Memorial Day in a state of unshakeable sorrow. She had met her son; she knew how he died. He had been a twenty-year-old infantryman staggering on the field, riddled with bullets, arms torn from shrapnel from a cluster bomb, gasping for a drop of water.

David Angvall's death, alone and ironically cruel, angered Matt, and he fought a lump in his throat as he read more of Sheila's memoirs. He knew a solution would be found. He had modeled a winning scenario many times before in his musings about the *Ultimate Warrior*. The Ultimate Warrior regenerated destroyed limbs and accomplished self-repair on damaged parts. He was equipped with sensors to detect poisons and secreted a pharmacopoeia of specialized antidotes. He possessed the power of self-reproduction. The Ultimate Warrior would generate his own clone army as enforcements. He did not need anyone. No one mourned his pain.

Matt was filled with delight in conjuring feature after feature for the Ultimate Warrior. He recalled the name Branch thought of on the spur of the moment, *Polis Games*. He was more than psyched, and his father even seemed supportive. He would leave the wimpy stuff like catering parties and designing pastries to his sister, Elle. But he, Matt, would become the celebrated founder of an awesome game company, one with even an intellectual-sounding name. He now felt much better. He smiled and fell asleep.

CHAPTER SIXTEEN

THE T-GATE

The next day, Quintana's words echoed in Ericca's mind. *The heart requires closure in the form of evidence, evidence indisputable and final.*

She knew she had every reason to be happy. What she had known in her heart for so long was true. She was a descendent of a magical lineage. Her father had never really died.

She browsed through portions of *Green Basket, Blue Cup*. She marveled how the search for her father had revealed a totally unexpected glimpse into the bewildering world of Ringgolds and Saplings.

The serious and speculative words in the book were a distant voice as she sat on Spike fingering the Time Token. She had never used this round subway token from Maxine Weaver. She knew where she might find this relic useful, but she did not need Albert or Leonardo to lecture her about the perils of tinkering with time.

A phrase from the book caught her eye...*the Cosmic Rider reappears to rescue the Silver Guardian and the Black Gardener.* The phrase was excerpted from a prophecy found in southern France. Albert looked on and knew what Ericca was contemplating. He interrupted her thoughts with an admonition: "No, Ericca, I would strongly advise against plotting your strategy based on an ambiguous prophecy from a book that has not even been written."

Ericca had been contemplating the statuette of the centaur for several minutes. Albert read her mind again.

Albert argued, "You have no idea what the prophecy really means. The Cosmic Rider can be many things, if indeed the translation is precisely right. Those words were taken from the ruins of a site dating from Egyptian times. The Silver Guardian could be many things, malicious demon or benevolent daemon. The Black Gardener could be an actual dark-skinned person or someone who is hidden. Those old prophets liked talking in circles; saved them from ever being wrong."

"Furthermore, have you ever heard of the term *self-fulfilling prophecy* or *circular thinking?*" asked Albert sternly, "It is very strange having such a thing as a Q-aisle, where you can read the books yet to be published. We never had such a thing in my day. We considered travel to the past a fanciful concept and nothing more. Think how loopy things get when the future is in constant flux with people traveling to the past to tweak this and that..."

At the mention of *circular thinking,* Leonardo popped his head from the blanket and said in agreement, "I think Albert is right this time, my dear. Think of what has just happened. Quintana Castle peeked into the future and discovered her son's identity in a book he writes after he finds his true name. But the book would not have existed if she had not discovered it. Do you see the dilemma? In math, circular proofs are an absolute no-no. In computer science, this would be the nightmare of an endless loop, where the future revises the present and the altered present revises the future in an unending loop. Think of this scenario: She tells him his real heritage, he rebukes his mother for abandoning him and does not write the book, she therefore never discovers his name, he never rejects his name and writes the book having found his name by some other means, she then discovers his name, and ad infinitum in an endless cycle of flux and alternate futures."

Ericca listened patiently. Albert and Leonardo were in agreement and not squabbling, which was a good thing. They were smart and well-meaning, but at times tiresome and overly theoretical. But theory was secondary now. She knew what she had to do. She had to return to the T-Gate to travel across time and

CHAPTER SIXTEEN

space to Sagetooth.

"My esteemed dears, pardon me for sounding presumptuous, but please set aside linear time just this once; time really does move in benevolent circles," said Ericca lightheartedly as she began stuffing Spike into her backpack. Albert and Leonardo made muffled protests as their faces were squashed under the weight of the library book. With a quick note to her mother, they were soon out the door.

The Q-aisle was empty and quiet today. Ericca browsed the shelves of the majestic hall in private. She pondered the chess set of blue pinstriped figures displayed with the plaque...*Hammond Spiro...the LOGOS Corporation...in the spirit of fair play*. She thought of Daphne's words...*the SPIRO Corporation was pretty heavy handed in the takeover of LOGOS Computers*. Sometimes people differed on the definition of *fair play*.

She found the carved doorway leading to the T-Gate and soon was strolling in a dimly lit hallway that reminded her of a huge subway station. She peered into the round pool near the entrance, and studied the markings on the capstones bordering the pool. She walked around as in a trance, studying the ripples in the pool, nearly bumping into someone also walking about the pool in a state of preoccupation.

"Oh, hello, Ericca...What bring you here?" he asked.

"Oh, hi, Dad, just exploring a little. What brings you here?" stammered Ericca with an expression of guilty surprise.

Branch held the Q-computer in one hand. Apparently, Matt had been good enough to lend it to him. "You do know what this place is, don't you?" asked Branch.

"Umm, yes, this is the T-Gate," replied Ericca.

"That it is. I am actually waiting for my train," said Branch.

"What?" replied Ericca with a note of anguish. She suspected his purpose here.

"My work is done here. And now I think I deserve some rest, so I am headed back," answered Branch.

Ericca knew his purpose. He had accompanied Sheila Angvall to the afterlife as was his role as a Ringgold. Now he was headed back to Sagetooth, away from the world of Saplings, away from her. "But you don't have a ticket," she protested.

"I actually do. The Every Eye helps in many places," he said as his hand came out of his pocket. He stood above the engraved eye in the raised capstone and turned his hand so the jeweled ring faced the engraved eye. A mirrored ball rose in the pool, rotating slowly, sending projections of light and shadow into the hall. The deserted hall now rang with the clang and buzz of a subway station. Lights flickered and a whooshing sound came from two dark corners in the back.

"Careful, you want to be standing near the lamps when the tunnels open. They'll keep you warm," said Branch, walking closer to a column with a bright sconce light. The light had a metal shade perforated with a pattern of stars, the constellation Orion. Ericca huddled next to him, glad for his comforting presence, searching for an argument to persuade him to stay, studying the array of stars in the sconces. She recognized the constellations, Taurus, Capricorn, and Sirius.

Two loud whooshes of cold air made her freeze and shudder. There were now two arches in the distance clothed in shimmering blue. Above her the sign read *T-Gate Outbound*; across the aisle the sign read *T-Gate Inbound*. Then, out of the arched tunnels came a scream like screeching brakes applied with awesome force. A subway train slowed to a halt at the platform. Hoary letters on the train read *Sagetooth*.

"This is it, I'm afraid, Ericca. I'm sure I'll see you later," said Branch reluctantly, kissing her forehead.

"But let me go with you...we can fix things," pleaded Ericca.

"No, you can't. You don't have a ticket. It is not your time," said Branch with finality.

"But I do have a ticket," retorted Ericca. She opened her palm to show the bronze subway token.

Branch chuckled and replied, "That's a very nice thing, but

unfortunately that won't work today, not for this train." He turned and waved goodbye as he walked through the automated doors of the subway train.

Before Ericca could scream in protest or voice one last goodbye, the train departed with another shrill shriek and blast of cold, and the shimmering ball in the pool disappeared once again below the surface. Ericca stood alone once again in the dim, empty hall. She clutched the Time Token and thought she could almost hear Albert and Leonardo say things in smug approval.

But things were not over; she was not done. On a sudden whim, she held the Time Token over the engraved outline of an ankh in the pool's stone capstone. She felt a tug; effortlessly the token dropped on the capstone, conforming to the outline of the ankh as it touched the stone. The token lodged in the eye of the ankh, now glowed with a scintillating gold light that reflected on the water and the framed paintings decorating the hall.

The undulating ripples in the pool painted a scene of a party in the formal garden of a large estate. Well-dressed men and women in a variety of fashions paraded by, fluted glasses in hand, chatting gaily. She even thought she saw a man with droopy eyes and a thick mustache in the crowd and a slight man with delicate features wearing a collared tunic. The scene shifted to an airy ballroom lined with statues. Branch stood in the room, looking quizzically at her from the surface of the pool.

"Ericca, I just wanted you to know I had a safe trip to Sagetooth, and everything is fine. This place is really happening, just as I remember it. You may even recognize some people here," said Branch. He stood near the open double doors, where a woman frolicked in the sunshine with her young son. Ericca recognized them as Sheila Angvall with her son, David, appearing just as he had that day at the Memorial Monument.

"Well, I've got some work to do now. I can't say I hold a lot of hope in this working out, but everyone deserves a second chance. Hopefully I won't end up again as an oil lamp buried in the trunk of some antiques dealer or worse, a celebrity accessory," he said with a wry smile.

The scene faded. The colored ripples swirled about to paint another scene, one of a twinkling night sky shrouding a mountainous desert punctured by the rattle and hum of airplanes and machine guns. Branch spoke to her from a fighter plane high in the air out of the range of antiaircraft artillery.

"Looks like I made it. But I have to warn you, this is a real crapshoot. Your buddies Albert and Leonardo have probably already explained how things tend to follow the most probable course, a destiny determined as much by who we are as by karma. And even if things don't follow probability, things can still get messed up. When you walk out of this hall in a few minutes, you may find things completely different, completely screwed up, or basically the same. Just cross your fingers," he explained to her from behind the headgear of his pilot suit. His voice was muffled, but he gave her an encouraging thumbs-up before turning his plane away from her with a roaring screech.

Now the ripples showed only the night sky with occasional bursts of light and sound. Bombs exploded on the ground. Missiles fired with bright bursts of light. Planes dodged the rapid rounds of artillery. Then the scene faded completely, leaving Ericca to gaze anxiously into the pool for the first sign of what happened more than thirteen years ago.

Branch enjoyed being a fighter pilot. He was quite good at it. He had a long history with wartime situations. He liked the fact that as a fighter pilot, unlike those other situations, he had relatively little risk. The missions he typically flew were conducted at high altitude and away from the menace of truck-mounted machine guns. His missions tended to be quite successful, thanks in no small part to the finesse of his squadron partners, Taurus Twenty-One and Mistletoe Thirteen who each flew their own specially equipped planes.

Taurus Twenty-One's role was to locate the target with pinpoint accuracy. Once located, his role as Orion Four was to send the laser-guided bomb on an irreversible course to the designated target. This technology had been perfected over many bombing missions, and was known for an incredible success rate in hitting military targets and deftly avoiding collateral damage. Throughout it all, no small debt of gratitude was due to Mistletoe Thirteen, who flew at a low altitude to provide visual confirmation of the target. He also took good before-and-after photos to send home.

Branch had played over and over in his mind what had happened that night. The night had started uneventfully, with the usual preflight checks and processes. This would be his last mission before going home, home to his new wife who was expecting their first child. It had not been an occasion to ponder the responsibilities of Ringgolds, the importance of protecting the time tunnels, nor the relative triviality of this Sapling conflict. Rather, it was a moment of celebration for a long, satisfying string of successful missions with partners who shared his intensity and sense of fun.

The mission was proceeding flawlessly until they came under a rapid flurry of enemy fire. Mistletoe Thirteen was panicked. A message came that radar-guided missiles were headed their way. Their last target approached.

Taurus Twenty-One radioed, "Target within range. Cosmic Light to launch in thirty seconds."

Mistletoe Thirteen, frantically dodging machine-gun fire crackled over the radio, "Ready to go. Target within sight."

A few seconds passed. Branch, in his Phantom fighter plane, waited for the light to appear in the monitor showing the target had been designated. He was about to send confirmation and begin his dive towards the target when he heard a tentative voice over the radio. It was Mistletoe Thirteen. "Target off mark. Collateral target identified," he said over the disruptive background of machine-gun fire from the ground.

Branch heaved a heavy sigh. He was running out of fuel. He could not continue flying at this altitude with a two-ton bomb. He was looking forward to the lift he would get from unloading the monster. But now he pondered. Collateral target usually meant a civilian facility, an orphanage or hospital strategically located among military targets. The enemy was Machiavellian without knowing the first thing about Machiavelli.

"Identify target. Over," he queried over the radio.

"Not sure, sir. I would guess an orphanage," came the muffled voice. Branch thought cynically, The next generation of barbarous Saplings. Then he thought of his unborn child. If his child were orphaned, he would want the child to have a chance. He could not launch the bomb.

But he hardly had a second to think, because the panicked reports from Mistletoe Thirteen now registered a helpless intensity. Branch listened. Taurus Twenty-One was quiet. He had to do something. Mistletoe Thirteen's plane lacked the power to muster a quick escape. Branch navigated to within shooting range of ground fire and launched his assault. At once fire was deflected from Mistletoe Thirteen, and directed ferociously at him.

His own words played in his mind: *the most probable course …* *determined by who we are.* He stood again at a pivotal point in time, poised over destiny in the form of withering heat. His plane was on fire from missiles which had found their target. The parachute he remembered using sparked with embers, ready to wrap his mortal body once again in a flaming shroud as inescapable as a sarcophagus. He thought quickly; there were pockets of refuge here, tunnel trams, more frequent in this region than others. The key was finding the moment to jump.

The plane exploded in a fiery spectacle. Flames singed his hair and he shielded his face. But he was free from the rain of fire and debris. He was in a bubble now, a tunnel tram. He floated to the ground without the deathly acceleration of gravity, *moving through space with neither the push of time nor the pull of weight,* a shadowy figure dissolving gently in the silent mountains.

Ericca watched the night of darkness and fire. The hall echoed with her gasps, the muffled sounds from the pool, and then the clink of the Time Token popping out of the capstone. The pool became opaque and still. The token looked just like any other subway token. Ericca stifled a sob as she returned the token to her pocket. Outside, she squinted between tears in the bright sunlight of the spring day. She averted the blank stares on the subway and sat huddled against the window, staring distantly into space as the train chugged home.

Then, Quintana's words returned to her, *a Sapling predilection toward stubborn attachment....the heart requires closure in the form of evidence, indisputable and final.* The next stop was the M-Gate for the Memorial Monument in Central Park. She gathered herself, wiped her eyes, and swung her backpack over her shoulder bravely.

Outside, small children played on the Memorial Monument. A handsome replica but a wonderful piece just the same, she thought. Sunlight glinted on the pool. Stuffed animals and flowers lay at the base of the ship. She ran her hand over the smooth, engraved glass hull as she had so many times before. Her hand had memorized the names:

...*Chun Lee Ang, David Angvall, Catriona Anthony*
...*Reginald Arthur.*

She ran her hand over the glass again. Then she opened her eyes. Her eyes now welled over, but this time with joy and relief. *Branch Archer* was not on the list.

Ericca went home and found things pretty much as they had been except for a pile of letters. She contemplated the neat stack on the desk next to the centaur statue. It was as though the letters had been there all along, something she just now had the time to mull over. She knew what was in those letters, having read them each multiple times over the past years.

The envelopes bore a multitude of different stamps and return addresses. A few had no return address at all. Here and there were spots and smudges, a raindrop, a tear, a smoke burn, an ink stain.

She flipped through the letters as one might browse a scrapbook or family album. The oldest letter was sent about ten years ago and was among the few letters addressed to both Ericca and Sophia.

Dear Ericca and Sophia,

I am glad to report that after a disastrous crash and unfortunate episode as a prisoner, I am now recuperating in good hands.

I am overwhelmed with joy to hear about Ericca. I've never seen a more beautiful baby. I hope to be home soon, just as soon as I am able to travel. The rest of my squadron has gone home with appropriate medals, including Daemon Skye, the awesome Taurus Twenty-One, and Nicholas Bard, the fearless Mistletoe Thirteen.

I am so glad to hear you are both well. See you soon.
With love,
Branch

The letters to Sophia were few. The most recent, from two years ago, had been returned to the envelope with the adhesive flap pressed firmly. The letter was sealed, and even now Ericca chose not to read it.

She opened another of the earliest letters, received when she was just about seven, just learning to read.

Dear Ericca,
I am in remarkably good spirits today, and amazingly, I have remembered. It is your birthday! Every seven-year-old deserves a special surprise, and I have sent one care of Ray Bender. I suspect you have inherited my compulsion toward uncovering secrets, but no spoilers. All my love and happy birthday.

Dad

CHAPTER SIXTEEN

Ericca tried to remember the gift from Ray Bender. Oh, of course, she thought, one of my favorite books, one she learned to read on her own and had practically memorized: a story about a pilot who crashed and was saved by an antique collector. The story took place somewhere in Central Asia and was written with beautiful calligraphy:

> The antique collector nursed the pilot to health, and introduced him to the beauty and history of the region.

> But there was a catch: The pilot agreed to help locate relics lost in time and divulge their secrets. *Levitate Along...Matter Mirror...* the pilot gave the antique collector the secret commands for flying carpets and magical walking sticks. The antique collector called the pilot *Djinn*, for the supernatural tribes that once roamed the area. He joked that the pilot might agree to be his personal genie and live always at his beck and call inside an enchanted vessel. The pilot smiled; he was known at one time as *Genu*, meaning branch of the world tree.

> The antique collector had uncovered many precious relics: carpets, pendants, amulets. But he wanted the ultimate prize, the famed Every Eye which, it was rumored, would be found in a labyrinthine cave, guarded by bears and serpents. The pilot warned against this exploit but finally conceded and equipped them both with headdresses to mimic ferocious bears.

> They found the cave and navigated the dank and convoluted passages. They fought and defeated the bears guarding the entry and proceeded to

confront the serpents that lurked in shadow and swamp. Instead of slithering monsters, though, they were welcomed by three maidens, lovely and pale in the limpid glow, with shining coronas of hoary locks.

The maidens led them to an underground well, where at the center was a mirrored ball, the Every Eye. The well bubbled and rippled in shimmering blue. The maidens settled to their tasks, chatting and weaving. The pilot and the antique collector watched as their delicate fingers gingerly manipulated fine skeins of thread through spindle whorls and looms.

But the antique collector was not content to observe. He wanted the enchanted orb, glimmering eerily in the cavernous hall. He asked the maidens innocently if he might make a wish; he was, after all, just a tourist. They agreed but indicated the cost of a wish was the surrender of the wish-seeker's heart. The antique collector gave the pilot a nudge. The pilot agreed; his heart was his own, no matter what enchantments were invoked, and woe to anyone who tried to steal it. The pilot tossed his heart into the well, a heart of such fire and integrity it gleamed like a brilliant red jewel in the water.

At once, the pool glimmered with a playground scene. A small girl bounced between a bronze climbing sculpture and her father. But all this dissolved as the antique collector's sinewy fingers grabbed the red heart from the well and grasped for the mirror ball. The maidens stopped their weaving and stood up in frightful rage. Their shiny coronas erupted into writhing, threatening serpents. They turned their wrathful visages on the pilot and the antique collector as they now groveled on the edge of the well. The pilot flattened himself on the ground, pulling the antique collector with him, just as the mirror ball turned to reflect the grimacing faces of the outraged maidens.

Then, to the relief and surprise of the pilot and the antique collector, still flat on the ground, the maidens became still. Their gruesome expressions were frozen for eternity, turned to stone by their own reflections. The limpid light faded to gray, the water in the well turned to impermeable stone. The Every Eye shattered, sending shards every which way; one particularly sharp sliver lodged itself in the antique collector's eye, blinding him to beauty while filling his mind with insatiable greed.

Little by little, every bit of moisture turned to stone, every bit of root, moss, and vegetation withered to black. But from the swirling storm of glass shards sprang a fantastic beast. The winged horse flew toward the shaft of light high in the cavernous cave and disappeared with a soft whoosh of its iridescent wings.

The antique collector and the pilot ran frantically through the passages and were relieved to find themselves once again in the sunlight and familiar scene of mountains and wide blue skies. But things were never the same. The antique collector returned to New York with his cache of relics, lacking the crystal orb but with another prized relic that he exulted over in secret. The pilot would forever search for his heart.

Ericca looked fondly at the book, *The Last Pilot*. The book was an old favorite filled with all the fantastic things she liked to imagine. And as she mulled over the stack of letters, she thought, somehow everything makes sense now. She reached for the latest letter, date-stamped that very day. The handwriting was wobbly, as if scribbled on a moving train.

Dear Ericca,

By now, you should be back among your friends and all those who insist on a progression of cause and effect. But you have never lived in their world of leaden landmarks and stolen symbols, not really — past, future, cause, effect, right, wrong, here, there. Instead, you and I wander the circles of time in enchanted pursuit.

I cannot be with you now. But as you follow the spirals of logic in your mind, you will discover why. Know, though, that I am well, amid surroundings that have a nostalgic charm, doing what truly fascinates me. I wake each day and see the same glorious orb that glints through your window; I sleep each night under the same riders and archers that twinkle before your sleepy eyes.

Tell Matt thanks for the Q-computer. I hope to return it shortly. Tell him his gadget has stood the test of time. But since I don't know what guises will be necessary for my next visit to New York, I'd like to keep it just awhile longer.

I know what you are feeling. And I admit all the poetry in the world would not help things much. And I apologize, for many things. I forgot to give you your birthday present the last time we met, so I am sending it now. I hope you like it. Happy birthday.

Love, Dad

Ericca read the note again. She fought back a sob. She could barely decipher the address, *Pazyryk Valley, Altai Mountains*. The stamp showed a scene of stark, snow-capped mountains and barren tundra.

She fingered the object wrapped in paper in the bottom of the envelope. She unwrapped the paper to reveal a round pendant on an orange silk chain. The pendant was made of gold, with six bands of spirals and braids with motifs suggesting coiled serpents and sun rays. At the center was the figure of a winged horse, a woman's profile, and a swastika. Ericca thought of the fashion show as she fingered the shiny medallion. The scrap of paper in the package read:

> Just something I found in my travels. Don't worry. It's not a Ringgold relic, so it wouldn't set off any subway sensors. But it is thousands of years old. If your friends ask, tell them it's a *Svastikah*, which means 'being happy' in Sanskrit.

Ericca tried on the pendant. Albert and Leonardo, who had sensed her mood and managed to stay quiet, now burst out with their compliments.

"Wonderful, dear, that looks absolutely exquisite on you. Wouldn't you agree, Leonardo?" exclaimed Albert. He really wanted to say something to the effect of *I told you so. It does not do to try to undo the events of the past. You may have gained memories, but remember what I said: Events tend to follow a predictable trajectory.*

If he had launched into his diatribe on the perils of time travel,

Ericca would have found her backpack, and produced the library book *Green Basket, Blue Cup*. She would have shown Albert that the future as broadcast in this pivotal book was unchanged. Her father's reversal of his own bodily demise did not send shock waves through time. She opened the book now. The dedication to Quintana Castle read exactly as it had before. The introduction was as she remembered.

> ...the symbol of the green basket and blue cup has intrinsic meaning to us even today. These two symbols date back thousands of years to the civilization of the ancient Egyptians, where they signified the papyrus of the fertile Nile Delta, ruled by Osiris, and the blue lotus of the drought-ridden Nile Valley where Seth had dominion.

> But now, when vestiges of the ancient world populate only our trinket galleries and fiction racks, we still find meaning and insight in the symbols of old. Today we contemplate astounding scientific and technological progress — the manufacture of wormholes in stabilizing clouds of frozen atoms, cloning of life, automated warfare.

> Today we exalt the blue cup, a crystal grail representing the ascendancy of cold intellect, disjoined from the heart, the senses, and the comforting mythology of our tribal ancestors. We are as blue shadows in a lonely and bewildering wasteland.

Such lofty and ominous words, she thought. She was glad to have proof that her forays into time did not disrupt the overall fabric of things, but at that moment, she did not want her happy mood to be ruined by more unhappy ruminations. She closed the book and returned it to her backpack.

CHAPTER SIXTEEN

She peered at herself in the mirror. Her father was alive. That she knew. A collection of fond memories was now hers. A shadow crossed her face momentarily as she pondered his words... *I cannot be with you now.* But she looked up again, and she saw a girl with a shining gold pendant and the broadest grin imaginable.

The next evening, Ericca listened carefully for sounds from the apartment next door. Nicholas Bard...Mistletoe Thirteen. She remembered the images from the T-Gate. She fought back the urge to blame Nicholas for her father's crash. She persuaded herself that it was not Mr. Bard's fault that she and her mother were still alone in the world.

She remembered Daemon's words to Sophia that night at the Skye Tower: *Branch was a great guy with a big heart.* Ericca couldn't help herself from thinking with anger, My father's compassion saved this Sapling, the pathetic man next door. Then the words... *individual meaning...personal justice* came to her.

Familiar sounds of a phonograph came through the thin walls. Nicholas was listening to jazz alone in his apartment. He had once talked to her about those "...truly great jazz artists, Russell Malone, Ray Charles... artists who captured a mood, a certain time and place." She thought she might interrupt his musical enjoyment and ask him to talk about his years as a pilot; maybe he would even have some recollection of his squadron mate Branch Archer.

If she had, she might have heard rollicking tales of young men sharing camaraderie and excitement at the prospect of destiny-defining conflict. They had spent afternoons together, jogging barefoot on the rough gravel roads around the military base, hoping to harden the soles of their feet. The enemy knew their feet were soft, unlike the native guerrilla fighters who grew up without the assurance of shoes from infancy. Downed pilots and prisoners were often confined by simple confiscation of their shoes. She might have heard of an incorrigibly social and mischievous Branch Archer, well-liked and admired by all, often rumored to appear for multiple social calls simultaneously.

But this evening she doubted he was in the mood for telling old war stories, or being sociable at all. She had found a crumpled piece of paper outside his door. Not knowing what it was, she opened it and read the message, a letter from Daphne:

Nicholas,
Crumpled as a doll
In a Frankenthaler painting
Solemn as a shadow
In a Kollwitz drawing
Lonely as the echo
Of a whisper in space

I cannot be with you. You will always live in my heart.
Goodbye.
Daphne

Ericca was confused. She could not help thinking of Daphne sitting by herself in her apartment in Seattle, nose pressed to the computer screen into the wee hours of the morning, pondering line after line of cryptic code. She thought of Nicholas, contemplating yet another discouraging letter from the Veterans Administration Hospital or another night alone, chatting with strangers on the Web, falling asleep unshaven, amid the disorder of books and vinyl albums in his dusty apartment. She thought of the millions of souls locked in impossible, impenetrable loneliness...*blue shadows in a bewildering wasteland.*

She thought of her father, thousands of miles away in the mountains of Central Asia. She pondered possible explanations. Branch battled back from death only to reject the world that plunged him into the nightmare of an impossible dilemma. *Nostalgic charm*...her father's words occurred to her now as she looked again at the centaur statue. He was right, she thought, Ringgolds, with the wisdom of the ages, would find much to reject in the world of today.

CHAPTER SIXTEEN

The quiver of love through the arrow of time read the dedication on the centaur statuette. She sighed. She had a hopeful thought. Maybe it would only be a matter of time before the pilot recovered his heart. The soft, expressionistic sounds of jazz filtered from next door as Ericca drifted off to sleep.

CHAPTER SEVENTEEN

The Gorgon Glade

School was out and already temperatures in New York were hitting record highs. Ericca and Elle mopped beads of sweat from their foreheads with the backs of their hands as they hurried through Central Park. They took care not to get their hands dirty, even as they rolled carts brimming with pastry boxes behind them.

Today was Father's Day and a special occasion in many ways. Elle's new business, *Polis Pastries*, had been selected to cater an important party. This party was none other than a birthday party for Quintana Castle's dog, Tau. The garden party was to be held in a part of Central Park that Ericca had never visited before, a sculpture court called the *Gorgon Glade*.

Behind them today were Miguel, his aunt and uncle, and Miguel's father, the esteemed pastry chef Mr. Lujan, rolling carts loaded with party paraphernalia: flowers, tablecloths, silverware, plates, and goblets.

Miguel and his relatives were jubilant. Apparently, Elle's idea for a summertime activity had the enthusiastic support of both her mother and father, who then arranged for some first-rate employees. As it turned out, Mr. Lujan was more than happy to help, and the inclusion of his relatives meant they were spared from deportation proceedings.

The last in this retinue was Matt, who walked disconsolately behind, carrying nothing but his Q-computer and one small pastry box. He grumbled to himself about the silliness of the whole thing.

CHAPTER SEVENTEEN

He had never heard of such a thing: a huge catered party attended by Manhattan dignitaries for the purpose of celebrating a dog. At the thought of this ridiculous obsession with small pets, he thought of Tory. She was sure to be there with her new accessory, of course. Once Pluto had been returned to his original owner, Tory had wasted no time in procuring a comparable replacement, a Chihuahua named Cyclops. In fact, Tory now behaved as though Cyclops had always been her only dog; she scarcely even acknowledged Pluto. What was it with those dogs and owners, he thought, before berating himself for following the silliest tidbits of celebrity news.

Actually, Matt had good reason for his poor mood. He was helping his sister only because he needed a loan. He still badly wanted the turntable he saw in the dressing room of the Gravity Bar. But as it turned out, his plans for selling his Ultimate Warrior game had not panned out. The Q-computer would not be available on the mass market for some time due to manufacturing issues. Evidently quantum replication was not quite there yet.

Even without the fortuitous combination of hardware and software, he had been hoping for some significant income for the summer. His family had some major trips planned, and the fixed allowance his parents promised would not cover everything. His Ultimate Warrior game had been a runner-up in a war-game-simulation contest. The prize in the contest was a trip to a combat-simulation site in a secret location in Nevada and a check for a large amount. He would have been ecstatic to win, but instead he had been a runner-up. He received an encouraging letter of thanks acknowledging his talent and young age and not much more. The agony of being an also-ran was heightened by knowing that his twin sister was getting notoriety and being paid handsomely for, of all silly things, designing one-of-a-kind decorations and treats for fancy parties.

"Hey, wait up," he shouted as Elle, Ericca, and Miguel grew more distant. He was here to help, after all. He saw that they had circled a path a few times now.

"We're a bit lost," announced Ericca. She remembered the picture of the Gorgon Glade from the dossier in Maxine Weaver's desk months earlier, but now the trails and paths of the park seemed like a mesmerizing maze.

"Well, you can't be *a bit* lost. Either you know the way or you don't," asserted Matt confidently as he puffed to catch up with them. "Let's see the map," he said as they all stopped under the shade of a large black walnut tree.

Matt was glad to be useful and quite proud of his spatial-navigation skills. "Let's see, we're here, and the Gorgon Glade is there, just beyond Bethesda Terrace and the Literary Walk," he explained helpfully. "We need to turn left, that way, *un tour gauche*," he continued, glad to practice his remarkably improved French. They followed now as Matt led the way through the familiar corridor of bronze busts.

When they arrived at the fountain and benches where the Empire Poets Society usually met, they saw only a smattering of people. They passed the stone balconies of Bethesda Terrace, where crowds gathered about the fountain and clumped in front of tables watching chess games.

Ericca stopped for a moment, letting her companions go ahead when they passed the Memorial Monument at the Thyme Terrace. There were the usual crowds of tourists, and small children in the company of adoring adults queued up for the Thyme Train. She and her mother had visited the Memorial Monument just as they always had. They had contemplated the columns of names on the smooth glass hull, and the inscription on the base:

A vessel for the brave,
A barque in place of a body…

They had placed a bouquet of flowers in their regular spot, with the many mementos that always accumulated there this time of year. Ericca thought of how grateful and privileged she was. Her father's name was gone from the list. Then, as if echoing her happy thought, her mother mentioned that it could be an unusually busy summer. Daphne had contacted her and invited Ericca to visit. Ericca was tickled. Being in Seattle while most of New York labored under oppressive humidity would be awesome.

"Your father also wrote that it might be possible for you to visit him, though the flight will be very long and tiring," added Sophia. Ericca brightened and was giddy with excitement.

"Also, George has invited us to visit him in France," continued Sophia. Ericca was caught by surprise. She knew her mother was still dating him, but to her, he was still *Mr. Plantagenet*. She smiled back pleasantly. "That's great, Mom...I'm invited?" she asked tentatively.

"Oh, of course you are," replied her mother, as though surprised by the question.

Ericca was not a specialist in adult relationships, but she did know some things from her mother, who had a special window into those things.

Ericca noticed half-heartedly the developing relationship between George and her mother, not wanting to acknowledge the possible role this new relationship had in her father's continued absence. She always categorized the feelings between Sophia and George with other Sapling sentiments. She thought with faint snobbery, George is a Sapling, silly, sentimental, weak. He could never replace my father.

But discarding these thoughts, she smiled again and said agreeably, "That's wonderful, Mom," she said, "I've never been to Europe. Matt and Elle will be there this summer. Maybe we'll see them there."

Now, as she trailed behind her companions, Ericca turned toward them and yelled happily, "Hey, Matt, hey, Elle, guess what? I'm going to Europe this summer!"

Albert and Leonardo, in the blanket folded in her backpack indicated their approval. "Ahh, for some real wienerschnitzel and sauerbraten," said Albert nostalgically.

"And some heavenly Italian cappuccino and biscotti,"

reminisced Leonardo wistfully.

Elle was already at the Gorgon Glade when Ericca caught up with them. Elle busily directed them as they unfolded the tables and chairs. The glade was an amazingly beautiful spot in Central Park, frequently closed to the public for private events.

The courtyard was ample and square, with a perfectly symmetrical arrangement of privet hedges and benches around a circular pool. At the center of the pool was a statue in marble. The statue showed the winged figure of the horse Pegasus rearing up on its hind legs, in rapid escape from the youth Perseus, who triumphantly stood with his sword and the glaring Medusa head in hand.

On the edges of the glade, along the border of privet hedges were three fountains, each with the carved stone figure of a woman. The two fountains facing each other in the courtyard showed the immortal Gorgons. "Those are *Stheno* and *Euryale*," remarked Miguel.

"Oh, really," replied Ericca in wide-eyed fascination. "How do you know?" She would have thought their names were *Maxine* and *Sybille*.

"I read the plaques," answered Miguel sheepishly, pointing to the bronze plaques in the base. The Gorgon figures in stone had wings, sharp tusks grew from the nostrils, and their nails were brass claws like razors.

In contrast, the center fountain featured the feminine form of Medusa, not as a gruesome monster but as a delicate mortal nymph whose headdress of entangled snakes was a cruel curse: Medusa, the Roman monster and slayer of men...the *Medha* in Sanskrit...the Egyptian *Maat*, supreme Earth Goddess. Mythical symbols of corrupted and buried significance, Ericca thought, recalling Sybille's words.

Ericca knew the Greek myth of Perseus, who slew the Gorgon Medusa and gave her head to Athena, the Greek goddess of war. Athena bore the frightful visage on her shield. Elle, who was an expert in all things mythological, would have been happy to engage in a thorough discussion of this myth. But she was at that very moment busily straightening the tablecloths and not disposed to an explanation of the significance of the statues around them.

Elle was trying to adjust the tablecloths so they were perfectly flat and hung evenly over the table. Matt was helping her, though he was not being very helpful, giving the tablecloth an impatient tug as Elle gingerly adjusted her end. Finally, Elle said angrily, "Forget it, Matt. Why don't you find some dragons to slay or rocks to throw," and walked over to correct Matt's ill-tempered tampering. Matt, already hot and frustrated for reasons of his own, strode off in a huff, giving a final spiteful tug before walking away.

"He just wants to sabotage this whole thing," muttered Elle as Ericca approached. Elle started to unpack the boxes of plates, glasses, and goblets. Ericca marveled at Elle's incredible planning and organization. Elle arranged the stacks of porcelain plates and rows of cut-crystal glasses neatly on the carefully straightened tablecloth. The plates were unlike anything Ericca was used to using. Not the standard white plates of catered events, instead, for this event, Elle was using scallop-edged plates decorated with colorful faience motifs featuring bees and swirling lines. Elle met Ericca's curious gaze and replied, "Quintana Castle asked for these things. *Faience* was originally developed by the Egyptians, who likened brightly colored faience objects to the brilliance of the sun, moon, and stars."

Elle explained further, "This is to be a very special event for her. Quintana Castle, the reclusive Manhattan philanthropist and heiress of the Sax fortune, has decided to signal her reentry into public life with an event that will unmistakably announce her intentions to all, friends…and enemies."

Elle lifted a large bouquet of sunflowers, already in a weathered stainless-steel watering can, from the cart and placed it on the table. "And of course she wanted plenty of my specialty, *ever-blooming sunflowers*," she said enthusiastically.

"That's so totally awesome, Elle," said Ericca admiringly. She could not imagine the amount of work Elle had poured into this event. Actually, she could; Ericca had spent many an afternoon and evening in the past weeks with Elle, hammering out spreadsheets estimating the quantities of tableware, spun sugar, linens, boxes, carts...an incredible amount of little things, which they tracked meticulously. This work had paid off, though. Polis Pastries was now already booked all summer for events of all kinds, some even as far away as Seattle. Elle and Ericca took great pride in this, even as Matt sulked.

A few guests had arrived. Other caterers providing an array of dinner items were assembling their offerings. But Ericca pondered Elle's remark...*friends and enemies*. Ericca could not help wonder what she meant by that.

Quintana Castle was a charming old woman, adored for her style and appreciated for all her efforts on behalf of the New York City Library and other causes. But Elle was now bent over the pastry boxes, and not able to provide a full explanation. Her small skinny hand worked alongside Mr. Lujan's brown gaunt hand as they carefully lifted each spun-sugar figurine to its designated position.

They stuck glassy figures of winged fairies on candy spirals in the salads, flowers, and platters of crackers and cheeses. Cupcakes with chocolate frosting and rainbow sprinkles, adorned with spun-sugar motifs of stars, moons, and suns, drew admiring glances from all. Candied webs delineating the forms of archers and centaurs topped crystalline spears on the tray of beef and lamb steaks.

Ericca looked up from the frenzied preparations to glimpse the lined, painted face of Vivian Spiro, walking with Daemon Skye. Quintana's enemies, she thought. She now pieced together the bits of conversation she had heard. The LOGOS Corporation was once a computer company founded by Taliesin Sax, Daphne had said. She remembered the excerpt from the newspaper: Quintana Castle was married to Taliesin Sax and expecting their child when Taliesin died. She remembered Quintana's words in the library:

those responsible for Taliesin's death would not hesitate to murder his son.

She looked at Vivian Spiro talking amiably to Daemon. Tory and Regi walked close behind them. Tory was wearing yet another ensemble that coordinated with the shirt on her new dog. Regi looked as he did that afternoon during the Empire Poets Society meeting, with a white tank top that displayed his carved, muscular shoulders and a large pendant around his neck.

Ericca could not understand why someone as prominent and respected as Vivian Spiro would harm anyone, let alone an individual as brilliant and creative as Taliesin Sax had been. But now she remembered Miguel telling her once about his visit to the LOGOS Corporation. The company developed a lethal array of herbicides with no other purpose than use as a weapon. Their early success as the Spiro Corporation was built on enormous profits from military contracts.

Ericca remembered Quintana's words in the library; Taliesin had built his considerable fortune from his computer business. He had achieved his lifetime goal of creating his own success, independent of his inheritance as the heir of the *Hats & Sax* retail conglomerate. He was at a supremely happy point in his life and was expecting a child.

But he was anguished by the overseas conflicts of the time, considered part of the early stages of the Tunnel Wars in Ringgold circles. Taliesin became active in the antiwar movement. He used his own capital to finance lobbyists, think tanks, and activists who attacked the administration and the huge military economy propelling its policies. He was successful and undoubtedly drew the notice of those with the power and money to eliminate pesky activists with impunity. He also had valuable secrets in the patented intellectual property of his company, secrets the Spiro Company vied for despite his continued refusal to sell.

Vivian Spiro and Constance Gordon now looked straight at Ericca from across the fountain. The face of the stone Gorgon snarled in the background. Ericca thought of the visage of

Medusa on the aegis of Athena, corrupted femininity chained to serve the goddess of war. Ericca remembered Sybille's sardonic wit: *Constance Gordon's duplicity and pettiness would be enough to wither a titan or pave a jungle.* She remembered the words overheard in the Gravity Bar…*elimination of pesky activists.*

Ericca's musings were interrupted by a sudden silence in the gathering as Quintana Castle approached the podium in the center. With the severed head of Medusa in the background, Quintana addressed her guests.

> Dear friends and family, it has been too long since we celebrated Taliesin's birthday, but today, on what would have been his seventy-third birthday, I have invited all of you to mark a very joyous occasion.
>
> I have spent many years away from the public eye, and for good reason. I have been in mourning over the death of my late husband, an event of horrible significance to myself and our society as a whole.
>
> For Taliesin represented many wonderful things, not just the incentive of material reward in our system of free commerce, but also the spirit of innovation that does not stop with complacency and inherited success. He represented compassion in the ruling class, a genuine compassion, the lack of which has led to the demise of many a proud and arrogant civilization, but not just compassion, but the energy and courage to act on compassion, a will and determination that may have cost him his life.

Quintana paused and looked through the crowd directly at Vivian Spiro, who met her gaze with a blank, unblinking stare.

Quintana continued, "But today I stand before you not simply to commemorate my personal loss. I have happy news. The son I bore more than thirty years ago has once again returned to my life, and has matured to adulthood. He is a delightful young man, full of the charm and brilliance of his father. I can scarcely contain my enthusiasm. Ladies and gentlemen, please welcome my son, George Sax, on this, the most wonderful of all birthdays, and not incidentally the best Father's Day ever."

The guests clapped as a man in dark-blue suit approached the podium. George bent over to give his mother a peck on the cheek and acknowledged the crowd with a wave of his hand. He addressed the crowd. "I am so happy you are able to be here for this happy event. I have to admit I was very surprised to meet my mother; surprised and beyond happy. But surely, my recent celebrity would be a clue as to my true heritage."

He smiled. The crowd chuckled, all except Vivian Spiro, who maintained her blank non-expression. George continued, "It is my hope that I will live up to the compassionate and visionary legacy of my father, and also that everyone here absolutely has a fabulous time this evening."

With that Quintana returned to the podium and smiled slyly. "See what I mean by charm," she said and then added, "We cannot forget to commend our brilliant caterers tonight. Ladies and gentlemen, please show your appreciation for Elle, Ericca, the Lujan family, and all the dedicated and talented staff of Polis Pastries for the incredible treats this evening."

To Elle and Ericca's flabbergasted astonishment, all eyes were turned toward them. The crowd erupted with thunderous applause. They blinked as bright lights flashed and paparazzi aimed their cameras as they stood by the dessert table.

"Oh, my gosh," whispered Ericca to Elle, "...we're going to be celebrities!" They put on their most glamorous expressions, before breaking down in fits of giggles. Later they would marvel at how grown-up and professional they looked in their chef's shirts, labeled with the logo for Polis Pastries. They were now immortalized in urban legend and lore, and would each keep the photo from the news clip for posterity.

The party was nearing a close and Ericca finally found a quiet moment. She looked among the remaining guests seated at the elegant tables, lingering over coffee and dessert by the fading light of day. She spied Maxine Weaver sitting upright with her customary dignity beside the small, bird-like figure of Ray Bender.

Maxine looked up with a warm smile when she saw Ericca approach. She had not seen Ericca since the fashion show, and she was sure much had happened since. "Ericca, my dear, do sit down and enjoy this wonderful lemon-thyme gratin you and Elle prepared," she said.

"Well, it was actually mostly Mr. Lujan who made that, though I gave him the recipe. Sheila Angvall recommended the recipe to me, you know," admitted Ericca with a grin. But the mention of Sheila Angvall made Ericca sad, and now she asked in a low voice, "You know, Sheila Angvall wasn't guilty. And neither was George Sax." It felt strange uttering that name, *George Sax*, the name that had represented mystery and possibility for so long.

Maxine replied pensively, as she nibbled her dessert and sipped from her coffee cup. "Of course not, but you will find, my dear, the affairs of Saplings are never as straightforward as one might hope." She raised her brow, and nodded toward Daemon Skye and Vivian Spiros, still chatting at a corner table.

"But I know Daemon really only cares about preserving the better artifacts of Sapling civilization. I read that in the *Underground Encyclopedia*," Ericca argued.

"Hmm, funny you should mention that publication. And who do you suppose writes the *Underground Encyclopedia*?" asked Maxine with a faintly ironic smile. "No, you shouldn't believe everything you read, even in the Q-aisle. But you're right, the real culprit has not been exposed, and may never be. He or she has powerful protection, protection from people who are capable of befriending prosecutors, politicians, antique dealers, even radical poets to advance their ends," continued Maxine, this time looking toward the slight figure of Vladimir Poe. In the fading light of dusk, Ericca could just barely glimpse the carved, coiled top of

Vladimir Poe's walking stick. The *Antique Collector*, she thought.

He stood alongside the tall, lithe figure of his daughter, Rebecca Poe. Daemon and Vivian strolled over to talk to the two of them.

"You are right. Ringgolds generally take only an advisory role in the affairs of Sapling society, but Ringgolds are not immune to the lure of power and prestige that fascinates most Saplings." Maxine paused, and then continued, "You know Rebecca Poe, don't you?" Ericca had seen Rebecca at the Empire Poets Society meeting and also glimpsed her as she flailed at security guards at the Gravity Bar.

Ericca recalled the dossier on Rebecca on Maxine's desk, and the exact text of graffiti identified on the Empire Poets Society dossier: *Of Hollow Patriarchs and Stuffed Mandarins.* Ericca met Maxine's eyes, and Ericca knew she had her answer.

In the distance, Rebecca smoothed her long, silky hair and turned her slender frame ever so slightly to show the gold ring that pierced her navel and the red heart charm floating above her taut abdomen. The smooth, tan belly was painted. *Henna tattoos, my mehendi Mirror Maid signature,* Rebecca explained once when Elle noticed the painted motif of intertwined swans. Rebecca looked toward them now with a glimmer of defiance, before turning her enchanting smile once more to Daemon and Vivian. In that look, Ericca saw a blithe disregard for authority, and she knew at that moment who was the real graffiti artist.

"Of course," Maxine explained, "...as often happens in Sapling affairs, the quest for truth is secondary to appeasement of the powers that be. We have cleaned up the graffiti everywhere, and currently there is no pressure to reopen the case."

"But these statues and pieces of art are replicas," argued Ericca. "Daemon stole the originals."

"Perhaps," replied Maxine patiently, "but from the official standpoint of the Metropolitan Tunnel Authority, the case is closed. We actually have more serious concerns than eloquent graffiti or monument-swapping."

Ericca knew what Maxine was talking about.

"We have equipped the tunnels with state-of-the-art sensors that detect explosives or other substances that disrupt matter. We are still fine-tuning the calibration. You probably know by now that sometimes the sensors cause false alarms."

Ericca thought about the security alerts that had forced evacuation of the subways. Matter disrupters, she thought. That would be the Tory Torus.

Maxine was nearing the last bit of her dessert. "But not to fret, my dear...I hear you have a wonderful summer ahead of you. I look forward to hearing about your adventures." She pressed Ericca's small hands between her fleshy palms and took a final sip of coffee. Just then she noticed the gold pendant around Ericca's neck. "Another relic, I see. That will definitely help you in your adventures," she said as she took Ray Bender's arm.

Ericca looked down at the pendant as the couple strolled away. She remembered distinctly her father's assurance: *this is not a Ringgold relic*. She chuckled to herself.

The crowd gathered around the fountain for what would be the crowning spectacle of the evening. Elle had made Matt in charge of producing a magic show that would be certain to astound the sophisticated and elegant company. Elle stood nervously as Matt unveiled his surprise.

"Welcome, ladies and gentlemen," he announced with a slight falter. "I am so pleased to bring you the finale of the evening, which I dedicate to Sheila Angvall. Most of you never knew Mrs. Angvall, except perhaps as an alleged criminal and graffiti artist. I, however, knew her as a talented horticulturalist, a tireless supporter of Central Park, and above all else, a shining citizen who made the biggest sacrifice ever." The crowd murmured in agreement; many of them knew the complete story of Sheila Angvall.

Matt looked down at his notes and continued more confidently. "She is no longer with us. But I feel sure she is in a place of good, and that she is now looking on as I pay her this tribute."

He held his Q-computer so images were projected in the ever -

darkening sky above the fountain. A hologram showing the young Sheila Angvall appeared.

"Sheila Angvall was a New York native. She grew up in Brooklyn, attended public colleges, and eventually became a school nurse. She married and had a son named David. Though she was a busy working mother, she found time for her favorite hobby, the study of the plant life in Central Park. She eventually became a recognized plant expert and local tour guide. She shared her love for the natural world with her young son, whose favorite pastime was to explore the verdant glades and monuments of Central Park."

Matt paused to change the projected hologram. The audience sat in hushed attention at the image of David Angvall as a small boy playing on the Alice in Wonderland sculpture.

Matt continued, "Know that Sheila Angvall never committed any crime. Her abiding love for the monuments and public spaces of this city was second only to her love for her son. Know also that, like Taliesin Sax, she took with her in death secrets that others might exploit for personal gain."

Matt waited with his eyes lowered as the audience sat transfixed. He continued. "One of Sheila's greatest accomplishments was the cultivation of the corpse flower, an undertaking that has frustrated botanists worldwide." He raised the veil over the centerpiece on the table to reveal a very odd-looking plant with a large vertical tuber, and broad burgundy petals, emanating a strong smell.

"This plant, a specimen of *Amorphophallus titanium*, has fascinated botanists for years and was even designated the official flower of the Bronx one year. That weird smell emanates from the central spike, or *spadix*, and attracts flies for the purpose of pollination. The lengths we go to for a date!"

The audience chuckled. "Anyway, the military has studied this tropical plant for possible uses. Botanists have puzzled over it, and believe the corpse flower is related to the very first flowering plants and water lilies back in the Cretaceous Period some one hundred and twenty-four million years ago," explained Matt.

Then he said in conclusion, "I knew Sheila Angvall. She was a woman who lived in New York for seventy years and died alone in her apartment a few months ago. Her son died on the field of battle at the age of twenty. It was just this tragic death that Taliesin Sax sought to address in his lifetime. And tonight I applaud them both for their spirit and contributions."

Everyone had been quiet and motionless during the show, including Ericca. But now she took a quick look around. She saw Daemon clapping, looking right at Matt. Then, in the growing shadows she saw Vivian Spiro quickly exiting, followed closely by Constance Gordon.

She turned to Elle, clapping enthusiastically and looking at Matt with an expression of astonished pride. "I can't believe that was Matt," exclaimed Elle.

Ericca nodded in understanding. They were so used to thinking of Matt as a typical boy, a particularly sulky boy of late.

"I'll definitely have to help him get that turntable," added Elle as she looked proudly toward Matt, who now stood under the spotlight while hordes of Manhattan dignitaries and celebrities waited to shake his hand.

The guests were gradually leaving. As Elle and Ericca busily packed up the plates and glasses and cleaned the remnants of dessert, a group of very stylishly dressed girls came by.

"Sssh, those are the dancers from the Gravity Bar. I think one of them is the one who almost clobbered her friend with a hairbrush," whispered Ericca. Elle gave her a look of acknowledgement before ducking under the table.

As they crawled on the ground, picking up pieces of uneaten food, discarded napkins, and dropped tableware, they listened.

"That Ted the Titan, the Amorpho-whatchamacallit…wouldn't you like to get a handle on that?"

"Whaddaya talking about, girl? That dorky thing? You can definitely do better than that…"

"Hmm, how about Regi Arthur…"

"Sorry, he's taken. That Gorgon there isn't the only thing with claws..."

"Hey, how about the poet? He's very cute."

"His name is George Sax. Weren't you listening? Anyway, check out these flowers, incredible, the perfect shade of yellow...I suppose they don't need them anymore..."

Elle and Ericca laughed. Ericca hissed a stern "Sssh" as she heard Albert and Leonardo protest the unfortunate term *dork*. They heard the clink of the floral centerpieces leaving the table.

Finally, only a few guests remained. The lawn was restored to its initial pristine state. Miguel and Matt folded the remaining tables and chairs and loaded them on carts to be returned to the storage shed. Ericca finally caught up with Matt. Tentatively taking his arm, she said with small smile, "Matt, great speech. I never would have guessed."

"Well, I really liked Sheila's ideas for my Ultimate Warrior game. And I really liked the notebook she left me," he said grinning sheepishly as he picked up the folded chairs and lined them up neatly in the storage shed.

"Oh, yeah, what did she say in her notebook?" asked Ericca.

"Well, I can't tell anyone. That was part of my promise, a special promise that can never be broken," answered Matt.

"Hmm, like the secret of the ever-blooming corpse flower?" asked Ericca good-naturedly.

"That and so much more," replied Matt, looking up with a serious look. Miguel came over, and stacked a few more chairs.

"Awesome speech, Matt...I think every important person in New York congratulated you personally, from the mayor on down, everyone except for..." Miguel paused. He had noticed Vivian Spiro's silent exit; evidently, so had Matt.

"Well, I wouldn't expect anyone from the LOGOS Corporation to be excited by my speech. I would think they were here tonight mostly to witness a word of warning," replied Matt.

"A word of warning?" asked Ericca. She could guess what

Matt's explanation would be.

"Quintana Castle drew the battle lines tonight. She knows the forces at work that destroyed her husband have not rested and will continue to harass her and her family. She replied in no uncertain terms that she will not hide from them any longer. She will fight their every attempt to destroy her and hijack her secrets."

"And the secrets of Sheila Angvall?" asked Ericca.

Miguel and Ericca looked at each other. Miguel grimaced at the irony of his moment of pride in the gleaming lobby of the LOGOS Corporation. LOGOS...*living organism genotype ownership and simulation.*

Matt thought of Sheila's notebook and the story of David Angvall, a new recruit on the front lines for the first time. He was killed his first time in battle and as he wandered in a delirious haze, rapidly losing blood, his final glimpse was of green fields exploding with cluster bombs intended for the enemy, surrounded by water and vegetation poisoned by rainbow herbicides. Matt had avoided the cupcakes with rainbow sprinkles all evening.

Matt felt tears flooding his eyes. He thought of Sheila Angvall's funeral. He had attended the short service at the Memorial Monument with his father, Elle and Ericca. Daemon Skye was there as well, holding a silver box containing a gold barque. To everyone's surprise, Daemon offered the priceless Egyptian artifact to the funeral attendant who set the boat into the shimmering pool. Matt thought of the sight of the golden boat floating away before disappearing into the vortex at the center of the pool. *A vessel for the brave.* He wiped a tear.

Elle walked into the storage shed with a sunny smile. "Oh, there you all are...I think we are all done. The place looks great!" she said enthusiastically. She looked at their glum faces. "What's wrong? We're done. We pulled it off, a spectacular event. Quintana said she was so pleased with us, she'd like to hire us again for her next event...Isn't that great?" asked Elle.

They nodded in agreement and walked out of the shed onto the lawn, which was now empty in the dusky gloom. Miguel joined

CHAPTER SEVENTEEN

his father in packing up the last pastry boxes and said thank you to Elle. With a wave, he headed away, rolling the remaining cart along the deserted path.

Elle and Matt looked around for their parents. Sybille and Quint were saying their final farewells to Quintana, who now stood by the winged Pegasus statue over the fountain. The light of the moon reflected in the pond and glimmered in her gray hair. Quintana held the white Samoyed on a leash beside her.

"Tau, you were marvelous tonight. Did you have any idea so many people would show up for your birthday?" she said, affectionately petting his fluffy mane.

Then she turned to Quint and Sybille and said, "Thank you so much for coming. What a wonderful evening."

"Brings back old times, I'd say," replied Quint with a smile.

"Well, you know what they say: history repeats itself," answered Quintana.

"Yes, but never like this..." interjected Sybille.

"Yes, the world of Saplings today can be terrifying," replied Quintana. She bent to stroke the dog beside her with her spotted hand. She added, "But that is something we have chosen for ourselves, isn't it, Tau?" The dog looked up with a happy expression in his soft brown eyes.

Quintana gave them each a hug, and then turned to Elle, Matt, and Ericca. "You were just wonderful tonight. We should definitely do this again," she said graciously. Then she gave them each a hug and shook Matt's hand even as he looked down shyly.

Finally she gathered her coat and bag. "A Sybille Nix Label original," she said to Sybille with twinkling eyes. Turning to Ericca as she held Tau's leash, she said, "Be sure to visit me this summer in the Q-aisle, a nice place to stay cool. And do enjoy yourself in France with George and Sophia."

She waved and departed down the path with Tau, creating the eerie specter of a wizened old woman in the company of a ghostly white dog in a narrow, dark corridor of elm trees.

Elle and Matt gathered their belongings. Matt carefully packed the corpse flower back into its pastry box. "I'd like to send it to your father. I think he'd get the joke if I told him it was meant as a replacement," he said to Ericca with a grin.

Then he added, "Speaking of trips, be sure to tell your dad thanks. My Q-computer not only survived the trip through time, but now it's even better." He reached in his pocket for the device, which he now flexed in his hand. "See, not brittle plastic and rigid metal anymore. This is awesome. I can drop it now without breaking it. That'll be great this summer."

Ericca acknowledged the thanks with a slight smile. She had been so caught up in the events of the evening, she hadn't even thought of Branch. Now she missed her dad and instinctively reached for the pendant around her neck. *Svastikah*, she thought, meaning *be happy*.

Elle and Matt headed into the gloom with their parents, shouting, "See you this summer," and waving in farewell.

Ericca looked around for her mother. Sophia was waiting, standing next to George by the statue of Medusa. They were chatting. "Come along, Ericca," called her mother, waving her hand.

Ericca grabbed her backpack and headed toward them to a chorus of cheers from Albert and Leonardo, who evidently were getting tired and were anxious to leave. Sophia and George had left the glade and were ahead of her on the path. Ericca looked wistfully at their shadowy shapes side by side in the gloom.

Ericca scurried to catch up with them, growing anxious at the darkness that now enveloped her. Then, to her surprise, her mother turned around. She gathered Ericca in her lean, strong arms. And, peering through the canopy of trees at the crescent moon, Ericca felt as light and secure as a branch swinging in the wind.

Acknowledgements

The chess set described in the chapter *Blind Chess* is based on a collectors' chess set by the Mexican sculptor Lowe. The *Pazyryk* carpet described in the chapter *Pluto* is based on the rug by that name that is part of the collection of the Hermitage Museum in St. Petersburg, Russia. The painting *The Sun* by Yue Minjun, described in the chapter *The Proletarian Prince*, is an actual painting. The opera *Turandot* by Puccini, described in the chapter *Pluto*, is based on a fable by Carlo Gozzi, which was in turn based on a poem by the Persian poet Nizami. The Cobra car is based on the AC Cobra, a collectors' sports car. Motifs throughout the book are based on ancient Egyptian and Scythian art. The combat scene in the chapter *The T-Gate* draws on the book *War For The Hell Of It* by Ed Cobleigh. Many of the scientific concepts in this book are discussed more thoroughly in books by Brian Greene and Amir Azcel.

Various painters and musical artists are mentioned in this book, including the German Expressionist Käthe Kollwitz and American painters Jasper Johns and Helen Frankenthaler. Among the musical artists mentioned are the rappers Nas and the Black Eyed Peas.

Mention is made of various historical figures, including the writer Sir Walter Scott, the physicist Robert Oppenheimer, and mathematicians John Nash and Kurt Godel. The characters of Albert and Leonardo are loosely based on Albert Einstein and Leonardo Fibonacci. *Alice in Wonderland,* by Lewis Carroll, is mentioned, with notable quotes based on this source. The Alice in Wonderland sculpture is based on the bronze sculpture in Central Park by José de Creeft, donated by the publisher and philanthropist George Delacorte in 1959. The actual sculpture does not feature Humpty Dumpty. Rebecca's poem in the chapter *The Proletarian Prince* echoes T. S. Eliot's 1925 poem "The Hollow Men." Descriptions of the museum pieces in the chapter *The Q-Computer* are based on information from the Metropolitan Museum in New York and the Hermitage Museum in St. Petersburg.

About the Author

Author and illustrator Rowena Wright is one of those rare individuals who dream with the left brain. She reluctantly admits to a long fascination with ancient history and an aversion to housework and exercise. She counts herself among the graduates of the University of California at Berkeley and Cornell University. She lives in Seattle.

For more information about Rowena Wright, visit www.finialpublishing.com.
E-mail her at goodreads@finialpublishing.com.

THE TUNNEL TIMES

CLASSIFIEDS

AFFORDABLE TEMPORARY HOUSING SOUGHT
Family emergency leads to housing crisis.
Accomplished young scientist seeks
temporary housing. Manhattan. Contact
Miguel at The Ringgold Room.

HOUSESITTER WANTED
Guest quarters available for cheerful
housesitter. Must be responsible and
organized. References required. Contact
Quintana Castle c/o The Ringgold Room.

Why is Miguel looking for a new place to live?
For clues, visit the world of Saplings and Ringgolds
on the Web at:

www.polisgames.com.

Printed in the United States
59445LVS00004B/172-216

9 781933 791074